Malcolm Berry

The Foulks Rebellion

Rutsatz Publishing
Blaine, Washington

Library of Congress Control Number: 2011905401

ISBN 978-0-615-47308-6

Designed by Sloan Mgaba
Author photo by Riley Folsom

Printed in the United States of America

For my mother and father

The Foulks Rebellion

Prologue

Viola Ferrari pulled the rental Chevy off I-80 into a dismal motel somewhere in the wind-blasted high desert south of the Great Salt Lake. It was mid-September, and still hot. All afternoon she'd felt a presence nearby, but she shook it off as part of traveling in a lunar landscape. Popping the glove box, she found the reservation she had secured for the motel. An overnight stop here was crucial for Ferrari. She needed a few more hours of preparation before confronting the notoriously uncooperative commander at Dugway Proving Ground, an hour's drive south.

A dark, shockingly attractive woman of forty, Ferrari was interesting to men on various levels, and interesting to women too, and she knew it. But she was a serious government lawyer, fixed on her career, had never been married, and rarely fell into the kinds of liaisons that she had seen destroy women in the US Attorney's Office. Prosecuting federal crimes was slippery and sober business, requiring high intelligence and the ability to think fast in a federal courtroom crammed with niggling bureaucrats and vicious defense lawyers. And there was this – the dirty, nerve-wracking political business she was heading for now, field investigations her department head simply did not trust the FBI to do without prejudice.

The very reason she was in this God-forsaken hole testified to her special status in the agency. She had been lead prosecutor in several trials dealing with illegal uses of Brain-Computer Interface, a brilliant medical breakthrough lately twisted into high-tech brainwashing by spurious research outfits and software engineers. As an expert in the legal aspects of mind control research, Viola Ferrari had been sent to Utah for two reasons. One, nobody else in the department knew a damn thing about the field. And two, the Senate Judiciary Committee had specifically ordered an expert from the US Attorney's Office to come out to Dugway and ask some questions. Somebody in Washington believed the people running these *experiments were up to no good.*

Clicking on a lamp, she closed the curtains and washed up, then phoned her mother at the nursing home outside Chicago for the daily check-in. Satisfied, she snapped open her laptop and began her night's work.

Corruption at high levels of government always involved elected officials. Long experience told Ferrari that if there were criminal activity going on at Dugway, the evidence was likely to be crumpled into departmental doublespeak and eventually tossed in the archives. She would proceed with extreme deliberation, back up everything, trust nobody. If the Army had been playing dangerous and illegal games with people's heads, she would need irrefutable evidence, and nobody was going to hand it to her.

She would never get it.

In the morning the wind blew hard as she pushed south on 196, analyzing for the hundredth time the legal traps they would place in her path. She was going seventy-five when the explosion rocked the left front of the car. A blowout! Instinctively she slammed on the brakes. The car swerved violently across the center line. She released the brake pedal then and the car straightened, banging wildly from the front tire. With all her strength she managed to stop the car in the middle of the road. Another vehicle had closed in and now pulled up behind her. Gasping and still gripping the wheel, feeling the adrenaline surging through her body, she watched in the rear view, unable to think clearly as a thickly-built man in a dark suit approached, pulling on leather gloves.

Her brain said, "Cop?"

He reached the passenger door and opened it, leaning in without betraying any emotion. She saw his lips curl. Men often did when coming in close and realizing how beautiful she was.

"You okay?" His voice was neither soft nor hard, tentative, almost as if he were not accustomed to speaking.

"I think so," she blurted out, still battling the lingering horror. "This damn car better have a spare."

"It does," the man told her. "I checked."

A look of confusion came into Ferrari's dark eyes as the man reached toward her, grasped her head in both hands, and twisted violently, snapping her neck. Immediately he moved her lifeless body back behind the wheel, maneuvered her right foot onto the gas pedal, pushed it down to the floor, grabbed her laptop from the back seat, dropped the Chevy into gear and leaped out of the way. Before he was back in his non-descript sedan with the muddied license plate, he heard the car roaring off the highway and rolling over.

Part One – The Escape

1

At eleven p.m. in New York on election night, the President of the United States took the stage at Madison Square Garden.

On Holotech monitors scattered through the arena, President Sol Burligame adjusted his tie under a banner that read, "God bless the New Freedom Party." He rubbed two fingers along his brow, observed Vice President Billy Hellman moving forward, and strode toward the podium to accept responsibility for his second term in the White House. Once again Burligame had dominated the voting instruments across the nation. The sixty-two-year-old President made a convincing show of competence, a sturdy man with thick lips and stately nose below curly brown hair speckled with silver. A glaze of contentment was fixed on his cello-shaped face. Even considering the deep violet gashes around the eyes – the result of the three-year airborne pathogen pandemic thought to be spread by ordinary pigeons – Sol Burligame looked every bit the most powerful man on Earth.

The tallies were in. Only twenty-three percent of the people had cast their ballots, by far the worst turnout in US history. Of those, less than half had chosen the Burligame-Hellman ticket, yet this meager result was enough to re-elect the President and Vice President.

Sol Burligame gazed across the carefully orchestrated pandemonium. What he saw rather than adoration was the vulgar pomp of election night politics. Holding a powerful hand out as if to still the waters, he slipped on a baseball cap bearing the word, "Coach." On cue a tumultuous roar arose from twenty-eight thousand paid political cronies at the Garden.

"The people have spoken," the President bellowed over the

din. "It looks like we're back in the batter's box!" The audience went berserk, screaming over the band's spontaneous blaring of *"Hail to the Chief."* Baseball bats, the emblem of Burligame's presidency, bashed against the floor in a thundering three-four tempo, causing the enormous structure to quake in paid political ecstasy.

Vice President Billy Hellman leaned toward Burligame. "I've got business to take care of," he said. Sending a cursory wave to the cameras, he walked out.

2

Three thousand miles west, at home overlooking the Strait of Georgia, Progressive Party Congressman Victor Sligo felt the rage twisting his stomach into knots as he watched the jubilation in Manhattan. The phony spectacle at the Garden made him want to smash something. Four more years of Burligame, this complacent stooge for the ultrawealthy, and his unchained pit bull of a Vice President.

It was after eight p.m. The supporters and the press were gone, following Victor's expected triumph in Washington state's second district. He needed to keep himself composed in order to take a clandestine call from Massachusetts Senator Hal Riske, the minority leader. A call he had during his long public life never thought would be necessary. But he and Riske, and others, had seen the gathering storm early in the campaign. If the voters failed to show up again this November, there would be rioting in the streets. The government would come under siege.

Victor Sligo was a hard-bodied compulsive athlete of fifty, three inches over six feet, lines already creasing his face from half a lifetime in public service. He had been on the cover of two national journals. The first was *Ironman.* He was the first sitting Congressman to finish the Kona Hawaii World Championship. A year ago he had appeared on the cover of *The New Republic,* along with two dozen other collaborators in an electrifying socio-economic battle cry called *Strategies for Survival in a Corporate World,* a national expression of outrage over the mismanagement of the federal government by Vice President Billy Hellman and his henchmen in Washington. Among the contributors were respected tax and banking and health specialists, urban visionaries and industrialists and retired diplomats, cops and CEOs, expressing broad avenues of social change, all looking toward the perilous terrain of participatory democracy. Walls quaked and curses spewed from the windows of the Executive Office Building for a week after publication of the *Strategies for Survival*

The Congressman glanced at the illegal black transceiver on his desk. The Code Thirteen. Any moment it would begin blinking, he was certain, and the life he had built over so many years was going to come crashing down. He yanked a beer from the fridge and hurled the cap across the marble countertop and drank hard from the bottle, then stood before the big Holotech TV screen broadcasting the President's speech around the globe.

The truth was, Victor Sligo actually liked the President. A decent man, not as sophisticated as JFK, certainly not as intelligent as Thomas Jefferson, but a man, as they say, of the people. And at the same time the chief puppet of the New Freedom Party – the Newfies – rigidly controlled by Billy Hellman and his hand-picked gang of sycophants, the lobbyists, the trust fund babies and the moguls of the financial industry, pathologically devoted to their own profit margins, even at the expense of the nation's economic health.

Draining his beer and reaching for another, he smirked as the Vice President walked off the platform. He understood. Billy Hellman was so universally despised he could not stay in the public eye for long. He was probably heading off to blackmail the Pope or beat up a couple of boy scouts.

Too disgusted to watch, Victor flicked the remote, but the television didn't turn off. Of course it wouldn't. As if to pour acid on his wounds, the Holotech defaulted to I-Media programming – the planet's controlling television monopoly – whenever the President was speaking. Rage pumped through his chest. He lunged at the TV, gripped both edges of the wide screen, and cursed in the President's face. Where the hell is Riske, he roared inside his head. A gentle female voice muted the words of the President.

"Are you requesting exit?" purred the voice.

Victor screamed into Sol Burligame's placid face, "Yes, goddammit! Exit! Exit!"

The voice with infuriating calm said, *"The President will be finished speaking in eleven minutes."*

Congressman Sligo exploded. Snatching heavy gloves and a crowbar from the front closet, he ripped his door open and stormed out to the home module at the street. With a violent *crack* he tore the door off the box, and smashed clear through the two 220-volt laser fuses. A second's searing blue flare, and he was in darkness. The house was deadly silent except for the diminishing undercurrent from the covered lap pool. Likewise the whisper of the government-supplied airborne pathogen detector. Everything discharged. He peered through the soft drizzle into his living room. The huge screen powered down to a flicker.

"Yo!" an irritated voice called from behind the dark two-story Tudor house. "Victor? What's going on?" Two or three other voices chimed in. Lost people in search of light.

In his tantrum Victor had forgotten his staff, including his wife, were watching election night coverage in the guest cottage. He had been left alone to brood in the house.

Candles sputtered on in the cottage. The athletic congressman jogged back to the house, found a flashlight and hurried down to the basement to fire up the emergency generator. He did not want to miss Riske's call. The anger roiling in his head formed the question: how soon would somebody round up enough armed citizens to storm the White House? Tonight the country simmered with a lethal mixture of unfocused anger and suspicion over the election results, streaming in on the Web all evening. The signs were undeniable. Insurrection was imminent. Nobody could predict what was about to take place, but Victor feared the worst. It was hard not to think the nation was about to be torn apart.

A politician half his life, Victor Sligo's world view was divided into the powerful and the powerless. Only might could take on might. As ranking Progressive on the crucial Ways and Means Committee, he knew he could be more effective even in the minority in Congress, than in jail. And as one of the most popular political figures in the nation, he understood once the insurrection began, Vice President Billy Hellman's first response would be to make all the leaders disappear.

3

Back upstairs he found Purvis Courtman flicking off his pocket flash, grinning at his boss as the lights came up. Courtman was his chief of staff.

"Must have been a power conflagration down at the substation," Courtman said. Like Victor, Courtman was a tall man, but much too thin, a bassoon player turned social activist in grad school, pursuing a career in politics at the start of the hopeful Clinton years. At the age of sixty-one he bore the iconic image of Ichabod Crane, the long, loose body, the deep-set dark eyes. The chief of staff had a precious wit and was influential in his own right in the halls of Congress. Victor had once called him "my fool." Courtman's response had been, "Hey, it takes a fool to pay a fool." His job was to remind the Congressman it wasn't serious. It was just human life under a microscope.

"Conflagration, all right," Victor said. "But it's not energy trouble. It's bugs. What you call a second termite."

The chief of staff chuckled. He made a squishing gesture with his surgical gloves, the translucent germ protectors he was never without.

More voices came from the dark yard. Three people entered the house – the other essential staffers, led by Nel Sligo, the congressman's proud and feisty wife. The sense of defeat came with them. All were prepared for what was coming: the traditional election night guilt, the railing against the pestilence in Washington. The New Freedom Party had now won three straight presidential elections. This time there were fewer votes cast than ever. Without instructions the giant speechwriter Sloan Mgaba, former Central African refugee ready at any moment for government treachery, fixed drinks.

The youngest staffer, crisp five-foot-five BJ Lichtenstein, took his place by the mantle. BJ was Victor's political advisor and staff worry-dog. Taking a scotch from Mgaba, he looked to the lanky congressman.

Victor crossed one arm over his chest and pinched the bridge of his nose with his other hand.

"Anybody got any cyanide?" Nobody laughed.

"You've all seen it," he said, voice still raw from a weekend of yelling at rallies. "Of the measly one-quarter of the electorate who bothered to show up, Burligame picked up forty percent. So in reality nine point two percent of total registered voters went for them, and they won! I just can't get my mind around it. Worse than Calvin Coolidge!" By tradition on election night, he wore an Ironman Finisher tee shirt over a black turtleneck, khaki slacks and white running shoes. His chiseled features were grim, and the riveting indigo blue eyes moved among his people, feeling the misery, the unspoken resentment, the defeat.

"In case there's any doubt about the matter, the rudder's about to come off the ship of state. Catastrophe is unavoidable, guys. There's no choice left. Anybody wants to jump ship, go ahead. I'll still respect you in the morning."

All eyes went to the Code Thirteen. The staff had been briefed. Senator Riske was about to make some radical declaration, and all hell was going to break loose.

Nel Sligo stood holding her drink, watching him. She was an attractive woman of average height, elegant in her close-cropped silver hair and sinewy physique, tougher than any man present. She had already removed the makeup and fuchsia suit required to stand with Victor during his acceptance speech half an hour ago. Now she wore a loose-fitting silk blouse and tailored shorts, her work attire. In her husband's honor she had pinned an Ironman button on her sleeve.

"You won your seat," she said needlessly. Her voice was lackluster. "You're an institution in the House of Representatives. Re-elected for your eighth term." No smile came as she spoke, no admiration.

"Yeah, my constituents are happy," Victor said. "But the viper's still in the Oval Office."

"And so is the President," Courtman said. He scratched nervously his weekend stubble of beard, and recited the rest of the damage. "Alex Holiday took thirty-eight percent. Twenty-one percent to Ms. Park. Who would have believed those numbers six months ago?"

Nobody knew what to say. A clock ticked somewhere.

Diminutive, cocky BJ Lichtenstein was not a man to suffer in silence.

"I'll tell you what happened. Besides the fact that Holiday

has the integrity of a three-toed sloth! All the strategic plotting, the fund raising, the damn potato salad! Useless! The mass of voters are mindless baboons! They heard Julio Reese right on Public Television tell them not to bother voting, and they didn't!" He pulled a pen from his breast pocket and tossed it end-over-end in the air and caught it neatly, mimicking Julio, the popular octogenarian with his signature white mustache. "Just like that! He picks up his pencil and flips it and tells the country, 'Why bother to vote?' So the voters stayed home."

Sloan Mgaba snorted and shook his great head. At six feet two and three hundred pounds, Mgaba made a large impression, and the deep French-accented bass voice expanded it. He spread his huge hands. "It was Ms. Park. The New Freedom Party paid for her campaign."

He was right. Whatever tricks had been employed to keep voters away, the New Freedom Party had won the old-fashioned way, flooding the weakest opponent's campaign with cash. "Naderizing," they called it. The target was Georgiana Park, the first Asian-American woman to command a major political party. Ms. Park had stunned the nation by picking up twenty-one percent as Green Party's presidential candidate. Votes that would probably have put Alex Holiday in the White House, had the Newfies not poured so much money into phony I-Media "newscasts" for Georgiana Park's campaign.

"Check the polls tomorrow," BJ said, shaking his head sourly at Mgaba. "Sure people voted for Georgiana. But Julio Reese was the principal actor. Walter Cronkite reincarnate! And you *know* the guy! You didn't bother to work on him! You could have got your rear end off the couch and –"

"Hold it!" Nel interrupted, shooting BJ a stern look. "You're still on the wrong premise. Both of you. Anybody who didn't vote for Burligame voted *against* him, and it didn't matter who they voted for. We knew all along Holiday is just another well-connected East Coast pretty boy. All talk and no guts."

"Phew!" BJ scoffed, one arm propped on the mantelpiece. He sipped his whisky and pouted. "They twisted people's brains till they didn't show up at the polls!" He was whining, but he didn't care. The hard campaign was over.

"Look," Nel snapped. "Everybody. Get off the pity pot. All

the election shows is how much work we have to do."

"Geez! Give it a rest, woman," BJ muttered.

Without hesitating she crossed the room and slapped him hard across the face. The short man's head flew back. His drink crashed against the stone fireplace and splashed on his pinstripe suit. His face pinched tight, and he glared up at his boss's wife, strangling with humiliation.

"Nel! Stop it!" Victor snapped.

"There won't be any rest now," Nel spat at the short man. She spun back to face her husband. "They're not going to destroy my country!" She was steel with rage, her lips barely moving as she spoke. "Now we know nobody can win in a fair election." She crossed her arms on her chest angrily. "Where is Riske with his big ideas?"

But they did need a rest. They needed to analyze, check fundamental premises, curse missed opportunities. Climb out of the fetid cesspool of politics, and have a look down in to see what new malignancies were forming.

Lichtenstein was on his knees, dropping shards of crystal into a napkin. He stood up then, all five and a half feet of him, one hand holding the napkin, the other gingerly brushing his $2,000 Versace suit. He smoldered, but was unable to look at Nel.

She felt his anger, and pressed her palms together and placed them against her lips. "I'm sorry, BJ. That was inexcusable." Again no smile. No glimmer of remorse came into her eyes. "I just feel so… violated."

At that instant the green led light on the Code Thirteen began to blink.

It was as if a deadly gas had entered the room and paralyzed them all. Each of them sank into private fears, careers, loved ones, the dreadful reality of revolution. Finally Mgaba, nearest the desk, picked up the postcard-size device, and held it up for Victor. "At least they haven't blocked this from working," he said. "So far."

Courtman immediately crossed to the window and closed the curtains.

In the candle-lit darkness, the light blinked like a series of firecrackers going off.

The Code Thirteen was essentially a closed cell phone network, a video transceiver engineered to slip under the vast satellite system owned by Communication International, I-Media's parent group and one of the world's dominant corporate powers. Paranoid Progressives had produced the device, signaling off a private satellite on randomly chosen frequencies. It was operated by an invisible cadre of technicians, initially thirteen angry geeks who had created the network as a defense against the all-seeing eyes of CI.

Everyone's attention locked on the small screen. A man's face appeared. He looked stressed, large-jawed, solemn. His eyes were steady.

"Senator," Victor Sligo said.

"I'm going to strangle him," the man said. "With my bare hands." His mouth grinned, but his eyes smoldered. "What's the consensus out there in Washington?" The voice was sour with resignation.

"Congratulations on your win, Hal," Victor said. "I believe this last straw broke the donkey's back. What are your –"

"Wait," BJ Lichtenstein burst out, and rushed toward Victor, eyes bulging, arms shooting out to grab the Code Thirteen. *"Don't do this!"* he pleaded, terror-stricken, but Victor shot a palm straight into the shorter man's face. Quickly Nel and Mgaba grabbed him and dumped him roughly into a chair.

"I hate them as much as you do," BJ sputtered. "But you can't sacrifice the entire country like this!"

"BJ." Courtman spoke like a cop addressing a prisoner. "Hear the man out."

On the screen Riske said, "Trouble in River City?"

"All over the land, Senator," Victor said.

Riske looked grim. "We're activating the committee." His voice was raw with feeling, and filled with peril. Staring at him, Victor's face turned to granite. "We should commiserate over drinks," Riske said. The joints at his temples were grinding. Nobody spoke. It felt as if all the air had gone out of the room. BJ shook off Mgaba's hand but remained seated, thinking of his wife and daughters. Sloan Mgaba, deeply involved in the revolution in the Central African Republic for half a decade, watched Victor's eyes. Purvis Courtman bit his lower lip. He had no instinct toward martyrdom. Nel moved away from BJ to stand beside her husband. In a rare display of affection she touched his back and they stared side by side at the digital image of the Minority Leader of the Senate. He had an extraordinary largeness to his craggy features, a man born for Mount Rushmore. His thick thumb touched his chin. Immediately Victor dug into his desk, found a small white envelope, and tore it open. Inside was a hand-written code only several officials had ever seen. He scanned the card quickly and switched his focus back to Riske. The senator's forefinger and thumb touched his left earlobe, then moved to the tip of his nose. The middle finger touched his lips, and hung there a moment. Then he clapped his hands once, loudly.

Instantly the face faded into the black plastic.

Nobody breathed. Without a word Victor took up his raincoat and his tan fishing hat and moved toward the door, snatching up a flashlight on the way. BJ jumped at him, grabbed him by the arm, obviously terrified, and whispered "What are they going to do?"

Victor nodded toward the door. They all understood immediately. Nel led them to the broad foyer and they found their coats. In another moment, five figures were moving down the driveway and into the winding street, walking east toward the highway, hunched against the damp night.

4

They made their way silently into an uncertain mist. Half a block away, light slashed from a doorway, and a woman emerged. She came quickly into step with Victor and his entourage. The woman wore a black raincoat and red spike heels, with luxurious blond hair obviously taking a beating in the moist night. She spoke with her head down, not making eye contact. The heels clicked loudly on the wet sidewalk.

"Saw your house lights cycle down," she said. "Figured you heaved a grenade at your television. What happened?"

"Same as," Victor Sligo said.

A black car slowed, and they all moved instinctively away from the curb until it passed.

She continued. "Seventy-seven percent of the voters stayed home! Consensus was, what was the point of voting? CI runs the

White House. Remember what Hitler said? Control the media and you control the world." Her voice sounded like sandpaper rubbing wood, with round vowels and slow cadence. A southern accent. "CI funds the New Freedom Party, the Newfies finance Georgiana Park's campaign, and America's uncle Julio Reese tells people why bother to vote."

BJ Lichtenstein, on the edge of a nervous breakdown, muttered the oldest political axiom: "What nincompoops voters are."

None of it was a big secret. Ms. Park's campaign contributions could be traced back to offshore tax shelters created by Communication International. The corporation incubated and enthroned people like Vice President Billy Hellman. Over the past two decades, CI had snaked its way into controlling the technological and media aspects of several industries. As it grew, the overwhelming success of I-Media TV meant that CI now dominated television, the Internet, and worldwide communications systems. None of the other two hundred or so TV networks could compete.

CI had even managed to muscle through Congress a new Cabinet department from the old FCC – the Department of Communications – and had a former Communication International executive, Dr. Hunter Tyne, appointed Secretary of Communications.

They walked on in gloomy silence, three in front, three behind. Large and combative Sloan Mgaba was at the center of the front line, flanked by Victor and Purvis Courtman. All three were tall men. Mgaba's broad shoulders occasionally touched one of the others with his swinging gait. Close behind, Nel Sligo watched her husband's back, her posture strong, her eyes sweeping to the side and occasionally to the dark street behind them. Behind Courtman, the blond woman moved with equal strength and vigilance, observing the perimeter. BJ hurried along between the two women, soaking wet, contemplating his options.

The group turned down a busy highway. The late evening rush of cars hissed homeward, fully one-third of them made in China. Victor sensed sinister government instruments recording their movements. But he could show no fear. No kneejerk reaction, no weakness. Suppress the urge to strike first, allowing no counterattack. St. Stephen's Home for Boys had brought him into adult life bruised and tough. Assume nothing, and reveal nothing. Every handshake will become a closed fist.

Between lampposts at a noisy section of highway, he stopped. The staff huddled around him. He spoke deliberately, his face steel, his lips not moving.

"Riske said he's going to kill him with his bare hands. He meant Hellman. He wasn't being metaphorical. He wants to talk strategy to bring down the government."

"What?" Nel gasped. Then instantly she gathered herself in, and spoke to the sidewalk. "A coup? Has he lost his mind? Have *you?"*

BJ was moaning, "Oh my God! Oh my God!" while Purvis Courtman studied his surgical gloves, repeatedly snapping the wristband. Only Mgaba stared back at Victor, rain dripping from his immense face, lips pulled back, half-consciously emitting an animal growl.

"You all understand the stakes," Victor said. "We're going to Philadelphia the week before the Inauguration. We're going to watch a football game. Each of you has time to decide whether you're in this or not. I will be there."

He glanced at his wife. Nel was unable to respond.

Finally Mgaba spoke. "Sometimes you either take a stand or crawl away on your belly," he said. "Count me in."

Victor gazed at him. "You have young children at home, Sloan. You need to –"

"Count me in," Mgaba said again.

BJ spoke up. "I need to speak to my family. But –" He sent a pleading glance to Courtman.

"Don't look at me, Licky. Hellman needs to be lined up and spanked, and sent back to Hell, if they'll let him in."

"Yes, but –"

Courtman turned away, blew out a deep breath, then wiped rain from his face. He said to Victor, "Don't ask me to drive a tank down Pennsylvania Avenue."

BJ appeared about to burst into tears. "Fine," he mumbled. "I'm in."

The blond woman peered into the darkness. Victor raised his chin at her. "Arrange transportation, will you? Book five hotel rooms. One suite where we can talk. Have your people scan the place for bugs. Use cash. Make the reservations in person."

He said to the others, "They're going to brainstorm with a

bunch of radicals. Free thinkers, pissed-off bureaucrats." Looking at the wet ground, uncertain of his next move. "God only knows what's coming! This might be the last time we –"

Suddenly the blond woman's arm slashed the air for silence. A moment later a government chopper roared into sight, its severe spotlight playing along the center strip. Instantly they separated into the darkness.

5

Neither had spoken since returning. They were getting ready for bed in the fine master suite, furnished with her parents' antiques from the family sheep ranch on San Juan Island.

Nel had been unable to concentrate. Her fears were locked on their four children, all grown, all vulnerable to retribution by enemies in the administration. If they joined this madness – it was impossible to know what awaited them.

Victor slipped a pillow under his raised knees and stared at the ceiling.

"They've been planning this for two years. The Pentagon's involved. A lot of extremely nervous people," he said. "Most of the Progressive caucus. The Armed Services Committee, Intelligence Committee. From what they tell me, huge support from back-home constituencies. I'm amazed it hasn't leaked. Couple of Newfies in the Senate and a bunch in the House. Some general's leaning on the National Guard. Plus the FBI. Possibly a member of Cabinet. The whole point is to do this without bloodshed."

Nel felt stricken. Her mouth had gone dry. She did not respond.

"Too bad John Lee Davis is only the number two guy at the FBI. Hellman still can't figure out how to get rid of him." He was balling and opening his fists, a sign of anxiety she had seen a thousand times. His face was tormented.

"Two years?" Nel said finally. "So it's not about this election?"

"It is about this election. But it was inevitable. Too much fresh blood on the floor of the House."

She looked at him sharply. "Meaning?"

Victor drummed his chest with long fingers, a sign he was debating whether to reveal – or conceal – state secrets. Then his face clouded, as if he'd turned a corner into a dark alley.

"Why didn't you support me in front of the staff tonight?" he said stiffly. "I told you I was going to Philadelphia and I expected you to stand up beside me. This thing is deadly serious. Those people have to know we're unified."

"God, there you go again!" She crossed her arms on her chest and turned away, unable to meet his gaze. "Can't you ever –" It felt like he was suffocating her. "The world is going to hell around us and you have to have an ego tirade?"

"Are you coming?" he demanded through clenched teeth.

"I don't know, I don't know! It's all going too fast. Don't attack me."

Silence hung like a wet blanket in the room. An ego tirade. He knew she was right. His insecurity had come clawing to the surface. He hated it when she was right.

She waited another minute. "There's always blood on the floor of the House."

Pressing his lips together for a full ten seconds, he made his decision.

"Too many lies from the White House," he told her. "Too much information blocked off." His face went hard, and a raw edge came into his voice. "Besides the resistance, the political extortion… Remember Viola Ferrari? Two months ago?"

She felt strange suddenly. Her nerves jangled.

"Viola Ferrari? A government lawyer? Killed in a car crash I think. Something suspicious about it."

"It was no car crash." He forced himself to calm. "That's what the US Attorney's Office reported initially, from local law enforcement. She was an Assistant US Attorney. Died in the middle of nowhere down in Utah. First they said she was on vacation. It's possible those bastards –"

"What's Viola Ferrari have to do with this Riske business? You never mentioned her name."

"It's Need-to-Know. Highly classified."

She waited.

"Okay, it's a ticking time bomb in the back rooms on the

Hill. Shortly after her death some anonymous Justice bureaucrat got all guilty and talked to the Crime Subcommittee in closed hearing. Claimed Ferrari was investigating brainwashing experiments out at some government facility in Utah. Wouldn't say his name. Smart guy with a high-pitched voice. But that's all he knew. Or that's all he would say. You could tell there was more. The FBI verified his credentials, and then they wouldn't back him up or make any move toward opening an investigation."

"Brainwashing! Wait. I'm remember now," Nel said. She was twisting her wedding ring. Turmoil rose suddenly in her body. "It was all over the Internet, her death, I mean. A cult following started up! They were comparing it to the Karen Silkwood case. Who was it? This anonymous guy? He must have known something."

"He showed up with a mask on his face. Just like in the movies! That's why I remember that weird voice."

"He did *what?*"

"It happens. People testify against organized crime, drug lords. Anonymous whistle blowers who don't want to get blown away. It's legal."

"Yes, but −" She felt like she was being pushed into a storm against her will. "Why didn't the FBI act? What happened? The story just went away?" Her blood was churning. Were they killing people now? Young women doing their jobs?

"We got stonewalled trying to investigate. It came from the White House. They forced the US Attorney's Office to clam up. Staffers went scurrying around trying to get information − and that's when the hammer fell. It turns out the files were sealed by executive privilege."

"The President? Burligame? Why would he −"

"Billy Hellman. I'm sure of it. Everybody at Justice knew it was bullshit! She was on assignment! We had screaming sessions in Committee. People wanted to storm the Executive Office Building and beat the truth out of Hellman! But there was nothing we could do. The FBI said it was an accident. Case closed."

Nel said quietly, "They had her *murdered!*" She felt herself closing down, her head filled with disbelief and anger. "Why would they −" she started, and stopped. "I saw it on the Web. She was beautiful, incredibly intelligent, a real workhorse. Maybe on track for Attorney General. If the Progressives ever get in again." Tears welled behind her eyes, surprising her, and she had to pull herself back from the sudden grief.

Victor scanned the ceiling. "Her family requested an autopsy but it didn't reveal anything. No doubt somebody knows what happened to her. We've been doing brainwashing since Korea," he said. "You have to wonder how many people disappear trying to figure out what the hell's going on in this great land of ours."

"If it turns out –" She felt herself losing control. "If it turns out they were involved in her death for investigating government crimes –" She did not know where to go with these words, but heard herself say, "I swear to God I'll rip Billy Hellman's heart out of his chest!"

Her vehemence startled both of them. Nel felt the paranoia poisoning her stomach.

The wind howled outside, rattling the windows.

Nudging up close to her, Victor spoke in a whisper. "So Riske thinks he can get half a dozen senators to cross the aisle if it gets to that point. That still wouldn't be enough to impeach. That's why he's moving on other… fronts." He leaned in close to her ear. "He has some Cabinet secretary, I don't know who, maybe it's St. John. Maybe he can influence Burligame to wake up and take action."

She was staring at him wide-eyed, her fear no longer containable, too much at once, gushing out. "Is Riske on some kind of *suicide* mission? A couple of loose cannons and a Cabinet spy, and he's going to start a revolution? Is he insane? You'll all wind up in prison! Or worse! Look what they did to Viola!"

He misinterpreted her foreboding as betrayal. Suppressing a flash of anger, he rolled out of bed, crossed to the laptop on his dresser and found the *West Coast Paper* Website. "Did you read Molly Bee tonight?" He read the San Francisco columnist's warning in a hoarse voice.

"*'Again we have disgraced the Founding Fathers by failing to show up at the polling stations. Why don't we just sell our children into slavery? We have become a nation enslaved to the sitting authorities and their minions on Wall Street, suckered by the trinkets passed out by Communication International. They have beat our democracy into so many shares of stock. They terrorize the tired, the poor, the huddled masses into not voting, with their obscene lies and their rigged statistics. Pay attention, America. The jaws of oppression are clamping down on the throat of ordinary human decency!'"*

Reading from the laptop in black silk pajamas, her husband looked up at her, bewildered and angry. "Wall Street must be elated! They'll throw a fucking ticker tape parade for Julio Reese!" He turned and swung both fists repeatedly, slowly, against the dresser, chanting, "Goddammit! *Goddammit!"* He whirled around, shooting a fiery glare at her. He slammed his fist against the dresser. "I'm going to Philadelphia. I'm going to risk everything I have to pull this country out of this black hole its gotten itself into." Breathing hard, studying her for any sign that she disagreed. Nel did not blink.

"Are you coming?" he shouted again. Immediately he felt the fear of losing everything. She was the grounding force his career had been built on. And this election, this foul stench across the land, was the worst nightmare of his long public life.

She folded her arms across her chest and stared back at him. She said, "I am going to find out what happened to Viola Ferrari."

They had been married twenty-seven years. She had seen the rage erupt countless times, sometimes over matters of injustice to people, sometimes over a lost cell phone Either she took her own stand, or he simply locked her out of his world. Nel knew what Victor's world was. Years had passed before he told her the truth about the orphanage, about the beatings, the lies, the hysterical kids and the violent men running St. Stephen's Home for Boys, about the Christmas Eve one of the masters, Chester Swaggart – nobody present would never forget his name – gathered all two hundred elementary school boys in the auditorium, and called six-year-old Danny Haggarty forward. Swaggart calmly announced, holding Danny by one wrist, that he had shoved a governess, and without looking delivered a savage blow to the boy's face, yanked him up from the floor, smashed his face again, hauled him up bleeding and screaming and smashed him again and again until the boy finally passed out with half a dozen other faculty members watching. He then calmly announced no student was to touch any adult at the school.

In Victor Sligo's world, there would always be fire-breathing dragons, and there would always be injustice, and he would never cease fighting against them until he was dead.

Nel had drawn some advice from Purvis Courtman. Either she ignored this man's raging and vigorously guarded her own self-awareness, or she and the children – all four were young then – would suffocate. Courtman's estimation of his boss was grudgingly respectful and at the same time realistic. "Great men," Purvis had told her, "are a pain in the ass."

Victor glared at her now, fists banging against his thighs. He resembled a karate master in his black silks and bare feet. Tufts of hair pushed from the top of the pajamas. At fifty he still had a full head of straight black hair. His face and body were powerful from a lifetime of athletic achievement. He was an irrepressible, compulsive, opinionated, passionate man. And he was a winner. A Victor.

"When you're finished bellowing like a she bear in a leg trap," she said coldly, "we'll discuss it."

"I'm at fault," he snapped. "Is that it?" He whipped his arm through the space between them, then spun around to find some place to focus his anger. He wandered around the house, finally retreating to his workshop, part of the broad three-car garage. The rhythmic murmuring of the generator calmed his breathing. His mind went in circles at the enormous folly of taking on the administration. Civil war was a real possibility. Riske was going to bring in the military. How many people would die was incalculable. But people would die. Six hundred thousand died in the War Between the States. Not unlike that war, this was a matter of suppression of the human spirit. The course of democracy had gone askew, and the people would have to rise up. Victor Sligo would be among those leading the charge.

6

The night had been wretched. Soothing a ragged headache the morning after the election, she fixed herbal tea and struggled through an uninspired half-hour of her ritual martial arts forms. From there to a shower and the jade-tiled Japanese tub, where she tried to let her mind shut down and feel the ancient currents ripple through her body to release negative energy. But it wasn't working.

She felt anxious and worried. Shadows murmured through the house. Unexpectedly, something in the whistling wind brought her mother to mind. A montage of strength and despair and humiliation that had lingered on her mother's face throughout the year Nel was at home with her on the island to help her through the horrid struggle with the airborne pathogen pandemic. The memory had lingered in Nel's mind like a tortured inkblot. Her mother had not succumbed to the sickness, but was now bitter and old and had lost her vigor. No scientific research had ever explained the origins of the pandemic. Some nonsense about pigeons.

In the large kitchen, bald and pudgy Merlin in his crisp white apron was already preparing the congressman's breakfast. Nel waved a pinky at Merlin and took her tea, a croissant and slice of watermelon back to the family room. She sat listening for him; then, frustrated, she tightened her robe about her and hurried upstairs.

Victor was standing naked at the mirror, shaving.

"Get any sleep?" he asked on the upstroke under the chin.

"These politicians?" she said. "You know what they remind me of? A clown on stilts that came to San Juan Island once with the circus. With a big orange top hat and a red nose that honked when he squeezed it, and when he shook his leg a dwarf clown dressed just like him came out of his pantleg. It was so inane."

The razor slid along his hard jawline. "Nothing has been decided," he said, his indigo blue eyes holding hers. She glared at him in the mirror, until suddenly words gushed out as if a cork had been removed from her mouth. "My world's being turned upside down! How am I supposed to feel? First you tell me maybe they murdered Viola Ferrari. Then you tell me you're going to start a revolution! What if they kill *you!* Or throw you in a cell and lock you up forever. What am I supposed to do – just stop my life and join your crusade? You see a cliff and you just have to jump! Everything changes, Victor! Governments change. People figure things out. Presidents get run out of office." She took small raspy breaths while he watched her, holding the razor to his cheek. "Stop and think what you're doing! Just let them play their games while we build up a coalition with the Greens and the non-voters! Don't do this. Don't wreck our lives."

It was a variation on their routine over many years. She disguising her fear that she might lose control, dissolve into a blubbering basket case, and he concealing his need for approval in the Great Decisions demanded of a man of his caliber. Nel hated being afraid as much as she hated growing older. And Victor could never admit how badly he needed Nel to convince him he knew what he was doing.

Finally he turned to face her. Feelings swarmed like lost bees through their bodies.

"I know it's bad," he said at last. The look in her wide brown eyes never failed to both strengthen and soften him. "The wheels are in motion." He splashed water on his face, took the towel she was holding, and dabbed his cheeks. "I guess what I want to say is, I'm going to Philadelphia and I want you to come. No, don't look at me like that."

Nel glared.

"Look. I don't know what happened to that woman. If it was foul play, it just proves the administration will stop at nothing to do whatever they intend to do! On top of that, nobody votes! I don't know what's going on any more than you do. And I'm not going to let it go on."

"Stop it, Victor! Just stop it!"

"And I can't fight them without your support. Don't ask me why." Instantly he regretted the words. Nel grabbed the nearest object, a bar of soap, and slammed it down on the tile floor.

"That's a sucker punch, Congressman!" she yelled. "I'll come for my own need to monitor you and those clowns on stilts," at the same moment Victor was yelling at her, "Don't flip out, Abigail –" and each waited for the other to finish the sarcasm, and both started again and stopped and finally Nel said, "Don't kill yourself to save your country. You're not that important, okay?"

7

Forty minutes later a Communication International security van came out of the November fog into the circular driveway. Merlin started out, putting on his disgruntled face, but Victor, in his silk bathrobe and slippers, waved him away and walked outside himself. The heavyset Russian in her hooded company coveralls did not speak. She simply handed him an invoice authorizing repairs, including a bill for labor plus a $1000 charge for willfully destroying CI property. Failure to respond would result in legal repercussions and loss of service. Holding his temper down, he read her name tag. It wasn't Lyubov Karchovna's fault that he'd ripped out the laser fuses to get Burligame out of his face. Still, he felt the blood pulsing in his neck. Not intending to frighten her, he managed to do so by presenting his steely visage.

"I am a United States Congressman," he said, watching her diminish as he handed her back the invoice. "You are doing your job and I appreciate that." His voice rose. "You are to repair this module immediately, and return to your office. I want you to personally give your supervisor this message. Kindly tell him if he sends anybody around here again trying to intimidate me, I will see to it that he spends the next year stringing cable in the desert of eastern Washington. Leave me the bill for your labor." Lyubov Karchovna backed steadily away, looked down at the paper, then grinned and winked in an unspoken conspiracy with him. She turned to the module, and began to undo the havoc he had created the night before.

Before the Christmas season the staff generated contact lists and learned how to program prepaid, untraceable phones for the trip east, and spoke to their families, trying to avoid the word "treason." Victor spent a week in D.C. on post-session committee work and sending condolences to his melancholy colleagues from his condo on Fulton Street. He resisted looking Riske in the eye when he bumped into him. All over the Federal City he could feel the undercurrent of suppressed rage. Something was going to crack.

He did look at the people standing in lines winding along the grimy sidewalks off Capitol Hill. The D.C. Hunger Project had set up a highly visible food bank. Officials from Atlanta to Providence distributed transit coupons enabling low-income residents to travel to Washington, and spend half a day on the hunger line to pick up a ten-family package of genetically enhanced Korean grain, along with dried soy beans and vertically grown veggies from Sri Lanka, and Japanese fruit powder. Enormous video screens on street corners featured organizers challenging the authorities to look out their windows and observe the state of the American dream.

At home, Nel made repeated attempts to connect with John Lee Davis at the FBI, and other acquaintances in the Justice Department, as well as doing futile Web searches on Viola Ferrari. Davis was on vacation and unavailable. She could find no trail to follow. Information was old. Web sites had been taken down. A Seattle federal prosecutor told her as horrible as Viola's death was, it was probably best to let it go. The US Attorney's Office deemed it inappropriate to discuss the matter. She was stonewalled every step of the way.

8

Lincoln Financial Field was perfectly named. Not only was it jammed to the nosebleed seats with the raunch and glitter of commerce, but it afforded the lathered-up crowd an adventure in pay-per-view slaughter, millionaire gladiators slamming each other senseless for fun and profit.

They fumbled to their assigned seats dressed as locals in jeans and football jackets and ski hats. Victor added a gray handlebar mustache and sunglasses. Both of them could feel government agents lurking in every row. They had left details of Riske's meeting in the hands of the blond woman. Before Christmas an electronic packet had arrived in BJ Lichtenstein's daughter's email at Western Washington University, containing reservations at the Gouverneur Morris Hotel and a variety of vouchers, including a colorful photo of Philadelphia Eagles cheerleaders, female and male, in a mildly pornographic frenzy of cheerleading.

Every eye contact shot adrenaline through their bodies. In the uproar following the Eagles touchdown, neither of them noticed the short man with the backwards baseball hat leave his seat just in front of them. A beer vendor with a massive neck and thick shoulders lumbered down the row and dropped into the vacant seat, hoisting the cooler into his lap. Then somehow a beer was between Victor's feet, the vendor was gone, and the short man was back shouting at the players. Victor reached for the container, not fully aware what he was doing, and noticed the top bore a drawing of a church bell, made with some kind of water pen. On the bell the number 3.

Tapping Nel's knee with his, he held the beer low in his lap with his
thumb over the drawing. She looked. He removed his thumb. The
drawing had already smudged out. It was gone.

Maybe the bell had a jagged line down the middle of it. As
if it were cracked.

Congressman Sligo drank the beer and crushed the container with one hand. He whispered to Nel what he'd seen. A bell,
with the number 3 written on it. Three bells? What time would that
be? Bell three? Belfry? The next contact at the belfry? A church on
Third Street? Yes. It must be downtown. The belfry arch at the old
North Church tower. No. That was Boston.

In the taxi on the way back to the hotel – they passed up a
couple, zigzagged two blocks and flagged the next one – Nel took a
shot in the dark.

"Where's the Liberty Bell," she asked the pleasant, mid-
fifties driver. She studied him from her front passenger seat – the
open sheepskin jacket revealing a muscular shirtless café-au-lait
chest. Like many others he wore the gray armband representing a
parent who was forced back to work over age eighty by the Older
Americans Act. The government provided meaningless jobs for sen-
iors, in security and attending parking lots and school playgrounds, to
pay for the Social Security quagmire.

"Independence Hall," he answered with a shrug. "Everybody knows that."

"Is it open at this time of year?"

"Yup. Open all year, just on Mondays. Used to be every day
when I was a kid. One of those government cutbacks."

She felt oddly nervous and relieved at once. She said, "You
were raised here?"

The man flashed her a beautiful smile. "Yup. Right in North
Philly. I'm L'Ouverture."

She held forth a fifty dollar bill, one of the new ones with
the image of John Wayne on it.

"Well, L'Ouverture, will you be good enough to not remember this ride?"

"What ride was that," the cabbie said.

They decided Victor should show up at Independence Hall
at three o'clock Monday afternoon. For Nel, the message on the

beer container was just encrypted enough to cause the wrong party to pay no attention. If they were mistaken, they had lost nothing. Whoever it was would try again. Victor was too powerful to ignore in an assembly of this magnitude. His understanding of the inner machinery and sleaze of government would be vital to an uprising. No palace coup was going to take place without him.

Before he left the hotel, Nel stood before him with trepidation in her eyes, touching his arm.

"This could be a setup. They could bag a bunch of patriots." She held his eyes forcefully. "They'll lock you up for treason, Mister Congressman, and they'll love it. They'll parade you through the streets like –"

"There'll be no locking me up!" he told her, moving toward the door. "Sure it's dangerous. Hell, so is driving into the Capitol parking lot every morning."

"For God's sake be careful," she said.

He did not mention that if something went haywire – if it was a setup – the government would not bother to arrest him. That would be a mistake.

The worst place to have your worst enemy is in prison. Everybody knows that.

This time he wore a striped rugby jersey and sweats and a man's blond wig and wraparound mirror sunglasses that made him look like an Australian football player on holiday. He felt oddly out of body, but in the violent smash-and-dash of downtown Philadelphia, he blended in with the crowd.

Walking past a cobblestone alley, he spotted half a dozen middle-aged women ambling along carrying fishing tackle. In search of dinner for the family, he assumed, dressed in cloth coats and scarves. Music blared from somewhere. He clenched his teeth and felt the guilt boiling in his belly. A desolate feeling rose with it. Poverty was becoming institutionalized across the country.

It was indeed football weather, gray but not raining, about forty degrees. A smear of industrial yellow blurred the horizon above New Jersey. Victor wandered across downtown to Independence Hall, gawking at the old brick spire, feeling acutely self-conscious, constantly planning an escape route. As he passed into the Visitors Center, a slim National Parks guard nodded at him and shifted his eyes toward a low archway leading to a side room. There, another guard spotted him, and again flicked his eyes toward a door with a velvet rope across the front, joining two brass stanchions. Casually the guard, built like a fire plug and wearing a crocheted gray armband, crossed toward the door. This time Victor hesitated. A setup? He glanced at the guard's eyes but saw nothing. His body felt like a hair trigger as the guard waddled in front of him and disconnected the red rope, never looking at him. The stakes were much too high for errors. Before Victor could come to a decision, the guard opened the door and walked into a tight hallway. He followed, tearing off the glasses and wig as he walked.

The hall ended at a narrow stairway. As he descended the steep stairs, he saw himself trapped like a rat in a dungeon. His heart thudded in his ears. His forearms tingled. He steeled himself and pushed on. At the bottom, another door opened onto an unadorned basement hall. Crates and barrels of antiques, possibly Revolutionary War relics, lined one side of the hall. Feeling completely spooked by now, Victor follow along the hallway, past a dozen large white doors, around a corner to a dark corridor. At the end of it was yet another door. A crack of light outlined the bottom.

As he warily approached, the door opened. A harsh-looking female Navy lieutenant looked him over.

"Congressman," she said. "Please." And moved aside to let him pass.

Perhaps twenty people chatted in a large, exquisite meeting room. Each one looked up as he entered. It was in fact a replica of one of the Capitol's small committee rooms, thickly carpeted, the walls lined with portraits of historic figures. Several people were seated at a fabulous oval-shaped oak table so large it must have been constructed on the premises. He recognized fewer people than he'd expected, a couple of the Progressive Party power elite, a Pentagon official in civilian clothes, some people he recognized connected to D.C. think tanks, and in her signature sky-blue one-piece suit, Michaela Velasquez, age ninety, venerable elder stateswoman of American culture. He'd expected to see his rebellious FBI friend John Lee Davis, a man long determined to cut the legs out from under the administration, but Davis was not present. Several strangers were, however. Some still wore what appeared to be disguises. One man he did not recognize was actually wearing a coonskin cap and fringed leathers, dressed to resemble Davy Crockett. A wide door at the opposite end of the rectangular room opened suddenly, to reveal an underground brick-lined alley. A fabulous silver Chinese-made Mao Zedong Rolls Royce purred outside. The car door closed, the Rolls hummed off, and Senator Hal Riske and one of his staff people came in. The staffer shut the door and, with a motion from Riske, locked it. Victor Sligo, accustomed to clandestine meetings, wondered why he had been directed through the main entrance of one of country's primary tourist attractions, where he might have been observed.

He wasn't long in wondering. Abruptly a man stood beside him, with sandy hair and a thick neck and crooked nose – the beer vendor from the football game. Now he was dressed in a tan jacket and brown slacks, and conveyed an authoritative presence.

"Congressman Sligo, thanks for coming." He extended a large hand, and spoke with a slow, lyrical, cowboys-around-the-fire twang. "Bert O'Donnell. I'm with NSA. Glad you made it. Any problems?" Without waiting he said, "Sorry to bring you in upstairs. We were concerned about drawing too much attention in the tunnel. Several others came in disguises, using the upstairs entrance. How was the beer?"

So the National Security Agency was involved. Who else had been conscripted into this ring of desperadoes? How deep did it go? Assessing the group, he wondered what they could possibly hope to accomplish, Hal Riske and a bunch of people Victor didn't even know running this mutiny. Whose allegiance had been tested? Who were the spies? Which of them were acting out delusions of grandeur? And who would gun down the Vice President in a seizure of passion and destroy whatever plans they laid? Victor's eyes swept the room, and all he could see was failure.

9

Shortly they were seated. The severe military woman and a man dressed in a Revolutionary War costume began serving coffee in pewter cups. Hal Riske occupied the seat of power, perfectly groomed but quite overweight in a black silk suit complete with the upside down American flag pinned to his lapel. On his left was his chief of staff, and on his right the wizened senior Senator from New York, Joe Zola, whom Victor knew to be armed. Riske noisily sipped coffee, nodding at a dark man opposite him in an interesting rust-colored suit with white lapel piping. Victor recognized him: Admiral Sukwant Singh, former Chief of Naval Operations and now chairman of the Joint Chiefs of Staff. Singh's very presence in this room was a great way for him to lose everything he had spent his life working for.

But the same was true for all of them.

A single knock came to the door Victor had entered. Several people looked up in surprise. The door swung open. Instantly the female lieutenant was at the door. The short guard moved aside, and there stood Purvis Courtman, in his touristy LL Bean lavender out-fit, gawking anxiously around the table. The young Naval officer recognized him and moved aside. Courtman spotted Victor, and rushed clumsily to the last empty chair next to his boss. He looked nervous.

Courtman noticed somebody. "Sage!" he whispered loudly.

Victor looked. A gaunt man with flowing white hair stood at the end of the table making odd faces at Courtman. He whispered to Victor that Dr. Sage Kuushmann was an old physicist friend who ran the military communications network down in Groom Lake, Nevada, once known as Area 51.

Senator Riske shot Courtman a look, and began. His voice was reserved, his deeply lined, Hell's Kitchen face unreadable.

"We're meeting in this historic place to visit the necessity of taking our government back from people whose intentions do not relate to the common good." He swept his eyes through the group that counted Hispanics, Jews, African Americans, an Asian man with his thumb on a tracheal voice chip, five women, including one black, and one Pacific Islander; the Archbishop of the Eastern US, and an older person of unclear gender representing the Unemployed People's Alliance. He examined a notepad. "A cadre of professional people are meeting elsewhere, creating shadow Cabinet portfolios, defense options, avenues to pursue in the event of public violence and mass arrests, and wrestling with transfer of authority and Constitutional questions. We expect to be here until something concrete is resolved." He paused. "Now. We have asked you folks here for a brainstorming session. There is a lot on your minds. We are, ladies and gentlemen, up against the wall."

Immediately the politicians began grumbling about the state of the nation, each obviously intending to speak his righteous umbrage until somebody interrupted. They flogged the primary issues until Victor began feeling drowsy – Control of Congress by lobbyists, Hellman's cronies at Communication International, *blah blah blah,* Senator, billionaire profiteers and Asian governments looming, crisis in the voting booth. Victor was drifting off. His chin was on his chest. Take the bastards out to the woodshed! The FBI shackled, unable to investigate high crimes. Information blocked by the White House. The death of Viola Ferrari still unexplained –

Victor snapped back to the meeting. His eyes blurred through the room. Ferrari's name had startled a few of them, but the rest were reading the agenda and yawning behind coffee cups while Riske intoned his fried-chicken and bunting response to all this dissident blather. Beside him, Purvis Courtman's eyes were glazed as if nobody was home.

At this moment the NSA man O'Donnell burst out, "Excuse me, Senator! The country is going to hell in a shopping cart. We have a lot of authority here, as well as many independent thinkers ready to form a cohesive body and take action." His thick face turned to steel. "Apparently you have an organized meeting *elsewhere!* Is there a point to this? What the hell are we doing here, Senator? Or are you just monitoring this infantile whining so you can stroke your oversized ego, and then drive home in your Rolls Royce pretending you're a fucking patriot?"

It felt like a tree had crashed through the ceiling. All the air in the room compacted. A cup dropped to the carpet. Courtman stomped on Victor's foot, then looked innocently at Riske.

"Amen!" shouted a woman with a tight Afro and a vivid yellow dashiki. "We have flocks to tend, Senator! We know these issues. We know what's wrong! They're pushing us right to the brink! Now somebody just brought up Viola Ferrari. Her case perfectly demonstrates the evil personified by this administration." She glared at Riske. Her nostrils flared and her lips twisted. "Nothing leaves this room, Senator. I want you to tell me what you know about Viola Ferrari. Right now."

A series of emotions flashed across Riske's face, only visible to the hardened politician. Guilt flickering to embarrassment, morphing to indignation.

"Ms. Webster, I'm sorry," Riske said, quickly erecting a wall around himself. "We have a lot on our plates today. Can I get back to you?" Turning to his staffer, pointing at Webster and whirling his fingers.

She snarled openly, but held her tongue. At the same moment Victor's own frustration boiled over. He called out, "The other day you were ready to strangle Billy Hellman with your bare hands!" Simultaneously, the radical Mayor of Cleveland, Kareem McCandless, shouted, "No wonder people aren't voting! What kind of message are we sending them? The party leadership's reduced to a bunch of barnyard chickens!"

Others began shouting. Riske slapped a hand hard on the ornate table. "All right! These are troubled times, people," he shouted over the din. "I'm just as tormented by these events as the rest of you. Dammit, everybody, calm down!" But he was *smiling*. Victor saw it. He was creating chaos for *fun*.

Victor found himself envisioning horny old Ben Franklin preening in the Chippendale mirror upstairs, nattering at young John Adams to get the rest of them to cease this verbal brouhaha, and Adams telling Franklin to go fly a kite.

"I am yielding the floor," the Senator from Massachusetts said. "Before doing so let me state that our dilemma is so similar to that of the Founding Fathers, I imagine their first meeting to have been much like this one. Fear and mistrust must have underlined the profound human yearning for liberty. Now we are seeing the collapse of the democratic process. We must hang together or –"

Ms. Webster and Admiral Singh both interrupted at once. Singh spoke louder.

"Right. Thank you Senator," he snapped, closing down Riske's voice. "We must hang together, yes, but I'm damned if I'm going to stick my neck in the noose in defense of a bunch of Progressive Party –" Singh flailed a moment, unable to find the word. "Poopers!" he snapped. "The Pentagon has developed a first-strike offensive scenario in the event the Vice President attempts to –"

"There you go, Admiral," roared Senator Zola, surprising everybody. "You're the reason we don't let the military make decisions! You people are just as dangerous as they are!"

"Stand down, Senator," screamed another broadly deco-rated officer beside Singh. All three men jumped up, glaring and rat-tling their swords like drunks in a bar brawl. Angry people fired off their salvoes. Nearly breaking a finger jabbing his tracheal chip, eighty-year-old Doc Nguyen, CEO of VoteAmerica, gasped, "Stop this bickering, fools! We can get this baloney at the corner store! If the looting and pillaging hasn't started yet!" At the same moment Archbishop Goldberg grumbled to the stranger sitting beside him, who happened to be Purvis Courtman, "I had to fly clear from St. Louis to listen to this? The Philadelphia Eagles played better than these guys!"

A wild cacophony ensued, exalted strangers spewing their vomitatious clichés to get the country back to where it had never been to begin with. Someone insisted that Congress should be gassed, and he was already at work on the air conditioning system. A woman thought they needed to start with one premise – that Sec-retary of Communications Hunter Tyne, the love child of Adolph Hitler and Satan, known as the whacko of the Wasatch, was respon-sible for the poor voter turnout, and he needed to be lined up and shot immediately. Another demanded that failing to vote be consid-ered a felony, and perpetrators should be forced to live in D.C. for a week. Anybody connected to the financial services industry should have their taxes audited and their urine tested. Lawyers should be barred from running for public office. Vicious and immoral ideas flew around the angry table. Riske's staffer and the Navy lieutenant wrote frantically. Purvis Courtman sat with his mouth hanging open, his head swiveling from person to person on his scrawny neck.

Finally Ms. Webster rose. She fixed Senator Riske with a fiery gaze. *"Not to belabor the point."* She leaned forward, both fists on the table. "I want a full investigation into Viola Ferrari's death," she said through clenched teeth. Before he could respond over the echoes of a dozen others, Webster said, "I knew this woman, Senator. She was a great resource to our nation, a coura-geous fighter for justice and human decency, an uncommon trait within the US Attorney's office, not to say anywhere in govern-ment! Her death was no accident! And they're covering it up! The FBI, the US Attorney's Office, and the Congress! Maybe the White House! Those are high crimes and misdemeanors, Senator. You want a goddamn revolution? This is where it starts." She slammed the table with a stiff palm. "Right here! Now what are you going to do about this?"

"All right," Senator Riske sighed. He touched a thumb and forefinger to his nose. "I am aware further inquiry is needed regarding her death. In view of your esteemed reputation, and the fact that you have willingly stepped forward at risk of dire consequences – as is true for all of us – and in consideration of –"

"What?" Admiral Singh sputtered. *"For God's sake, spit it out, man."* At the far end of the table, the bulky NSA man O'Donnell continued staring with blatant pleasure at Webster, and shot a thumbs-up at Singh without speaking.

"Ms. Webster." Riske's tone was disrespectful and acerbic. "The investigation will be reactivated immediately. I'll have the Utah Highway Patrol report faxed to you. If we receive new information you will be informed. The report is absolutely confidential. Your eyes only. Do we understand each other?"

"For now," Webster breathed.

10

In the momentary silencing of bickering voices, the Davy Crockett figure rose, the fringe of his leather jacket flapping, his light beard giving him a much-too-youthful look. He had removed the coonskin cap. He acknowledged Riske with profuse hand gestures.

"We're obliged to you for making this meeting happen." He was an attractive man of about forty, fair-haired, six feet tall and slightly built. The close-cropped blond beard and pleasant voice brought to mind rolling fields and hay wagons. He was steady of eye with an ironic quirkiness about his long face. He chatted with one hand in his leather pants pocket, looking about in a boyish fashion, drawing the angry individuals together, although later nobody could say why exactly he seemed so compelling. But every person present would go home to talk about this strange, reasonable man.

"People like us are meeting all over the country. They're just as frustrated and just as disorganized as we are." He gazed wide-eyed around the table. "What we need to do is get these people into the herd, instead of letting them run amok all over the back forty. We want to understand why people aren't voting. That is a problem. Instead of beating our brains out looking for what divides us, we want to develop a strategy building on what already unifies us. And we need to do it in a way that gets people's attention fast. Here's what I suggest." Holding one hand in the air, he described an arc across the ceiling. "We hire an airplane with a big sign trailing behind it: *'Taking over the government. Go to Rebellion.com.'* We fly it all over the country. Especially Saturday nights, around sports stadiums and malls."

Nobody reacted for a moment. Who let this guy in here? Is he nuts? The Representative from Northwest Washington state rose. He liked the sound of this man's voice.

"I don't believe we've met. I'm Victor Sligo. And may I say, sir, you have an astute political mind there. That's the best idea I've heard since the unification of North and South Dakota."

Somebody ejaculated a single bolt of laughter.

"My pleasure, Congressman." He smiled genuinely. "Edwin Foulks. I'm in transportation."

"Well, Mr. Foulks. Delighted to meet you." Victor's mind was slipping sideways. He could feel his face flushing. He could not account for the sudden sensation that he was looking at – what was it? – his long lost *brother?* The costume was so quirky. Had Riske invited him? And what was his real agenda, speaking out so calmly in the face of clear and present danger to the republic, with this pathetic fantasy about an airplane and a sign?

Admiral Singh snapped his fingers at the Navy lieutenant standing behind him. He whispered, "Security clearance?"

She consulted a notepad screen and nodded once, brusquely. She said loud enough for everyone in the room to hear, "Bus driver." Courtman looked at him. His brow wrinkled.

A voice called out, "What's this *Rebellion.com* Web site say?"

"It says, turn off your TV and go vote," Edwin Foulks said.

Around the fabulous table, people shrugged, shook their heads, and prepared to move on. Riske was obviously enthralled.

"Well, hey," Foulks continued, smooth as butter, but with that childlike reserve. He looked like he should have been leaning on a Blunderbuss. "We're creating an insurrection here. We need to change our thinking about some things, particularly how to remove, or maybe I should say *rearrange* the sitting administration without destroying the country." He looked pleasantly around the table, connecting fluidly with each pair of eyes. Nobody but Edwin Foulks could detect the blood-mingling *plunk!* each time he reached another person, first the women – the intellectuals, then the writers – and then the men, Archbishop Goldberg, then the politicians, and finally the military people. "Change your thinking," he articulated softly, as though he were speaking to Martians or third graders. "We all understand the problem. The other side has the entire access to government locked up and a lot of people are suffering because of it. They win all the elections, even though hardly anybody's voting, and everybody in this room's stumped about what to do about it, even Governor Alex Holiday, who I can't help noticing is not present. So we need to change our thinking." The steady, determined boy-next-door feeling permeated the room. Women were raising eyebrows at one another and trying not to smile. Purvis Courtman was contemplating Foulks' campaign for the Presidency.

"I believe," Edwin Foulks said, "we need to ask Vice President Billy Hellman to tell the country the truth about what is taking place, and who he actually represents." He shrugged absently. "Maybe he'll do it."

The rough and tumble Mayor of Cleveland said, "Son, you've wandered into the wrong meeting. The Dada convention's down the hall." Some moaned and grinned queerly. Others were caught up in his unfathomable innocence.

"I am completely serious," Foulks said. "Turn off that TV, and go vote. And read Ms. Webster's epic work." With shy deference, he held an open hand toward the woman in the yellow dashiki. *"Strategies for Survival in a Corporate World."*

Iona Webster blushed through her perfect oak-hued skin and said, "I was just the editor, honey."

"Thank you. Now look." He pulled a large carrot out of his leather pants. "We've been paying too much attention to the carrot, and not enough attention to the stick."

The Progressive renegades stared. Ms. Webster and Mayor McCandless exchanged a look that suggested they'd stumbled into *A Charlie Brown Christmas.* Edwin Foulks reached under his seat and retrieved a collapsible metal rod, maybe an old car antenna, which he extended until it was about three feet long. With a twist-tie he fixed the carrot so it hung beneath the rod, then held one end of the rod on top of his head and frantically tried to snatch the carrot, just out of arm's reach. The leather fringes of his jacket flapped as he whipped his long arms out, and he yelled, "Whoops! Come on, carrot! Come here now!" But no amount of cajoling would get that carrot into his fist.

He turned and took a few steps toward Victor Sligo. The two men stood facing each other. The carrot dangled between them. Victor felt a profound intimacy churning in his body. He was being drawn into a powerful force against his will. He wanted to pull back, but at the same time was content where he was.

Nobody breathed.

"Congressman," Foulks smiled easily. "I'm starving."

For three seconds the two men held each other's gaze. Foulks appeared perfectly calm, a benign pleasantness in his bearded face. Victor was mesmerized, breathless and flooded with energy. Blood boiled through the back of his head. The younger man's wide eyes were the electric gray of a storm at sea. Victor felt gripped, held captive by this man's imagination. Into his mind came the old riddle: "If you had no elbows, how would you eat?" He grabbed the carrot and snapped half of it off, then held the piece of carrot in front of Foulks, who took a bite out of it. The tension collapsed. Everybody laughed. Hal Riske clapped, and immediately other government people began to applaud. The temperature had changed in the meeting room. People felt somehow safer.

For the seven-term Congressman, it was the defining moment in this subversive caucus. Later he would tell his staff he felt as if they had stared into one another's eyes for minutes, and finally Victor understood he had to surrender. His mind had simply stopped functioning. The state of the nation had become irrelevant.

Twice before he'd felt a similar sensation. When Nel gave birth to their first child, the baby had grabbed Victor's extended little finger and held on for dear life, and the tears had flooded his eyes. The other moment was a violent crash he had witnessed as a freshman in Congress. He carried a woman from the burning vehicle, and as he held her in his arms hearing the ambulance shrieking toward them, he felt her breath leaving her, and she gazed at him with crushing tenderness as she died.

The meeting pushed on for some hours. Nervous options came to the table, expanding the margins of both the sublime and the unthinkable. Edwin Foulks, in spite of his preposterous Davy Crockett persona, his carrots and surreal notions, spoke to each individual around the table as if the two of them were alone on an island, and he drew their feelings out like cocoanuts falling from trees. Finally, he plopped in his chair and stretched his long legs, ignoring the applause and bewildered nodding, and placed his fingertips to his eyes and massaged them gently, as if his contact lenses were burning. Victor Sligo's mind cleared. He felt something leave his chest. His immediate thought was, what kind of fumbling outfit is this? We've fallen down the rabbit hole! And whoever this Foulks is, with his country boy charm and his pretty face, there's no way in hell he can survive this train wreck of an insurrection we're pretending to launch.

Especially by sending up an airplane with a Web site advertising the insurrection!

Purvis Courtman had migrated to the side of Dr. Sage Kuushmann, the Groom Lake man. The two were going out for a drink after the meeting.

Senator Joe Zola, New York's powerful party leader, in his black suit and blue suspenders, still squinting in disbelief at Edwin Foulks, allowed a mild flicker of approbation to slide across his dry lips, then caught the eye of his longtime colleague Hal Riske and raised his vast and tremulous white eyebrows. Riske grinned at him.

"Life, liberty and the pursuit of Billy Hellman," Riske chortled. "We've brought the fanatics and the godforsaken into the political wasteland."

Victor was listening. "You don't really believe the Vice President can be taken down," he said.

"Any of that carrot left?" was the senator's answer.

11

Twice Nel had dreamed of Viola Ferrari's murder. It was an unconscionable horror that she felt strangely guilty about – almost as if a connection had existed between the two women that Nel had somehow forgotten. By the time they arrived in Philadelphia, her disgust with the blocked investigation into Ferrari's death, combined with her gut-wrenching fear for her own family, had brought her to a conclusion. She would have to do the investigation herself. The last thing the wife of a political figure wants. But nobody else seemed to give a damn.

Through standard government sources she quickly learned Viola had worked in Chicago. With BJ working one phone and she another, they managed to locate a Ms. Concetta Ferrari in Oak Park, a nearby suburb. She had no taste for detective work, and hated the questions she would have to ask. But it was Viola's family, she concluded, who would begin opening doors for her.

She was in the bedroom preparing to call the Oak Park Elder Care Facility when Victor returned.

His mind swirled with fractured images. He had to sit down and let them settle before he could think. BJ was ordering dinner on the hotel phone, and Mgaba stood in one of his lavish African robes and found a beer in the fridge and handed it to him. Courtman was still out with Dr. Kuushmann, and nobody knew where the blond woman had gotten off to. He stared out the wall-to-wall window at the fabulous Philadelphia evening trying to make sense of this excruciating dilemma. Was it even *possible* to progress, with ego-frothing bureaucrats and this Davy Crockett, this incorruptible dreamer at the helm of the sinking ship? And nobody voting? They couldn't take the law into their own hands. That was insane! They had no leadership, no core, no fire. This was the era of smash-mouth politics. They would need the same courage, and the same burning determination, that propelled the Founding Fathers to illegally break away from King George III. The streets ran red with blood. Hunger and violence ruled. It was a terrible time.

As he began, Nel came in from the bedroom.

"I don't know which is worse," he said. "Sticking with the government we have now, or casting our lot with that discombobulated mob. Those people couldn't organize their way out of a paper bag!" Not hiding his disappointment, he sketched the details. He noted a more formal meeting was ongoing with other high-level people at this moment. Among the nutjobs in the Independence Hall group, somebody was planning to gas Congress. What a redundant act that would be!

Shortly Courtman showed up loose with drink. He described the meeting with surreal flapping of his long arms and snapping the poly gloves. "It was like standing on your head playing a Sousa march while the pianist is pounding out the *Rach 4* and the conductor's giving you Tchaikovsky's *Concerto for Cello!* I had to hold on to the table to keep from falling on the floor." Turning to Victor, "Who were those people? That guy with the frontier outfit – I think he escaped from a Nineteenth Century riverboat burlesque!"

"A true Monty Python board meeting," Victor said. He dropped to the couch and hoisted his feet onto the coffee table, and admitted it. "I would say we got exactly nowhere."

"But like a good Christian nation," Courtman couldn't resist saying, "everybody at that meeting hated somebody."

"Except the kooky patriot Davy Crockett, who loves everybody and so far is leading this parade of unfocused zealots."

He told them about Edwin. His face, somehow angular and oblong at once, smiling and puzzling, pleasantly calling somebody's bluff every moment. The soothing voice, like a finely-tuned story teller scaring children around a campfire. Only then did he mention the NSA renegade O'Donnell and Admiral Singh and the inner city warlords, each with his own suspicions about the administration.

BJ Lichtenstein finally spoke. "Don't you people have any idea how *dangerous* this is?" He had taken to sitting with his phone in one hand and his notebook in the other, as though he was going to call his lawyer – or a taxi – any moment.

Courtman said woozily, "Well, nothing is as we sometimes think it must have been before."

They all looked at him like he should go lie down.

Victor turned to Nel. "Iona Webster really jumped in Riske's face. He's going to get her the report on Viola Ferrari's death."

His wife raised her eyebrows. "I'm calling her mother." Signaling BJ to come along, she walked into one of the bedrooms, checking notes in his notebook. She turned back to Victor and said, "I don't suppose there's any hope of us getting a look at it? I mean the FBI investigation?"

"I really don't know if there is one, dear," Victor said. "Accidental death's not a federal crime."

12

Concetta Ferrari was at the early stage of dementia. The evening charge nurse explained that phone visitors were not normally permitted unless authorized by family. When Nel pressed her about this, the nurse took a few seconds and said, "There is nobody. Her daughter passed in September." Nel then played her trump card: Congressman Sligo's wife, doing compassionate service work at the request of the US Attorney's Office, Northern District of Illinois. I see, the charge nurse said. And again asked her to hold. She returned with reluctant approval, asked for the Congressman's office number for verification in the morning, and warned Nel to be brief and not upset Ms. Ferrari.

For an eighty-two-year-old Alzheimer's patient speaking a second language, she was fairly together, if a bit obtuse and occasionally adrift. Nel approached her as she would expect to be interviewed herself knowing that her only daughter had been killed a few months past. With empathy and mindfulness.

"Ms. Ferrari! Hello! I'm Nel," she began too loudly. "Viola and I worked together in the office in Chicago."

"Oh, yes," Concetta Ferrari said. In the two syllables Nel could hear hesitancy and confusion and pride.

"I was hoping we could talk on the phone for just a minute or two about Viola."

"I miss her. My daughter." What she wanted was for the old lady to tell her how her daughter had died and who would want to kill her. She had to shake off the crazy thoughts, and she glanced at BJ, poised on the bed with his notebook ready, flashing on her own mother and the airborne pathogen pandemic that had nearly taken her life some years ago.

"I miss her also," Nel said, and the lie became true and sank into her heart. She had to turn away from BJ. "We were working on a case together, Concetta – may I call you Concetta?"

"Concetta, yes."

"When she left to go out West –"

"You pronounce it good."

"Thank you. Do you remember Viola coming to visit you before she left?" She caught her breath and squeezed her facial muscles tight. She'd gone directly to the damn murder!

"Coming to visit me?"

"She was going out to Utah, remember, Concetta?" Cradling the phone against her cheek and swirling her wedding ring till BJ finally pointed to it. "Some kind of brain experiments she was looking into. Brainwashing. Do you remember?"

"Oh, sure," Concetta said. Immediately Nel sensed she had broken through, and held up an open hand toward BJ.

"The Nazis, the airplanes, December 2nd, 1943. You think I forget? I don't forget. They blew up the boats. My hometown, Bari, in Puglia, and the sky blew up and kill people all over. Nobody said nothing." She paused, sniffled, and said, "Next twenty years they call it brainwashing." Her mind had shifted instantly to this horrific scene from her childhood. Again Nel collapsed into herself, and she reached for BJ's notebook and read the research she and BJ had hastily done online about Bari, on the Adriatic Coast.

"You probably remember this too," Nel said. *"'Se Parigi avesse il mare, sarebbe una piccola Bari.'"* She forced a gentle laugh.

"Parli Italiano!" shouted Viola's mother.

"No, no," Nel tried her only joke. *"Solo due parole."* Pause. *"Due, e parole!"*

Concetta repeated the old town joke in her language: "If Paris had the sea, it would be a little Bari." As she spoke BJ held up his notebook: "brainwashing".

She plunged back in. "Viola was going out West to talk to people about brain experiments. Did she have family in Utah? Anybody she visited?"

"Too many questions," BJ whispered.

"I don't. What is your name?"

"I'm Nel. Viola and I worked together, and I just wondered if maybe she left a message for me." She was yelling into the phone, and had to center herself with a few breaths.

"Viola, you know I think she came. Oh God. I think she came but didn't leave nothing, just the little record she gave me, and you probably want to know, she told me about Ten. A man. Ten, *capisci?* Somebody Ten. I think Ten, maybe looking for him."

"Ten?"

"Then after she die a man came. Somebody, a man. C. Told me some, what he call? Big mucky-mucky in America gets very mad at my daughter. See? I remember!"

Nel's heart jumped. "He came to see you? Was it the FBI? You said this was after she —"

"No, C." She made a sound like a soft snort, and repeated it. "No, C."

Again BJ held out a calming hand, and this time actually touched Nel's fingers where she was twisting the wedding ring, rubbing her flesh raw. She glared at him. BJ went back to his notes.

"No see?" Nel said calmly.

"You listen!" Concetta yelled at her, the voice rough and painful. "A man name 'C'. He cry, he slobber like little boy! You understan'? Said his name 'C' and he work in office with Viola like you and he cry because Viola dead!" An agonized sob came through the speaker, and it was all too much, all wrong, and Nel was so far out of her terrain her mind simply stopped working. A brusque female voice came on the phone.

"Ms. Sligo? I'm sorry. We'll have to go now." And she hung up.

For five full seconds BJ and Nel sat looking at the phone.

"This detective work sucks," she said. Then, "What just happened?"

Taking a few moments, BJ interpreted the conversation. There was the Luftwaffe attack on Bari during the war. Then, more recently, there were three people she spoke about, and at least one came to see her, and maybe two. The daughter talked about "Ten." BJ presumed Ten had something to do with her trip to Utah. "C" was another one.

"C felt awful about Viola's death," BJ speculated. "Maybe even responsible, it's hard to tell. Maybe he killed her. But then there's this third guy, the big mucky-mucky, who apparently was mad at Viola. He had no name." He shrugged and looked up at her. "She has a temper, that one."

"Okay. Thanks." Nel rose.

"Oh, and Viola left her a little record," BJ said, reading the notes. "Probably some family thing. So one is tempted to believe there's no laptop with Ms. Ferrari. No notes, no documents, probably nothing."

"All right," she said grimly. "I want you to get on the Web and start checking the two thousand government sites and all the federal listings for somebody named Ten, and everybody you can connect to this whose name starts with C. Start with the US Attorney's Office, Northern District of Illinois. And the whole damn state of Utah."

13

Patiently Victor and Courtman described for Nel and BJ and Mgaba the radical approaches to tyranny under discussion across town. Mayor Kareem McCandless would make voting mandatory, and impose community service for failure to cast a ballot. Meanwhile he had launched a city investigation into voting improprieties without the slightest clue whether there had been any. The yellow dashiki woman was in fact Iona Webster, editor of the *Strategies for Survival* Victor had contributed to, and also the first African American woman to play in the NFL as a place-kicker. Her strategy was to persuade voters to grow beans, pass them on to new voters, then continue the cycle, create a sort of urban-pride-democratic-agrarian culture thing.

"Beans!" Courtman blasted out, draining the last of his cherished Old Hickory.

BJ had to get his licks in. "We could do a bean poll. But seriously −"

Mgaba pushed his thick lower lip out at BJ. "Open your mind, Lichtenstein. One hundred forty million registered voters failed to show! This not only brings people into a voting conspiracy. It feeds people."

"Perfect!" spat BJ. "People standing in line at the polls farting!"

Courtman noted, "An old friend was there from a secret military installation in Nevada. Intimate with Communication International's operations. Sage Kuushmann. He thinks he can flood the continent with an external satellite overlay, which would create havoc with the government's communications grid for say twenty-four hours. Something like the old Star Wars idea. Then have a fast vote. See if anything changes when I-Media's unable to broadcast its propaganda."

One man had traveled all the way from an Air Force base in Thule, Greenland, to advocate a vote of no confidence in the White House. As he recounted this, Victor opened the door for two hotel employees who wheeled in dinner on carts, fussed with trays and wine, and left.

Mgaba rechecked the premises for bugs. While he worked he said, "The vote of no confidence is useless. Everybody would vote along party lines. The Newfies hold sixty percent of the House. There's no way. No way." He laughed haughtily. As always, Mgaba had his truth, and it was correct.

Courtman whispered, "But Sloan, he's going to slip sodium pentothal into the air conditioning system! He wants to *mindfuck* four-hundred and thirty-eight United States Representatives!"

Victor let loose a belch of laughter. "I don't know whether that guy knows who I am or not, but he looked me right in the eye and said, 'Who knows? Maybe some of those assholes in Congress will finally tell the truth!'" He threw his napkin down and laughed till his eyes watered. "I don't know what's in the Thules up there in Greenland, but I want to get me some!"

Nel Sligo chuckled with her husband, wondering who else in all of Congress would think that was funny.

She asked him, "Where did you send the blond woman?"

"I didn't. I thought you might have," Victor said. "Probably schmoozing with the governor."

The National Security Agency man Bert O'Donnell had had a word with Victor. He'd told him with that odd cowboy intonation, "If this little rebellion takes off, get out of the country immediately. Hellman's completely psychotic when it comes to enemies."

Somewhat lubricated, Courtman needed to amplify this. "Without doubt Billy Hellman is the real enemy here. He's inarticulate, muscular, violent, and he has the moral character of a runaway train. He's xenophobic and a skilled and malicious liar. He doesn't care a fiddler's piss about his own public image. He's the perfect enema. I mean enemy."

"And those are his good qualities," said Congressman Sligo.

Courtman spewed out Hellman's bio as he collapsed into a big leather chair, unscrewed another fifth of bourbon, and reloaded. They all knew the story, but just let him babble. Rising from the EPA's fabled Region Nine solid waste division, the nation's nuclear waste dump, Hellman had eventually snatched one of Nevada's two House seats, where he encountered and immediately reviled Victor Sligo of Washington state. Hellman was as ruthless as he was ugly. The nuclear waste connections led naturally to the chemical conglomerates and then to Wall Street, which in turn opened the door to the secretive global power elite and the embodiment of the New World Order within the US, Communication International. Eventually, of the Burligame administration's twenty-seven indictments, firings, replacements and suicides, Billy Hellman had elbow-lifting connections in twenty-one cases, and was implicated in the removal of one Supreme Court justice, three Cabinet members, half a dozen undersecretaries, and a White House legal counselor.

A phone hissed somewhere, an urgent, one syllable *sssst!* Mgaba reached into his jacket and grabbed it.

"Please?"

Immediately he turned to Victor. His face drew tight. Air blew noisily from his large nostrils. He opened his mouth to speak, his face a mixture of disbelief and pain, but he merely said, "Thank you," and clicked off.

"What?" Nel said.

Mgaba looked at the phone in his enormous hand, and back to Victor. "The blond woman followed your Davy Crockett guy from Independence Hall. He went straight to some private airport out in Lancaster County."

"How did she know who he was?" Victor was obviously alarmed. "Why follow him?"

"I have no idea. But he's now the loose cannon on the ship. He's at a private hangar, apparently renting an airplane. She says he's fabricated some kind of huge Mylar sign, and he's getting ready to take off. He's actually going to do it!"

Victor leapt to his feet. "Wait a minute! He can't do that! They'll kill him! Jesus Christ, where's my coat? I've got to get out there. Nel, call a taxi. You're going to have to head off the Gestapo if he actually takes off. Shit!" He slapped a hand to his forehead, already wondering why he needed to protect this strange man. "Damn that guy! They'll run him down to Guantánamo, and nobody will ever hear of him again. Nel! You'll have to deal with Manicotti! Right now! Get Courtman with you. Tell him anything you want! *He is not dangerous!* Don't let them shoot him down! Tell him he's drunk! Anything!"

Nel caught her breath. Manicotti was the Philadelphia Chief of Police. The most powerful law enforcement man in the country. "But that's not even Manicotti's jurisdiction! He has nothing to do with –"

"I'll call you as soon as I can learn anything." Victor was shouting orders. "Sloan, come with me. We've got to stop the guy before they arrest him!" He was pulling on the shiny green Eagles jacket, grabbing a last sip of beer, and stuffing his phone in his pocket. "BJ, give me some money. I can't use my name. No plastic! And stay here!"

Lichtenstein scurried about looking for his wallet, realizing he would be left to handle the media if anything weird happened. A battle was taking shape in his mind.

"Maybe I'd better go with you, Congressman. In a situation like this you're going to need –"

"Damn it, man, get me some cash and man the phones!" Victor bellowed, Captain Ahab about to lower the boats. "Somebody has to hold the fort! Purvis, listen! Are you sober?"

"Relatively," he slurred.

"You need a phone and you need to be at police headquarters." To Nel he yelled, "Manicotti controls this whole state! I know you despise him, but you have to tell him I'm handling it! If you don't he'll go out there and take over the goddamn thing. He'll destroy the kid and take the credit! The feds'll put his balls through the wringer, and we don't want that. The way he was operating in that meeting, he's probably too naive to save his own ass."

"So you want to throw *me* in the firing line?" Nel shot back at him. "What if it's some dumb publicity prank?" But she knew from long experience once Victor went frenetic like this, twenty mules couldn't pull him off his course.

Mgaba said hastily, "Oh it's no prank. The blond woman believes he's serious. And she's never been wrong yet."

"That's why she followed him," Victor shouted, a manic tintinnabulation in his voice. Then, squinting at the windows and the air conditioning vents he said just above a whisper, "Foulks. That's his name. Edwin Foulks. Dammit, he's like Moses with a straw between his teeth! We can't let them grab him. He's a child prodigy at the county fair about to fall off the roller coaster!" He glanced at

Nel. She stood with one hand on her hip, observing him as if he'd lost his mind. "Hey," he said to her. "Don't ask me what's going on! I don't even know myself! Edwin Foulks is one of us. Look, go with Courtman, will you? Don't give me that look! You know how to handle these people. Purvis will just piss Manicotti off with all his political baloney, and the guy's a right wing hardass!" He was speaking so fast the words were jamming together. "Where's my goddamn phone?"

"In your pocket!" they all shouted.

"Great! Why the hell can't you people –" he muttered as he felt for the phone. "All right. Nel, keep a phone handy. Purvis, go with her!"

She moved quickly to Victor's side. "You'd better get a grip on yourself, Congressman."

"Look, Dear –"

"You don't even know this man. So calm down. If he's the second coming of Jesus, we'll know soon enough!" She was getting caught up in Victor's mad fervor, already boiling inside with the thought of dealing with Chief Manicotti. But she was Victor's anchor and had to contain herself.

"Saddle up, Mgaba. BJ, if you hear from anybody who attended that meeting today, stall 'em. I'll be back!" He dashed out the door before anybody could slow him down. Within minutes, Nel and Courtman had settled on a plan, made some calls, and were on their way out the door. Courtman turned to Lichtenstein.

"Hey Licky!" he snapped. "Check out the Web site! Maybe the whole thing's an elaborate Newfie trick to embarrass us!"

BJ Lichtenstein didn't hear. He was already taking control, wondering what was going on, and why he was always the one left behind.

14

BJ didn't much care for Gouverneur Morris's fabulous presidential suite. He didn't like being on the road at all. In spite of the nagging and the constant criticism at home, he loved his over-priced condo across the bay from Sunrise. The pool, the roiling spa, the ravishing women at the country club, the security, all of it. He had a beautiful home. Leah had her own Lexus and her own career in real estate. He took care of himself, he was good-looking and smart, and he shot in the low eighties on the Arnie Palmer golf course.

He was just never at ease in his own skin. That was the problem.

In profile he thought he looked like John Kennedy, the wavy dark hair and strong face – if you ignored the sloping chin – although BJ was shorter and Kennedy was dead. Leah had commented on them both, early on the strong face, then later the weak chin, after lavishing him with creative sex until well into the third week of the marriage. He took a whooshing handball swing to admire his physique. Yeah. He was looking good.

But he had to get to work. That load of stuff Nel needed done. Look up everybody in government.

BJ Lichtenstein began to suffocate in the cage of his middle years. He couldn't seem to get through a single hour without heavy judgments about his wife. Her muttering to herself, her acquisitiveness, her whining. But on the road he envisioned Leah lounging by the sauna with her sexy girlfriend Binny, the long dark legs parted, perhaps a white towel wrapped close around her. BJ contemplated Binny's fine body, a well-worn fantasy that involved Binny and BJ sweating in the sauna together.

But he had to get to work. Get online. Everybody in government.

It was a long taxi ride to Frank Ney Field in Lancaster County. Victor and Sloan Mgaba jumped out at a large open hangar among several dark buildings. Excruciatingly bright light poured out onto the tarmac. They burst into the hangar preparing to knock Edwin Foulks unconscious if necessary to prevent him from doing something unspeakably foolish, if not actually fatal.

Standing beside an aging Cessna 400, Edwin was engaged in an animated conversation with a man the color of dark chocolate, with a beefy body under a worn powder-blue tuxedo. His bow tie hung undone around his thick neck. Both men were laughing. At that moment the blond woman appeared from a back office, looking disheveled and exhausted in her red suit and heels, just flipping closed her cell phone. Coming forward, she stood sternly beside the airplane and fumed at Edwin Foulks.

Mgaba immediately took charge. Believing the deal was already done, he shot forward and shouted, "Sir! This man is being sought by federal authorities! Don't you let him have that airplane!"

The big man turned to Mgaba and Victor. His demeanor switched instantly to disdainful arrogance.

"I am certainly not being sought by federal authorities," he growled. "Who the hell are you?"

"No, *him,*" Mgaba gestured frantically at Edwin. "Him! He's got treason on his mind and he'll never get away with it!" Victor, surprised how pleased he was to see Foulks again, called out, "Edwin! What's wrong with you, man? You know you can't do this! You won't last half an hour!" Victor caught himself. He had intended to express his congressional indignation at this man doing something so patently stupid. But none of those feelings surfaced.

Actually, he might have been feeling a bit envious.

The fringed leather costume was gone. Now Edwin wore a tan winter jogging outfit – hooded jacket and sweatpants, complete with faded stripe down the leg. Across his slim chest was the single word, "Airborne." Gazing at them with pewter-colored eyes, he nodded ironically, his soft grin telling them he understood everything. The smile was all out of synch with what was taking place. Even stranger, his face seemed to cast a soft light against the side of the plane's silver fuselage.

"But that's not the main thing on your mind, Congressman," Edwin said. The smile was genuine, the voice at once commanding and soothing. As Victor and Mgaba struggled to prevent a horrible injustice, Foulks was acting like it was Sunday at the beach.

To his own astonishment, Victor agreed. "That's right. You haven't consulted me with your scheme, and I don't like it. I'm not used to people doing things without my approval. I am a United States Representative, and people need to listen to my opinion!" He turned to nod at the man in the tux. "Especially about acts of sabotage against the government."

All the breath went out of him. Where did that come from? Of course that's what he was thinking! But that was none of this guy's business. Victor was very nervous telling the raw truth like that. He opened his mouth to say more, half intending to lash out at

Foulks, but his thoughts somehow flushed through his bloodstream. Foulks had read his mind. The man in the tux nodded vigorously, as if he and Edwin shared some deep secret. Victor felt caught in some invisible conspiracy. With no effort he and Foulks had established a bond back at Independence Hall, and now the man was going ahead with this patriotic suicide mission without further discussion, and Victor had whined about his own vast self-importance. Spreading his hands out, pained disbelief on his face, he wanted to demand Foulks get in the taxi so they could deliver him to a padded cell. Instead he heard himself ask, "This banner we've been hearing about. Is it for real?"

"It's for real." The blond woman gushed out her daily quota of words all at once. "It's hung out on those goalposts on the airstrip waiting for the hook. High-tech halogen-threading. You can read it a mile in the air at night!"

"You people understand," the man in the tux started, his voice articulate and rich, "The time for talk is over!" Holding his great hands clasped together and pointing thick index fingers at Victor and Mgaba, "And you should damn well know it!"

Mgaba shot back, "You should damn well know he's asking for a lethal injection!"

"I'm sorry," Edwin broke in effusively, his fine tenor warbling on the cool air. "This is Mr. Toon." He looked up at him. "Alonzo, isn't it? Congressman Victor Sligo." As he spoke he reached down for a stuffed gunny sack, and took a step toward the open door of the plane.

"Call me Spit," the big man said. "I manage this airstrip. What you're seeing here, gentlemen, is a man taking action!" Unceremoniously he opened the top stud of his white shirt. "Pardon my clothes. I also play blues in a club. This guy –" slapping Edwin on the shoulder – "has a protest to make. That last election?" He shot a loaded look at the blond woman. His voice dropped half an octave. "You got to be the lady who called these people."

She smiled acidly.

"Congressman. Get this. I was cheated out of my vote, but I don't know how they did it," Toon exclaimed.

"Mr. Toon!" Mgaba said. "Congressman Sligo has not come here to –"

Toon paid no attention. Edwin was already busy in the

cockpit. Suddenly the motor came to life, a violent whooshing howl that sent the visitors' hands to their ears.

"I'm a thinking voter," Toon screamed at Victor, leaning in close, ignoring the roaring aircraft. "And I'm fed up. And I'll tell you why. The absentee ballot came in the mail 'cause I don't vote on line, no way, not the way politicians cheat on the Internet." The engine noise filled the night. Toon's face twisted against the turbulence. "No offense, sir. I filled out the ballot, Progressive all the way. But I never sent it in." His chubby face was grim. The lips pursed into a pout. He glanced at something under the wing, grabbed a big wrench and a spray can of Astrolube, and pushed by Victor to crouch down and adjust something, then popped out and signaled to Foulks, a single finger twirling shoulder high. He put a hand on Victor's back and moved him away from the screaming airplane. He shouted, "In other words, I never voted."

Victor could smell the night club odors on him, whiskey and cigars and late night jazz. But he was seriously alarmed about Foulks. It was not the time for whining over spilled elections.

"He's taking off!" Mgaba boomed. "Toon! Get him out of there!"

Toon crossed his thick arms, the big wrench in his hand tapping the air. The two-seater Cessna began to roll.

"But I still can't figure out why I didn't vote!" Shaking his big head, Toon grunted loudly, waving the wrench. "It doesn't make sense! Me? A hard-core ghetto liberal? Spent my life in North Philly till ten years ago when I came out here and bought this place. Watch it, Crockett! Easy, brother." The airplane rolled into the bright lights outside. Swinging an arm overhead and pointing repeatedly down the runway, Toon moved aside as the roaring increased. They watched the plane roll away. The tiny wing-tip directional adjuster shot a blue streak into a snowbank beside the tarmac.

"I'm not going to let this happen!" Victor shouting now, strange sensations flooding him as the Cessna taxied toward the runway. "They'll shoot him down before he's in the air ten minutes! Goddammit Toon, stop him! They'll arrest you too! Inciting to treason!" He felt elated. But in his mind was the sure knowledge that Edwin was flying to his death. It was like sinking into a warm whirlpool, the screaming engine, the fear of this man killing himself for a cause too big to grasp. And at the same time an eerie warmth seeping into his chest.

The Cessna was five hundred yards down the tarmac, where Edwin had climbed out and was checking something at the rear. Toon was smiling, caressing the heavy wrench. "We fought for co-operative public housing, and they beat that down. We fought for abortion rights, and they beat that down. We fought for inner city schools, and they beat that down." His face was grim. "You know what the city water tastes like down there? And the sewers! And the rats!" He looked hard at Victor, with neither anger nor accusation. The words came from deep in his chest, rich and evocative. "You surprised somebody'd do something like this?" Waving the wrench toward the aircraft. "That's a man with a lot of courage, there. Somebody has to speak for all the hungry voices and all the power-less voices and all the broken voices. For some reason nobody has ever explained to me, people like you don't hear those voices." Pointing a thick finger at Victor, he balanced the wrench across it. They both watched the wrench tilt slowly to one side, then the other. "It could be so simple. Just taking care of folks. Everybody getting what he needs. But when the needs of the needy people somehow have to pass through people like you, rich white folks already in control of everything, what happens is, you people just want too much." A finger of his other hand came to the end of the wrench, and with the slightest nudge, the wrench clattered to the ground. "And that's what happens." He held up enormous empty hands, his large glistening face firm, eyes blazing.

Victor was shaken. His face tightened against his own guilt at his role in government policy. "Well, dammit, man! What do you suppose –" His brain flooded with a completely reckless notion. For a mind-numbing instant he struggled against the consequences. The end of his career in Washington and possibly the end of his life. But he would go down in a blaze of glory, that was certain.

He started running toward the airplane. Mgaba yelled after him, then grabbed Toon by the shoulders and demanded he stop Foulks. Toon stared after him, then looked at Mgaba. "This man comes out here with his cockamamie idea and I thought, yeah, somebody got to do something radical. Everything is so wrong, so real wrong with this country, ain't no voting about to fix it. Ain't no democracy about to fix it. Ain't no Congress about to fix it."

"What?" Mgaba yelled. "He just told you what he was going to do? Just like that?"

"Yup," Toon said.

"You realize it's a federal offense to incite to treason against the government?"

"Yup," Toon admitted, eyes on the runway.

"Are you insane?" Mgaba bellowed.

"I don't believe so," Toon said, grinning broadly.

Victor was racing behind the Cessna, squinting to the opposite end of the runway at the goalpost-shaped stanchion, where Edwin had fixed the cable and a seventy-foot-long halogen-threaded banner. Finally he caught up and yelled at Edwin to open the door, then began beating on the freezing wing, screaming at the top of his lungs. At the far end of the runway the plane stopped. Victor yanked the door open and pulled himself in.

Edwin Foulks was slipping in contact lenses. He looked over, blinking, and adjusted his headset.

"Hey," he said. "What took you so long?"

Sucking in air, trying to look angry, Victor managed to gasp, "What do you think you're doing?"

"Going shopping," Foulks said. He listened to Toon on the radio a moment. Then turning the Cessna into the wind, he eased the throttle forward, and roared down the runway. In moments they were airborne, then peeled back to the airstrip and dropped directly toward the goalposts. The aircraft jolted when the hook snagged the cable, and they soared into the pitch black night.

15

Downtown, Nel Sligo and Purvis Courtman had succeeded in arranging a 7:30 meeting at City Hall with ice-veined crime-buster Giuseppe Manicotti, Chief of Philadelphia's finest, often quoted on I-Media national talk shows, obscenely self-promoting, demonstrating what he insisted was his "presidential demeanor" to whoever would listen.

She knew trying to persuade Manicotti of anything was a terrible idea. But he was powerful enough to stall the authorities till Victor could corral Foulks. Already she sensed this was bigger than it looked, and Victor had made it plain – too many unpredictable people were connected to the Independence Hall crowd. This kid in the sky with his banner was inviting a catastrophe. She had to persuade Manicotti to get the feds to back off.

They met in Manicotti's colorless office. The police chief, in his mid-fifties, was thickly built, five-ten, with a receding V of tight-cropped hair and the grizzled look of a military veteran. He brooked no insubordination, and was not moved by Nel's plea for understanding. It fact it made him laugh.

"You're telling me this man's got some sign advertising insurrection against the United States? But it's just a joke? And you're telling me he's perfectly sane but really isn't? Is that it, Ms. Sligo?" His voice boomed through the hallways of Police Headquarters. "And I'm supposed to do *nothing?*"

"Technically," Courtman said, pressing down on his shaking legs, "it's not your jurisdiction. The Congressman simply asked us to come here to –"

"Jurisdiction my ass!" Manicotti growled. Without seeming to notice, he jammed a pinkie into his ear and scratched wildly. "I don't care if it's a choir of singing nuns from Wyoming Seminary!" His voice had bullets in it. Studying his little finger, then looking Nel dead in the eye, "It's a national security matter. If this guy's a terrorist, he'll be detained. Doesn't matter whose jurisdiction it is." His voice brought to mind an electric pencil sharpener. Grrr-whish! In! Out! No extra words.

"Chief Manicotti!" Nel stood, unsure of herself, but holding his small dark eyes with hers. She had changed into a cashmere sweater and short jacket, and rather tight cream-colored pants. How do you reason with a thick-skulled redneck? Surely he wasn't a complete fool. "We both know you are in a position to influence federal authorities in handling this situation. The fact is," she said, weaving through a minefield, "this man is protesting the poor voter turnout. That's all. It is perfectly legal."

The police chief stared at her. The stare morphed to a glare. *"What?"*

"Voters not showing up at the polls," Nel said. And immediately felt ridiculous.

Courtman wanted to shut her up, just threaten the cop with repercussions from the governor. But his threat clogged in his throat, and he kept silent. He couldn't remember the governor's name.

Backing a step away, Manicotti dropped his gaze heavily to hers. Through hard lips that barely moved he said, "You tell Sligo something for me. He's not going to come in here whining about a fair national election that re-elected my Commander-in-Chief!" He paused to examine her figure in an overtly sexual fashion. "And tell him not to send a woman next time!" He stepped away from her. "Voters, my ass! Excuse me, Ms. Sligo. I've got a city to police!" And he waved a hand at the door.

Unaccustomed to being dismissed, Nel stood her ground. Her eyes went to slits, and she hissed through clenched teeth, "You will regret playing with me, *Chief!*"

Immediately Courtman grabbed her arm and moved her away from Manicotti's desk. Staring at her with his eyeballs bulging, Manicotti pushed a button on his desk and snapped, "Kowalski. Code orange at Ney Field. Now!"

In the media room, a junior reporter stuck on the police beat was reading. She was a tall, attractive young woman, twenty-three, full of spunk and bored out of her mind. Hearing the hubbub, she straightened herself up and, shoeless, glided down the marble hall to eavesdrop. Immediately her heart began to race. She discovered she had no notebook, only the company phone tucked into the tight side pocket of her jeans. What was the wife of Congressman Victor Sligo doing here at this hour? Why the heat from Manicotti? She could feel a story bubbling up in her stomach. In her eight months experience, Raven Menez had already learned politicians only speak to journalists for their own advantage. Never spontaneously, and almost never truthfully. At the same time she had begun to seriously question her employer, *US Times-Philadelphia*, the extreme right wing print division of Communication International. But Raven needed the experience, and she was developing her portfolio while her editor twisted her reporting skills into what passed for news at the paper.

Throwing on a coat and shoes, she followed Courtman and Nel out of the building, managing to open the big glass door while wiggling a hand into her pocket. She withdrew the phone, touched the "record" key, and moved in.

Nel was slapping her purse against her thigh. She muttered,

"That sexist prick!"

Courtman turned to her. "You don't suppose Foulks actually took off?"

Nel stopped on the sidewalk to button her coat. Raven Menez stopped three paces behind. "Now all we've managed to do is alert the police! They'll chew him to pieces. Manicotti'll probably bring in the –" Courtman's phone chirped.

"Mgaba! Where is he?" He listened a moment. "Oh, Jesus!" He stopped walking. Nel watched him anxiously. "Victor's on the plane!"

She gasped involuntarily. "They've take off? We've got to get out there!"

"They've taken off with the sign flapping big as life!" With sinking horror, Courtman swept a hand across the sky, imitating Foulks at the Independence Hall meeting. *"Taking over the government!"* he whisper-shouted at Nel with a distorted grimace. *"Go to Rebellion.com!"*

Instantly Raven Menez turned on her heel, making herself say aloud, "Ney Field. Code orange. *Rebellion.com.*" She was back in City Hall in a flash, to call the night city editor. Jiggling the phone in her hand, she visualized promotions, a new car, breaking a fantastic story of one man taking on a corrupt federal government. Maybe he'd even kidnapped a US Congressman for some kind of protection! And not some backbencher, but a true voice of the common man, Victor Sligo! But the city editor! She'd never... With a blaze of comprehension she knew she could not call in the story. Not yet. Her only choice was to race out to Ney Field. On the way she'd get hold of her mentor, Molly Bee, the *West Coast Paper's* powerful columnist out in San Francisco. Maybe this was Raven Menez's ticket to a real career.

16

Naked BJ Lichtenstein was busy in the warm marble-tiled bathroom when the phone jangled.

He found the phone on an end table. The drawer was open, with a gilt-edged Gideon Bible inside.

"This is Michaela Velasquez. May I speak with Congressman Sligo, please?"

"Ms. Velasquez! Hi! Well gosh!" He snatched up the Bible to cover himself, then hurried back to the bathroom, pressing his thumb over the phone camera, fumbling into his underpants. He fell on the tile floor with a harsh thud.

She must be downstairs!

"Victor? Are you all right? My phone video's out."

"Yes, uh, no," he moaned, "it's BJ Lichtenstein! I'm the political advisor. How are you?"

"Have I reached the presidential suite of the Gouverneur Morris Hotel?" The tone enormously dignified and grating.

"You have. I'm terribly sorry, Ms. Velasquez. Congressman Sligo is out. May I take your number and have him return your call?"

"No. I'm coming over there. Turn on your television. Look up that Web site. And order up some brandy."

"Yes, ma'am, I'll see if –" What was he supposed to do? His balls throbbed, and he looked down to see he was crushing himself against the sink.

The line went dead.

He stumbled toward the wall-mounted television. Waving the remote at it, he dropped to the couch, still in his jockeys, and looked up to see the distorted image of some sort of flag flying above a huge crowd. Zooming in, the camera caught it with blazing clarity: *"Taking over the government. Go to Rebellion.com."*

Oh my God, he did it! Everybody in America had to be watching. He closed his eyes in disbelief. A strange squealing sound came involuntarily from his mouth. His hair was standing on end, and he wondered where his phone was, and what he was doing in his underpants. He had to warn Sligo before Homeland Security came out and blew Edwin Foulks to smithereens, taking the revolution with him before it even started. And brandy, yes, get some brandy.

17

He was scared, all right. Yet there was something calming about cruising half a mile over a geometry of silence, the blue lights of the Main Line west of Philadelphia winking at them. The city of eight million glowed like an electric mushroom across the eastern horizon. Behind the Cessna the banner flickered its message. The compressed gas threading would withstand fire or hurricane, and was powered by a tiny two-volt igniter. The super-lightweight banner could be read for a mile across the greasy smear of night.

Edwin Foulks was placidly humming while Victor imagined the calamity that was about to take place. He believed Foulks had succumbed to a childlike fantasy. Regardless how appealing or genuine he seemed, the man did not comprehend the consequences of reckless actions.

But Victor liked him. He felt drawn to Edwin the way an adolescent is drawn to an eccentric uncle. This curious feeling made him all the more edgy. He was not accustomed to coming under another man's spell. Victor was a powerful, confident man himself, a leader of men, and he wielded his power skillfully. He didn't care much for the adoration of others, particularly a country boy with a tender voice and bright eyes and a Pollyanna attitude.

So what was it?

"I have to explain something to you. They're going to shoot you down. It's not an option in a terrorist action. That's what this is." Victor squirmed in the old leather seat. "That banner. If Mgaba is smart enough to tell the authorities I'm on board, it might save your life."

Edwin turned to look at him. "Or they'll kill both of us."

"Or they'll kill both of us. We don't want that. You get it? Even if it is a great cause. We don't want to die by pulling a stunt so incredibly stupid —"

"Hey, look! There's the new mall!" Just ahead were the flood lights, the enormous parking lot defining three hundred acres of the American dream.

"I'm trying to tell you, you can do more good alive than dead. Back on your farm or wherever you come from. Anything's better than the government locking you up on terrorism charges in a rat-infested cell in Cuba!"

"You politicians, you know interesting things." He glanced again at Victor. Immediately Victor's brain felt loose inside his skull. It was perfectly clear what was happening. This man had neutralized his normal denial routes. And Victor didn't care. He was waiting for his anger to emerge in the face of somebody trying to bend his will. But there was no anger. He saw floaters behind his eyes. Fingers massaged his brain when Foulks looked at him. And sitting side-by-side, he heard an odd low-frequency rumble, like flatcars passing through a railroad crossing.

"Politicians are like magicians pulling doves out of their hats," he actually heard himself say. "It's all illusion." What he intended to say was, politicians are real people with families and fears and insecurities, and an enormous responsibility to protect the American way of life. He wanted to sound like Alonzo Toon, commanding and concerned and genuine. But he was no Alonzo Toon and he knew it. Instead he said, "We always get what we want. It's like a magic act. People vote for our acting skills. We're constantly perfecting the illusion that we're doing something constructive." His mind lined up the Ways and Means Committee, paranoid roosters clawing over their turf. "The truth is, politicians spend about fifty percent of their energy taking perks and orders from corporate interests, and another forty-eight percent getting re-elected. Right from the beginning."

"That leaves only two percent for public service," Edwin said. "Look at all the citizens down there! I think I see a Ferris wheel!"

Victor gazed down. "As long as you create a stirring illusion, that's enough. You erect a foundation you can perch on, like building a medical research facility or funding a Navy base in your district. Make a lot of noise doing it. Give ego-jacking speeches at graduations – social causes, unemployment. Make jokes about God. Make them think your opponent's entire life objective is to screw the voter. Or his wife." He studied Edwin's face, utterly calm, in another world. Why was he telling him all this? "You're sitting on a teeter-totter all the time, and your opponent's on the other end, shooting darts at you with lobbyists' money. So the question that preoccupies Congress is, how do I get that bastard off my teeter totter?"

"You're awfully cynical," Edwin said.

"Well. There is the media, who hate us. And the opposition, who devote their lives to making us look like idiots." Laughing nervously, "Nobody knows! God, I never talk like this! How I do my job's none of the public's business. This East Coast air's curdling my brain. Graft and corruption in every lung!"

Edwin banked to swing back across the mall, and they could feel the tug of the banner. They could make out a hubbub below, people pointing, rushing back and forth, cops flashing in, and the odd flare that almost looked like a gun discharging directly toward the Cessna and its belligerent banner, glowing like a rocket's red glare, like bombs bursting in air.

18

BJ stared mortified at his phone. The come-hither voice of the answering service girl told him his call was very important to Congressman Sligo. A staff member would get back to him shortly.

He clicked back to the Web site on the big Holotech TV.

Rebellion.com featured a stunning reproduction of Picasso's *Guernica.* Superimposed as a rider on the agonized bull was a leering Billy Hellman, drawn to resemble the devil, cracking a bloody whip, his eyes shooting fire, his mouth an executioner's black snarl, the fringe of gray hair smoldering on his head. It was a horrific but accurate rendering of the Vice President. Under the drawing a bold-face note proclaimed, "Mr. Hellman goes to Washington."

Studying the screen, BJ took a moment to search through Courtman's travel bag for a bottle he knew would be there. He tore off the cap and took a quick slug, and scrolled down.

Below the *Guernica* was a collection of essays circulating underground for a year, edited by a woman whose name he'd heard tonight before the chaos erupted – Iona Webster. The volume was titled, *"Strategies for Survival in a Corporate World,"* a series of sound proposals submitted by professionals in many fields, a vision of the country in which its citizens practice the extraordinarily simple principles of participatory democracy. The introduction to the volume was VoteAmerica's study on the spectacular decline in voting over the past three elections, breaking the pattern of more than a century. The text brought to mind the 1787 *Federalist Papers* explaining the new US Constitution. BJ took a moment to read the prologue, a stern warning by Thomas Jefferson: "It is incumbent upon the citizenry to express its displeasure with sitting government; otherwise, the populace would do well to stay home and slop the pigs, for pig-slopping, while bearing a resemblance to the function of government at its basic level, will at least lead to healthy swine."

The New Republic had called the *Strategies* "fundamental solutions to human turmoil and suffering, an unprecedented merging of corporate muscle and tested democratic principles. These are the unequivocal strategies for creating a caring and visionary society."

Within sixty seconds of the first pass over the Mall of Brotherly Love, hundreds of people had checked into the Web site. An Ontario lad of about ten with a pair of binoculars spotted the red decal on the nose of the Cessna, and screamed to his daddy, "Look! It's a Canadian flag!" Immediately people all around him were popping open cell phones.

Within four minutes sixty-five hundred hits were recorded on *Rebellion.com*, and panic began to blow apart the opening ceremonies at the fabulous new facility. Phones jammed first the 911 emergency line, then the Homeland Security emergency number. Things were escalating quickly.

Racing madly toward Ney Field, Raven Menez heard the first report on her car radio. People were screaming into phones, shaking fists, and cheering at the banner soaring above the glass ceiling at the new mall. The message by this time was circling the globe on every Communication International affiliate on the planet. The plane had been in the air for perhaps twenty minutes, and the message was already appearing on Web pages from Bora Bora to Lappish villages above the Arctic Circle. Somebody was taking over the government of the United States. Go to *Rebellion.com*.

But nobody was mentioning Congressman Victor Sligo. Only Raven Menez knew he was on the plane.

19

At home in his fortified condo village in Cherry Hill, New Jersey, National Security Agency Deputy Administrator and sometimes beer vendor Bert O'Donnell was studying his monitor, networked into highly sensitive material at his office on Arch Street in Philadelphia, feeling more astonishment than he normally permitted himself, even in the calamitous daily drama of the NSA. He was completely oblivious to events in the sky across the river. For the past half hour he'd been puzzling over a classified Senate order directing a specific individual at the US Attorney's Office in Chicago to send a subordinate out to Utah to investigate illegal mind-control research. It was against procedure and completely unethical. But it was the Senate.

Iona Webster, a tough cookie he'd met only this afternoon at Independence Hall, had brought up Ferrari's case in a raw confrontation with Senator Hal Riske. For Bert O'Donnell, a man with a finger on every national security pulse in America, the look on Webster's face made him twitch just enough that he had dug into the matter – unethical, but not without precedent – to learn what the hell was going on. He liked Webster. Not only did he like her, he thought she was the sexiest, smartest, meanest woman he'd met since his third grade soccer coach.

Over the years since his divorce, he'd taken to discussing political intrigue and affairs of the heart with his Chesapeake Bay retriever, Lucy. Talking it out with Lucy helped him keep his sanity, as well as his very high-prestige job.

But he wasn't ready to confess his feelings about Webster. Not yet.

"Now, what's wrong here," he asked the dog in his fine cowboy-tinged baritone, perusing the classified Senate order on his monitor. "The man directs the Chicago office to send somebody out West. Check into this mind-control business at Dugway Proving Ground?" He read from the decrypted order, "'We have been advised a member of your Criminal Division is skilled in the precarious legal-slash-moral interpretations of mind-control experiments and procedures.' So this Ferrari woman goes to Utah, and somebody knocks her off *before she even arrives!* Why would he do that?" He examined the screen again, noting the recipient, a mid-level Assistant US Attorney. Whispering to the handsome copper-colored dog, "Is this not the slickest part of our job? Reading everybody's private mail in the entire government! Don't you go telling anybody, you hear?" And, aloud, "But why? What were they doing that was so…? And why Chicago? That's a sure jurisdictional battle with the Salt Lake City people. Ah. Wait. Obviously Ferrari's the expert. Maybe it's in her thumbnail. Or in her caseload."

Spinning back to the computer, he tapped in a long coded inquiry, feeling an almost sexual elation, but quickly discovered that US Attorney's Office files related to Viola Ferrari had been sealed by executive privilege, somebody in Cabinet or the White House. "I bet even you know who would do that," he said to Lucy. He rubbed his stubbled cheek. "So let's see. This man spends two years organizing this uprising. Then some business is doing brain research, God knows what for, and he orders a federal prosecutor out to investigate. FBI concludes no foul. I can't help thinking whatever the research is about, this mind control thing… It must connect to… Suppose… What if…" He blew out a frustrating breath. "You're going to have to tell me, Lucy. I don't get it." The electronic routing code on the order seemed vaguely familiar, although not the normal one for Senate activity. But there was no confusing the electronic signature of the man giving the order. It was Senator Hal Riske.

Gripping the dog's big jowls, O'Donnell said in his best Desi Arnaz accent, "Lucy, you got some esplainin' to do!"

The red Terrorist Alert phone suddenly blinked. "Fuck!" he said. "Now what?"

A frighteningly monotone voice said, *"Level Five alert. We have a breach. Ops responding. This is a Level Five alert. This is not a drill."*

Immediately his mind raced through the Level Five chain of command and his place in it. He pressed several buttons on the same secure crisis line, and was briefed by the duty Signals Intelligence Directive officer at Fort Meade, known as "Mother." Verified unarmed foreign aircraft over the Main Line area west of Philadelphia. Thousands watching a banner bearing a message threatening to overthrow the government. Possibly millions viewing the Web site. Local interception pre-empted by DoD. Preliminary confirmation by NSA. US Naval Station Philadelphia already scrambling. No radio communication with target. Orders: detain with prejudice.

Holy shit! It's that screwball at Riske's meeting! He's the guy flying that plane!

They were about to seize the aircraft. It would force the so-called insurrection into high gear completely unprepared. O'Donnell's people had already responded – but he was required to confirm digitally that he had received notification. The Pentagon had the ball. Half a dozen other agencies would have to respond within the next sixty seconds. Either he confirmed, or he would face trial for conspiracy to sabotage the United States government. Guilty or not, it would be bye-bye pension. Adios career. Public disgrace. May as well blow his brains out right now. Homeland Security always pissed and moaned, but domestic threats snagged by NSA's massive Signals Intelligence spider web had to be passed on to DoD. The only catch was "Detain with prejudice." This was old Patriots Act jargon for a legal chain of command requirement under the category VUA – Verified Unarmed Aircraft. DoD first responders will order the aircraft down. In the unlikely event of resistance, the aircraft will be deemed a terrorist suicide mission, and will be shot down following authorization only by the President or the Vice-President.

O'Donnell entered another long set of numbers on his keypad. Decoded, his confirmation read, "Assume unarmed non-combatants." This was a signal to make absolutely certain before they shot up some drunken college kid out for a joyride in Daddy's aircraft. Maybe it would keep the pilots off their triggers for a few critical minutes. It was all he could do. He could almost hear the pair of Skyhawk Intimidators at the nearby Naval airbase shrieking to the attack.

So the thing had begun. O'Donnell felt a surge of patriotism infused with real revulsion. The old familiar hatred sputtered in his chest, his decades-old loathing of Billy Hellman and the gutless sycophants he'd set up in government. Hellman was still in Congress when O'Donnell signed on with NSA, cocky little bastard on the Clean Air and Water Subcommittee, up to his neck with EPA and the toxic waste mafia out in Nevada. Crooked as a corkscrew willow. He had spearheaded the drive to deregulate toxic substances from national air quality standards. It turned out an outfit called Communication West had illegally slipped a couple of million bucks into Hellman's run for Congress. Somebody had blown a

whistle, connecting the dots between certain chemical manufactur-
ers, Communication West, and Hellman's Nevada PAC fund. It all
stunk like hell. Of course Hellman weaseled out of it. The man running Communication West's research division at the time was a
militant control freak named Dr. Hunter Tyne.

Ten years later Communication West was Communication
International.

To continue his career with NSA, O'Donnell was forced to
repress his contempt for the Vice President, but he had developed a
few intimate acquaintances who shared his disgust with the direction the nation was taking. This was the very reason Senator Hal
Riske had come to him eighteen months ago with his whispered
proposal to develop a group interested in destabilizing the government, in the event President Burligame won re-election. Now it
looked like Riske had some nasty shit in his own septic tank. And
not only that. Here was this Crockett guy leaping into the firing line
in the sky over Philadelphia! Where did anybody get that kind of
balls? What was Davy Crockett's real name? Peoples? Everyman?
He couldn't remember. He'd have to check his recording from the
meeting this afternoon.

O'Donnell could only hope he was sane. If he was, the insurrection may have actually begun. If not, the man would probably
be dead within an hour.

20

Chief of Police Giuseppe Manicotti was satisfied that his instructions to his aide Maria Kowalski would produce an immediate
code orange alert to the Air National Guard command center. The
fact was, he felt like hell. It was the ulcer. The venom produced by
his standoff with Sligo's wife had dripped into his stomach like battery acid. What was going to happen was, the Air National Guard
would call the plane down, arrest the guy, and Philadelphia's rough
and ready chief of police would again look like the man who called
the shots. And that frigid little cunt, that congressman's old lady,
could go piss in her hat.

* * *

People were milling about bumping into each other, frantically shouting into phones, scanning *Strategies for Survival* with their Web tools, some just staring up, faces contorted in outrage or delight or spiritual wonder. The message was amplified one hundredfold by Picasso's nightmare image made more horrific with the addition of the Vice President bearing the blood-drenched whip. Already excessive phone use was overloading local cell towers. Internet junkies were cramming both the Orishimo and the Hutchinson telecom satellites, closer in geocentric orbit than military satellites, but smaller, with systems not designed for wholesale panic in cyberspace. Processors were slowing down, spitting out information in unknown languages. Foul humor written in email toilets across America was turning up in response to questions. Who is responsible for this? Where do I sign up for the revolution? I may not have voted in the last three elections, but by God I'm voting for this! Where are the Marines when we need them to blow this terrorist out of the Pennsylvania sky?

Toon and Mgaba stared in twisted fascination at the TV in the small airfield office. The Cessna made another swoop towards the mall, accompanied by two blinking dots closing in fast. Military vehicles were already arriving at the mall, lights whirring, bullhorns blaring at the vast and still-growing crowd. A mini-revolt was already taking place in the parking areas and inside the immense glass-enclosed shopping mecca. Teen-agers, instantly recognizing the mother of all parties, had swarmed to the mall, and were dancing on car tops and climbing light poles, some actually screaming for the plane to dive into the glass roof. Toon had been on the radio since take-off, pleading with Foulks not to hurt his airplane. The insurance would never cover an act of sabotage. But Foulks refused to respond. On his scanner, Toon listened to angry air traffic controllers, and suddenly heard the dreaded high-pitched squeal replace human voices.

Mgaba's eyes went wide with fear. "What's that?" he demanded.

"They've shut down civilian communications," Toon yelled. "Homeland Security's in it. That boy's in the fire now!" The two men were staring at each other, neither wanting to come to the awful conclusion, when a car shuddered to a stop outside. A young woman in jeans and leather jacket pushed into the office just before Toon got to the door to shut her out.

"I'm Raven Menez, *US Times.*" She was disjointed from the hectic drive and listening to the frenzied activity on her radio. To Mgaba she said, "Are you the manager?" Mgaba simply pointed at Toon, still in his blue tux, looking like anything but an airfield manager. Raven didn't blink.

"Will you be good enough to tell me when and where that plane is going to land?"

"Which plane is that, ma'am," Toon said pleasantly enough.

Raven stood her ground. She reached for her phone and clicked it on "playback". They all listened to Courtman frantically telling Nel the story.

"Will you tell me what is going on at the Mall of Brotherly Love?"

"Oh," Toon said. "You must mean that new mall?"

She took a breath and let it out, not taking her eyes off the big musician. She hoped her phone wouldn't ring just now. She'd left a message in San Francisco.

"I'll try once more." She softened her eyes, glancing to Mgaba and back to Toon, her mind replaying one of Molly Bee's fundamentals: *empathy.* You want the interviewee to trust you. Show empathy! "Sooner or later," she said, "somebody was going to go postal and try to bring down this poor excuse for a government. Can one of you confirm for me that Congressman Victor Sligo is on that plane circling over the new mall?"

Toon stared at her as though she had just come in from Jupiter. His mouth opened and closed as if he couldn't make himself repeat something so ludicrous. Mgaba said nothing.

"Is this a publicity stunt?" she demanded. "This is about the last election, isn't it? Look, everybody knows what a blow this must be to Progressive Party leadership. How far will the Congressman go before he admits Sol Burligame is going to have another term in the White House?"

With no ability to be intimidated, Toon simply pointed a thick finger back at Mgaba. "If you want to talk politics, he's your man."

Already she knew this was way out of her league. She steeled herself for obfuscation and lies, but she was so nervous her mind went blank. On the way here, she'd tried Molly Bee's number, the one she'd used for the year she had taken all three of Ms. Bee's on-line journalism classes at Penn. Although they had never met face-to-face, a kinship had developed between the two women, the brightest-student-and-the-compassionate-professor kind of relationship. Bee had fully encouraged Raven's speculative graduate thesis on the ultra-secret Society With No Name, the organization Raven guessed was spawned from the loins of the Illuminati and the Council on Foreign Relations, using the Bilderberger group as midwife.

Now she needed a way to draw information out of these two guys. Both seemed like decent people. They weren't nervous. Why should she be?

"Do US Congressmen often take off from here and go joy riding?" Raven's voice sounded to her like a high school reporter interviewing a football star.

"Oh yeah," Toon said, laughing. "All the time." Mgaba, the public relations man, pulled himself together and said, "What's a nice girl like you doing in the newspaper racket? You ought to be – what do you think, Mr. Toon? A brain surgeon?" He winked at the man in the tux.

"Just a minute, this is a serious –" She was looking past them at the monitor perched on the countertop. She was clearly in the right place to get hard information. Nobody else knew Sligo was on the plane. It put her in an interesting position.

Toon studied her, then actually took her hand and examined it. "Could be. Or classical piano. You play music, miss? You have those long lovely fingers. If I was a piano keyboard, I'd just love to have you –"

"Gentlemen!" Raven needed to yank herself out of this deteriorating mess. "Have you looked at that TV in the past minute?" All eyes turned simultaneously to the screen. It looked like a World War II dogfight in slow motion. Two US Marine Skyhawk jets screamed across the sky, then slowed to a crawl as they approached the tiny Cessna. Spotlights flashed along the cockpit, and at the instant the satellite cam zoomed in for an excruciating close-up, the man flying the plane seemed to be – was it possible? His palms were pressed together, and he was *bowing* in a Buddhist-style acknowledgement to the fighter pilots.

Was this some kind of cartoon?

In a fit of journalistic angst she blurted out, "Do you realize nobody else on this planet knows there's a United States Congressman on that plane? Look at that! They're going to shoot it down! Are you just going to let it happen?" She glared at the two of them.

Toon, long a man of the street, looked at Mgaba. "Girl's got a point."

To which in exasperation Raven Menez stamped her foot and yelled, "I'm a woman, dammit! And nobody else knows about this but you two and me! Now do something!"

21

None of them had any way of guessing what had taken place in the past five minutes between Cherry Hill, the Pentagon, Langley, the White House, and remote Queensland, Australia. Although Mgaba had a bad feeling about the feds taking control of air communications. And this little lady with the recorder and the tight jeans, well, she was pretty sweet.

By Level Five procedure, NSA had confirmed with the White House and the Joint Chiefs. Homeland Security's terrorist division was in it. This took place in one minute, thirty-five seconds. Already the Skyhawk Interceptors were airborne, the two youthful pilots spazzed with anticipation of skirmishing with a realtime night bogey, weapons activated, gloved hands tenderly stroking the launch mechanisms. By coincidence the Chairman of the Joint Chiefs of Staff, Admiral Sukwant Singh, had returned to D.C. and was having a late supper in his elaborate Pentagon office with FBI Deputy Director John Lee Davis. Singh, five-foot-nine with militarily cropped black hair, born on the island nation of Fiji, in reality served at the pleasure of the Vice President, although no military person would ever admit this aloud. His politics were unknown – except to John Lee Davis. His profile suggested high intelligence and unswerving patriotism. When the crisis line blinked, Admiral Singh listened to the report on the phone, showing no emotion. Quietly, he let Davis in on the flying insurrection taking place over the new mall up in Philadelphia. It took only moments for Davis to key in. Some two years previously, Davis's elder daughter's godfather,

Senate minority leader Hal Riske, had warned that when the pressure for change built to a critical mass, some rather unseemly events would signal the insurrection. Christmas Day, Riske had told him of the meeting at Independence Hall. But Davis had declined attending. He simply needed to go his own way.

Davis was the first deputy director over six feet six inches tall, and the first male FBI operative at any level to wear his hair in a carefully-groomed pony tail. He was a direct man, schooled on the street, not equipped for nonsense or diplomacy. This missing bureaucratic element had cost him at shot at the directorship of the Bureau during nomination hearings some years ago. The pony tail hadn't helped much either.

One burning objective kept John Lee Davis serving at the ugliest building on Pennsylvania Avenue: in time a pathway would become clear to bring down the despicable reign of Billy Hellman. When the path revealed itself, Davis intended to show up, bulldozer roaring, to ground Hellman to dust. Right where he belonged.

The people from Independence Hall were moving. Both Singh and Davis could see the immediate future. "What's for dessert, Sukwant?" Davis said.

Singh nodded once to his aide, authorizing the pilots to communicate directly with the Commander-in Chief, who was away from Washington on a family holiday at an undisclosed location.

Singh leaned in close to Davis when the aide left. "I was thinking crème de Billy." He continued softly, "Oh, by the way, this afternoon up north the name Viola Ferrari came up. Do you know that name?"

"Barely." Davis was too busy to read the papers. Some Justice lawyer. An accident.

Singh said, "Apparently there are still more extra-curricular activities coming from across the river. We're being kept out of the loop. I'll update you."

Davis tossed his napkin down in disgust. More of the same. It just never stopped.

At this moment Singh's aide, a head-chopped Marine lieutenant in full dress, returned poker-faced. He reported the news Singh already feared. Only a team of Secret Service operatives in the southern hemisphere knew where "Havarti" – today's code for the President – was. It would be several minutes before he could respond. So the fate of the insurrection was already jeopardized, but for the wrong reason. The safety of the nation was in the hands of a dangerous crackpot, Vice President Billy Hellman. Hellman was too volatile, too egotistical, totally unpredictable in an emergency. His first instinct would be to start blowing things up. Hellman could create a nightmare nobody would ever recover from. In his position, with his imperious arrogance and his paranoid mindset, he could spiral what might be a legitimate expression of dissent against the government into a blood bath.

Right now national security communications were jamming up. Web traffic north clear to Boston was on the fritz. Maybe it was sunspots clogging their network. The interagency links were acting a little sketchy, like a run on the bank, as if everybody in North America was suddenly plugging in their hair dryers all at once.

The two Marine Skyhawk Interceptors, Harrier-type subsonic thrust vectoring defense aircraft, were in tight, carefully observing the trailing cable, signaling and scanning radio frequencies, demanding the pokey Cessna land immediately. Foulks looked around surprised, and bowed again to the pilots, both by now in sexual interlock with the weapons launch buttons that triggered eighteen-ounce AHS missiles – Autorectified Heartbeat Sensors designed to terminate personnel and send the aircraft into remote pilot mode. The pair of thirty-two million dollar aircraft could not fly at 150 knots for long, and Edwin Foulks knew it – as did many nine-year-olds following the pursuit on the Internet. He hoped his friends had produced a good pair of contact lenses as the Skyhawks sizzled past. He sent both pilots a big smile.

Beside him, Congressman Victor Sligo was drenched in sweat in his nylon football jacket over a dress shirt and sweater. His head hammered a sonic beat. He had to piss. In fact he was going out of his mind. He was whispering a love note to Nel, imagining his children's faces and mourning the grandchildren he would never see. He was preparing to die – a concept alien to his entire being – in a blinding fireball any moment. He said over the drone of the Cessna, "All right, Foulks! On our way to Hell, why don't you let me in on your plan?"

Foulks didn't bother to look at him. Waving to the starboard Intimidator, he said, "Plan? What plan was that? Did you have to be somewhere?" As he spoke he was banking again, this time west-ward, back towards Ney Field. He watched the port side pilot fall back and growl into his microphone. Hearing the anxious howl in the congressman's voice, Foulks said, "We might make it. Just hang on."

Eighty feet away, Marine Captain Bernard "Buzz" Kalo-malokulei, was demanding instructions concerning resistance from a Verified Unarmed Aircraft.

"We believe it's a prank, sir," he radioed his base com-mander. "VUA, repeat, VUA. In fact, sir, the pilot is bowing to me, and to my wing man, Captain Tuieasosopo. We believe it's a luna-tic, sir, pulling some kind of lunatic stunt. He will not respond to my command. My guess is we are being observed by twelve to fifteen thousand civilians. Awaiting orders, sir."

The Naval airbase commander stalled. Nobody could make a decision without executive order. During this three and a half minute period, the White House Communications Agency was fran-tically trying to get through to the President. The WHCA Zarella satellite operated on a frequency similar in amplitude to the east coast communications network's Orishimo satellite, at this point suffering extreme overload and worrying technicians monitoring the forty-foot screen at the underground Command Central six floors beneath the White House – the War Room. The normally glacial scene was bordering on frenzy. Half a dozen staff officers shouted at a room full of technicians at computer stations, while all watched in disbelief the worldwide communications overlay on the enormous screen, illustrating not only the military traffic, but also the situation flooding private networks west of Philadelphia.

Into this chaos came the evening cleaning lady, Ms. Flotilda Lament, wearing her dowdy cleaning lady pinafore and her security chip, pushing a cart bobbing with cleaning supplies. She was hold-ing an ancient cell phone in her gnarled hand. Hobbling straight into the command pit, she approached a stressed technician unhappily clicking on his keyboard and squinting at his monitor as if it were giving birth. "Hey, Sarge," Ms. Lament said, "something's wrong with my phone. I got to call the grandkid. It's his birthday." And she shoved the little mobile phone in his face.

She did this about twice a year. Somebody always helped.

The technician at first brushed her hand away. Then glancing at her, seeing the weary plea in her eyes, he took up the phone distractedly and dialed a number.

"Nothing," he shrugged. "Must be the battery."

"No, it ain't that. Look." She pointed to the battery icon on the phone display. It was full.

"Huh," he said. He looked back to his monitor. Then up at the massive worldwide screen, the tracking devices moving into Australia, already fading. Flashing red warning signals in southeast Pennsylvania had begun to spread westward across the country. Feeling a strange turbulence in his bowels, he turned back to Ms. Lament.

"Lemme borrow this." He was already racing away.

She called after him, "Yeah, well, it's my grandbaby's birthday, so –"

Thirteen seconds later the techie interrupted a heated conference among his superiors, who in eleven more seconds reported to the shouting generals that the wayward aircraft everyone had been monitoring had set off such a blitz of Internet use, a worldwide communications collapse was imminent. And even as they spoke, like the crashing of a million-light chandelier in the opera, the War Room screen, the most elaborate and costly array of technology north of Cape Canaveral, went blank.

People gasped. A bird colonel standing beside the White House Chaplain bellowed out, "What the fuck's going on?" Down in the pit a Spec 4 snickered, "There is a God!"

Two seconds later the screen sputtered and returned to life.

Upon which, amidst cheers, the chaplain sang out, "You're damn right there is!"

Forty-five seconds later the Director of the Secret Service threatened to reconfigure the body parts of the AIC running the Presidential detail in Sydney, Australia. But he got nowhere. The coded message returned to the War Room: President Burligame cannot be reached for twelve minutes.

22

In actual fact, Sol Burligame was sipping a mojito, basking in January heat at the Prime Minister's private estate outside Toowoomba, Queensland, a short helicopter flight from the nearest spook command in Brisbane, reading his tourist dictionary, *Let Stalk Strine,* and munching on the local variety of utter martyr sandwich. He had taken exhaustive measures to be unavailable except in a dire national emergency.

Somebody would have to get Vice President Hellman off the dance floor up in the White House ballroom.

Amid curses and threats, the Secret Service got back to Admiral Sukwant Singh, enjoying a succulent crème brulé with FBI Deputy Director John Lee Davis at the Pentagon. Over Davis's smirk, Singh authorized communication between the two Hawaiian pilots engaging the Cessna 400, and "Limburger" – the Vice President of the United States.

Purvis Courtman and Nel Sligo were dashing out of Philadelphia in a banged-up Hummer taxi, weaving through looky-loo traffic out to Ney Field thirty miles west. She frantically pressed codes into her phone trying to contact Victor, leaning her face against the window searching for explosions over the new Mall of Brotherly Love. Across the endless suburbs her mind created bloody plane crashes and exploding missiles. She felt her husband's body parts flying everywhere. Her cell phone wasn't working. She heaved it at Courtman, screaming at him to reach Victor, reach anybody! All he had to do was tell the authorities who was on the plane.

Courtman finally put the parts together. Obviously these people were intent upon shooting down an aircraft bearing a seditious warning, armed or not. A message to the proletariat. Nel was right. Nobody had the slightest idea who his passenger was.

But communications were plugged up. It had to be the damned banner Foulks was flying. Everybody was on their phones at once, on the Web site, twittering and tweeting and bleating, yelling across backyard fences.

There was one last chance.

Courtman's own phone was already dead. He remembered the two mobile Code Thirteens. He was in possession of one, and

Victor carried the other. Both were credit-card-size, voice-only models. He fumbled through his long leather billfold and yanked out the small black unit, at the same time trying to keep Nel together.

"There's only once choice left." He pursed his lips, wishing he'd brought his good Old Hickory along. "We've got to tell the feds that guy kidnapped Victor. It's our only hope."

She blanched, then grabbed Courtman by the lapels, hauling him half out of his seat. "He *kidnapped* Victor?" she barked.

"Yes, yes," he gasped, struggling against Nel's considerable strength. "The Davy Crockett guy kidnapped him. We have to get through to Victor! Don't you see? Otherwise, they're going to shoot him down!"

"All right, Congressman, this is it!" Foulks was gathering his nerves, while Victor was seriously thinking about praying for the first time since his fourth child was born. "The initial objective is secured. Everybody in America is now on the Web site."

"You can't be sure," Victor managed to say. "People will think you're just another deranged Progressive who forgot to vote." Foulks had revealed his escape plan. It sounded as smart as skiing into the crater on Mount Saint Helen's.

At that instant his mobile Code Thirteen hissed. It had to be Courtman. He ripped the device from his pocket.

"Courtman?"

"They don't know you're on the plane, Victor! All land communications are falling apart thanks to your host."

The Intimidators were abeam and aft, flicking hypnotic strobe lights at the cockpit. The pilot of the starboard jet appeared to be gagging into his headset and shaking a fist at the Cessna. The rear pilot had to contend with the banner, flapping dangerously in so much turbulence; thus the strobe actually accentuated the message. From the ground, less than twelve hundred feet below, the scene resembled electronic dominoes flashing madly across the night sky.

Admiral Singh had immediately contacted the Vice President's chief of staff, Leora Psybysch, whom he knew to be present in the Ball Room, and then Colonel John Vuolo, duty commander of the War Room. As the VP's guard dog and chief consultant, Psybysch never let Hellman out of her sight. (She pronounced her name

SHI-bish, thought to be of Gypsy origin, which Washington insiders translated as: the most wretched of all God's creatures.) In less than sixty seconds, Billy Hellman himself burst into the War Room in his lush London green silk suit, smiling from one cauliflower ear to the other, followed immediately by Psybysch with her trademark revealing blouse and shawl, a slit black skirt and a murderous sneer. Hellman was a powerful, densely-built man, a fringe of gray hair forming a horseshoe around the back of his head, almost teetering on the balls of his feet, spewing confidence, five-foot-four on a tall day, strong as a tank. He blinked constantly. Practically leaping into the Command Center hub, he stared wild-eyed at the huge screen. Red circles pulsed west of Philadelphia.

"The President's away," Hellman screamed in his berserk tenor. "I'm in charge here! Colonel, what the hell's this guy doing?"

Colonel Vuolo snapped a glance at Psybysch and relayed the scene. "You understand, sir, our entire communications network is —"

"Gimme a transmitter," Hellman bellowed, eyes glued to the screen. The grin had not left his severely lined face. He looked in fact like a smiling Chinese shar-pei. The colonel motioned with his chin at an airman before a flickering terminal. Hellman jumped with raw agility to the terminal and snatched up the airman's headset.

"Skyhawk One, Skyhawk One, let's play ball." He winked at the stunned airman. He had produced a poor imitation of President Burligame.

The pilot's response sputtered through a dozen speakers. "Negative, sir, Voice ID not accepted, sir."

"Listen up, Captain," roared Hellman. "This is Limburger! Are we clear?" He snarled at the screen like his face was about to explode.

"Roger that, sir. You are clear."

"What do you see? Talk to me, son." He breathed noisily through his pug nose, like a boxer between rounds.

"The guy won't respond, sir. We've tried everything. He keeps smiling at us! I'll tell you frankly, sir, I'd really hate to —" A cacophony of squawks flooded the speakers, followed by yet another spasm at the main board. Voices groaned across the War Room. Then out of nowhere came a female voice.

"Victor! Victor! You have to talk to them! Tell him to switch on the National Emergency Frequency and tell those pilots who you are." The speaker squealed, and the voice said clearly, "kidnapped! It's your only chance."

The Vice President's eyes went tight with confusion. His face crunched up like a red cabbage as he listened to the female voice. He had heard it before.

On the Cessna, Foulks slapped the stick. "Kidnapped? Why didn't I think of that."

"You jackass!" Victor shouted back. "What were you going to do? Just let them shoot us down?"

"Well… yeah. Think of the publicity!"

Nel's voice came in a desperate yowl. *"Victor! Do it now!"*

Immediately Foulks flipped a switch on the overhead panel, and called out a frequency number. Suddenly the cabin was filled with voices. Almost calmly he said, "Go ahead please."

Toon's voice came through from the airstrip.

"Crockett! Crockett! Dammit, pick it up!"

"I'm here, Mr. Toon."

Another voice pushed through hard. "This is the Vice President of the United States, Mr. Crockett! I want you to land that aircraft immediately or you will be shot down as a terrorist. You have five seconds –"

Hellman stopped. He squinted at the floor.

Nel had wrestled the Code Thirteen from Courtman in the taxi. She yelled into the tiny microphone, "They'll confirm your voice pattern, and they'll let you land somewhere! Just tell them –" Incoherent squawking came through the Code Thirteen as the Hummer taxi peeled into Ney Field.

Billy Hellman was a man who remembered faces and voices. To his glimmering black shoes he muttered, "Victor. Well, goddamn. That's Victor Sligo." And to Leora Psybysch slavering beside him, "That was his wife, that voice! That fucking irritating Progressive from Washington state. He's on that plane."

Edwin Foulks was dropping fast now, heading northwest into farm country. He was smiling.

"Captain!" The Vice President had thought it through. One of the true enemies of the government was about to go down in flames. What the hell. The country would be better off without him.

"Sir!"

"On my command you will launch two AHS missiles at the occupants of the aircraft. Prepare to fire." His voice echoed furiously through the War Room. The speakers hissed and wobbled.

"Yes sir, but with all due respect, sir –"

"Prepare to fire!" The Vice President's voice bellowed into the droning Cessna.

Victor heard. His heart was in his throat. Both fighter planes fell behind instantly. Turning to look back, he could almost see the pulsing lock-on signals light up their cockpits. Nel screamed till her lungs nearly burst. Billy Hellman put on his severe, tough-decision face. Each pilot had a thumb on the launch button. Hellman opened his mouth to shout the command – and the War Room screen went black. Background noise on the radio fizzled to scratchings. *"Fire!"* Hellman roared, just as the entire Eastern United States communications system collapsed. It took with it the Zarella satellite and its billion-dollar failsafe network, along with the entire Worldwide Web.

Fifteen seconds later Courtman and Nel burst out of the Hummer and sprinted to the office, where Toon, Mgaba and Raven Menez were listening in terror as the wall speaker sputtered and slid down through octaves like a stoned trombone. Then, only static.

The two Skyhawks were suddenly flying with dead guidance systems. They were essentially lost in the pitch black sky west of Philadelphia. Emergency procedure required a scan through civil frequencies – which they already knew were gone – followed by activating the antiquated radio that broadcast through the Zarella satellite network. It was dead. Captain Tuiasosopo nearly heaved his hand-held radio through the roof of his cockpit before he realized they could navigate back to base by actually looking out the window. It was a novel concept.

Six floors below street level at the White House, the Vice President of the United States smoldered with rage at the very hub of command in the War Room. He fired his clenched fist full strength into a steel filing cabinet. He did not break any knuckles, but he put a nasty dent in the top drawer.

23

Chaos erupted at Ney Field. Fully-armed FBI assault squads showed up in a bright blue Sikorski chopper, half a dozen growling Nanjing military jeeps, and a fire truck. They thundered through the place bearing flood lights, crowd control gas-pellet weapons, loud-speakers and at the moment useless mobile data computers. Quickly a Ground Command Center was established, orders snapped out, Toon's office locked down. Dark-clad and booted agents moved into position to detain, and if necessary destroy, the Cessna 400. It had all happened so fast, the Homeland Security people, roaring in at the same time, were left with ancillary work, sealing the perimeter, following the crossed runways beyond the edge lights to ensure no terrorist subjects had spilled into the community, and cordoning off civilians in the parking lot. Fearing media hordes were racing to the airfield, Homeland Security AIC Carlotta Pfister dealt with the civilians personally. One by one Agent Pfister, wearing battle dress camos and full anti-terrorist gear, questioned the people present – Courtman, Nel, Toon, Mgaba, and Raven Menez.

Except for Menez, the others had hastily agreed on a story to tell the feds moments before their arrival.

"Who was flying that aircraft?" Pfister demanded of each of them.

Only Toon could possibly answer. Nobody else had a clue. He swaggered up to Pfister when she pointed at him, grinning pleasantly, puffing out his great chest to make sure she appreciated his fabulous blue tux.

"Everything you need," Toon told her in his mellow bass, "is on my desk. The man registered as a D. Crockett." He smiled at her, his great dark face shining in the floodlights. "D. Crockett," he repeated slowly. "In the address field, he left a post office box in a place called Van Zandt, Washington. Out west," he told her. "Where states are square." Clinging to her professional demeanor, Pfister, a thickly-built but soft-spoken career Immigration and Customs Enforcement officer, took Toon to the office and made hard copies of all January activities at Ney Field, recorded his voiceprint, and took a surreptitious and illegal voiceprint polygraph. Toon appeared to be telling the truth. The pilot had registered the social security number of the governor of Tennessee, and had presented Toon with an outdated pilot's license issued to some other D. Crockett from San Antonio, Texas.

Something extraordinary was also taking place at the National Security Center. Millions had followed the bizarre incident on the Web until the moment of its catastrophic blackout. Already, not thirty minutes after the Skyhawk pilots had returned to base flying on the seat of their pants, reports were being directed to NSC concerning the location of the Cessna. They were catalogued and checked out laboriously, sightings filed with the CIA, FBI, the Bureau of Land Management, SETI, the White House and the Boy Scouts of America.

"It's here, all right. A single-engine Cessna, water damaged, no sign of survivors. It's in my pool! In the back yard! I presume everybody swam to safety."

"Last sighted passing over the Statue of Liberty, heading north. The starboard engine was on fire. It landed in New York harbor. Six people and a dog began rowing to shore in a rubber dinghy. That's when my mom came in and I had to go to bed."

"I am an amateur astronomer. I managed to photograph the pilot with my telescope as the plane cruised overhead. I'll send it on to you. The pilot bears an uncanny resemblance to Vice President Hellman. Looks like one of those wrinkly Chinese dogs with a smile on its face."

It was as though all the repressed anger and frustration of a citizenry weary of lies and dirty politics, had burst out with adolescent revenge. Some pissed-off pilot saying he was taking over the government single-handedly? Well by God, it's about time!

Shortly, Police Chief Giuseppe Manicotti roared up, siren wailing, in his armored Nanjing Police Avenger, followed by two carloads of serious young cops. They poured out and established a perimeter around the Avenger as the chief emerged, still in police blues and scrambled-egg saucer hat. Primarily Manicotti was here because everybody else was. He had scraped together something resembling a show of force for the media. Since he had scoffed at Nel Sligo's warning for him to ignore the matter – thereby completely outwitting himself – he knew he was going to be embarrassed if the word ever got out. Manicotti squinted through the crowd, wondering what threat he could hang over Ms. Sligo to keep her quiet.

In the corner resisting the urge to photograph the scene with her phone, Raven Menez prayed she hadn't made a dumb mistake not notifying her editor at the *US Times* when she had the exclusive. It was around the globe by now. She watched Manicotti's noisy arrival. Something startling and ugly came into the Police Chief's eyes. She followed his gaze directly to Nel Sligo, looking terrified, eyes closed, arms clutching her torso, shivering in her short cashmere jacket. The Police Chief took a few steps toward her. Raven saw Nel's eyes pop open, and instantly Manicotti spun on his spit-shined heel and strolled in among the two-dozen uniformed figures surrounding Alonzo Toon. Raven began to feel deeply conflicted. It was as if a film of her life had paused at this moment. She felt the presence of her hypercritical editor, and the entire fanatically conservative staff at the *US Times*. Molly Bee came to mind, a courageous woman true to her convictions. Within, she felt the vice of her narrow life – her family, her loneliness, her unmentionable desires. At that instant, she saw everything Manicotti symbolized in his ludicrous presence, as he swaggered around City Hall. A whisper rose beneath the shouting Homeland Security people. She heard it clearly. "Get out before it's too late!"

Overcome with this thing blazing like a sunburst in her chest, Raven walked directly toward Ms. Sligo to speak to her about her husband and maybe just stand close to her to warm them both.

Manicotti had backed out of Toon's office, unwelcome, and was approaching Ms. Sligo. He ignored the busybody reporter coming beside her. The chief was confident he would have the right words for her in the next five seconds. He was in his element.

Nel looked at him. Fury billowed in her face.

"Ms. Sligo," he said to her. His face was smug. "The only reason your husband –"

"I told you to stay out of this," she snapped, a reedy finger pointing at his chest. "This scene is under federal control. I'll be seeing the governor in the morning about you! Now get out of here!"

Manicotti's mouth dropped open. His blood boiled. He had not struck a woman in months. But he was lurching forward. He was going to club her and then arrest her. He came at her, unthinking, a hulk of uniformed testosterone.

Raven Menez instinctively moved forward, ready for action. Agent-in-Charge Carlotta Pfister, a thicker version of hard-bodied

Nel Sligo, stood with the landline in one hand and her walkie-talkie in the other, waiting for results of the Laser Iris Scan the Marine pilots had taken on the man flying the Cessna. She'd heard Nel's angry words. Now the big police chief was lumbering toward Nel, and Pfister yelled, *"Chief!"* and stepped toward him. Manicotti, consumed with rage and barely able to hear anything, lifted both big fists in front of him but glanced aside just enough to prepare for an attack. At that instant Nel Sligo came forward, shifted her weight onto her back foot, and with her front leg launched a fierce kick straight into the police chief's sternum. With a stunned *whoof* all the air went out of him. He went down like a sledge-hammered bull. Nel pulled back and Pfister moved over him, a wary referee. She did not speak. Gasping, Manicotti pulled himself up, pressing his chest, floundering for his demolished dignity. Unable to breathe, glaring at Nel and then at Pfister, he wheezed, "This isn't over, woman! You're gonna wish you never laid eyes on me!"

Fumbling sideways, he signaled with a jerk of his head for his men to move out, and he was gone.

Raven Menez was holding a hand out to Nel when a phone jangled. The female agent stood holding the Homeland Security landline with its yellow cord winding back to Toon's office.

"Pfister."

"You're not going to believe this." Jeffrey James, her technician down at Fort Holabird, was giddy. "The iris scan's in. We ran it twice. The man flying that aircraft was the Secretary of Communications. It's Hunter Tyne."

"What did you say," Pfister ejaculated.

"Yep. No question about it. Iris identity's just like DNA, boss. Million to one chance it was not him."

"The Secretary of Communications." Her voice had gone flat, unencumbered by emotion. Then she added, "Aw, shit."

"Any suggestions?"

"Not for you," Pfister told him, quickly coming to herself. "I'll pass this upstairs immediately. Good job, James."

Finally Raven Menez, as of thirty seconds ago a former reporter for the *US Times*, steeled her nerves and approached Congressman Sligo's wife. Breathing shallowly, Nel turned to face her.

"You were fantastic!" she gushed. "Wow!" Then, embarrassed, she added, "Hello. I'm Raven Menez."

24

Besides Foulks himself, one other man could guess how he did it. Across the Delaware, at his condo in Cherry Hill, NSA deputy administrator Bert O'Donnell watched the Web self-destruct. Calculating roughly, he allowed the Homeland Security's borrowed Army lab the same time to decipher the Laser Iris Scan that it would take him to feed Lucy, and listen to the last track on the Lynyrd Skynyrd CD. He fixed himself a glass of milk and half a dozen Oreo cookies, walked to his balcony and looked out at the dreary heavens where two satellites were scrambling to reconfigure themselves. He truly loved being paid to monitor the planet's electronic communications. The ultimate perk for a born spook like O'Donnell, decrypting secrets that could destroy people, secrets he'd learned to track simply by doing his job. This one was a particularly audacious trick. A renegade grad student at the University of Washington ophthalmology lab, the nation's primary source for iris scan technology, had developed the ability to imprint an iris identity on contact lenses. Incredible! It would only last a few hours, but it was good enough to fool a scanner moving at high speed. Emails that O'Donnell came privy to by ordinary NSA snooping – any recent reference to iris scanning technology tripped the wire – told the story. The UW kid feared they might produce some monkey's ID in their lab – but it was pretty comical they could replicate the eyeball imprint of a Cabinet secretary, "especially," he wrote, "a prick like Tyne." It would appear that he had delivered the contacts to Davy Crockett.

It was all part of a monstrous joke that nobody knew the punchline to. Tyne, one of the most despised public figures in US history, was appointed to Cabinet as part of an exceedingly sinister arrangement. Through O'Donnell's worldwide spook network of men and women taking joy in swapping secrets, he had come to understand it this way: Communication Internal had guaranteed to a virtually untraceable international organization – O'Donnell believed it was the group referred to in tabloids as the Society With No Name – that Sol Burligame would win the election four years ago. In return Hunter Tyne, former research director for CI, would be named Secretary of the new Department of Communications.

Just thinking about Hunter Tyne made Bert O'Donnell decide he'd better go back in to the city tonight. Ms. Sligo was probably in more danger than she realized. And he didn't want Iona Webster leaving town without seeing her again.

25

Three thousand miles west of Cherry Hill, the *West Coast Paper's* popular columnist Molly Bee deciphered the upheaval from her downtown condo until the Web collapsed. It surprised her that she hadn't seen it coming. At least not this way, only two months after the election, initiated by some anonymous Dudley Doright who not only had the courage to pull off the flying banner shocker, but, according to unconfirmed blogs, had managed to kidnap the ranking Progressive on the House Ways and Means Committee along the way. Three or was it four years ago she'd devoted a full column to Victor Sligo, a trench fighter in the war against Communication International and its mushrooming fungus in Washington. Bee's modest tribute to Congressman Sligo had half-intentionally drifted into a vitriolic diatribe against the megacorporation, and she'd nearly crossed the line into serious libel, referring to CI as *"corporate elitists in their Gucci jackboots and offshore wealth, electing their henchmen into high office, with their clenched-fist approach to human dignity, clogging the aisles of Congress with their leering lobbyists and their tax tricks, and their commitment to Liberty and Justice for all members of the board."*

The publisher, a renegade descendant of the Hearst family, had nearly lost his lunch when he read the column. Storming into Bee's unmarked sixth-floor office, he slammed the early edition on her desk, apoplectic with rage. The woman was abusing some of his major advertisers! He ranted and barked long enough to make his point, then waited five days to monitor results. Worldwide subscriptions to both the diminishing paper and its moneymaking Web side had moved up. National advertising had jumped a full point. Among the thousands of emails in support of Molly Bee – the woman whose photo had never been published, and whom nobody could identify if they saw her on the street – the weekly journal in DeQueen, Arkansas, voted to elect her "DeQueen Bee."

Within the week, the publisher had presented her with a framed, hand-rendered copy of the column. It hung on her living room wall beside her personal life-size poster of hall-of-famer Kirby Puckett laughing with Molly's little brother, gazing up at Puckett and clutching a catcher's mitt.

Sol Burligame was elected by close margins twice. Both elections featured surprising third-party advances and diminishing voters. And the damned *US Times*, Communication International's darling instrument read by half the Internet users in America, had predicted the results. What aggravated Molly's suspicion more than anything else was the voters staying away in droves. A genuinely distressed nation, evil circulating in Washington like vultures gnawing at a carcass, and the voters not showing up. It made absolutely no sense. And nobody in the country could figure it out.

She'd stayed up late thinking sideways and backwards, and reading the most inane blogs looking for clues to subversive activity at the voting booth. The most outrageous was some nutjob who called himself "Slickwatch," who not only singled out Public Television commentator Julio Reese as an unwitting stooge for Billy Hellman, but who also claimed computer chips were growing in the brains of voters from eating fast food hamburgers, and somebody was programming them to not vote.

Cheers for the Internet's clandestine underlayers! A place for frogs and princes.

When the old FCC was elevated to the cabinet-level Department of Communications, and suspected sociopath Dr. Hunter Tyne was named Secretary, the world of media journalism had truly gone to hell. Tyne, shepherded through Senate nomination hearings by Billy Hellman, immediately deregulated the industry, virtually wiping out all competition for CI and its flagship television outlet, I-Media.

Why would people not vote to stop this kind of behavior?

She sat before a live feed of the renegade airplane over the new mall, waiting for the pilot's next move. She'd been observing for about ten minutes when the Web crashed.

Temporarily disabled, Bee decided to take her shih-tzu, Dolly Mama, for her evening walk, then returned to the common area of her condo. A bearded man read the paper behind the counter of a coffee stand. A sign said, "Jimmy Boyd's Flood Relief."

"Got a chocolate chip cookie left, Jimmy?"

"Saved you the last one," the man said. He reached for a napkin, dropped the big cookie on it, and winked at her. She dropped a buck on the counter.

In the elevator going back to her office she read the note scribbled on the napkin: *"Call I."*

Molly Bee was a quiet woman of thirty-five, a bit taller than average height, with short hair the color of faded gold, a round face and wonderful hazel eyes that made people believe she could see right into them. She tended toward dark knits and wool in the cool San Francisco air. And she was pathologically private. Nobody in the condo knew what she did, and nobody at work knew where she lived. Of the millions who read her column, *Trying Times,* virtually nobody could identify her on the street. Occasionally an acquaintance commented, with comic irony, that she bore a sort of sideways resemblance to President Sol Burligame. To which Molly would roll her eyes and grunt her displeasure.

Settling herself at the desk, she allowed the imperial shih-tzu to clamber into her lap, then reached for the landline, turned on the scrambler, and touched in Iona Webster's cell number, hoping at least cell service was back to normal.

"Hey," she said when Webster answered. "You still there?" Through Webster, Molly had learned earlier in the evening – on threat of death, or worse – of the vaguest outline of events at Independence Hall this afternoon. Just before the blackout, Iona Webster's name had been mentioned on the I-Media newscast as editor of *Strategies for Survival in a Corporate World,* reprinted on Davy Crockett's Web site. It was hard for Bee not to connect the insane flight of the *Rebellion.com* banner all over the Internet, with Hal Riske's mutiny a few miles away.

"Oh, I'm here all right," Webster said. "Watching the end of stupidity as we know it. Maybe."

"What's going on at the mall?"

"Davy Crockett," Iona said, in her lilting, ironic tone. Molly could almost hear her smiling through the phone. "I swear this man got up and took control of that bickering bunch of bullies like Jesus talking to the multitudes. He was cool. The man was the real Davy Crockett, and I ain't lyin'. You should have been there, girl. He's gonna bring up a real hullabaloo." Then reverting to her normal inflection she added, "We'd better meet. I'll be home in the morning."

"Nothing definitive yet?" Bee was thinking of tomorrow's column. "What's his agenda?"

"Just wait," Webster said. "Do your magic. Now, do you remember a woman called Viola Ferrari?"

"Sure. US Attorney. She died, and then I don't know. Lot of the usual dumb blogging on the Web, and then I was going to do a column, but there was nothing to write. I remember feeling sick about it, and then –"

"That's the one. I interviewed her last year for a piece I wrote about women in federal law enforcement for *LA Magazine*. A very cool person, I mean a real, warm, professional woman. So listen to this. We're on a good phone line?"

"Always." Bee reached for a notepad and pencil.

"I have this itch. The place where it's itching I'm not going to tell you, but our friend Senator Riske, he's going to fax me the initial report from the Utah Highway Patrol on Ferrari's death."

"You lost me. What happened?"

"You know what happened. They rubbed her out. In my group, the ombudsmen's association, there's a woman who talks to an ex-AUSA guy, Assistant US Attorney from New Orleans. Now in private practice. His totally uncorroborated inside story is that Ferrari was getting too close to real bad stuff, and she had to be taken out. They were close friends, and he says they spoke on the phone the week she died."

Molly Bee listened, mind-boggled, remembering now the photo of a beautiful, serious woman. Remembering that the story reeked of foul play but none was uncovered. She was already reaching for her computer before she remembered the Internet was down.

"What bad stuff?"

"Some of her prosecuting experience had to do with brainwashing, waterboarding, torture by federal agencies, that kind of thing. So they moved her around the country as an expert prosecution witness sometimes. Now get this. Ferrari was also an expert in a related field about how you connect brains and computers, I can't remember, the way they help stroke victims to say things without talking?"

"Yes. BCI. Brain-Computer Interface," Molly said.

"What I'm getting from the guy in New Orleans is Viola

was chasing down people connected to brain experiments they were doing without medical authority. Sounds like Frankenstein, I know. But there's too many loose ends. Apparently she was onto something out there in the desert in Utah, whatever it was, and somebody stopped her. *Then!* I finally connected with my source at the FBI and I got routed around the country and wound up in Salt Lake City – that's where it happened – and you know what they said? I still can't believe it. They said the investigation's over. It was an accident!"

It was the kind of material that makes the journalism business exciting, heart-wrenching and hard work, all at once. Bee scratched behind the dog's ears, allowing the information to settle in her mind. She began to feel a little nervous.

"Okay. Let me know when you get something from Riske," she said. Then she added, "That poor woman! This really sucks!" Then, "This Davy Crockett guy. Maybe something good could come of it. I can't believe I'm saying this. Me, the queen cynic from the school of hard knocks."

"I feel you," Webster said. "In the end, good will conquer evil, right?"

"Yeah, right," Molly Bee said.

26

When east coast phone service came up, she called her Justice Department source at his private number.

"Hi," she greeted him. "It's Molly."

"Ah," the source said. "You've heard the voice flying in the wilderness." The accent completely Minnesota.

"You can't say the administration hasn't been asking for it. Do you have any comment from the government?" Knowing perfectly well none would be forthcoming.

"I can't talk to you," the source said. "You know that. We're assuming the guy is a terrorist. I will tell you the psycho-profile so far suggests no intent to harm Sligo. Personally I think it'll be a big mistake if the Progressives are in this. This pilot crashed a party looking for a cheap thrill, and found himself in the lion's den."

"The liar's den?"

"Molly—"

"We both know the crazies are coming out because of the low voter turnout. It's not just the crazies either. People are sick of this stuff. People are sick of dirty tricks and lies!" She was struggling to keep from shouting at the source, but her blood was boiling. "Everybody in the country knows there are crooked people at high levels of government. And I personally have a right to be outraged about it."

"Yeah, yeah," the source mocked. She could feel a sort of helplessness behind his sarcasm. She reached for the notepad before her and scanned her notes. Her hand was steady.

"Why don't you tell me right now, off the record, what's the connection between the low voter turnout and the New Freedom Party winning all the elections?"

His pause was only half a second. "Come on, Molly. What do you want from me? I'm really handcuffed with this thing."

"Fine! I'll tell you what I want!" she exploded. "An Assistant US Attorney named Viola Ferrari died under mysterious conditions while looking into illegal mind control experiments in Utah!" She hated when she lost control, but the situation required it. "Somewhere in the US Attorney's Office they know about this! Now I find out the FBI shoved the investigation into her death under the rug! What is that? That's bullshit, and I want to know what's actually going on."

"I understand your feelings. But we're not going there."

Molly pushed. "Who's the authorizing body on BCI experiments? The Surgeon General? Did Ferrari open some door that was so dirty the feds had to come in to close it? Is that why she died? Is that why your people covered it up? No wonder this Davy Crockett guy started a revolution. With this kind of corruption everywhere you turn!"

"You're sticking a knife right in my heart, you know that? Just a minute." Molly knew this man. He would be pacing right now, putting his pipe in his mouth without lighting it. He knew she would never expose him. "All right," he said when he returned. "I'll say it once, absolutely not for publication." He hesitated. When he spoke his voice was barely audible. "The only reason I know about this is because her death rocked the entire US Attorney's group very seriously. The Federal Bar Association went berserk. People quit. You're right, she was the legal authority on mind control research. Maybe somebody thought Communication International was using the Army to do mind control research without proper sanctions." His voice darkened. "You know their history."

"CI? Why would CI be using the Army for anything? Was this a government contract? Who sent her? Where are the records? Why Chicago? Why didn't the Salt Lake City US Attorney –"

"That's all I know," the source said. "And you never heard me say it. You know the rules."

She jabbed the pencil down so hard against the notebook that it broke. "So you're clearly suggesting the cause of Viola Ferrari's death was not a car crash."

Silence. Molly had to regain her composure. She tossed the broken pencil into the trash.

"Off the record," she said. "You hate CI as much as any decent person, don't you?"

He said nothing. But his silence was enough.

"All right. Where can I go with this?"

"Jaap Tenkley," the source said slowly. He spelled the name. "Okay?"

"Okay. Thanks."

Within thirty seconds she had begun tomorrow's column. Reaching for her Mac to do a Google search of Jaap Tenkley, she cursed aloud when she realized she still had no Internet service, then touched in the phone number of a colleague on the White House beat, Lulu Xiang. Lulu had nothing new on Viola Ferrari. "Okay," Molly said. "Give my blessings to Joel." She added in her notebook, *"CI. You know their history."*

27

Although it was after hours, BJ Lichtenstein had made an attempt to speak with someone working late at Viola Ferrari's office on South Dearborn Street in Chicago. But there would be no information leaving the building. He'd then miraculously gotten through to the Congressional Data Service, and received a call-back with the news that nine prosecutors in the Chicago US Attorney's Office had names starting with C. Two only worked anti-terrorism plus identity theft, two were assigned to Project Safe Neighborhoods, one was the resident Organized Crime guy, and the other four were women. Checking with the Oak Park Elder Care Facility, he found nobody had signed in to visit Concetta Ferrari with the initial C.

The mysterious Ten produced the same result. The virtually unknown registry of US government employees turned up 309 non-military people whose names started with "Ten," and BJ did not have the foggiest idea what to do with this information. In a seizure of optimism he checked with the FBI going through Victor's usual channel, looking for felony records of a "Ten" alias, or a federal indictment or warrant with a name that sounded like Ten. What he got from the Bureau was their peculiar doublespeak for "it's none of your business."

Which was a shame, all things considered, since only last September, confidential FBI records would show, as would the Federal Prisons Supervised Release databank, that a former inmate named Jaap Tenkley had disappeared from supervised release, and in fact had surfaced in Alexandria, Egypt, a sovereign nation with no extradition treaty with the United States.

At the same time BJ was monitoring developments from the mall on the Web. When the television had suddenly gone black, and nobody on the staff would answer their phones, and Ms. Velasquez finally showed up with her breathless tale of Davy Crockett charming the pants off everybody at Independence Hall, he got the picture. Somehow, the Congressman was on that plane.

The old lady did not bother to remove her coat, a fabulous, hooded faux zebra, achingly fashionable in Paris, and she dumped herself unceremoniously on the couch. Getting her relaxed with a drink, BJ paced the rich carpeting, running a twitchy hand through his thick hair and feeling his own heroic nature rising. The camera began rolling in his head – spokesman for the bereaved, BJ Lichtenstein, longtime advisor and close friend of the late Congressman. Yes, with some persuasion he might consider an appointment to serve out the Congressman's new term, if asked.

So they were out of communication. Ms Velasquez smiled at BJ, rather naughtily for a person of her age and stature, and asked if he would pour her another brandy.

Eventually, Courtman called on the landline from Ney Field to explain. There had been a dogfight. The Cessna had disappeared from the sky. Maybe he was dead. Maybe Davy Crockett was nuts. They were on their way back to the hotel.

28

Before midnight, the restored I-Media network reported the brutal kidnapping of US Congressman Victor Sligo by a lone assailant known only as Davy Crockett.

Photos, prints and interviews were scooped into evidence bags at Ney Field. During the frantic invasion, Alonzo "Spit" Toon was having the time of his life. He'd worked up a little ditty, a sort of jazzy-rap number describing the scene for his fans at the club next Saturday night. The whole federal government had plugged up his toilet, messed with his paperwork and stepped in his boxwood shrubs, and treated him with the customary bureaucratic disrespect. Homeland Security, the FBI, the Navy, the Secret Service and some other outfit he'd never heard of, plus that pompous fool Manicotti, had all been made to look like idiots by the man who'd rented the Cessna 400. They tried to nail Toon as an accessory to kidnapping, said they'd take his license, bulldoze down the airstrip, all those diddly white threats, so he just told them what they wanted, signed what they put in front of him after a visit from his attorney, and added couplets to his new ode, "Ney nights." Or maybe he'd call it, "White bread don't cut no mustard." Watching the lady somebody said was Sligo's wife knock the chief of police on his fat behind made Toon clap right out loud, and that Mr. Courtman came over and clapped right with him, the one in the silly vest and tie made him look like a scarecrow.

It was time to get out the horn.

He drifted as quietly as the powder blue tux would allow behind the few people still left, working the valves of his cornet. Black-booted agents were firing up their Nanjing Jeeps and climbing in the chopper. People were coiling up landlines. The wife, wrapped in a blanket Toon had found for her, didn't know which way to turn. She stood in front of him, shoulder-to-shoulder with Raven Menez and Mgaba, while the tall thin guy, the scarecrow, hung around with his hands in his pockets.

Everybody was leaving.

Half the time he didn't know what would come out when the brass touched his lips. Would it be *The Saints? Georgia?* He started to blow, and they all turned around. Toon was wailing out a raw, broken-glass version of *America the Beautiful.* He had to stop for a second to compose himself, and he wiped his brow with a handkerchief and looked for all the world like Louis Armstrong.

29

After penetrating interviews with the FBI, Homeland Security and what felt like a dozen other agencies, Nel Sligo, Courtman and Mgaba were escorted against their wishes back to the hotel by a pair of battle-dressed agents. They were devastated, frightened, half in shock. It was two a.m.

With sanitized frustration, the feds had quizzed Nel about D. Crockett. How had the Congressman managed to be in harm's way when Crockett took off? Was there any prior relationship between them? Did Nel feel there might have been political motivation in the kidnapping, asked the one with the shabby black suit and double chin.

"Of course it's politically motivated," she'd screamed. "What do you think that banner was about? A church picnic?"

"But, Ms. Sligo, your husband represents the opposition, the Progressive Party! What could this man possibly gain by –"

She was worn down and genuinely fearing for Victor's life. "Wake up!" she snarled, baring her pure white teeth. "My husband is missing! Now go find him!"

Nobody asked what she and her husband and his staff were doing in Philadelphia.

She had no clue as to the real identity of D. Crockett, nor the slightest notion what business Congressman Sligo might have had out at Ney Field.

BJ was standing at the door with a drink in his hand when they finally dragged themselves in. Nel said, "Have you heard anything?"

"No. I'm so sorry, Nel. But your husband is the toughest man I know! There's no way he's going to –"

"All right, stop, stop!" She jerked a thin hand in his face. Nel felt like her world was coming apart, and now she noticed a strange, disheveled woman sitting in a recliner wearing a zebra hide coat. She looked half dead.

"Who's this?" she demanded.

Courtman coughed. Then Nel recognized her.

"Ms. Velasquez! Oh, forgive me, I –"

"He's missing, isn't he," said the old lady tenderly.

Nel immediately dropped onto the couch. Her mouth opened wide, as though she were about to scream. Then she reached up and took the drink Mgaba was holding out for her. "He's missing," she said with no inflection. And added, "In action."

"Maybe there was something I could have done," Michaela Velasquez moaned.

All evening Courtman had been immobilized with a case of terrified procrastination. He was contemplating a call to Washington as soon as his phone came back online, intending to rage at Homeland Security. Then he'd get hold of Admiral Singh at the Pentagon, to ascertain the search for Sligo was legit and not coming from the White House, where the devil knew what might transpire. He needed an update on Senator Riske's next move – certain that a bourgeois revolution had been launched – and he needed to convince himself that it would be to his advantage to stay the course, if somebody would just stand up and lead the damn rebellion. It wasn't going to be Edwin Foulks! Edwin Foulks was a carrot-wielding flake on a crusade to get himself a footnote in history. Maybe his plan was to haul in the carcass of the dead Congressman, find a retarded street urchin to play Davy Crockett, and claim the million bucks reward. And spend the rest of his life on the last clean beach on Earth, the Bikini Atoll, learning how to speak Marshallese.

Maybe that was what Foulks had planned from the beginning.

The only part that didn't fit was that Victor Sligo was too

smart to let that happen.

Courtman stood beside a thermal cube, at last feeling some warmth creep up his legs, listening to Nel and Michaela Velasquez apologize to each other, a bourbon in his hand from a bottle he didn't remember opening.

Where was that Menez girl? They would need local media standing by to get out fast press releases, and she was connected locally. Not that he didn't have several dozen reliable contacts in D.C., plus the entire press corps back home in Washington state – but this kid was here in Philadelphia, and she obviously admired Nel, and she wasn't old enough to be mistrusted. That novice desperation was always refreshing.

"Sloan."

The big speechwriter was just leaving. "Enough!" he yawned. "I'm going down to my room. I've got to get a shower and get to bed. I stink and I'm dead tired. Call me if anything develops."

"That reporter out at the airfield. Can you get hold of her?"

"It's two o'clock in the morning. Can it wait?"

"You're not too stinking tired to realize we have a life-threatening crisis on our hands." Courtman moved a step toward Mgaba. "Are you?"

"Fine. I have her number." Mgaba slumped against the door jamb. "She is to compromise her entire career for us, am I right?"

"Just call her, your lordship."

Michaela pushed against the sofa and slowly rose. She was gaunt, her rouged face chiseled by a lifetime of forcing her will on people who could do something for her. She was so exhausted from the long day she looked like a ghost in the fake zebra coat.

She said, just above a whisper, "I'm already hearing from my people abroad. If our government should collapse, heaven forbid, some sort of national bankruptcy... Some people are going to get very upset about this. This damn fool Crockett storming the Bastille all by himself!"

BJ thought he was supposed to respond. He opened his mouth, but Mgaba cut him off.

"I was there," the big man said, moving back toward the group. "I'll tell you what –"

BJ snapped, *"They* could make a run for the White House!" He glared at Mgaba. "We have a one-man air force and Mr. Ways and Means jerking the rug out from under Billy Hellman!" Without intending it he laughed hysterically for one full second, then slammed his mouth shut.

Nel whirled furiously around at him. "Lichtenstein, are you drunk? Are you insinuating my husband is stupid?" At the same moment, Courtman had crossed the room with the hotel phone, heading for Mgaba. Nerves were poking through flesh all over the room. Caught in the middle, Ms. Velasquez was having trouble understanding staff dynamics.

"Are you going to call Menez," Courtman spat. "Take the phone! I've got work to do while you people sit around sniping at each other." He shoved the phone at Mgaba, but Mgaba's huge hand slapped his arm.

"Hey!" Mgaba growled. "Calm down. Don't forget the priority here, *Purvis,* is to get Congressman Sligo to safety!" His voice was rough and commanding.

Ms. Velasquez tried to get out of the way, but couldn't quite make it.

"Damn you, I know the priority, Mgaba! I told you to call that girl!" Courtman pulled back and unintentionally pushed against Nel. Instinctively Nel moved in to separate them, whipping her arms out like a referee, banging an elbow into Mgaba's chest to back him off, pushing on Courtman's shoulder, furious that these morons would play power games when her husband's life was threatened.

"People!" BJ also tried to take charge. "Let's have some cool heads here, folks –" Then Michaela was in the fray, looking into Nel's fiery eyes. They were in a scrum, Mgaba and Courtman gripping the white hotel phone, BJ wiggling in against Courtman, Nel shoving at both tall men, her eyes falling to Michaela's, angry at everybody, tasting blood, not understanding what was happening here, and Michaela opposite her in that ridiculous zebra coat saying, "Ms. Sligo, Nel, Nel, it's all right, what he's doing is –" But Nel couldn't stand it. She was spitting through clenched teeth, tears flooding her eyes, "No! It's not all right! Victor might already be dead! This is how they get rid of their enemies!" Grabbing wildly for the phone with no idea what she was doing, Mgaba just pulling back a big open hand to knock Courtman out of the way, when suddenly a fist was pounding on the door.

"Federal agent! Congressman Sligo! Open up, sir!"

30

Nobody moved. Ever so gently, Ms Velasquez, crumpled against Courtman, touched Nel's cheek. In her face was a century of compassion. Up against the two women, Mgaba and Courtman glowered at each other. Holding his breath with an arm extended against Mgaba's chest, Lichtenstein placed a finger to his lips. His instinct was to simply be quiet until the intruder went away. But Nel's voice fractured the air.

"Just a minute!" She pulled away from the stunned staff and the old lady. She whispered huskily, "Everybody sit!" Grabbing a tissue, she blew her nose and pulled the door open.

A thickly built man in a gray suit and black winter coat stood before her. Straight sandy hair, crooked nose.

"Ms. Sligo," he said with deep weariness. The others craned their necks toward the door. "Bert O'Donnell," he said, "National Security Agency. Pardon my coming down so late at night. I believe we almost met at the Eagles game the other day. I was selling beer."

"Of course," turning, vastly relieved to see this man without knowing why, tears burning her cheeks, still shaking with embarrassment and rage. "It's been an awful day. Would you mind if –"

"Forgive my violent knocking. I really should come in," O'Donnell told her.

It was approaching 2:30 in the morning. O'Donnell greeted Ms. Velasquez formally, a comrade-in-arms. Gazing quickly around he realized at once he'd made a stupid error. Iona Webster was not here. How could she be? He had connected her to Sligo's group without a second thought. She was probably already at home in LA.

He said to Nel quietly, "Is the room secure?"

"Yes."

Everybody sat, shooting nervous glances at one another. He explained to Nel his small role in the survival of the aircraft. He needed to come downtown to let her know her husband was safe. "There's a simple GPS tracking device built into airplanes. The Pentagon was in such a froth about their systems failing they just forgot about it. The congressman landed safely and destroyed the beeper. That's all I know."

Nel listened feverishly. "Thank you," she said.

Courtman said, "I suppose you found us thanks to our new

acquaintances in jack boots bringing us back here."

"The whole damn town knows you're here," O'Donnell said. Turning back to Nel, "The man's launched a riot. Crockett, I mean. I assure you there was no kidnapping."

"That's correct," Mgaba said, his voice thick and exhausted. "The Congressman just leaped on the plane. I would imagine to save that man from execution."

"This is madness," Michaela Velasquez now spoke up. "Mr. O'Donnell." She studied his large haggard face. "Senator Riske said nothing about his people's intentions. What is actually happening? Is NSA engaged in this? Is the military up to speed? That ungodly Hellman – he won't do anything stupid?"

O'Donnell's eyebrows shot up. Riske. He saw his computer screen at home, Riske's order to send Viola Ferrari to Utah. Instantly he told himself, thank God Iona's not here. He was not going down that road.

"Hellman likely won't be in this," he said to Ms. Velasquez. "As you know, the commander in chief of the military is the President. Congress gets no say. In the event of imminent threat to the nation's security – and that's what this is – it's all extremely high profile. Burligame will have to take charge. He'll be back in the country before dawn. And no, NSA is not engaged. Nobody predicted this. We're in a wait-and-see mode. I know nothing about the military's response. Just what's on the news."

"Still," Courtman said, "They won't stop till we're all locked up. I'm amazed they let us go tonight." He strained not to wonder what O'Donnell knew about the Code Thirteen. He didn't dare ask. Nobody spoke. O'Donnell shifted himself to stand up.

"I needed to know about that airplane," Nel said without conviction. Her face was tormented. "But I still don't understand," studying him, fiddling with the wedding ring. "Why are you here, Mr. O'Donnell?"

He rose, and said without hesitating, "People are monitoring Congressman Sligo's electronic communications – and yours – as potential terrorist threats. In my work... I'm able to get wind of things fairly quickly." He reached in his jacket, and handed her a coded white card. "It is possible that I'll know of the congressman's activities, or of other people's activities regarding him. Tomorrow evening, go to a public phone and insert this card. When the phone rings, hang up."

She moved closer to him, but the look in her eyes was not trusting. Their eyes were level. Her voice sounded strange in her own ears. "My husband told me this afternoon –" She had to collect herself. "The meeting you attended. There was some discussion about Viola Ferrari." Her eyes were riveted to his, her lips thin, two fingers working on the wedding band. "Nobody in government is willing to –" Something was happening to Nel's blood pressure. Her face was flushed. Her hands would not cease dancing about. Suddenly she spat out, "My husband is missing! And now NSA shows up here! Why? I think you know what happened to him! And I think you know what happened to Viola Ferrari!" She had become a lioness lashing at her prey.

Michaela Velasquez came beside her, taking a hand in both of hers. "Nel." Turning to Courtman. "Has she eaten tonight?"

O'Donnell's loathing of his own government had begun to gnaw at him like a cancer. Which was why he had landed at Independence Hall. He was torn by fear of failure and possibly prison, or worse, pulled in every direction by career and family and the crushing reality of what could happen. But he had come here mostly to have a minute with Iona Webster. Now Sligo's wife had turned it into an inquisition.

"Ms. Sligo. Please listen to me. This is the worst possible moment to be investigating a government conspiracy. If this insurrection has any inertia to it, you will not find a single door open. You won't find anybody to talk to, much less tell you the truth, as long as this thing is moving. You can only –"

"Don't give me that!" she shouted at him. "A woman was *murdered!* Probably by government agents! And now they have my husband! That must be clear to you by now! You tell me when is the right time to investigate!"

"They'll kill me as quick as they killed Viola Ferrari!" O'Donnell said harshly. He was struggling for control. He forced himself to think, her husband is missing. The woman is scared to death.

They were nearly eyeball to eyeball. He said, "Anybody with any connection to Crockett is living on the cliff's edge!" He heard what she heard in his voice: guilt, shame, panic. She had every reason to believe they had Sligo locked up somewhere.

For those few seconds, Nel gripped his eyes with hers, feminine and powerful, clawing into his reality. She could feel him succumbing. O'Donnell reached into his jacket pocket and withdrew a brown notebook. He looked down and found the page he wanted, then copied names and numbers in an awkward left-handed scribble onto a fresh page, tore it off, and handed it to her.

"Your husband's plane landed safely," he said again. He turned toward the door and pulled it open, then turned back. "That first number is Fred Geschwantner. Retired Utah state investigator. You're going to want to talk to him. The other one's Viola Ferrari's boss. Nobody knows where he is. You will need data from Viola's files, and the files have been sealed by executive privilege. And her laptop's missing. I'm sorry." With a preemptory nod, he left.

Nel sent Michaela Velasquez away in a cab, but not before she insisted on being informed the instant anybody learned anything. She embraced Nel, and then BJ Lichtenstein perhaps a bit longer than was necessary, and promised they'd get together soon. Before they all collapsed, Nel assigned to BJ the job of finding Viola Ferrari's superior in Chicago. O'Donnell had written down the name "Jerome Tse". Between the two of them, neither conversant with third-world names, they were too wiped out to come up with a likely pronunciation.

"It's pronounced like the letter C," Mgaba muttered sleepily. "Jerome Tse."

"Huh. Like the man who came to see Viola's mother," BJ remembered.

31

Foulks and Victor sat at a large hand-hewn oak table in an industrial-size kitchen painted completely white, surrounded by farm people, the men with square beards and coveralls, the women in long severe gray dresses and no jewelry. All were squeaky clean. They were sipping strong black tea following a crack-of-dawn breakfast of cornbread and ham and eggs and potato pancakes and bowls of fruit and milk that both men had to force themselves to drink. Nobody spoke during the meal, except for grace offered by the oldest of them, a woman of indeterminate age, maybe sixty-five, maybe ninety-five, with a completely smooth complexion, her hair in a snow white bun pulled back so harshly you flinched to look at her. She spoke with a sort of Philadelphia German accent.

"You know, you do resemble that politician," she said at last, her voice coming like butter to the ears, well-churned but sweet. Turning to look down the long table, "Remember that commissioner? He stopped in to see if we would vote for him?" She pronounced the word "voet," addressing another older woman who was apparently blind, who tapped the table in a gesture of hilarity. "He thought because we're Mormons we would voet for him. But you see, we are Mennonites. Not Mormons." She chortled somehow without a sound coming from her white lips. "He could not tell a Mormon from a Mennonite! And wanted us to voet for him! The dear man. We explained the Mormons left Pennsylvania quite some time ago."

There was a long silence. A few heads dropped low as if in prayer, and some even shook. Neither Foulks nor Victor could figure out if they were supposed to speak, or if humor would help, or what to say. And the way the others stared at them without a hint of emotion, it was as if nobody ever spoke at all around here except the old lady. These were devoted, working people. It showed in their hands and their silence.

"We don't vote," one of the men in coveralls said. Victor looked down the table. All stared at him silently. No clue to who had spoken.

"Well, I –" Foulks kicked Victor's shin. The matter was not up for debate. "Hmm," he said. Still wearing the tan hoodie with the word "Airborne" across the chest, Foulks studied his teacup. Everybody sipped in unison. The hands returned to the clasped position before them. It was like having breakfast in a Grant Wood painting.

After what seemed like an hour, the old woman said, "You are nice people."

"Well, yeah!" said Edwin Foulks happily. Cocking his head, waiting.

"Why are these men looking for you?"

Foulks started to pull out his pocket knife, caught himself, and went stiff. "Remember we told you last night? We have started a rebellion against the government. Your government!"

"You mean our town? Altemenschen? Whatever for?" She must have forgotten their convoluted story from late last night, when they had arrived battered and frozen on an ancient motorcycle.

"No, ma'am," Victor said. "Not your town. The United States government."

"Oh. That's different then." She smiled. A piece of silverware tinkled to the tile floor, and somebody bent to retrieve it.

"These men run the government in a way this is designed to only help the few at the top," Victor said.

"Oh, yes. That is what we do also." She nodded sagely. "We all take care of each other."

"Yes, no, I mean... How to explain? Everybody else in the whole country is against them. You see?"

"Of course. Just like us." She formed a triangle with her scarred farm hands flat on the table. "But why are you running from them? If you started a rebellion, don't you want to finish it?"

Edwin Foulks was barely controlling his patience. "Sure," he said. "But one thing at a time, missus. First let me ask you something. Do you ever –"

"No questions!" The same male voice came rough and threatening. Again nobody seemed responsible for the words. Nobody so much as twitched. One bearded person was rubbing a gnarled knuckle with his thumb. Congressman Sligo, utterly out of his element, watched the play of the thumb and the knuckle across the silence. Was this the leader? Nobody blinked. He watched the farmer long enough for spiders to mate and their babies go to college. Finally the man made eye contact. His eyes were severe, a deep blue, but not without compassion. He held Victor's gaze sternly.

"Philadelphia Eagles," he said. The voice not quite so rough. "You are a bird watcher?" He stared, and began grinding his teeth. His jaws clenched. A sound seemed trapped in his throat.

Victor recoiled. Looked down at the shiny green Eagles jacket he still wore, now grimy from last night's wild escape.

"Uh, no sir, it's –" Was he joking? Nobody could be that detached. He found the man's gaze and tried to smile.

Edwin clamored to the rescue. "It's football! Don't you people –" But he heard himself asking a question, a dumb one at that, and he closed his mouth.

"Foot-ball," hyphenated the farmer. With exaggerated confusion he looked around to the others. Edwin and Victor looked
with him. A few of them, men and women, were clenching their
teeth or pressing their lips together. A woman was rolling her eyes.
What was it? Repressed Mennonite angst about to boil over? One
man with a bull neck and shoulders was looking cross-eyed at the
wall over Victor's head. His face began to quiver, almost as if he
were having a heart attack. His cheeks puffed out. Tears began
pouring down his huge face. Suddenly he threw his enormous hands
against his face and began shaking all over. The others looked in
surprise. Holy Jesus, Victor thought, he really *is* having a heart attack. Then like a troop of clowns bursting in, the charade collapsed.
The bull neck man exploded with laughter. All of them began
shrieking, gasping, cackling at one another. They roared across at
each other, slamming the table with thick hands, sighing and weeping. One woman had fallen sideways and was biting her neighbor's
shoulder, clutching his arm and laughing hysterically.

"Well fine," said Edwin Foulks over the din.

"Oh, Lord," the football man said, holding his cheeks. He
squinted through tears up at the old lady. "When you said —" Unable
to finish, he practically balled with laughter. "That guy thought we
were Mormons!" And he began banging his forehead on the table,
while others shrieked all over again, screaming out the old lady's
lines.

"You are a bird watcher?" somebody bellowed, and they
burst out all over again.

The old lady meanwhile sat smiling like the cat who ate the
canary. She reached out and took Victor's hand. "You boys are
good sports," she said.

A woman declared, "That is really awful tea. Are we out of
Starbucks?" This set off a new round of laughter. The youngest man
present, about seventy, told them when Victor said they were only
taking over the US government, and the old lady had said, "Oh,
that's different," he had to hide under the table, and he'd just about
peed his pants.

Somebody was brewing coffee already. Introductions went
around. The oldest farmer's name was John Zander. He said he'd
missed the daring rescue last night since he went to bed regularly at

7:30, and asked them to tell it again.

"It was like Pearl Harbor," Victor Sligo began, caught up in the humor. "Jets were everywhere, buzzing like mosquitoes."

"Two of them," said Foulks.

"Right, and suddenly they just vanished! We didn't know until you people told us what happened. Then I tried turning on the TV last night down the hall there, but it failed to come on. The whole east coast communications network, down the toilet! What's a Holotech TV doing on a Mennonite farm anyway?"

"We watch," said Elizabeth Zander, the white-haired woman.

"We actually did have a plan," Edwin Foulks continued.

Victor reached for a coffee pitcher. He was feeling vastly relieved. "Do you happen to have any cream?"

Everybody laughed. "Do we have cream?" asked William Freund, of the bull neck. With his severe crew cut and burnished face, he looked like an FBI man in undercoveralls. "Ask an udder question." The farmers flicked their fingers at him.

Victor said. "Anyway, we landed somewhere. This bumpy old airstrip. Scared the hell out of me."

"There was a vehicle waiting?" Jerzy Zander asked this. The man of the Eagles joke. "But if you'd never been here before, how did you –"

"There was this old motorcycle. He went straight for it." Turning to Foulks, "Where'd that motorcycle come from, anyway?"

"Amazing," Foulks said, wiping his mouth. "The woman said she'd leave it there, out by that unused runway, with a map to this farm. That woman from the little gathering at Independence Hall."

"What woman?"

"I don't know. All dressed in red. The blond. Remember?"

"Oh. Really?" And then, "Come outside a minute."

Victor hauled him out to the front porch.

"Foulks," he said, and had to shift his eyes to stay focused under Edwin's steady gaze. "You have to quit being so blasé about this, man! They've been chasing you for eight hours. They probably got an iris scan on you in the plane. Your fingerprints are all over the place. Voice pattern, face ID. Hell, man, didn't you ever have a driver's license? There's a national manhunt going on for you and some pain-in-the-neck Representative you took for a joyride in a stolen aircraft! You threatened to take over the government!" He leaned close, and whispered tight-lipped, "They haven't extermi-nated you yet, pal. But let me make a little prediction: when they find you, they will!"

They returned to the table as tiny Sister Margaret was enter-ing. "Excuse me," she said. "The Web's back on."

Immediately Foulks was standing. "You have the Internet here?"

"Of course," Sister Elizabeth laughed.

He returned in a couple of minutes, wearing an ironic grin. "The Web site's been taken down."

Sister Margaret coughed. Her skin was pure white and as thin as paper, but she had a stern manner, and now she held up a stern hand and said, "What are you expecting to happen?" A minis-cule suggestion of a grin puckered her lips. She looked like a mad New England grandmother who'd just done in the neighbor's gold-fish.

All eyes went to Edwin. He did withdraw the three-inch pocket knife this time, unfolded the blade and held it to his ear, and tested the edge with his thumb as if he were listening to it.

He was expecting, he said, the undoing of Vice President Billy Hellman. If the plan went correctly, President Burligame could go down with him. Collateral damage. Others could go down as well.

As the blade touched his soft beard, in his gentle voice Edwin told them he'd spent a year studying Iona Webster's life-altering document, *Strategies for Survival in a Corporate World.* Then out of the blue he had been invited by his activist techno-geek friend in Greenland to the Independence Hall meeting. On the way he'd conceived the actual flight plan. Flying over the new mall would cause an unprecedented flooding of the Web, conceivably shutting down communications satellites worldwide – cell phones, the Internet, and government information lines. The Greenland friend hooked him up with the insane grad student at UW who had created Hunter Tyne's iris ID contact lenses. But Edwin never dreamed that a powerful United States Congressman would go along for the ride.

"The thing I want," he said, closing the knife, "is to get to the real truth why people are not voting. If we get that, everything else will fall into place. That will finish Mr. Hellman, I imagine."

"You don't know why people ain't voting?" This was Lester Zander, another brother, with a voice so deep you had to listen at the bottom of your ears to hear him. He had huge hands, broad shoulders, bib overalls. His head was as shiny as the hood of a new Farmall tractor. "I thought you knew."

"No, sir," Edwin said. "I don't."

The big man turned to his neighbor. "He don't know why people ain't voting." The voice sounded like the middle notes of a euphonium.

"Huh," said the neighbor, the woman who had been biting his shoulder.

With some effort he turned back to Edwin. He grinned a big, grain-fed grin. "People ain't voting because... because..." Looking down the table to Sister Elizabeth, who waited for him, head cocked slightly, eyes bright. "I can't remember." The others laughed tenuously. Turning to Foulks, "I can't remember."

Foulks and Victor exchanged a shrug.

"Uh, well, that's fine, maybe you'll –"

"I can't remember," he repeated. "To vote. See, that's what's happening. I get real milked up to vote," he explained, showing the milking motion with both hands. "I even saw that Julio Reese fellow on the Public Television telling everybody to don't vote. Then all of a sudden it's the next day and ..." He flopped open the great shovel hands. "I forgot!"

"All is not lost, brother," Edwin told him pleasantly. "At least you remember that you can't remember." He waited a moment for Lester to get this and unleash his vast grin again.

Victor added, "I'd be a happy man if all my opponent's supporters were like you."

"Hey," Lester agreed.

Sister Elizabeth said, "You politicians are strange people."

To which all the brothers and sisters laughed.

"Everybody knows that," Edwin said, laughing along, not so sure what was so funny.

It was crucial to Sister Elizabeth that they find a way to let Ms. Sligo know her husband was safe. She needed to know where Nel was.

"The Gouverneur Morris Hotel?" she said. "How odd!"

"It's not that bad," Victor said.

She smiled. "Our milk collection man, Mr. Smith. This is the end of his route, all the way from King of Prussia. He's here very early. And you know, his wife is an auditor at the Gouverneur Morris Hotel. A lovely couple. Mennonites, of course. Very discreet. I will call Mrs. Smith."

Unhesitating, Victor said, "The message is that I'm fine and I'll contact her where the clowns walk on stilts in a few days."

32

The two men were walking along the straight dirt road between fields. It was cold with a high yellow-gray overcast. You could smell snow over the horizon. They had volunteered to pick up the paper out on the highway, half a mile further.

"I've got to get back to D.C. Congress is out, but the Intelligence Committee is meeting and I have some things to discuss. Plus I have to find my staff. And figure out what kind of crimes they want me for." He was buttoned up against the chill in an oversized red-checked hunting jacket and black rubber boots, German Army wool pants and a red Snoopy hat. He said, "I feel like Holden Caulfield lost on the subway."

"You could pass." Foulks stopped in the road and looked up at the taller man. Victor stopped.

"You do understand they're coming for me. You can't be around. Even with that silly hat on, people might take you out when they come for me."

Victor thought about this. He said, "I admit I haven't decided what to do about all this yet, Foulks. But I will say this. I do believe you're the craziest son of a bitch I've ever met in my life."

At the end of the road, where it met State Route 897, they yanked the *US Times-Philadelphia* out of a bright yellow paper box. Victor tore it open, not certain if the world was looking to rescue him, or gun him down.

There it was: a two-column color photo of himself, taken

last July as he finished a triathlon in Bellingham, under the fiery red headline, *"Congressman Sligo Kidnapped."*

The entire front page was crowded with stories about the events of the previous day. The two men stood reading in the gray midday chill, mesmerized by the paper's almost entirely made-up story of the airplane ride over the Mall of Brotherly Love, complete with incredible photos of two blistering Marine Corps Interceptors intending to blow them out of the sky. The *Rebellion.com* banner was displayed in vivid color. There were sidebars about Victor's recent eighth win in Washington's second district, woven in with his work on Ways and Means and other committees; stories about the Web collapse, the satellite overloads and heroic efforts at NASA to get them back on line; and at the bottom, under a flap advertising potatoes at $1.99 a pound, was a photo, obviously taken by a cheap cell phone, of complete chaos in the White House War Room as the military communications network crashed before their eyes.

Victor said, "Can't wait to read what Molly Bee has to say."

"Not in this paper, you won't."

Accounts of White House response filled the center pages, including file photos of figures involved in the fiasco, among them White House legal counsel Tenacia Friggie, who had her hands full determining who could say what in response to the crisis. Edwin burst out laughing when he saw Ms. Friggie's name and photo.

Press secretary Joel Babylon gave his usual elaborate obfuscation of the administration's actions. "A source in the War Room claims that Vice President Hellman saved the life of a great American, US Representative Victor Sligo, in the culminating moments of this bizarre event," Babylon said. "For national security reasons we cannot confirm Representative Sligo's whereabouts. In the absence of the President, Mr. Hellman has brought the full weight of the United States government to tracking down the alleged kidnapper and bringing him to justice." Unaccountably, Babylon was pictured reading the statement with a grin plastered across his handsome face.

The double layout on pages fourteen and fifteen contained more photos and what passed in the *US Times* for information. A nationwide search had been launched for a mysterious man only known as "D. Crockett," either from San Antonio or a post office box in rural western Washington. San Antonio was a red herring.

An FBI check in the tiny community of Van Zandt revealed that the town actually had not had a post office since 1977. A Dashiell Hammett Crockett of Skagit County had come forward, but investigators believed the kidnapper to be under age ninety-seven, neither sight-impaired nor wheelchair bound. Mr. Crockett was escorted by Paratransit back to his residence at Western State Hospital.

Yet another sidebar examined the embarrassing blunder of the Laser Iris Scan captured by Marine Corps Interceptor pilots in pursuit of the phantom Cessna 400. The chairman of the Joint Chiefs of Staff himself addressed the issue in an impromptu statement late Tuesday evening.

"High tech instrumentation is fallible," Admiral Singh told the *Times*. "The rumor that the LIS scan identified the Secretary of Communications is exactly that – rumor. No definitive identification has been released by the Defense Department."

Homeland Security's ICE Agent Carlotta Pfister explained her agency's role. Initially the logo on the nose of the Cessna had been identified as a Canadian Maple Leaf. The decision was automatic and instantaneous. Threat from a foreign power. Homeland Security had stepped in. Only upon examining video from Captain Tuiasosopo's flyby did they recognize the imprint on the renegade aircraft not as a Canadian maple leaf, but a man's hand with the fingers curled, painted bright red. It seemed to be blowing the nose of the Cessna. Some kind of little joke by the owner of the aircraft.

The Laser Iris Scan had erroneously misidentified the pilot.

Secretary of Communications Hunter Tyne was unavailable for comment. The paper was playful enough to print a photograph of Dr. Tyne tripping on the steps of the new DComm building. Beneath the photo was the single word, "Moonlighting?"

The paper took its stand through acerbic weekly columnist Osceola Stone.

"What's with all these people freaking out at the new Mall of Brotherly Love? Haven't you ever seen an infomercial before? Just another fanatic pushing his product! Look, we all read that *Strategies for Survival in a Corporate World.* More jumping on the Doomsday wagon! More socialist flogging at private enterprise! What made America a grand nation was not the picayune jabbering of the fringe loonies! It was the solid entrepreneurship of visionary men and women creating powerful communities, bringing schools

and industry, conquering poverty, and undoing the staggering welfare imbroglio left us by a century of self-indulgent Progressive
whiners. Of course it's a corporate world! Who else will pick up the
tab to straighten out the planet, but those whose primary interest is
to market goods and services only a functioning economy can pay
for? Iona Webster, give me a break!'"

On the big white porch Foulks found the story he wanted.
He read aloud, "The entire nation is on high alert to locate Congressman Sligo and the man the media is calling 'Davy Crockett.' A
one million dollar reward has been posted by the Burligame administration if the kidnapper is found and brought to justice."

Victor looked at him. "I could turn you in."

"Ever ride the rails?"

"No. Especially not in a blizzard."

"That Code Thirteen thing of yours. Can you still use it?"

"Too risky. By now they'll be monitoring every move my
staff makes. Puts everybody in jeopardy. My family, you, me, the
Mennonites." He stopped. "They can't catch you," he said.

"I hope not. So you know where I live. I think I'll try to get
home and work out the next move from there."

"You haven't told me the rest of your crazy plan."

He hesitated. "You weren't listening. We're going to get
them to tell the people what's really going on. Then see what happens."

"The people don't give a damn," Sligo shot back. "They
won't vote."

"When they hear the truth, they'll vote."

"Foulks! You have the ego of a mouse backstroking down a
river with an erection, yelling out, 'Open the drawbridge, I'm coming through!'" He tried not to smile.

"You politicians and your little rodent images."

Outside, the first thin flakes of snow were falling.

Victor turned to survey the broad, clean landscape. Wind
drummed against the house. "All right, Mister tell-the-truth. What
are we waiting for? We have ground to cover."

33

O'Donnell had scared BJ. Too blitzed to sleep, he'd found an all-night Warp Zone where every variety of techno-trash was sold, and he'd picked up a case of twenty-four throw-away phones, in hideous shades from canary yellow to weathered-barn purple, and all the store's plug-in scramblers.

At seven-thirty in the morning, they regathered. At the window overlooking the concrete-and-glass Legoland of downtown Philadelphia, Sloan Mgaba was muttering to himself, head bobbing, shifting his bulk from one heavy leg to the other. He was praying. BJ was burrowed in his notebook. At the house computer, Courtman surfed groggily through the news.

"All right, people. We have a man missing," Nel said, organizing her thoughts and willing herself to suppress her growing desperation. "BJ, what do you have on Jerome Tse?"

"Uh, nothing yet." He grabbed a house phone, called down for breakfast, and opened one of the new phones and an instruction booklet.

"I'm calling this Fred Geschwantner, whoever he is," Nel said. To Mgaba, "Get us on a plane home."

She picked up the other house phone and found the number O'Donnell had given her.

"Wait," BJ said. "Hang on. It's gotten way too real for that. I'm suggesting we use these prepaid phones. It's how drug dealers communicate with their sources."

"How would you know," Mgaba said.

"CSI," the little man said.

A soft knock came to the door. Courtman flicked a glance at Nel, rose, and cracked it opened carefully.

For a second the six-foot-three chief of staff thought it was a trick.

"Hi," said a soft voice. He looked down, and a woman in a motorized wheelchair was looking up, not smiling, not anything. Just looking at him.

"Hi," he said, pulling the door open.

"Ms. Sligo, please?" She was well dressed, with short light hair and an understated gold necklace over a white blouse, her eyes matter-of-fact and clear. Her left hand was somewhat gnarled against the controls of the wheelchair.

He tilted his head in his charming, disarming fashion. "May I ask your name?"

"Smith."

"Fine, Smith. Just a moment." Then Nel was at the door in her white shorts and a black pullover, looking tortured and sleepless. She bent forward and held her hand out. Smith took it.

"I have a message for you." Her mouth stretched in a gesture that might have resembled a smile.

Nel waited.

Smith moved her upper body forward. Nel bent further down. Barely moving her lips, she said, "Your husband will contact you where the clowns walk on stilts in a few days."

"Oh, dear God!" Nel was weeping, holding the woman's hand, her other hand to her mouth, turning to look back for Courtman. "Come in, come in," she choked, still holding Smith's hand, pulling as if the power chair would glide forward with her.

"No, I can't, I –"

"You are an angel," Nel gushed, not knowing what to call her, dropping to her knees and looking into Smith's eyes. A hundred questions came to her mind. "Did you see him?"

She pushed the toggle under her hand, and moved forward a few inches into the suite, and explained in a low monotone that her husband collected milk, and was given the message by the Zanders. There was no possible doubt. Victor was going home.

Still kneeling beside the young woman, Nel wiped her face and said, "I can't tell you how much this means to me. Your husband –. Do you have children?"

"Seven," Smith said.

"Seven!" She checked her impulse to exclaim, "No wonder you're in a wheelchair." Smith was already backing out the door. "Where can I get in touch with you?"

The woman shrugged. "Here," she said, and turning the chair, she whooshed silently down the hall toward the elevator.

"Thank you, thank you so much," Nel called after her.

34

They had to refuse the offer of a pickup truck from the Zanders. It was just too dangerous. If they were stopped it would lead the cops straight back to the farm. Jerzy vociferously insisted he drive them to wherever they were going. They refused to reveal their destination. Jerzy pushed harder. He always wanted children, he said, and now these two youngsters had come into his life and he wasn't about to just abandon them. Sister Elizabeth managed to bring him to his senses, suggesting he drive them as far as Lewistown, and introduce them to Dr. Horst Spangloss, a man she called a "fellow traveler," who would certainly be of some assistance.

The Zanders loaded them up with more food than they could consume in a week. Somebody had located clothing for Foulks so that both men resembled dairy farmers stumbling out for the five o'clock milking on a frosty morning. As for Jerzy Zander, he wore his coveralls and white long johns and Carhartt coat, and a ratty black watch cap. They headed west in Jerzy's overheated 2000 Lincoln Navigator, a vehicle the nearby nunnery had donated to the farm when the last two sisters had been shipped to a nursing home way over in Blue Ridge Summit. Everything felt out-of-body. Foulks rode shotgun and whispered over the *Times* stories, while Victor sat in the back watching the impending storm, feeling the rumble of the road through his German Army pants and contemplating what he would do after prison, and whether Nel would wait for him.

Real Radio came sputtering through the eight speakers. The search for Congressman Sligo had widened since last night. Checkpoints plugged up roads across southeast Pennsylvania and New Jersey, the entire turnpike and western Maryland and the jagged hind leg of West Virginia. Every car rental, airport, bus and train depot in the United States and Canada was being monitored. The *Rebellion.com* Web site had disappeared, but in its place, like a million phoenixes rising, came an armada of angry new sites, as well as old Progressive hangouts reinvigorated in the sudden euphoria of rebellion. Behind the voice of morning commentator Sarita Chavez, you could hear restrained glee drifting out across the land, as though the Progressive ideology had been locked in the basement for years, and had finally managed to get one hand free.

"Secretary of Communications Hunter Tyne has been vacationing in Greece," Chavez reported. Immediately Victor pushed forward from the back seat, and asked Jerzy to turn up the volume. "Dr. Tyne was not amused by the suggestion he was piloting the renegade aircraft carrying Congressman Sligo."

The sound bite hissed in on cue. "I might sue that man," Hunter Tyne's staccato voice filled up the Lincoln. "I've been here all week. My fiancée will join me today, and we do not intend to be harassed by the paparazzi." He added gruffly, "Avoiding you people is not illegal for the Secretary of Communications!"

"I met Tyne once or twice," Victor recalled from the back seat. "One of those yo-yo Capital Hill photo ops. My staff meets your staff, we pretend we want to play tennis some time. It was like talking to Jabba the Hutt. The man was about as warm and fuzzy as a machine gun. I felt like giving him a *'sieg heil'* when we left."

President Burligame was returning immediately. He was scheduled to address the nation tonight from the Oval Office.

It was still before noon and snowing hard. They were all jittery. Occasionally Jerzy's big hand swept across the windshield wiping away condensation. They were driving northwest into the Appalachians. Traffic diminished as the weather worsened. The black Navigator sizzled along the winding road, and as they slid around a bend, five hundred yards ahead at an intersection was a police roadblock. In the westbound lane a state patrol cruiser idled, the light bar flashing eerily in the storm, the trooper in his serious foul weather gear and Smokey hat holding up a gloved hand signaling the Navigator to stop.

"Here we go," Victor muttered.

Jerzy shouted, "What should I do? What should I do?"

It was Foulks who took charge. "Pull over, Jerz," he said. "Take it easy, big guy."

No accident was visible. No apparent reason for the trooper to be stopping people. They were halfway across the state. Even if someone had blundered onto the Cessna – shoved under a thicket of trees at the end of a deserted airstrip, banner and all – it was still a long shot that a cop twelve miles north of nowhere in a blizzard would be checking cars for an escaped terrorist and a kidnapped Congressman.

Victor grabbed the comic book that Jerzy had found in the

trunk, yanked his Snoopy hat sideways and let his face go slack. His heart double-knocked in his chest. In spite of the disguise he was preparing an elaborate tale for the trooper as he crammed a pair of dollar store red sunglasses on his face, sweating and pushing back against the once plush seat of the Lincoln, reminding himself there was no way in hell anybody could identify Foulks. He was thinking he'd chaired a thousand meetings with dignitaries – judges, presidents, governors and other elected criminals. Why in blazes should he be nervous now – when he heard Foulks' soft voice ask, "What's up, Officer?"

The trooper loomed big as a tree over the front passenger door. He took a moment to peer into the faces of all three men. Victor held his breath and drooled at the comic book. "Power line down half a mile ahead, sir," he told Foulks loudly, in the broken language bad weather brings with it. "You'll have to take the Richfield Road. Snowplow's already up there sanding." He flicked another glance back at Victor, cocked his big head slightly, and looked back at Edwin. His voice dropped half an octave. "Where you folks headed?"

"Hey," Jerzy Zander suddenly belched. "We don't have to take no Richfield Road. It's a free country, Officer!" Victor slid further down the back seat, cursing the old farmer. Foulks reached out a hand and touched Jerzy's forearm, then switched off the ignition key. He turned back to the state trooper.

The cop leaned in close and glared at Jerzy. "You can pull over here if you want," he said testily. "Power crew's coming tomorrow morning if the storm lets up." He glanced at Edwin, apparently the man in charge. Wordless communication passed between them, a furrowed brow, a twist of the mouth. The trooper reached out for the door handle. Edwin climbed out, but left the door open. Snow billowed in.

The trooper was a good six foot six, and Edwin had to stand back to squint up at him in the wind. They exchanged quiet words for a moment, perhaps an apology for the storm-stressed driver of the Lincoln.

Inside, Victor looked at the comic book, every ounce of his body focused on the trooper and Foulks and what they were saying. For half a second he contemplated shoving Jerzy aside and racing off in the Navigator. Surreptitiously glancing out the window, he observed Foulks studying the trooper's nametag, then taking a deep breath.

"Trooper Nesbitt?" His voice had an oddly burnished quality to it, authoritative considering the situation. Victor strained to listen. "We've been hearing about that guy with the airplane over in Philadelphia. You heard?"

"Yeah?"

Their eyes locked together. Trooper Nesbitt pulled back an inch, but his eyes stayed with Edwin's. He crossed his arms. His breath steamed through his nostrils.

"What if those people tried to get through this way?" It was a simple question. Maybe Nesbitt had been asked it twenty times this morning. Deliberation lined his face. It seemed as if he wanted to move his head aside, maybe to glance back into the car at the oddball in the back with the funny glasses. But his eyes lingered on Foulks. He grimaced. At the same time something that might have resembled a flicker of a smile came to his cold lips.

"FBI's got the country blanketed," Trooper Nesbitt said, his face conflicted, grinning with tight jaws. "Highways, train yards. Besides every airport and bus station from here to Montreal. They know the guy's got that Congressman, unless they ditched in the Schuylkill River, in which case they're both dead." He blanched, wiped a gloved hand across his cheek, and studied the glove. "You can't stop here, sir. This is a dangerous road. You and your friends better get –"

Foulks held up an index finger. The big trooper's eyes snapped to the finger, then back to Edwin's face. "You got to figure the FBI went to the Congressman's home, huh?"

"Yeah, you bet. I mean, I'm not privy to the details of the investigation, but they're covering the whole nine yards. Across the country and back overnight. Left people at his house, his offices. Checked out every D. Crockett in North America!" Now he did glance into the Navigator. Victor was staring directly at him. Instantly Victor crossed his eyes and stuck his tongue out. Then Nesbitt was back looking guardedly at Foulks.

"I suggest you get in your car, and drive carefully up the Richfield Road before I cite you for failure to comply."

Edwin's breath swirled into Trooper Nesbitt's face.

"Who's running the FBI investigation?"

Victor was certain the trooper was about to arrest them all.

"No idea. They just send us briefs."

"Who signs the briefs?"

"Dunno." He looked into the teeth of the storm. "I have to picture the orders posted at the barracks. Oh yeah. Name's Davis. Some upper crust guy in the Bureau. High priority." Eyes moving again to Foulks, unblinking. Already too much citizen input. He growled, "Now get off this road before I lose my patience."

35

Approaching the smear above LAX, Iona Webster called her office from the redeye as it descended. She retrieved a single message on her cell, the fax delivered from Senator Hal Riske. Although it was the crack of dawn, she did not hesitate to press in Molly Bee's private number up in San Fran.

"Here's the story," she told Molly's answering machine. "Case closed. Since she was a federal prosecutor from another state, the Bureau did a quote 'detailed analysis' of the crime scene. No foul play. No passengers. The car ran off the road, hit a boulder. Broke her neck. Nobody else in the car. ME says injuries consistent with sudden violent jarring just like the scene suggests. Everybody interviewed, the hotel, her office, the car rental, the mother, the whole nine yards. Plenty of cash and credit cards on hand. But no laptop." She paused. Fine. No need to editorialize.

After a lifetime in law enforcement, Fred Geschwantner still fumbled out of bed at six and got himself calibrated for the day, although he'd been retired a couple of years. He was back from his morning walk when the phone rang. In his slow-motion low-register voice, the voice of Smokey the Bear, he commiserated with Nel's fear concerning her husband, and told her he had been expecting her call.

"What?" Nel said, through the cheap rust-colored cell phone. "But how did you –"

"Well, add it up, ma'am. Your good Congressman's unaccounted for. You've taken up the cause of Viola Ferrari's death. I would imagine you've seen the FBI report."

"No, I —"

"And Mr. Bert O'Donnell mentioned you might get hold of me. What can I do for you, ma'am?"

"You can call me Nel, for starters. Yes, Mr. O'Donnell. So I suppose that is the question. What can you do for me?"

After inquiring about the state of her phone, Fred explained in his laconic, country boy fashion. He was in a position to access information without a) being fired; or b) influencing an investigation or a jury. In fact he was conversant with the Ferrari matter and believed facts might be forthcoming that he himself was not sufficiently connected to act on, but perhaps Nel was.

"What are you saying, Mr. Geschwantner?"

"I'm saying this. Before this horrible kidnapping of your husband by this rebellion dot com fella, out here in Utah most folks already knew this government was in trouble. And we're a conservative lot! When Ms. Ferrari was killed, right in that particular area, and then the feds clammed up on the investigation, well, ma'am, it seemed like in my mind I wanted to connect the two things."

"Viola's death and —"

"And the way the government handled it."

The former state detective fiddled around and said some strange things ever so obtusely — the scene of the accident, the impounded vehicle, Viola's occupation — until Nel finally got his drift.

"Are you suggesting I come to Utah to see for myself? I don't believe I can."

"And I doubt," Fred said, "whether you have the stamina for it, frankly. Or the presence of mind to do a rather delicate inquiry, considering your personal circumstances."

She was thinking, like hell I don't have the stamina for it!

"Yes, I don't know either. But I still don't follow your —"

"The situation may unearth other serious crimes, ma'am. But I cannot check into this as a former investigator for CJD. The state Criminal Justice Division."

Her face squinched up and her mind swirled. "May I get back to you?"

The departure took place quickly. Mgaba had arranged the Airporter to meet them at the hotel. When the hotel phone rang Nel assumed it was the Airporter driver. But no. Raven Menez was wishing to speak with her.

"Look," Nel snapped, "I've been through hell the past twenty-four hours, and I have nothing left. I'm sorry to be ugly with you." She automatically fell into a defensive posture with media people. During their brief meeting at Ney Field she'd been too distracted to hear about Raven's personal crisis. "If you'll leave your name with Mr. Mgaba –"

"Late last night I had a long conversation with Molly Bee," Raven interrupted, speaking quickly. "She wishes to expresses her sincere concern to you. She's been in contact with Iona Webster. Evidently Ms. Webster was here in Philadelphia at a meeting –"

"Meet me downstairs in two minutes," Nel said.

In fact it was four minutes later when the two women met again near the Airporter bus. Raven was in a state of liberation and confusion at once. She had quit her job last night in a sputtering battle with the *US Times* news editor, in spite of her witnessing part of the most incredible news event in a generation. She watched her roommate drive off in her car, and was shouldering a black backpack when Nel bounded out of the hotel, nodded at her, and kept moving toward the bus.

"Get in!"

Raven did as she was told. The others clamored after, all heavy coats and shoulder bags and cranky from lack of sleep.

Mgaba settled in behind the two women, who sat opposite each other as the mostly empty bus pulled away.

"Hello. How are you doing?" he said brightly. Turning to look at him, she smiled. She still wore the tight-fitting Value Village coat and her last pair of jeans and running shoes. She'd washed her shoulder-length black hair, and she'd located her bright turquoise earrings. "I'm tired, and hungry," she said. "And unemployed and broke. How are you, Sloan?"

He chuckled. "Better than that," he told her.

"You said you spoke to Molly Bee," Nel said.

"Oh, yes. I studied with her for a full year. Online."

"You never met?"

"Not face to face."

They watched what looked like orange and purple grease stains slithering up the sky to the east: the airborne organisms spawned from seventy-five years of hauling New York and North Jersey sewage out to international waters, until the putrid mass took on a life of its own and began to strangle the Eastern Atlantic. At sunrise the gasses projected what scientists called "Smog borealis." To the west, cold and gray. Maybe snow.

"I believe Molly wants to speak to you. Off the record."

Nel said, "Okay. Where are you off to?"

"I took my mom's credit card." She showed Nel her wide dark eyes and embarrassed smile. "I'm broke but I need to get to California. There's one of those no-frills cargo flights that goes to a Navy base in San Diego. Then I hitchhike to San Francisco and present my portfolio to the managing editor of the *West Coast Paper*. Maybe I'll get lucky."

Nel Sligo stared at her. Was she crazy? Just dump her life and leave? Raven Menez was a compelling and articulate young woman. Obviously Mgaba was smitten with her. And she was smart and progressive in her thinking. Last night Nel had felt a jolt of kinship with her after spontaneously kicking the chief of police in the chest.

"Where is this portfolio of yours?"

The younger woman grinned and pushed the back pack at her feet. "Well, actually, I –"

"Fill me in later. You're coming out to Washington with us. We need a staff media assistant. Can you –"

"Assist? Hell, yeah. I mean, sure!"

From behind them came Courtman's starched monotone. "May I remind you, hiring decisions require my approval."

"Oh, yes," Ms. Sligo said. "You have Mr. Courtman's approval." Raven felt Mgaba's big hand on her shoulder. Nel noticed.

At that instant she made up her mind.

36

"Mr. Mgaba." She turned to face him. "You and Courtman are going to escort Ms. Menez to Washington. I've got to get to Salt Lake City. I want you to get me on the next flight, and also book a flight for Lichtenstein to Chicago, overnight stop and on to Seattle.

Are you with me?" She hardly paused to breathe. "Raven." Twisting back to the young woman. "Do you have a laptop?"

"I do," Raven said.

"Get online and get hold of Molly Bee. Probably safer than her phone even if ours are good. You can reach her by your usual channel. Do you have that? Fine. See if she can talk to me on a safe line right now. BJ? Courtman, wake him up, will you?" BJ had fallen asleep with the phone to his ear and his open notebook in his lap.

"I think he's comatose," Courtman said.

"All right. He's got to see Concetta Ferrari. She is the key to this." She stopped. "Well, no. She isn't going to find Victor, I don't suppose." Nel was wired, sputtering on four hours sleep and a pot of serious coffee. "This Jerome Tse character. O'Donnell tells us he was Viola Ferrari's boss at the US Attorney's Office in Chicago. I'm willing to bet he's the man who came to see her mother. He's got some questions to answer."

"Tse," came BJ's shattered voice. He squinted with bleary resignation out the window. The busy morning traffic crashed past. "Where we going?"

"Raven, you're also going to take charge of these new phones. BJ. Where are they? I need one."

"In your pocket," Mgaba told her.

"Thank you ever so much," she said. Flipping it open, she redialed Fred Geschwantner's number. In three minutes she was booked on a flight to Salt Lake City where the retired investigator would meet her. What Fred explained was, "I can't release anything incriminating. I am retired and out of the loop, but I do know the law. And I want you to bring a very small flashlight and a very small camera, just in case." At this point Nel was flying too high to ask just in case what.

"Okay, Ms. Sligo. Here's Molly," Raven Menez told her, and handed the laptop across the aisle.

"Hello!" typed the screen. "May I express my heartfelt sympathy to you."

So it would be a discreet conversation.

"Thanks," Nel wrote. "I'm heading for Salt Lake City to check into matters I understand you and a friend spoke of just this morning. I suppose to divert my mind from the nightmare here."

"Interesting coincidence," Molly wrote. "The official report just arrived. It's been whitewashed. And I learned last night of a connection to –" A long pause here. Nel waited. "What the hell. I'm told by an unimpeachable source that the phone company might have a hand in what was taking place in Utah last fall. Sounds like playing mind games. I don't understand it, but it's probably true."

Nel was confused. She thought Molly was referring to Communication International, a thousand miles from illegal mind control research. What did she mean? Nel gazed out the window. They were on a freeway heading west past what looked like an enormous Navy base. The phone company was simple code for CI. Bigger than the government, operated by invisible billionaires in foreign countries, some you could not find on maps. Playing mind games. How could she not realize this? Now she was being told the FBI investigation was "whitewashed". Viola's death was part of a violent conspiracy to shut people up.

But about what?

She heard O'Donnell's warning. *The wrong time to investigate. No doors will be open.*

"Are you there?"

"I'm here." At this moment she felt a deep connection to a woman she had never met. There was no question of not confiding in her now. "I'm sending a man to visit relatives of our attorney friend. I wonder if you can break away and meet me –" Even after fourteen years in Congress, Nel was unable to proceed without true paranoia suddenly enveloping her. In mid-sentence, she opened the rust-colored phone and had Raven Menez press in the number she used to speak to Molly Bee.

"Yes," said the soft voice.

"It's Nel Sligo. How's the phone line?"

"Oh. Oh, well hi. It's good. I think."

"This is all so weird! It seems like we both have different people we're talking to. Maybe we have good information between us. Is it possible –"

"I can change some things. Where and when?"

They worked out the details. Nel would have to warn Geschwantner that the investigation was getting crowded, but no other option came to mind at this moment. Then Molly told her, "One thing. There's somebody in this named Jaap Tenkley. Do you know the name?"

"Tenkley! I just got the name last night. From a solid source. And the relative I spoke to, she kept going on about a man named Ten. That's got to be him. What do you have on him?"

"Nothing. He's in it. That's all."

"My staff's checking into it." She wrote down a note, then nudged Courtman and held up a finger toward BJ. "I was told to bring a small flashlight and a small camera."

"Okay. The other thing I have is this. The files have been sealed by executive privilege. In your position, can you –"

"No," Nel finished her thought. "No. I have heard this. I hoped you might know who would be at the bottom of it."

"It's impossible to find out," Molly said.

Before the bus was off the interstate she had gotten back to Fred Geschwantner, to run past him the idea of another body on this research project. The man sounded so accepting, so easy going, she hardly doubted it would be a problem. In fact, all Fred had to say was, "Nothing haunts a detective so much as an unsolved crime."

BJ had passed out again. Not at all sure of herself, Nel elaborated BJ's assignment to Courtman, who kept scratching his neck and looking at Menez with what might have been contempt or a sort of groggy lust, Nel couldn't tell.

"You understand, Purvis? He is to find out what was going on that made Viola Ferrari go to Utah! Her mother's in a nursing home in Oak Park, somewhere near Chicago."

Everybody was covered. Mgaba's job was to keep an eye on Menez. Courtman's job was to keep an eye on Mgaba.

37

Congressman Victor Sligo hadn't been snowboarding for years, but now he was, in the wet Appalachian snow, soaring over trees, not certain how this had come about, flying past a black skull and crossbones, and he gaped down into the bubbling filth where Billy Hellman operated a lemonade stand, and he rolled over moaning and sweating and then he was awake on the floor of the Lincoln Navigator, sweat snicking off his face.

Jerzy Zander pulled the car into the snowy driveway of a nondescript rambler on a nondescript street somewhere. No cars moved. Jerzy nodded to Edwin Foulks in the front seat.

"Maybe you can go ahead and see what's up," Foulks said. Jerzy got out, stretched his great bulk, and limped up the sidewalk, negotiated the unshoveled steps, and rang the buzzer. The door flew open. Jerzy looked up and down the street, and beckoned them in with a flick of his hand.

The dim living room looked like a bomb had just gone off. Dog-eared magazines and masses of newspapers occupied every surface. A pair of dilapidated church organs took up most of the back wall, one with a battered bench with the top missing, and sheet music and mouse droppings scattered inside. Lumpy overstuffed chairs with springs pushing through the bottom held magazines, busted toasters, computers, printers and disgraced kitchen implements. The place smelled like bad people had been doing raunchy things to animals.

"Hey! In here," Jerzy called from the kitchen.

Dr. Horst Spangloss stood filling a kettle at the sink. He was surrounded by a devastation of dishes, plates and unidentifiable flotsam, half-empty shelves containing ripped-open cracker boxes and dented cans of stew and cat food. He turned and smiled to them, a medium height, balding gentleman wearing a dirty white shirt and food-speckled tie and sweater under a baggy tweed jacket. He was gangly, a sort of simian swing to his appendages and a looseness to his jaw. Jerzy introduced them.

"Well, proud to meet you, Congressman!" he burst out, offering a hand. Victor held out a fist, and Spangloss knocked it with his. "You fellows have really got yourselves in a pickle, eh? The government's always got a bug in its heinie, and this week you're it! Tea?" Without waiting he spun around and put the kettle on the gas stove. "Bet you're starvin'! Some bread around somewhere, maybe some jam –"

"No, really, don't put yourself out, Doctor," Victor trying not to contemplate the contents of Spangloss's moldy larder.

"Horst. I'm not a medical doctor, so don't ask about that thing that keeps swellin' up under your other thing." Smiling innocently. "Seen the papers?"

"Just the *Times.*"

"Oh, yeah." He shook his head miserably. *"That West Coast Paper's* due any time. You know the television shut down last night with all this activity over there in Philly. Of course you're the ones who did it."

Foulks finally spoke. "Reason we're here, Dr. Spangloss –"

"Need a ride west, is that it?" He looked to be between fifty and eighty, with wire glasses that made him look older, but he spoke in a vibrant voice with missing word endings that sounded like down-east Maine. Pressing thin lips together and looking at Victor, "Miss your wife, I can tell. How about you, sir? You married?"

Edwin shrugged, trying to follow the strange man's mental mapping. "I don't recall getting married. Yes, we're heading west. Like pioneers of old."

Spangloss studied him, peering over the wire glasses. "You a Mormon?"

"Presently between religions," Foulks said. "You?"

"I am of the Church of Jesus Christ of Latter Day Saints. Once removed." He found this terribly humorous, and chuckled while he poured boiling water into a sorry teapot, then nudged his bony chin toward a photo of a glum young woman in a bulky sweater. "After that one, no woman would ever have me, once they got a close look." He turned and stood bolt upright for them to judge, thin graying hair uncombed, the nose like a chipped spool of thread. "Their loss. Now Congressman," wrapping the teapot in a dishrag and swishing it as he spoke, "The feds can't decide what to do. At this point they don't think you were kidnapped. Oh, no. They're after you for treason, fomentin' civil disturbance, lemme think, failure to comply with federal agents, abettin' a criminal act, national security violations…" Blinking at Foulks, "How'd you do that? That laser eyeball scan? I laughed myself sick when I heard that. Embarrassed the unspeakable out of Dr. Hunter Tyne! That might be your million right there, mister." He babbled on in his gangly fashion, reveling in details intimate to their journey the past eighteen hours. Victor's fatigue was already replaced with a sort of sick curiosity, standing in this foul little kitchen with no place to sit, listening to this odd man casually relating events nobody knew any-thing about, knowledge that would probably put him in prison if the feds came busting in.

"You people have started somethin' long overdue. Hope to

God some good comes of it. Could do. The Web's already soaked with one idea. '*Rebellion.com* Day!' The day the revolution started." He slapped the counter top, sending a decayed potato chip flying, then swished the pot again and poured tea in mugs. "By tomorrow we'll be in the 'post-rebellion era.' They're going to erect a statue for you, Congressman!"

"Yeah. In Folsom Prison!" Victor smirked, but Spangloss slapped him on the back in spontaneous approval, then pulled away and smelled his hand.

"We have food packed in Jerzy's car," Foulks hinted.

"Yes, no thanks, I just ate. Say, did Sister Elizabeth tell you about me?"

He rolled on while Jerzy hauled their gear from the Lincoln to a weathered car of indiscernible model and vintage parked by a collapsed fence at the back of the property. Shortly the big farmer departed, giving each a crushing embrace, choking out that he would remember them long after the cows came home. Spangloss chattered in his preacher's voice while he sprayed pure hydrogen in the air cleaner to get the car started and they rumbled west out of town.

He told them he'd been moving refugees all his life. Like his father before him. Reaching into the glove box, he said, "My dad did it with Jews in France. You people smoke marijuana?"

They lurched on through the diminishing storm toward Pittsburgh, then down into West Virginia to avoid police curiosity.

"What we're doin'," Spangloss said, "is going on down to Beckley. Ever been there?"

"Never been out of the state of Washington before a few days ago," Edwin Foulks said. Victor looked up. The seating arrangement was the same as in the Navigator, to discourage snooping strangers at gas stations.

"You've never been out of Washington?"

"Got everything I need." Foulks assessed a stump-crowded hillside covered with snow and a puny stand of hickory and ash. "Why Beckley?"

"The prettiest girls in America come from Beckley, West Virginia."

"Who said that?"

"Me. Didn't you recognize my voice?"

38

The roads grew narrower. He had chosen a circuitous route along lesser rivers. Before dark and after chicken salad sandwiches and homemade chocolate the Zanders had contributed, they entered Beckley, a city recently enriched by the design and manufacture of military weapons that wound up on battlefields in distant lands, protecting American interests.

Near Eisenhower Drive where it turns into Robert Byrd Drive, the city had developed several hundred acres into an industrial park, satisfying conditions to bring the US Army to the rescue of southern West Virginia's economy. Thanks to earmarks that had actually passed through Representative Sligo's committee, the Army had built a munitions plant here. A big one.

Not five hundred yards from the sprawling weapons factory, unobtrusively doing business with the military, was an Aztek air freight outlet. Spangloss explained with his busy voice and quick logic. A shift change took place at five o'clock. At that moment all kinds of electronic checking, vehicle monitoring, iris scanning, and intimate personnel sniffing took place. Then immediately after, the MP shift rotated, and the new group came on duty. That was the time to move.

"Old friends of the underground railway," Spangloss said, chin pointing toward the building.

Travel-buzzed Victor didn't like it.

"When did you last contact these people?"

"Couple years. Three. Look. I'm gonna mosey over. Sit tight."

It was 4:30. He found a smashed gray fedora, snugged it down on his square head, and walked hunched and muttering to himself into the Aztek office. They could see what looked like an anchorwoman jabbering on the evening news on a 56-inch TV screen inside the glass front of the building. Victor murmured, "What the hell can Aztek do? Shove us in the back of one of their cargo planes? We'll wind up in Saudi Arabia with some general's golf clubs!"

The minutes ticked past. The snow had stopped, but the temperature was dropping fast in the car. Lights powered up in the huge base parking lot. They felt like sitting ducks. Finally Spangloss moseyed back. He let out a nasal sigh.

"Oh, fine!" he sputtered. "Just terrific!" Looking like he'd just seen his mother shoplifting. Shaking his head miserably. "I can't believe this!"

"What?" Victor grabbed the shoulder of his tweed coat. "What, Spangloss?" Foulks was fearing capture. His guard had been down all day. Things had progressed all right, but now his stomach felt weird. He thought he smelled... Leavenworth.

"What nothing. It's perfect. There's a parcel plane leavin'" for points west at seven of the clock." He smiled, and they saw for the first time his greenish teeth.

"But there's a bit of a catch." He was speaking to Edwin.

"There always is," Victor hissed.

"My friend wants to meet you."

Instinctive rage flooded Victor's mind. He shoved the old man against the car door, both hands on his chest. The fedora went askew.

"You've done this your whole life? You fucking fool, you told somebody I'm out here?"

Spangloss clenched his awful teeth. "Not you. Him!"

"Jesus Christ!"

"*No! Him!* Davy Crockett!" He grabbed Victor's wrists and yanked them away and glared at him. Then to Foulks, "Says the country's finished if you don't pull off this rebellion! But right now these MPs are supposed to –"

"This is no rebellion!" Victor shot back. He looked like he was going to slug him.

"Oh yes it is! The feces has finally struck the oscillator, Congressman! But we can't wait here. We have to –" He stopped, gawking at the big screen in the office. They all turned. They were looking at a heaving throng of people taking over an entire city.

Victor immediately hunched down in his coat, pulled the hat bill over his eyes, and hurried toward the front of the building.

"No, wait!" Spangloss pleaded. "Dammit, man, the MPs are on their way!"

Victor entered the office. Playing on the big screen was what might have been midnight on New Year's Eve at Times Square, although it was mid-January. A million swarming people had gathered in a spontaneous, freezing riot in midtown Manhattan, bearing signs and coonskin caps. The woman at the counter was mesmerized by the screen, and failed to notice Victor.

A reporter was shouting, "...incredible outpouring of support for the man in the *Rebellion.com* airplane, the mysterious Davy Crockett figure nobody can find and in fact nobody can find any record of! Among the strange aspects of this increasingly bizarre event, Jamie, is that people seem to have forgotten a United States Congressman has been kidnapped! Indeed, speculation is mounting on the street here in New York that Representative Victor Sligo may have participated in his own –"

"Just a minute, Slobodan, apparently the National Guard –"

"Yes, I'm sorry, yes, Jamie, we have made contact with a... a Major General Yasuto Morinaka, I apologize if I'm pronouncing the name incorrectly, commander of the New England National Guard."

"You are to disperse immediately!" a commanding voice bellowed across midtown Manhattan and thundered into I-Media's national broadcast. It sounded as though Morinaka was addressing an army gathered on a hillside at Gettysburg. "You are creating mass terror! You are causing traffic problems that are a hazard to the city! Emergency vehicles are unable to get through! You have no permit to assemble in these numbers!"

Frenzied New Yorkers booed the voice. Obscenities poured from the crowd. Spangloss and Victor stood stunned, watching a million angry souls venting their frustration and disgust at their own government.

"God almighty," Victor whispered.

The woman at the counter looked up with a concerned twist in her small face.

"Oh, no!" she blurted out. Her eyes snapped out the window toward the Army base. "You can't be here! Get out!"

For half a second Victor's mind stuttered. He turned to see a fat sand-colored Jeep rumble through the gate of the Army base. Half a dozen MPs rode inside. Spangloss grabbed his arm and shoved him toward the door.

"Move! Move!" he shouted. "We can make it." Victor was already running full tilt toward Spangloss's rumbling car. The back door flew open. Edwin, at the wheel, was yelling something. Diving into the back seat, Victor hauled his long legs in as Edwin slammed the car into gear. Spangloss was still coming, gasping horribly. The car was already moving as Victor yanked the old man in with him. They roared off, the door still hanging open, fish-tailing out of the parking lot.

Everybody jabbered at once. Behind them, the jeep jolted to a stop at the Aztek building. Military cops poured out all the doors, pointing anxiously at the vehicle speeding away. Two of the armed MP's in their fatigues and white helmets dashed into the Aztek office just as the car slid around the corner, nearly out of control. Edwin banged his head against the window, and thundered down the main drag, spotted another crowded parking lot and wheeled in. Without so much as looking around, the three men abandoned the car and raced into a side entrance of an enormous warehouse-like building. Immediately they realized where they were: in the middle of the appliance section of the famous Beckley Kwalmart. The largest retail store in America. People were everywhere. The daily big sale was still on.

Victor stood with one hand covering his eyes, looking down at the shiny linoleum. His mind would not focus. He turned to Spangloss, breathing in raw gasps like an ancient horse.

"Your friend back there. Will she talk?"

"No. No, impossible," the old man whispered. Lines crinkled his brow. "I kept tryin' to tell you. They come every night at five. They'll be gone in a few minutes."

"This is nice," Foulks said, looking around as what seemed like five thousand people milled about the store. Pulling his hat down lower, he smiled through clenched teeth.

It hit him then like an ocean wave. The senior Progressive on the House Ways and Means Committee, fourteen years in Congress, was on the lam, wearing his red hunting cap and red kiddie sunglasses and a pea coat, staggering between the refrigerators and the dishwashers at a West Virginia Kwalmart. It almost made him smile.

"Those MPs might show up here," Foulks said, breaking Victor's trance. "They get antsy. Need some action. They saw us peeling out."

"I never knew what Jesse James felt like before," Victor mused. "Running from my own government! If these people recognize me, this thing is over."

Two minutes later, somebody did.

Simultaneously they all had to use the bathroom.

They formed a line at the urinals. A moment later the door swung open, causing all three men to look sideways in the wall mirror at two young men wearing the black and white checkered vests of the Kwalmart crew.

The taller one's eyes went directly to Victor. His head shook vigorously, and he pointed at his friend. "Yo, Rafael, holy smoke, it's Victor Sligo! Whoa! Hey, Congressman," he shouted. "How you doin'?" Smiling broadly, as if chance meetings with political fugitives happened every day in the bathroom.

Victor froze, looked down, waited half a beat, and said in an indeterminate accent, "No me! Wrong man!" and began zipping up before he was finished, wetting his hand and then his pants, while the other one, Rafael, said in his own thick accent, "No wrong man. Ju runnin' a rebolution, meester!" and pointing toward Foulks, "Ees Daybee Crockett, no?" And the first boy blurted, "Wow, my poli sci prof's gonna shit a Dick Cheney three-dollar bill when she hears this!" Rafael, a small dark youngster of twenty or so, pulled back and leaned heavily against the door. "Don't want no peoples see ju over there. They riot, man!"

"You're in my Kwalmart!" the student ejaculated. "I can't believe it! Congressman Victor Sligo, single-handedly saving the country, using my own private bathroom!" In a brutally symbolic move he ripped a paper towel from the dispenser. "Can I have your autograph? You too, Davy!"

Victor thought fast. Foulks was standing by the sink, arms crossed, wondering how Victor was going to handle this explosion back to reality. Still at the urinal, Spangloss looked gloomily down.

"All right, all right, fellows, yeah, let's keep that door shut." Victor worked up his good-guy-taking-charge persona. To the taller kid, "You, sir, would you mind just going outside, maybe find a way to close off the rest room for a couple of minutes. Obviously you understand our situation." But the boy just stared, slack-jawed, holding out the brown paper towel, then turned and shoved the Hispanic boy aside and raced out the door. Victor lunged at him but the kid was too quick.

"Get that guy back in here!" he demanded. Rafael turned obediently and rushed out, calling after him. Seconds later he returned.

"*Perdida,* Congress!" He smiled shyly. "No find. What, eh..." He made a strange face, the mouth stretched, his eyes closed down to slits. Then he opened his hands and said, "What?"

Foulks said, "Is there a back way out of here? Down that hallway maybe," pointing through the door the opposite direction from the way they'd come in.

"No. No."

"Diversion?" Spangloss finally spoke up.

"*No se,*" he said, squinting to understand. "*Muchas gentes aqui.* Kwalmart choppers!" he said proudly, like a trumpeting I-Media commercial.

Edwin said, "Pull your hat down, make yourself small, and get out the way we came in."

Victor pondered a moment. "It's all we have, gentlemen."

Rafael held up a clenched fist. "*¡Muy bien, Señor!*" he said intently. "*Vamonos.*"

They hunched down into their heavy coats and followed Rafael out, turning down the short hallway back into the appliance area. Immediately they heard a wild singing roar. Two hundred people and more coming, in a jammed semi-circle, clear out to the far aisles, cheering and screaming Victor's name, applauding with hands over their heads, shouting out Progressive slogans and jokes about Burligame and baseball. On the wall were half a dozen big Holotechs, all broadcasting the same unruly circus at Times Square. There was only one possible response. Victor removed his hat and looked squarely at the crowd. They roared and surged forward, and a large person in a tweed jacket yelled, "Okay, Congressman, you got our attention! So how do we get rid of that little pissant running the country?"

Clichés trickled like tickertape through his brain. He'd been here a hundred times. They wanted to hear about Hellman's dirty tricks, about the miserable minimum wage, and the "Doormat Congress" Victor himself was part of. But it all crumpled when he felt Foulks elbow him in the ribs and saw him jerk his head toward the side door. Victor knew what he had to say, and he had to say it quickly.

"The only way you can change things," he yelled to the back of the crowd, "is to vote! If you don't vote, it will just get worse!"

Grabbing his elbow, Foulks nudged him forward, then realized too late this was the wrong move.

"Davy Crockett!" somebody shrieked. "It's him!"

"No," he and Victor yelled at once. "No, it's –"

And from somewhere a voice cried, "Holy smoke, it's DB Cooper! Hey, DB! What'd you do with all the money!"

DB Cooper! DB Cooper! You could see a strange new thought fold over the crowd. Victor and Foulks exchanged a look. Yeah. That could work.

"Vote!" Victor roared again. And with a vicious reflex, "Damn you people! Get down there and vote!" He jammed the cap down on his head, located a side door, and started to run. The others were with him in an instant. Pushing through, led by little Rafael shoving and spewing orders in Spanglais, surrounded by calls and chants and sounds of support. Cameras flashed and children screamed. By the time they reached the door, the man in the tweed jacket was leading a new chant. "Down with Hellman!" he shouted, pumping a fist in the air. "Recall vote! Recall the President! Recall the Vice President! We want a recall vote!" And then they were all chanting as one, a thousand voices all across West Virginia, venting their frustration and anger as the three men finally burst outside, the crowd pushing and shoving among the airborne pathogen detectors and the home angioplasty kits, "Recall! Recall! Recall!"

39

Remembering everything a political consultant was required to remember never came easy for BJ Lichtenstein. He'd carried notebooks since high school, elaborate leather journals and drug store notebooks with cheap pink covers, and even a tiny unlined notepad his grandfather had left behind, bearing the label:

Arnold Lichtenstein
Fine Clothing
Indianapolis, Ind.

He pored through hastily scribbled orders from Courtman, notes from Nel's phone call to Concetta Ferrari, and half a dozen contacts in the Windy City. When he could get his bearings at O'Hare he found the car rental, grabbed the last one on the lot, and told the GPS to locate Oak Park Elder Care Facility. The map showed him where he was, and he decided to go downtown first, park illegally, and see what he could learn at the Northern District of Illinois US Attorney's Office.

Which nearly broke his spirit, that parking part. Old snow lined the sidewalks. It felt like about five above zero. A winter-splattered black sports car lurched along ahead of him. Suddenly it stopped in front of an empty space, but a yellow fire plug stood right at the curb. Even BJ knew the fine would be five hundred bucks. The driver did not hesitate. He zipped into the space, jumped out, a short, well-to-do gent, opened the trunk, picked up the yellow hydrant, tossed it in the trunk, and walked away without so much as a glance back.

Smooth move, BJ thought. Welcome to Chicago.

A reckless plan had floated through the edges of his mind on the flight. At last he was in the Courthouse. Today he wore the gray pinstriped suit and full length Loden coat he'd been assured made him look taller, and snappy dress shoes with a one-inch lift. He located the stairway, then took a big quiet elevator, a short hall-way, and entered a formal rotunda featuring a semi-circular official greeter's kiosk, which he approached feigning chest pains, and said to the kindly very dark-skinned woman, "Jerome Tse, please." Turning her head to the side as if looking for assistance and still watching the visitor with the grimace on his face, she said, "Mr. Tse is… is not… is… let me check my…"

"I'm his brother," moaned BJ Lichtenstein. With a loud breath, he pulled his phone out of his pocket and flicked on the camera, while pretending to reach for his identification.

"Oh. I see." Her voice was like sweet honey, but her de-meanor was closer to confused turnip.

And then she did exactly what he'd hoped she would do. She poked some keys on her computer, gazed uncertainly at the screen, and said, "May I have your name, sir?"

The rest BJ would tell the staff with phony nonchalance while he planned his future in the movies. What he desperately hoped, knowing that Tse hadn't been seen for weeks, and having not the foggiest idea how to locate him, was that the receptionist would pull up a list of emergency contacts or family members. Of course he couldn't guess what would appear, but the kindly lady could not guess that Jerome Tse's brother would suddenly clutch his chest, emit a ghastly shudder, and collapse. She gasped, grabbed a phone and spoke into it, then jumped up and ran through a door behind her. BJ also jumped up, zipped around to the computer, photographed the screen, and raced out the door and down the stairs. In the alley across and down the block between skyscrapers, he checked his work. Yes! He could not only read it, but there was the two-person contact list. In minutes he was back in the car, tucking the parking ticket into the jockey box, and heading for Oak Park, where Ernest Hemingway no longer lived.

Concetta Ferrari was asleep. Now acquainted with criminal behavior, BJ told the unit nurse the Housing Authority required that Concetta read over a document relating to her daughter's apartment in Chicago. He gave her plenty of time to freshen up and prepare for company, but did not expect to find a vibrant, disoriented and actually rather handsome old lady, her hair still black, her skin still olive, wearing slacks and a red sweater, vaguely calling Michaela Velasquez to mind.

He introduced himself as a colleague of Congressman Sligo, and reminded her Ms. Sligo had called last night, a call Concetta did not remember, although she did recall there was ice cream for dessert. He asked if she happened to remember the name Jaap Tenkley. Maybe he was her family doctor?

"Doctor is Doctor Amber Egan," she said with a straight face.

"Tenkley," he said slowly, as if he were teaching her to tie her shoes. "Ten."

"My daughter..." She pronounced it "dawda." Her eyes went to the upper left corner of the bright room. She seemed to disappear for a few seconds. He said the name a third time.

"It was long time ago," she said now. "I don't know, how do I know? From the jail."

BJ jerked back from his notes. Of course. A federal prosecutor. Where else would you look? But Concetta had closed off.

Surely she remembered a man named "C"?

"Oh, yes. He cried."

"Why?"

"He cried for my dawda, what's your name, you're a nice looking boy. You Catholic boy?"

"No, Concetta, I'm Jewish."

"Oh. Chewish?"

"Did you get the feeling your daughter worked for C?"

"Yes, no."

"Why was he crying?"

Concetta looked at Viola's studio picture on the dresser. She slumped into herself. She crossed her arms over her thin chest and stared at the floor, a Mona Lisa riddle playing at the corners of her mouth, and that was the end of the conversation.

Both contacts listed phone numbers different from the one O'Donnell had given Nel that nobody had ever answered. The first number did have voicemail that revealed nothing, but BJ left his prepaid cell number just in case. The other was a judge in Sawyer, Michigan.

So now a major dilemma. Tell the truth? Bullshit the judge? Just show up, maybe a two-hour drive for nothing? In the political profession telling the truth is never a realistic option, particularly to a judge. But strangely, Concetta Ferrari had softened him. She had touched a place in BJ that he did not know was there, and did not actually feel until he was back in his rented electric car. He cleared his throat, phoned Judge Michael Ward – and got lucky.

In mid-afternoon, he pulled into a wintery farmhouse. He'd told the truth. Persuaded His Honor, with great reluctance, to let him speak with his houseguest Jerome Tse, whom BJ's employer, Congressman Victor Sligo's wife, sincerely wished to visit concerning Viola Ferrari. He approached the newer frame home, half snowed-in, surrounded by out buildings and a big new garage.

Jerome Tse was not a bit Asian, as BJ had assumed. In fact he had Caucasian features and his accent was solid Chicago. He was well put together, about sixty, but stooped, melancholy, not entirely present. His hair was disheveled, and he wore a shabby Van Dyke beard and a solemn expression. He was nervous, or depressed, or broken-hearted. Or very sick. It was clear that Tse had serious things on his mind. He seemed pleased that Nel was looking into Viola's death, and after further ambiguities – and tea and biscuits the judge provided before he left for his usual Tuesday handball game and dinner out – BJ inquired about a certain Jaap Tenkley. Assistant US Attorney Jerome Tse fell onto a leather couch, stared in disbelief at BJ, and suddenly began weeping. He staggered out of the room, and returned in a few minutes to demand BJ produce his driver's license and Congressman Sligo's office number. Satisfying himself that BJ was genuine, Tse sat again and told him a fascinating story, clearly relieved to tell it. This was the clue BJ failed to catch. It was obviously an epiphany for him, and the beginning, or the end, of something. He sniffled and blew his nose, and spoke in a half-whisper.

"Viola came to me about certain activity people were doing out there in Utah. She wanted to look into it because it was big and connected to prior investigations about, I mean to say, prior investigations she'd been involved in. Touch-screen computers. Electronic ballot markers, computerized voting equipment."

"Voting." BJ's eyebrows crinkled.

"This time it was different. Illegal mind control research." A dry, frightening sound came from deep in Tse's chest. "Mr. Tenkley had been released from Greenville on September twelfth. He came straight to Chicago and had a visit with Viola, which released felons sometimes do, but I did not want to know what it was about. Because –" He stopped again. His cheeks filled up, and he blew out a great breath and said, "A very high level federal official was indicted by the Grand Jury in Tenkley's case, but he was never called and never formally charged."

"So he walked."

"He walked."

BJ practically bit his tongue off not asking Tse to name the official, even as an odd phrase came to his mind: big mucky-mucky.

"But the records are somewhere."

"All data concerning Viola Ferrari has been sealed by executive privilege," Tse said bitterly. "Without a court order – which in this case means going through Billy Hellman – we'll never see those records." His own phrase knocked the wind out of him for a minute. "Tenkley was prosecuted by our office and incarcerated for illegal medical research." His lungs made a ghastly stuttering sound.

BJ waited, then said, "Mind control research? What do they call it? Brain-Computer Interface?"

"That's right."

"Why did Tenkley come to see Ferrari?"

Tse pressed his lips together. "She sent him up. But as soon as he left her office, he disappeared. Failed to report for his first supervised release contact. Unbelievably, out of nowhere, the Senate Judiciary Committee decided to take action about the same activities. They had gotten wind of it somehow, maybe the usual political vengeance, somebody blowing the whistle on somebody, and I was supposed to make the decision to send Viola out there." He stopped and studied the animals half frozen in the pasture. "I panicked. The Judiciary Committee! Even though it wasn't our jurisdiction and no crime had been reported. And we were overloaded as always. They said it was 'Eyes only,' meaning I was to ask no questions and follow the order, because it was Defense related. Classified chemical warfare research going on at Dugway Proving Ground. The order from the committee told me to send a person experienced in legal aspects of mind control research. Viola was the obvious candidate..." He started again, and got hold of himself, and said, "That's why I went down to the House anonymously, that damn mask on my face and my voice altered... after she died. I went to the House, well, I believe it was the Subcommittee on Crime. I just couldn't bring myself to talk to the Judiciary Committee. I was after Communication International. They were the ones in Utah that Tenkley was delivering his research to. It was all in Tenkley's trial four years ago, but those files have been suppressed too! I never dreamed the power CI has with the FBI and with Congress. But what I did realize after my testimony was how completely stupid I was going to Washington to testify. My story was going to go straight to the White House! Who else but me would know anything? They killed Viola! Tenkley fled the country! All the files were wiped out!" The prosecutor's face turned inward, his lips thinned to paper, and he bared his teeth. "I'm next. It's only a matter of time."

"No, wait, Jerome, that's not necessarily –"

"Can it, kid," Tse said. "Okay?"

Involuntarily BJ moved his eyes back to his notes. Finally he asked about Greenville, which turned out to be the federal pen near St. Louis where Tenkley spent three years and eight months staring at the walls.

"Maybe his cellie knows something," Tse said. "Although

they rarely talk, unless there's an angle for them, and they only tell
the truth by accident."

"Cellie? His cell mate?"

"I'll get you a phone number. And then I'll ask you to
leave."

40

It was a four-hour drive south to Greenville through what
was fast becoming a blizzard. He'd probably have to fly home from
St. Louis tomorrow. Circling around Judge Ward's driveway, BJ
felt excited and at the same time half comatose with lack of sleep.
Tse had made it clear that nobody other than Sol Burligame was going to *call in* to a federal inmate on the phone. So he would have to
make the journey. But he did think enough to stop in the driveway
and call ahead to advise the prison that he was on his way to visit
one Rocky Mohammad, former cellmate of Jaap Tenkley.

The speed-talking young man who answered had a good
laugh when BJ told him his plans, explaining it took seven days to
approve a non-listed visitor unless he happened to be on the Federal
Law Enforcement Personnel list.

Damn!

He raced back to the house and persuaded Tse to give him
Judge Ward's mobile number. With considerable mental dis-
combobulation, the judge agreed to put in a call on behalf of an injustice which BJ was not at liberty to discuss. He found himself on
the Federal Law Enforcement Personnel list, and to his vast relief
was permitted a ten-minute, monitored and recorded phone call to
inmate Rocky Mohammad. Mercifully, the bad weather caused the
phone connection to be quite clear, right there in Judge Ward's
driveway.

Rocky had a memory, he said, like Moby Dick. He wasn't
forgetting nothing, and he wasn't forgiving nobody, and the usual
fee for electronic interviews was five cartons of cigarettes. Nine and
a half minutes into the conversation BJ was leaning back in the
crammed seat of the rental laughing like a madman, breathless with
the excitement of the novice detective, without the slightest memory

of Tse's warning that inmates were pathological liars.

"It's all he ever talked about," Rocky Mohammad gushed merrily. "He was gonna kill this guy Tyne. Tyne, Tyne, all night long. I don't know who the fuck Tyne was, but Tyne did the contracts that got Tenkley caught. I figured I could make some money off him if I could get his address. Then after a couple years it changed to going back to Chi and seeing the broad who sent him up. Ferrari. Ferrari and C. Prosecutor just with the name C. He was gettin out, and he was goin straight to Ferrari to blow the whistle on Tyne. Then about last spring sometime he changes his mind again. Now he's gonna put in a deposition on Tyne because likely Tyne was gonna do him as soon as he got out."

"Do him? You mean —"

"Yeah, that's what I mean. I don't mean fuckin *dance* with him."

"And?"

"And that's it, pal. What'd you say your name was?"

"It's BJ Lichtenstein."

"BJ? Fuckin BJ, man? You wouldn't last long around here with a name like that."

He'd heard it before, perhaps more subtly. "How many people have you told this to?"

"I tell everybody. Even that FBI dude who showed up the day Tenkley got sprung. But guess what? Nobody gives a rat's ass."

It took about thirty seconds to decide on his next move. He reviewed his notes, and made a heavy red circle on one item.

Back in Oak Park, the streets were shutting down, but he managed to slip and slide to the Elder Care Facility in time for dinner.

"Yes, oh yes, mister, want soup?" Concetta Ferrari offered, delighted to have two visitors in one day. She was now wearing baggy sweat pants and a pajama top, and slightly misplaced orange lipstick.

"Concetta." He smiled like a kid on Santa's knee. She smiled back. "Your dear daughter left something here on her last visit."

"My daughter?" The smile did not fade, but the voice did. "No. Nothing."

"A box of chocolates?" he prodded.

"Ah." She eyed him curiously.

"A magazine?"

"How you know this?"

"A little record?"

She smiled again, a motherly, head-shaking smile. "Little record! Soup always no spices, you know? I teach them to make *fagioli*!"

"May I see it?"

She slurped soup and stood rather gracefully for an old woman, and returned in a moment with a DVD disc in a plastic case. It was marked in computer printing, "Property of Maria Concetta Ferrari."

He snapped his laptop out of his briefcase and stuffed in the DVD long enough to see the most beautiful woman he'd ever laid eyes on speaking to a camcorder. "Assistant US Attorney Viola Ferrari, in the matter of Jaap Tenkley," and she stated her location and the date and BJ slammed the laptop shut, begged Concetta to let him borrow the little record for a few days, and was out of the nursing home before he could take another breath.

One more job to do, and then it was back on the silver bird for Seattle. He had to get back to Jerome Tse to confirm this was a bona fide videotape of Viola Ferrari. It was a redundancy he knew Sligo would demand. In fact he could almost see Mgaba sneering at him and scoffing at the little record from the little old demented lady from Oak Park.

The storm had moved east, but by the time he turned north onto I-94 for his second trip to Michigan, it was pitch black and cars were filling up the median strip. He slithered off at the Sawyer Road exit bone-weary, and found his way to the farm. The judge's pickup was still gone. All the lights in the house were off except what might have been candlelight in an end room. BJ felt a strange shadow cross before him as he got out, leaving the car headlights on, and walked through his own snowy footsteps toward the front door.

At first he thought the sound was a door banging shut, muffled by the wind. But that couldn't be right. The wind was down, and he rang the bell, then pounded on the door, a terrible darkness suddenly filling his chest, and he fell in the snow beside the house as he ran toward the dim light coming from the corner room. He was just tall enough to see into what appeared to be a bedroom, and he had to grab the windowsill and jump up, once, twice, and his heart nearly flew apart on the second jump, when he saw a body on the floor, a man, Jerome Tse, a small pistol in his hand, and blood oozing from the side of his head.

41

It was mid-afternoon over the Rockies when the small rectangular television powered up on the seatback in front of Raven Menez and the two men escorting her to Washington. Even at 44,000 feet. I-Media. There was no escaping it.

President Sol Burligame had some words for his people. Courtman waved to the business class host for another drink. Beside Raven, Mgaba blinked himself awake. Still two hours to fly. He was to make sure Raven had accommodations tonight, and get her to Sligo's residence sometime tomorrow. Whether Nel had made it back from Salt Lake City was another matter. She'd left with no real idea what was about to take place, except that Molly Bee was going to meet her there. At the same time, Courtman was to check in with his bald little friend Merlin, the Sligos' house man, make sure all was settled at home, and get ready for battle when she returned, and when BJ reported back from Chicago.

For now all three settled back to watch the President work.

Sol Burligame's face filled the screen perhaps three seconds before he began speaking. A simple timing error. Clearly the President was not aware his prickly grimace occupied every screen on Earth. His mouth opened wide, then dropped into a vast grin as he squinted down to his notes, a mirthless, steel-eyed sneer that would not have fooled a six-year-old. With a jerk he gripped his thick cheeks in both hands, bringing color to the flesh, making his eyes bulge. Suddenly he dropped his hands and clicked into his presidential demeanor for the camera.

"Good evening, my fellow Americans."

"Your holiness," Courtman greeted him, tipping his glass.

Sol Burligame was not given to press conferences, and in fact held only a couple a year with a specific agenda and timetable, facing reporters hand-picked by his press secretary, the ironic and well-spoken Joel Babylon. Babylon then handled the media. Courtman sensed he was going to see Mr. Babylon, the administration's serious funny man in the bowtie, shortly.

With surprising candor the President disarmed the *Rebellion.com* situation.

"I acknowledge the frustration many of you are feeling over the recent election," he said, in tones carefully rehearsed and modulated. "I was a bit shocked myself, and I expect to see many more people voting in the next election. As you know," confusion crossing the violin-shaped face, "turmoil has erupted once again across our land. It is not life-threatening to our democracy. But there are those who would circumvent the processes in place to tear down what our nation has built up. We can't allow this. We are a tolerant nation, but a nation forged in the defense of freedom by the blood of our citizenry." Timing the words precisely, "And we have more work to do to ensure equality for all Americans. To ensure that every man and woman receives a fair day's pay for a fair day's work. To ensure that honesty is rewarded and dishonesty is punished, from the teen-age hoodlum to the giant corporation. I admit it. We have work to do. Human nature will not change overnight. Perhaps not over a century. But we share a heritage that is certainly worth our patience."

"*Allez-y Sol! Foncez!*" grumbled the speechwriter Sloan Mgaba, wearing his African travel beads and square reading glasses. "Get on with it!"

Burligame heard. He removed his glasses and reached out to find his people. "I hear what you are saying in the streets and in your blogs. I am as hopeful, and at this moment as disappointed, in certain aspects of this great nation as you are. Remember, I am one of you. My parents were working people. Four generations ago, a Burligame played outfield for the old Boston Braves for twelve dollars a game. I struggled to get through college. When you cry 'foul,' I am listening."

He took pains to admonish Mr. Crockett. No seditious activity on our soil. Stop misbehaving.

"I took his protest to heart and read his cogitations on his

Web site," the President admitted. "My staff has intensely studied the *Strategies for Survival in a Corporate World.* I understand the Picasso parody. I encourage you to read what these scholars and visionaries have to say. Frankly, Mr. Crockett, I admire your spunk, if not your underhandedness." He frowned presidentially.

"But you made a mistake. A big one. While you were making your airborne protest, lawful under the First Amendment to the Constitution, you abducted a worthy and essential official of the United States government, Congressman Victor Sligo. Kidnapping is a federal offense."

"Blah-blah, blah-blah, blah-*blah*," chanted Courtman.

"Purvis, shut up," Mgaba said.

Courtman finally noticed that somehow everybody in America knew their secret.

"Hey," he said. "How do you suppose the entire planet figured out Sligo was on the plane?"

Across the aisle, Raven Menez shyly raised her hand to the shoulder. "I called in to my paper from that little airfield," she squeaked.

"You told the *Times* Victor had been kidnapped?" Sending her an admonishing look. "Shame on you!" And he laughed and held a hand up in the aisle for Raven to slap with a resounding zing.

The President said, "My prayers are with Congressman Sligo, his wife Nel and their family. I have insisted that FBI Deputy Director John Lee Davis personally supervise this investigation. Deputy Director Davis has ordered an extensive psychological profile on Mr. Crockett. We believe that Congressman Sligo will not be harmed, as this would be inimical to Mr. Crockett's intentions." Pausing to allow the citizenry a gasp of relief. "Mr. Crockett." He glared with uncompromising command into the camera. "Every man should be treated with dignity and respect. But this government will not countenance lawbreakers. You will be hunted down and brought to justice!" His face was deadly serious.

"Here comes the punch line," said glib Mgaba.

"Rebellion dot com," rapped the President of the United States, "will lead to capture dot com and from there to imprisonment dot com." He allowed the nation to absorb this demeaning humiliation of the uprising. "This is a government of men, not of laws!" he trumpeted across the land, misreading his notes. "You have a right to dissent, but you have no right to dissent unlawfully!"

In a blink he returned to his fireside manner. He was off the notes, against the advice of the entire brigade of 2,000 White House staffers. He grinned. "You want a civics lesson, my fellow Americans? Go ahead and read this *Strategies for Survival.* It represents a form of participatory democracy we all want our children to engage in. But I will remind you, ours is a vastly complex nation, with tremendous challenges! And we are a strong people. We will not be intimidated by opposition, or by insurrection! Let the word go out from this place: When the game is on the line, I will listen to you, I will listen to my trusted advisors, and I will act." With a gesture of stupendous dignity, he nodded to the huddled masses. "Goodnight, friends." In an instant, he was gone.

I-Media was taken off guard for a second and a half. A voice-over intoned, "We'll be right back." In the President's place came a commercial for a cough drop guaranteeing a lasting erection.

42

In the make-up alcove off the White House briefing room, Sol Burligame could feel the pressure fall off his body like hot rocks being pulled away. Burligame was a big man. He sweated a lot, and he stank when he sweated, and thus by long practice he refused to go before news cameras and their blaring klieg lights for more than thirteen minutes. In turn, setting this standard taught Burligame as far back as Lake Wobegone Junior College, to deal with his adversaries as well as the inevitable scum who collected around natural leaders, in language that would disarm both. And to do it with charm, voice inflection, and baseball imagery.

He joked with his core loyalists, "Who knows how far I could have gotten if I could speak like Martin van Buren!"

Both his press secretary and his chief of staff, Hussein al-Jakka – actually his second chief of staff; the one Billy had chosen for him was passing some time with the Nevada Department of Corrections – stood reading notes rapidly to each other at the second make-up station. It sounded like a college cram session. Joel Babylon was a younger, thicker Purvis Courtman. His graying hair came flat across his forehead. He was the most comfortable man in the entire administration, the only man in Washington still wearing a bowtie, given to sitting on the edge of the platform kicking his long legs out while defending crucial foreign policy decisions, and occasionally popping a yo-yo out of his pocket and slinging it down in answer to a particularly dumb question.

Under no circumstances could Babylon be mistaken for Hussein al-Jakka. Not only was the chief of staff utterly without humor, but he carried some 260 pounds on a dense Semitic figure five feet eight inches high. Among a long list of al-Jakka's favorite resentments was the obvious one: he had been chosen second. Burligame's first chief of staff had been indicted on a charge of public exposure. Only then did al-Jakka demonstrate his true strength of character – managing a staff of two thousand in the fashion of his adopted hero, Captain Bligh, and at the same moment demonstrating unwavering loyalty to the most powerful man on the planet. Not counting Billy Hellman.

Al-Jakka and Babylon loved and hated each other, sometimes simultaneously. Both were extremely intelligent. The President's chief of staff felt the burden to chastise his boss if he uttered the most innocent malapropism.

Now he happily touched Babylon on both cheeks and whisked to the President's side.

"Sir!" He always began with a fatuous display of admiration. "Well done! You have put the infidels on the defensive!" A little obsequious move there, calling the Progressives "infidels."

"Of course you realize you used the phrase, 'we are a nation of men, not of laws!'"

"Yeah?" said the President.

"You meant, 'a nation of laws, not of men.' Sir."

Sol Burligame looked up at his olive-skinned, wobbling chief of staff. "What are you mumbling about, Hussein?"

Patiently, fingertips pressing together to form a tent, Al-Jakka explained. He was articulate, brief, and struggled not to be condescending. Satisfied, he finished.

"So?" said Sol Burligame.

"So, Mr. President, next time you'll remember." The short man smiled. He had made the President a better man.

"Shit, Hussein, go away," said the President.

"Thank you, sir," he said, and touching forehead, lips and heart with pinched fingers, he retreated.

The media people grumbled and went outside for a smoke and flirted and told short raunchy jokes, and finally Joel Babylon came before them to do combat. He walked to the lectern cocky and quick in his hand-tied red silk bowtie and gray blazer. Instantly they erupted, fifty-eight questions from fifty-eight journalists. The press secretary didn't flinch.

"Thank you, people. I heard all your questions, and I will get to them all. We're in a modest crisis here and I need you to be civil. Only one question per reporter, please." He held up one finger. The thundering questions instantly arose again. Babylon yelled, "We need civility, boys and girls! The first person to shut up, I will answer his or her question! One question only!"

It took another minute or two for the mob to establish its usual pecking order. Which meant the *US Times'* venerable Washington bureau chief, Ellen Sheehan, went first.

"Joel, is the administration treating it as a crisis? You called it a crisis. The President said," reading her notes, "'harming Congressman Sligo would be inimical to Mr. Crockett's interests.' What does the White House believe are Mr. Crockett's interests?"

Babylon grinned. Another multi-sided question snuck in. Looking directly at Sheehan he asked, "And if not, why not?"

She smiled. "Exactly."

"Not a crisis, people." He found the camera and articulated carefully, "Not – a – crisis. Calm will prevail. Look, it's a natural political hiccup following a close election! Now, the government is going to find Mr. Crockett and he is going to have his day in court. It is the view of this administration that Mr. Crockett was weaned too early," Babylon said with a straight face. "We are hoping to locate his mother for a belated breast-feeding event." He pointed.

A reporter said, "Philadelphia's Chief of Police Giuseppe Manicotti informed *US Times* reporters that his attempt to rescue Congressman Sligo at Ney Field was thwarted by urban terrorist activity. Can you comment on this? Has a terrorist group taken credit for the kidnapping? Was Chief Manicotti injured? He appeared to be limping at his press conference."

Babylon smiled broadly, shaking his head, not quite laughing at the bizarre assertion. "No, no, and I don't know," he said, pointing to another questioner.

"If the government falls, what position will the President then hold?" a voice called.

Joel Babylon looked at the floor a long moment, long enough for another reporter to begin his question. The press secretary looked up and froze the second voice with a cold stare.

"If the government falls," he repeated calmly, looking directly at the questioner. "You said, 'If the government falls.' Have I blundered into the twilight zone here? If the government falls, the position the President will then hold is President of the United States! Where is my yo-yo? You know, I've forgotten my yo-yo!" As the press corps laughed at itself, Babylon snapped his fingers toward the handsome aide at the side of the room. "Erik, get that guy's White House pass! Take him on a tour of the Clinton bathroom. Mr. Utanoptuaq?" Pointing to another laughing questioner, the native Alaskan.

"Neither you nor President Burligame appears to be taking this matter with the seriousness suggested by howling mobs from Long Island to San Diego. The central issue of these demonstrations has been voting irregularities – ballot miscounts, computer failures and street-level paranoia about why people are not voting. How confident is the President that –"

"Hey," Babylon broke in, uncharacteristically short-tempered. "Don't bring voting irregularities in here! The President was elected, people! That suggests a process we call voting! I don't want to hear my private press corps reduced to a bunch of whining amateur detectives!" Slamming an open palm on the lectern. "I don't know from voting irregularities! Speak to the irregular voters!" He stood and walked briskly to the wings, and returned slinging down the bright yellow yo-yo with the red baseball stitching.

"May we limit our profundities to the subjects at hand?" He nodded to the rear. "Mr. Wildeman?"

"Joel, word comes from the War Room six floors below us that Vice President Hellman intended to blow up Mr. Crockett's aircraft just prior to the communications meltdown, knowing that Congressman Sligo was on board. Can you comment on this, and if so, what will –"

"Yes! I will say this. No word ever came from the War

Room to my ears, personally, in my career with this administration, and I can comment that whomever your source might be is probably confusing this building with some alternate universe he lives in." He pointed to a woman in the second row, then flicked his attention back to the rear. "Unless of course you're referring to Ms. Flotilda Lament, the downstairs cleaning lady." Again laughter rippled down the room. "Ms. Lament for all I know is a CIA operative loose in the War Room! Is she your source?"

Wildeman yelled, "Yes, actually, she is," and the whole room erupted in hilarity.

"In that case," Babylon said, "cancel my subscription!"

"Who is Davy Crockett?" boomed out another voice.

Babylon found himself sweating. "Thank you Frank. You have once again validated my belief that all journalists are fundamentally —" and he lifted a notepad to his mouth and coughed a word into it that sounded a bit like "assholes." At this moment a woman appeared in the doorway at the back. She was dressed provocatively, in a revealing rose-colored blouse and tight navy skirt slit halfway up the thigh. Leora Psybysch, Vice President Hellman's chief of staff, tended to prowl the President's activities in the shadows, particularly regarding the press. It was widely assumed she was spying for Hellman — ensuring that his personal mouthpiece, Sol Burligame, did not make any spectacularly stupid mistakes.

Many eyes, men's and women's, chanced clandestine glances at her.

For a variety of reasons, Joel Babylon truly hated her. She had no business in this room at the moment, and she seriously cramped his style. And other areas.

"Okay! We have about ten minutes. Who's next." A loud murmuring rolled forward. Some repeated, "Who is Davy Crockett?" and "Answer the question, please!"

He sighed loudly. "Davy Crockett was a Tennessee legislator and member of the US Congress for two separate terms, between 1827 and 1833. He was killed defending the Alamo by Santa Anna's forces during the Texas war of independence against Mexico." Pointing. "Yes."

"Come on, Joel!" bellowed the man in the back. "That's a yo-yo response and you know it!"

Leora Psybysch allowed herself a rare shadow of a grin.

The one thing Billy Hellman's entire entourage had in common, the fundamentalist zealots and the hand-picked team from S. and the CI lobbyists, was that they all despised the media.

"We don't know. If we knew you would know." Babylon looked grim. His lips compressed. He never exhibited anything less than absolute control over this mob. Sweat snicked under his collar. "But I can tell you this. As the President said – in case your crayons broke and you didn't write it down – the FBI has created a profile of this kidnapper. They have assured the President that Mr. Crockett will be incarcerated within forty-eight hours." Uncontrollably he faded a non-glance at Psybysch. "While President Burligame feels confident that Congressman Sligo will be returned safely, we are hauling out the Military Commissions Act of 2006 and dusting it off in the event that potential, I emphasize *potential* activity might warrant some immediate, brief occasion to facilitate Congressman Sligo's safe return."

An uncharacteristic silence fell across the press room for one full second, followed by a furious uproar.

"Are you suggesting the administration may declare *martial law?*" screeched a woman above the din. The words recoiled like a gunshot around the room. Reporters envisioned headlines igniting riots across the nation. A couple of people were already speed-dialing cell phones. Every journalist present knew this was Vice President Hellman's favorite threat.

"That Act suspends *habeas corpus*, and the President knows it," the woman wailed. "It's unconstitutional!"

"No. People, read my lips! This - is - not - a - crisis! I bring this up as a conditional consideration, just as you would buy flood insurance for some catastrophe that will probably never take place!" Babylon was losing patience. Manipulating this crowd was like juggling half a dozen live hand grenades blindfolded while a Doberman gnawed on your leg and your wife was telling you she was running off with your priest. He knew that any single word he uttered would be played back a thousand times in search of hidden meanings. At the same time, everyone present knew they were here at the pleasure of the Vice President. Anyone who fell out of Hellman's favor was back covering high school sports and writing obituaries in a heartbeat. Needless to say, the *West Coast Paper* was not represented.

But he had accidentally opened this avenue of questioning

while grating his eyes across Leora Psybysch's exposed breasts. He simply could not help himself. He felt sexual desire for the most vile woman he had ever known.

Hard questions boiled out of the increasingly rowdy crowd. If it was technically possible to fake a laser iris scan – which hasn't been proven – why had Crockett picked out Secretary of Communications Hunter Tyne to embarrass with that little trick? Whose head will roll at Homeland Security? Who ordered the *Rebellion.com* Web site dismantled? How long could the President continue allowing Billy Hellman to run the government?

That did it. Babylon stood, the gray blazer open, the bowtie too tight, cramped in the groin, but his striking features continued to focus on each reporter in turn, eyes level, and he tried to patch up with his lithe rhetoric what he knew to be a crumbling facade, a professional liar spinning fairy tales for the national media.

What they paid Joel Babylon $325,000 a year to believe was this: voters, and consequently the media, were redundant to the process of governance. They worshipped low interest rates, soap opera stars, basketball players and rap musicians. The collapse of the American way of life lay at the feet of Progressive ideology. The so-called "common good" was an antiquated sham that had never had any value in any government at any time in history.

Joel Babylon didn't like it. But he had tried stand-up comic work, and liked that even less.

Inevitably in the last minute somebody slipped in one more tough issue. It was the fabulous Lulu Xiang, I-Media defector and now *Webgoods* editor, a one-time lover of Joel Babylon and thus admitted to the cadre of reporters. Exactly as she had planned it.

Thin as a pencil and dressed all in khaki, completely bald, Lulu said, "We are told that new information may be forthcoming in the case of Assistant US Attorney Viola Ferrari." A shocked murmur rolled through the press room. "As a matter of fact, in her column today, Molly Bee made the point that –"

The sound of Bee's name shot a jolt of adrenaline through Babylon's chest. Molly Bee, anathema to the administration. He did not dare let Lulu push the President around with Bee's potent insinuations. He had to trump her, fast.

"Ms. Xiang, please," he interrupted, fumbling for a way to squelch her query. "We may object to Ms. Bee's nagging, but that's no grounds to arrest her. I'm sure she doesn't know this Crockett guy. Her function apparently is to bring hostility to American society. A bum denied his food stamps will do that." He examined the floor a moment.

Unperturbed, Lulu pressed on. "No, I was referring to the investigation into the death of Viola Ferrari!"

Nothing ever deterred Joel Babylon from his task. Other than Leora Psybysch.

"We've been all through that! Ms. Bee insists on acting the hornet in the ear of this administration. She has her repressed angst, and frankly I'm not interested in whose ghost she's hauling out of the grave this week!" Babylon could feel himself losing control. It was always the women. Always. "Look. Does Ms. Bee not call the police when she is threatened in the street? Yes! Is she safe in her home? Sure! Was she educated in a free society, on student loans and government grants? Probably! Don't you suppose her father is happy to know she lives in a country where –" His brain electrified for a split second. His hair caught fire, and he grabbed a sip of water and felt his mouth hiss. "Does Ms. Bee drive on roads safe from explosive devices? Drink clean water? Breathe clean air?" Some in the press corps were laughing now. The vicious media.

"Hath not a Jew eyes?" someone yelled. "If you prick us, do we not bleed?"

He looked up angrily. "The point is –"

Somebody bellowed, "Does the President hold a vendetta against Molly Bee? Is that the reason she has to live her life anonymously?"

And another heated voice, "Is that why you won't let Lulu ask her question?"

Babylon went pink. His fists clenched, and he knew this time they had defeated him. There was no place left to go. He sucked in a deep breath of White House filtered air.

"Ladies and gentlemen," he paused, and showed his disgust to all present. *"You* work it out. Good day."

43

Nothing was visible at all through the mustard-colored cloud blanketing the Mississippi Delta. The Aztek C130-H churned through the southern sky smooth as cream, big as a battleship, loud as an ocean, airlifting the world's goods from 100-milliliter vials of African plum bark extract to a forty-ton evaporator required yesterday at the San Joaquin desalinization plant. Every two minutes Victor and Edwin could hear the s*nick-snick whirr* in the fusion chambers of the jet engines. At this altitude the air was permanently puckered with earthly contaminants, the result of greenhouse gasses that eventually solidified in combination with industrial effluence burned into the air over cities for two centuries. Thus even the wonderful Rolls Royce 550 heavy hydrogen power plants required a scrubbing by chemical neutralizer at the input cone every 120 seconds to keep the aircraft flowing smoothly.

Foulks dozed in his cargo seat opposite Victor. He had that Jesus look about him again, Foulks did, the close-cropped light beard, thick lips and longish hair, the sculpted face. Asleep, he was safer to look at. Victor did not get that sickening hypnotic feeling from him. Something in his eyes wanted to make you fight him off, as if he was penetrating too deeply, and then you just surrendered. Now they were both dressed in Aztek red. The cargo master had insisted they dump the Mennonites' outfits for company uniforms that almost fit, complete with employee names sewn over the breast pocket, "Larry" for Foulks, and "Malcolm" for United States Representative Victor Sligo. Malcolm! He felt like he was supposed to be eating haggis and heaving a boulder over a barn.

Somebody tossed back the evening *West Coast Paper* at their first stop in Chattanooga.

"It's started!" blared the 160-point headline. Photos sprinkled the front page, prominently featuring the *Rebellion.com* banner flapping over the new mall behind a family with children sitting on their parents' shoulders. A one-column photo strip along the edge showed laughing faces, old people weeping, children pointing. Under each was a name and a quote, all variations on the statement by civic leader Jonathan Winter that read, "Return the power to the people!" below his photo with an upheld fist. There was the same vivid photo of the two Interceptor jets nudging the Cessna's air

space.

Victor thought he was losing his mind and his career with one incredible blunder. This man beside him had bet the farm on the most cockeyed premise, that he could make political leaders tell the public the truth. Maybe, if Santa Claus would help and the tooth fairy could join in, Foulks could shift the government into something resembling compassion with the millions of working poor, the uninsured, the disabled, the sick. Ironically, the Hellman crowd had burst in broadcasting their phony divine right to rule, and with them came the New Freedom Party clampdown on the populace, and a web of intrigue vastly more secretive and powerful than ever in the nation's history. I-Media constantly telling people how to think. It was a leering *1984,* where Big Brother wore a little flag in his lapel.

Even Julio Reese on Public Television, jokingly telling voters why bother to vote, and then catching that pencil and saying, no, no I was being ironic, get to the polls, your vote counts. Even that felt somehow subversive.

A small steel door opened, and a man in a pinstriped black silk suit and black leather gloves entered, closed the door behind him, and leaned against it. He was a powerful-looking person, stern of jaw and fixed of eye, maybe fifty years old, maybe younger, a touch of gray, broad shoulders and an expressive tan face.

"Congressman Sligo," he said neutrally.

The two fugitives flicked a look at each other. "Speaking," Victor said.

"Heinrich Eisenstadt. Happened to be in Atlanta last night during your interesting airplane ride. Got word that Dr. Spangloss might be bringing you down south."

Victor didn't quite get it, but he shook hands and allowed a question mark to come across his face. "A pleasure, sir."

"You don't remember me," Eisenstadt said. "This is my company. Aztek. I own it."

He remembered. Ten-grand-a-plate dinner somewhere, probably for Alex Holiday last year. Apparently Eisenstadt was here for a little discussion. Right now. The Congressman and his flying pal had fomented chaos in the streets. Wall Street had shut down. A movement had arisen out of nowhere to recall President Burligame. Somebody on one of the renegade television networks was already touting DB Cooper for President. And there was Molly Bee's column, *Trying Times,* in today's paper. A riot in the making. Had he seen it?

Still not sure which side the man was on, Victor reached over and took the paper from Foulks. Eisenstadt snatched it from his hands. His demeanor suddenly shifted. His face pulled down, and his mouth clamped into a tight V. Tearing through the sections, he found what he was looking for.

"Listen to this idiocy!" he growled, slapping the paper. He read the column aloud. It was headed, *"Rebellion dot common sense."*

"'Hallelujah! Somebody finally has found the guts to stand up to them. Congress wouldn't do it. They were eviscerated long ago." He sent Victor an adolescent smirk. *"The judiciary? In Billy Hellman's pocket. The voters simply stayed away in the last election. What's left? I'll tell you what's left: Davy Crockett! Somebody finally has awakened the sleeping dragon of resistance to political oppression.'"*

He was forcing the words through gritted teeth, and stopped long enough to fire a look at Foulks.

"Seat belts, please," rumbled a taped voice overhead. "Memphis."

Obediently Eisenstadt dropped into one of the seats facing Victor, and buckled up. Victor did not move.

"She can awaken my goddamn dragon!" His eyes went to slits, and he began a sort of piggy grunting. Victor reached out angrily to grab the paper, but Eisenstadt ripped it away.

"Steady, big fella," Eisenstadt admonished, the Lone Ranger settling his horse. Then immediately his voice became a circus barker, thundering up and down the scale, pointing, snarling. "You Progressives keep putting up goddamn *sunflowers* like Alex Holiday to run for President! Who's going to vote for this jackass? He's going to guarantee welfare for everybody in America with a cut finger!" Reading with pissy sarcasm, *"'The appalling irony of our times is that voting is irrelevant. The New Freedom Party wins the elections, and the smug sugar daddy behind the Party – Communication International – goes on controlling the country from locations that cannot be Googled!'"* The man was approaching apoplexy, slapping the paper against the bulkhead, going red all over, steam hissing out his ears.

"'The US Attorney's Office is collating CI's litigation history, including a dozen or so incidents involving voting machine scandals, touchscreen failures, and vote-counting miscalculations connected to CI contracts. True, all that has been cleaned up and monitored by independent agents. But one can't help wondering what CI is up to now.

"'Inevitably all this raises one of the seminal questions of our times: What happened to Viola Ferrari? A reliable government source – who demanded anonymity – decided to break his silence and told me Ferrari, an Assistant US Attorney, had been investigating unauthorized mind control experiments in Utah, and had reason to suspect involvement by Communication International. VoteAmerica reported last week the investigation into Ferrari's death was sealed by executive privilege. How is that possible? What are they hiding? Here is a voice literally crying out in the wilderness for justice, and the Justice Department responding, "Piss off!"'

"Give me that," Victor demanded, and snatched the paper from Eisenstadt's tan hands. To Foulks he said, "Maybe Nel's onto something. The way they're handling this, it wouldn't surprise me if they actually did kill her!"

"You're a politician," Eisenstadt said. "You know there's always people sticking there noses where they don't belong. But you also know what every politician knows. Business is the soul of this country. The *raison d'être*. The cash! Hell, Mr. Sligo, this woman comes barging into CI's operations, sure it's a horrible decision, eliminating somebody, but it's *business!* The same thing as –"

Leaping up, Victor slammed his fist into the side of Eisenstadt's face. "You sorry piece of shit," he roared. Eisenstadt ripped off his seat belt and started up, but Victor jammed a forearm against his throat and shoved him hard against the seat. "Steady, big fella!"

It was Edwin's turn to snatch the paper and continue reading while Eisenstadt nursed his face. Molly Bee wrote, *"This administration is breaking apart. Government will have to be recalibrated. This is exactly what Davy Crockett has insinuated upon the populace in the skies west of Philadelphia. We are invited to a rebellion. Here is what I suggest: Join the general strike. Demand a legal recall of Billy Hellman. Don't pay your taxes till the administration tells you why 160 million people failed to vote, after decades of corporate cronyism, unemployment and economic turmoil,*

*combined with phony bailouts and unspeakable crimes like the
death of Viola Ferrari. "*

"Tsk, tsk, that Crockett," Edwin Foulks said.

Eisenstadt groaned. He set to complaining about all manner
of Progressive stupidities when they were in the majority. Shutting
down the war with Iraq. The defense of the country shriveled to a
couple of people with paddles spanking drug runners at the borders.
Satanists, Eisenstadt said with a straight face, taking over the public
schools. Children encouraged to draw outside the lines, to – what do
they call it – eschew authority. "Pretty soon there'll be Boy Scout
leaders bunking with innocent kids, and everybody taking drugs and
having sex with their sisters. As for business," he smirked, "it is
well documented that the Progressives regulate financial institutions
so heavily, every time a CEO farts the watchdogs show up to check
for emissions violations! *That's* why the Newfies keep winning."

Victor was pretty sure Heinrich Eisenstadt was clinically
nuts. He said, "Why are you helping us?" Wondering if there were
any parachutes aboard.

"You mean why am I helping you?"

"Yes."

The lips went thin, but the sour grin held. "I happen to believe Billy Hellman is the most dangerous moron who ever entered
public life."

Simultaneously Victor and Foulks opened their mouths, the
Congressman to agree, Edwin to pop his ears. The CEO of Aztek
shot his hands over his head and shouted, *"Rebellion.com!"* and he
burst out laughing. As if on signal, the great engines roared, and the
plane began to descend rapidly. He gripped the arms of his seat, and
began spewing out a hiccupping paradiddle, looking at his astonished passengers unable to speak, weeping with laughter. "Taking
over the government!" he yelled, and fell into tongue-tied gasps.
"You're damn tootin', Crockett!" and the tears flooded down his tan
cheeks. His tongue bent along his lips to lick the tears, and this was
even more absurd, and he collapsed forward, snickering in harmony
with his thundering aircraft. He wiped his face with a blue silk
handkerchief, took a great gulp of air and stared with bulging eyes
at Edwin Foulks. He sniffled.

"That *Rebellion.com* flying carpet dragging down that
Cessna," he managed to say, but could go no further. Stuffing the

hanky in his mouth, he fell forward again, and the plane dropped
further, engines screaming, the wheels dropping with a howl beneath them, and Eisenstadt's entire body vibrated with sniffling,
slobbering laughter. Then he shot bolt upright and said, "I never saw
anything so ridiculous in my life." He laughed like a stuck record,
hu-huh, hu-huh, hu-huh, legs banging together, then touching his
jaw and wincing.

"Maybe we should call 911," Victor said, eyebrows raised.

"Hard to tell," Edwin said. "He might bust the defibrillator."

"Then!" screamed the CEO, "that fatuous clown Hellman
comes out and takes credit for saving your life! After nearly vapor-
izing you with those two Interceptors!" He stopped dead. The engines sighed and slowed. Bulge-eyed, mouth hanging open, he
stared at Victor. "You gotta love that guy," he said, and he heaved
his head back against the seat, mouth agape, gold fillings flickering.
He stared upward, post-orgasmic, silent.

They landed. With his dignified executive façade in place,
Eisenstadt rose and shook both their hands firmly, his mouth set,
chin firm, eyes steady. "Good luck, gentlemen," he said.

Victor looked up and said, "Sorry about the –"

"Glad to help," Eisenstadt said. And he turned and left.

After that it was Fort Smith, Oklahoma City, Lubbock, Tu-
cumcari, Palm Springs, Fresno, Grants Pass, Portland. At this point
two men entered, both strong and rather daunting. Dozing and starving, the fugitives were instantly on alert as the two men, dressed in
the Aztek red coveralls, sat opposite them. The bigger man wore a
nametag that read "Omari," and on his arm the gray band signifying
a parent forced back to work over age eighty. Victor wondered if
they were bounty hunters.

Shortly they were chatting, and the conversation drifted to
the interesting company CEO. A year ago his son's skull had been
crushed in a jetski accident. Eisenstadt's life had changed dramati-
cally. The formerly intransigent conservative had a close look at un-
derstaffed long-term care facilities for people with permanent brain
damage, prescription drug costs, the staggering rich-poor gap
viewed from this tragic vantage point, and other parents as emotion-
ally devastated as he was. The boy's experience had cracked Eisenstadt's heart open. He reversed himself politically, and became a

mentally unhinged philanthropist. The man called Omari articulated all this with enormously dignified calm.

Then they were taxiing at Boeing Field. The airplane made a wide turn, and stopped. The big cargo carrier had no portholes. Had there been, they all would have seen an eight-man FBI anti-terror squad moving intently through the industrial airfield in battle dress, armed, communicating on the half hour with the other units at SeaTac, Union Station, the state ferry terminals, I-5 rest areas and the Greyhound Station and every airport from San Francisco to Vancouver, waiting anxiously for Congressman Sligo and Mr. Crockett to return.

44

Two men and a woman worked on high alert posing as a street crew in Sunrise, near the Canadian border and half a block from the Congressman's house, speaking surreptitiously into collar mikes. Another female espionage person was returning by speed-boat from San Juan Island, where at five a.m. she had managed to place an invisible recording device into the false teeth of Nel Sligo's mother, Ms. Pearl Diamond. Other personnel tracked Victor's cell phone, pager and staff, as well as his twin daughters at a law firm in Seattle, and two sons, away together on a ski trip to Banff. A bored Homeland Security agent had eventually spoken to every citizen in Van Zandt, in the area along the Middle Fork and the South Fork of the Seyes River. He found no Davy Crockett, no terrorist enclave, no insurrectionist movement, no noticeable social discontent beyond the expected grumbling about Hellman and the constant sleeting ice rain. Van Zandt was in fact the most benign place he'd ever seen. The women were powerful, the men were handsome, and all the children were, well, children.

The FBI had fared slightly better. Agents questioning em-ployees at the Gouverneur Morris Hotel had been led to a closet on the twentieth floor where somebody had left behind a Philadelphia Eagles jacket. Crime lab analysis of the jacket's contents led to a list of 67,594 names of people who had purchased tickets for or at-tended last Sunday's losing effort against the Patriots. None of the names was Sligo.

As luck would have it, tall and spirited Desdemona B. Crockett had acquired her tickets on line, using her first two initials, from up in North Jersey, and happened to have purchased a fragrance of similar chemical composition to the one Nel Sligo wore and which was identified on the Eagles jacket. And piling one coincidence upon another, the fact that Ms. Crockett, age seventy-one, retired school librarian and martial arts instructor and registered Progressive, had a lifetime hobby of jumping out of airplanes, was terribly compelling news.

But what was truly unfortunate was that when the feds came to question her in their preemptory fashion, Ms. Crockett had become so upset she accidentally pushed one of the arresting agents down a flight of stairs at her walk-up apartment in Newark, and while the other agent was calling the medics, she had become frightened by a passing semi and had accidentally fallen against him, rather hard, shoving his cell phone into his face and breaking his nose.

Not far to the east, in the projects below Roosevelt Avenue in the Woodside section of Queens, New York, a shadow investigation was proceeding with salivating anxiety. High-tech sleuth and Manhattan Federal Building night janitor Jaroslav "Slash" Zewinta had followed with breathless fascination what he knew would be the defining political incident of the decade, only topped for sheer breathtaking *balls* in the past century by the attack on Pearl Harbor, the assassination of John Kennedy and the September 11th conversion of four commercial aircraft into guided missile systems. The entire experience had unhinged his mind since flicking on the Web last night and watching the little Cessna declare war on the United States government.

Then! Adding to this fantastic development, the great Molly Bee had weighed in with another sledge hammer blow to government malevolence, connecting the *Rebellion.com* protest to Communication International, and CI to the murder of Viola Ferrari! Brainwashing! At the time of her death, the US Attorney's Office would say only that Viola was vacationing in Utah when she was killed in a car wreck. What a crock of horse manure *that* was! Finally a national columnist had come out of the closet and told the truth. Even gave a government source. They knew Viola was investigating CI for doing dirty experiments. No wonder the damn Newfies keep winning elections! *Of course* CI was involved! They were involved in everything! Hell, Slash knew about them fifteen years ago. They were still called Communication West then, and they forced mind-bending drug experiments on Slash himself and his Army buddies down at Aberdeen. The same thing they were doing out at Dugway Proving Ground, where Dr. Whacked Brain himself, Hunter Tyne, ran the Army's other classified brain lab, on a contract with ComWest! They all knew it, and they all hated the damn Nazi. And here was Molly Bee, grumbling about CI and the Newfies controlling the voting booth, and trying to connect that to these brainwashing experiments in Utah. She was probably on the right track. Viola was probably murdered for sticking her nose too close to CI in her investigation. Man, this was *serious!* You never knew who would disappear! People just flat-out didn't talk about this. Then Davy Crockett hits the skies, and everybody who didn't vote comes pouring out to join the rebellion.

Somebody big like Molly Bee sniffing around CI could only lead to one place: Hunter Tyne! The company's ex-golden boy. And Tyne could only lead to the absolute baddest of all the bad people, Vice President Billy Hellman. *Son of a dung beetle!*

Slash poked a finger at the smeared black and white photo of the Secretary of Communications duct-taped to the lid of his garbage can. Tyne was fleeing a crowd of reporters, hand in the air, a grimace twisting his little mustache like he'd fallen into a blender. "The jig's up, tough guy," Slash growled. He heaved his last crust of white bread at the photo. Thus inspired, he spun aside and did a Gene Kelly glance over one shoulder. "Crockett's coming for you!" he sang, then spun his thick body around to face the photo from over the other shoulder and chanted, "Molly Bee's coming for you!" Then, to complete the dance, he whirled fully around to face Tyne. "And when they're done with you," he hissed between chipped teeth, pointing both gnarled index fingers at the photo, "I'm gonna eat you alive!"

45

It was a given within the community of mentally-distressed geeks that all degradation and misery on this planet could be traced back to Billy Hellman and Hunter Tyne. Archenemies of all human decency. Slash Zewinta believed the reason only one known mortal could break into CI's dark digital universe was because guys like Tyne made damn sure nobody could break in. In response to this, Slash had recently been upgrading his hobby of publishing on the Web the secret lives of these two public figures. Just to appease his two constituents – his cat, Mother Superior, and his penis, Yankee.

But actually connecting Hunter Tyne to Viola Ferrari's murder, this required a real leap of filth. It was like the Kennedy assassination, or FDR's drinking days with Stalin. You had to create an outrageous scenario, then turn official denials upside down, and hold the two pictures up to the light sideways. Slash loved the cyberhunt, seeking out dust bunnies left unvacuumed by administration goons as they cleaned up one step ahead of their own federal investigators. He felt the squeeze in his sphincter. His unrequited hate affair with Hunter Tyne was literally busting his prostate. The man was too devious, too laced into the government's protection system. But this time Slash had a whole new road to go down: Molly Bee was connecting the dots. What she knew and what Slash knew – together they might actually take on the Wasatch whacko, the drug pusher risen from the Army's hallucination farm, right where they found Viola's body.

Slash's shiny blue eyes bulged under a catastrophe of prematurely white hair. In a single long stride he was back to his red swiveling soda-counter stool. He clicked back to Molly Bee's online column. There was old Miss *Trying Times* herself – never with a photo, of course – and he knew instantly if he contacted her paper he'd be dismissed as a crackpot.

Whistling his twisted version of "Surfer Girl," Slash clicked into his friend's encrypted Website, a diligent electronic bandit and social disaster area known as Evileye.

"Do me a big favor, dude," Slash texted. He told him to check Molly Bee's column and said, "Whataya got new on Hunter Tyne? Lemme have it. I want his blood! How's ya mothah?"

It took more than four hours. Evileye – whose actual recorded birth name was Justice Will Prevail – was nothing if not thorough. Then came the almost incriminating evidence. As Slash read, blood whirled through his cranium, down his jugular vein, through his chest, into his fingers. Yes! He knew it! Evileye! You da man!

"You owe me, dirtbag," Evileye blogged back affectionately, from his tidy room over his mother's garage not far from Baltimore Harbor. "I timed out busting into that US Attorney's Office. Had to scramble out of there with my heinie on fire."

An actual FBI bogus Website, *savetherepublic,* got Evileye rolling. The Bureau used it for dirty tricks, misinformation, ways to screw people without official sanction. That's how he figured out where to go next. But, funnily enough, following FBI directions to the Public Access to Electronic Records, he discovered the Hunter Tyne's files now had to be accessed through the Justice Department. Obviously some IT techie at the Bureau hated Tyne's guts – but who didn't? Justice had the files hidden in the National Security Division archive, but the files on Tyne were locked by some kind of government baloney. "Inaccessible by Executive Privilege," it said. That frustrated Evileye for a full hour. Next he tried to penetrate Communication International, Tyne's old company. No way. Locked up tighter than the frozen passwords on Evileye's bank account. He was cornered. He had to go beg his mom for today's user code to get into Justice archives. His mother, Jane Doe, was another story altogether, a trusted employee deep in the inner sanctum of the National Institute of Justice. She wouldn't do a lot, but there were certain stones she might roll aside, in a case of national insecurity.

With Evileye's mother's insider password, a connection turned up in his search for Hunter Tyne's recent activity. Buried with the Star Wars plans and some phony plot to locate Weapons of Mass Destruction, was the link to Communication International's litigation history with the US Attorney's Office. Tyne had been CI's Director of Research. According to court document summaries – that was all Evileye could access – CI had been cited for mismanagement of touchscreen voting equipment in nineteen states. They must have figured this was a national security matter. There had been a trial five years ago, a file with the bold red asterisk that indicated a lofty government official had been implicated.

But nobody was getting into those documents. Not even

Jane Doe. All they had was the brief trial summary. But no results.

Evileye opened the summary. About five years ago a lab in Cicero, Illinois called REDACTED had been busted doing research on the brain stem and the hypothalamus known as "neurochemical programming" without a DHHS medical research license. Evileye knew about this. Slash had mentioned it more than once . This had nothing to do with medical research. The lab was experimenting with remote mind control, essentially computerized brainwashing! The prosecutor showed CI had contracted this lab in Cicero to do the research. And somebody from CI named REDACTED had signed the contract. He was indicted by the Grand Jury, but never charged. Right then the passcode timed out and the screen closed.

"Why, you dirty person!" Evileye gushed. "Sure Dr. Hunter Redacted wiggled off the hook. And so did CI. Who do you think," Evileye was later to inquire of Slash Zewinta, "who do you think ran the research? Who do you think takes care of the FBI? Who do you think?" And Slash's considered reply had been, "A big pizza pie in the sky, that's *amore!*"

46

Ecstatically Slash reached for his phone and clicked up the all-Web *New York Times,* but then clacked the phone closed and laughed at himself. They'd never cover it. But sure as hell that's why the files disappeared. Dr. Tyne was doing something unsavory. And he got away with it. And they covered it up. It would be damn interesting to find out who it was exactly who had executed his privilege to shut down those files. And way more interesting to... to... Slash leaned back on the swivel stool and gazed at the spaghetti-splattered window over the stove. Oh, yeah. To screw Hunter Tyne to the wall.

Wolfing down his last Hostess Twinkie and cracking his knuckles like they did in the movies, he clicked into one of those legit watchdog sites, *Government Incendiaries.* Tyne had a thumbnail bio there. They all did. Shortly he was amending Tyne's bio with some new details, recently released – Slash cackled as he typed in the phony citation – by the "Senate Oversight Subcommittee on

Cabinet Nominees." He used his own tag, "Slickwatch." He loved the name. Today he was after Hunter Tyne. But they were all the same. Slick Billy Hellman, Tyne, Satan, Osama bin Laden. Unsavory bastards every one, and Slash Zewinta, real American, psychotic Twinkie-wolfing sanitation engineer from Queens, had their numbers.

Straight people checked the *Government Incendiaries* Web site all the time. And to be fair he couldn't say *Tyne* was implicated in the Cicero trial. He had to say REDACTED was implicated.

More news poured in on the outrageous saga of *Rebellion.com*. Bloggers kept saying a US Congressman was aboard! Maybe kidnapped! Slash's head gurgled with speculation. He tore open the fridge and grabbed his last Dr. Pepper, then flopped in front of his keyboard, and immediately knew he was not getting into the FBI files. "You dirty rat," he said, in his Queens-mangled Edward G. Robinson accent, "you kidnapped my brothah!" Running through his list of hacker-acquaintances, he located a programmer calling himself Dalmatinke, who for an unspecified future interaction could get him today's official Northeast area FBI log for precisely ten minutes.

That would have to do.

In an hour he was staring at a transcript on his screen that nearly stopped his heart. The feds had grabbed a prime suspect, and it sure as hell wasn't Davy Crockett! He was reading about the detaining of Desdemona B. Crockett, 71, African-American female, 5 feet 11, 147 pounds, over in Jersey approximately sixty seconds after Special Agent B. Gessell had staunched the bloodflow from his wrecked septum and found his cell phone. As Slash read the tight legalese, he heard on his radio stream the ecstatic background chanting in the city: "DB Cooper for President!" Slash's favorite cult hero. *How crazy was that?* Within moments, Slash began to feel the pressure stir-frying his frontal lobe. He thought he was about to have a seizure. So much going on at once! He shot a glance at the cork board near his eating table. Immediately his fantasy-laced brain began filling in the missing pieces of history. Molly Bee putting the truth to Hunter Tyne, that was one thing. That was earthshaking. But this! This was unthinkable! This was as crazy as dung beetles.

Desdemona B. Crockett would have been under thirty at the time of the heist. Bold enough to disguise herself as a white man, hijack an airplane, demand $200,000 in small bills, and parachute out somewhere over southwest Washington state. DB Cooper was a rebel, a blight to law enforcement agencies everywhere, scorning everything held sacred in this country – and a folk hero to millions. People love to see the great suckered. Giants reduced to the dimensions of ordinary fools. The police, airline companies, the FBI, an entire battalion of DB Cooper fanatics – nobody could figure out whatever became of DB after the electrifying hijacking, hurting absolutely nobody, on the day before Thanksgiving, 1971.

For Slash Zewinta, the parts came together as easy as the day he glued photos of Billy Hellman on toilet seats all over Queens. On the fridge was a wanted poster of his genuine hero, the man who traveled under the name of Dan Cooper. It was part of Slash's ramshackle décor, like the pot pipe made of Mount Saint Helens ash, and the replica of the sexy leg lamp he and Darin McGavin both found so fetching in *A Christmas Story*. Incredible as it seems, Slash Zewinta's grandfather Mistoslav had been on that plane from Portland, and had later ignited the flames of social upheaval in Slash with the stunning image of DB Cooper leaping out over the Cascades with four parachutes and all that money. Slash, now himself approaching forty, held up beside DB's face the printout of a digital photo he'd just pilfered from an FBI/DIA joint Person-of-Interest file, of Desdemona B. Crockett.

The resemblance was uncanny. The initials were the same. Just add half a century to the high forehead and V-shaped face, create the full lower lip, adjust the height and weight. Maybe tack on a wig and false teeth. Even a sex change, and darkening of skin color. A chill spilled down Slash Zewinta's scoliotic spine. Accolades flowered in his mind, editorial cheers across the nation, a book tour, interviews with the gorgeous hosts of celebrity talk shows. In his hand was the ticket out of his mundane life.

Desdemona B. Crockett and DB Cooper were one and the same.

47

In escape mode at Boeing Field, Victor was working out a difficult but manageable strategy to complete the journey home, involving snowshoes and compasses, heading into the North Cascades and sleeping in national park huts. Edwin looked to be in pretty fair shape. Together, they could handle it. It would take a week but they would only be spotted by cougars, mountain goats, eagles and bears. The hard part was getting out of the lowlands unobserved.

"Here's what I'm thinking," he began. "If we can get some kind of disguises, we could hitch a ride out I-90 to Snoqualmie Pass. They won't be looking for us going east. I know some people might lend us some winter gear. Then we go north through –"

"I have my car," Edwin said.

"Oh. You have your car?"

"Well, sure. Omari's going to give me a ride to SeaTac to get it. You wait here."

Waiting for the Aztek men to finish their shift, Edwin confessed his deception. A month ago he'd paid cash – most of the money he'd saved toward a new chain saw – for a one-way flight to Chicago, and by bus from there to Philadelphia, and a stay at the Y. When the airline clerk asked his name, with a spasm of irony he'd leaned forward and whispered, "Tenacia Friggie." Friggie was the White House counsel whose name he found so delightful. His own name would have been picked out of a computer list somewhere and traced back. But any fool could call himself Tenacia Friggie.

Victor found a port-a-potty in the parking lot, where he could watch for Edwin, freezing but unobserved. Eventually, the battered green Subaru wagon appeared, gushing a plume of blue smoke. Victor flagged him down and leaped into the back seat before Edwin could stop. In minutes they were on the freeway, heading north into rainbow country.

48

Crossing the Rockies always felt barren and eerie for Nel. This time the feeling was closer to anesthetized terror – endless blue and white mountain ranges, the snowy forested landscape along the western edge carpeting her into Salt Lake City not knowing, simply *not knowing* what was about to happen, or where in this frozen land her husband was.

She found Fred Geschwantner first. He had described himself as "bulky, with a coat." In fact he was a big ruddy-faced man with a gray walrus mustache and broad shoulders and that deliberate way of speaking that brings to mind old John Wayne movies, where an ancient cowboy whittling on the porch gives directions to the frantic kid in agonizingly slow detail. His handshake was gigantic and warm. Nel allowed herself to feel some relief for the first time in days.

"Your friend in yet?"

Nel explained she and Molly Bee had never met, but her plane was due immediately, and even as she finished the sentence the flight was announced at the neighboring arrival gate. In a few minutes a youngish woman with short light hair and glasses and stylish wool overcoat approached with a lovely smile, shook hands and said, "Ms. Sligo. I thought that was you." Nel introduced Fred. It was Molly's eyes that were so striking. They were what people call hazel eyes, but just now were of a bright, deep copper tone with a hint of green, and looked at you steadily and without fear or nuance of any kind.

Shortly they were on a freeway getting one another up to speed, and then at a coffee shop on a sunny afternoon. Fred told them they'd better get straight to work.

There was the accident scene, a couple of hours west out of town. Then the vehicle itself, a rental Chevy smashed to smithereens in lockup here in Salt Lake. The Utah Highway Patrol report and the FBI investigation report, which Molly believed she had already seen. And there was Fred Geschwantner's unqualified speculation, based entirely on rumor and political hocus-pocus and Molly Bee's own columns, that suggested foul play was afoot, possibly at a high official level.

"But understand, ladies," Fred said pleasantly enough, "I

know nothing that is admissible. I cannot part with any state evidence and I won't do anything illegal unless it stands in the way of justice." He grinned from one tip of the walrus mustache to the other. "Where shall we start?"

Examining the reports required little relocation. They began in a Mormon-white basement cubicle in the older section of the stone-and-brick Federal Building on South State, where every person they encountered was Fred's oldest and dearest friend and how was retirement treating him? It couldn't be that good if he was back here.

In all essentials the UHP details jibed with the much more elaborate FBI report Fred had requested. The feds, though, had done interviews back in Chicago with Ms. Concetta Ferrari, with a Jerome Tse and Paul Gottschalk, head of the Northern District of Illinois US Attorney's Office. Statements were documented from a hotel south of I-80 where Viola had spent the last night of her life, as well as the car rental clerk and the responding officer at the scene of the accident, and both Utah state investigators, Malisimo and Fauliger, who determined the crime to be a high speed, one-car accident on State Highway 196, known locally as the Skull Valley Road. There was the ME report. High speed blowout, broken neck. There was the FBI detailed analysis. No forced entry, personal belongs intact. Everything fell together in a neat little package. No foul play. One dead Assistant US Attorney. Case closed.

All three sipped coffee for a few minutes. The trapped energy from their combined suspicions of these reports would have powered a small satellite liftoff from the Nevada test site.

Nel broke the silence.

"I am at a loss here. It doesn't ring true stacked against circumstances we're aware of outside this accident. But I don't know where to turn."

Molly poked at the FBI document. "Tell me something. What's a 'detailed analysis?'"

"Ah," Fred grinned. "It's the lower level of investigation. They see a clear-cut situation, ample non-lab evidence, no motive, no suspects, no family, they shortcut the crime scene stuff. It's too expensive and they're overworked like all law enforcement. It's common practice."

"How do we do the higher level investigation?" Nel asked

him. She was rubbing the ring. Too much coffee, not enough sleep. She'd never met Viola Ferrari, and yet there was something so compelling about the woman, the lingering questions, the fear that enveloped Nel when her mind took off into conspiracies and CI's need to control the world.

Tweaking his mustache Fred said, "It has happened before."

In ten minutes they were at the indoor police storage facility looking at the demolished black Chevy. Molly immediately wanted to know where Viola's laptop was stored. Fred's eyes went wide, and he referred to the personal belongings list.

"No laptop, folks," he said, nodding and shaking his head at once, mustache twitching.

A serious, silent Central Lab techie from Forensic Services showed up, snapped on blue poly gloves – reminding Nel she had to get hold of Courtman right away – and plunged into the wreck with strange chemicals and fiber analysis gizmos and aroma-detecting devices and infrared lights. Satisfied, they left the unit and at Fred's suggestion, partly to wait out the lengthy lab investigation, drove ninety minutes out to the scene of the accident, in the snow crusted high desert along the base of a triangle between the Great Salt Lake, Salt Lake City, and Bonneville Salt Flats.

This, Nel figured, was the actual, Wikipedia-certified Middle of Nowhere. The boulder as big as a semi stood forty feet off the road and bore the horrible scrapings of the fatal crash. Again it was Molly who asked the interesting question.

"Why would any sane person be driving down this road? Fred? The Skull Valley Road? I've not heard personally that Viola was using hallucinogenic drugs."

Fred was about to project his guess, when a cell phone jangled. Later none of them would recall Molly's question, coming at that exact moment, as all three reached in their purses and pockets. BJ Lichtenstein was calling Nel on her new silver prepay.

"Jesus," BJ shouted, his tone just below psychotic level. "Guess what? I can't believe it. Hunter Tyne's in this! I just practically witnessed Jerome Tse's suicide, Nel! I've got to get out of here. This inmate down at Greenville, Rocky Mohammad, sent me back up to Oak Park because –"

"Wait! Slow down, BJ!" She was moving toward Fred's Crown Vic, head bent against the chill. She climbed into the car and tried to calm him down. As the others returned, she listened to his incredible findings.

Driving back toward Chicago, BJ had let the DVD play on his laptop. A perfectly composed Jaap Tenkley, thin, federally-induced brush cut, his skin white as a lab coat, had a lot to say about the Secretary of Communications. The gist of it, sleep-deprived BJ sputtered, was that five years ago Tyne's people at CI had engaged Tenkley's lab to do illegal mind-control research and deliver it to some other phony medical research outfit somewhere in Utah. The guy coordinating the whole project was Hunter Tyne. No question about it. Tenkley admitted he was giving a deposition which would never hold up in court in order to screw Tyne.

"And then," BJ nearly screamed, "somebody in D.C. ordered Jerome Tse to send Viola out to Utah to investigate!"

All three were listening on Nel's speaker phone. Now former state investigator Fred Geschwantner smiled broadly.

"Dugway," he said, like a turtle emerging into sunlight, aiming a thick thumb toward the late afternoon sun. "Mainly chem-bio warfare stuff, but also the good Lord only knows what else." Nel told BJ she had the message, and she'd be back in touch with him right away, and to get on a plane for Seattle immediately. Looking back to Fred and the big grin under the wooly mustache, she could not help asking, "How did you know?"

"Well," he drawled self-consciously, "for one thing, Tyne and I live in the same town. There's not a man or woman in law enforcement around here doesn't know Dr. Hunter Tyne makes his peanut butter and jelly sandwiches with no bread. See what I'm saying? Maybe victim of what they call a hostile uterus." This was so humorous Fred snickered into his bulky overcoat. "Now, he did work for CI for many years, here in Salt Lake. Rose through the ranks to run the research division. Along the way rubbed elbows, I gather, with a Nevada Congressman named Billy Hellman. A very strange duck. He keeps a winter place over in Little Cottonwood Canyon, across the valley." Something made him hesitate. He looked at the two utterly charmed women. They did not speak. "I didn't know, for sure. But you'll have to forgive me for a huge indiscretion." He brushed both sides of the mustache. Nel felt like a child at the feet of a master story teller, anticipating further delights. Beside her, Molly was wishing she'd brought her recorder along.

"In honor of you two good people coming, I hired a lady of the night." He was clearly embarrassed. Checked the shine on his black boots. Looked into their astonished eyes and held the suspense half a beat longer. "To meet Dr. Tyne in a couple of hours at her place down South Jordan area. They've done some business."

Molly shook her head. "Why, Fred. I'm shocked," in the same breath that Nel felt a jolt in her chest and she asked, "And the purpose of this tryst is –"

He started the car, spun a u-turn and headed north, working his tongue around his cheeks as if the answer might be there. "I helped prosecute so many B and E jobs I believe I know every trick there is. Didn't dare get any help for this, as you observed back at my old office. People think I'm, well, whatever they think, they don't think I'd ever enter some Cabinet official's residence uninvited to illegally obtain inadmissible evidence when as far as we know no crime has been reported!"

"What are you saying, sir," Nel said. "Just to clarify."

He let out a long breath. If there was a single individual worthy of Fred Geschwantner's breaking his lifetime code of moral decency, it was Hunter Tyne. "There is such a thing," he allowed, "as a delayed search warrant." Then glancing at Nel in the mirror, "I believe we're going to break in to Dr. Tyne's place. Right now. I will take responsibility. Did you bring that flashlight and camera?"

The women blinked at each other, and Nel thought she heard herself say, "Are you out of your mind," and she thought Molly answered, "I hope so," but it was all a kind of a blur, maybe a high-altitude thing, and another phone rang and she thought it was BJ and she was going to tell him she couldn't handle any more, but Fred said, "Yes?" into his phone, clicking on the speaker.

"We have something, Fred," said a voice. "An eyelash. Probably hers. Gonna need a test."

He nodded. "Okay. Inform the Biology Manager we need rush analysis. As a favor." He hung up. "Things are moving faster than I anticipated, my friends. Anybody hungry?"

"Come on, Fred, give," Molly Bee said.

A mile passed at high speed.

"An eyelash is potential DNA-revelatory evidence. We can have it done now at very big citizen's expense unless there's a serial killer on the loose, in which case we have to get in line behind him at the lab. But who knows, maybe our guy is a serial killer. They can put three people on it and I'll lose my pension if... never mind."

"What?" Nel said. "Go ahead. We're already committed."

"Or should be," Ms. Bee noted.

"If Hunter Tyne gets wind that I'm investigating him, guilty or not, warrant or not, my rear end will be hung out to dry in some very public place."

All three shrugged at once. "It's your call," Nel said. And then, "I guess you already called it."

49

They drove not speaking back to Salt Lake, picked up some food, and then down the mountain range to Wasatch Boulevard in the approaching darkness, and finally turned east into a deep, snow-plowed canyon. Cars shot down at them from a day at the ski areas up ahead, but nobody followed them up the canyon. Shortly they turned down a truck road, passed a couple of fancy wrought-iron gates, and pulled up at the third one, and stopped. Fred turned off the lights, considered a moment, and drove the Crown Vic a hundred yards farther, around a slight bend, turned around and parked at the edge of the plowed gravel road. Now he shifted into his commando role, pointing out the barely visible pathway beyond the gate, where the motion detectors were located, and explaining how he was planning to enter the house – the highly recommended elbow-through-the-garage-window technique.

They had to blaze a trail through old snow for a short distance beside the gate. Then they were on Tyne's plowed driveway, darting along a row of cedars, watching for movement inside the fully-lit first floor of the huge house.

No dogs, no sirens, not a sound anywhere. Nel could hear her heartbeat. Her breathing was shallow, and she was sweating and freezing at once. Desperately she followed behind the others, the determined retired cop and the frightened journalist, and finally, miraculously, they were under the eave. A window cracked with a muffled *clink*, and they were inside a cement bunker-type dark four-car garage. In another moment Fred had in his hands a drawing of some sort and a flashlight, and they waited till he fiddled with switches in a breaker box, first putting the first floor in darkness, then instantly back to light, then switching off an alarm system, and they were holding hands and passing through a steel door into the pitch black basement. The women reached for flashlights. Fred's was the police variety, long and black, and he whispered a short prayer as they entered the basement.

"Lord give me strength," he said. "Will you look at this!"

Their lights slashed through a fully furnished office, lush crimson carpeting, paneled walls, bizarre artwork, along with various electronic centers containing phones, computers, a variety of Holotech screens – three of them on separate walls – and what resembled a freak science exhibit, a life-size mannequin complete with see-though skull swirling with fiber optic cabling connecting to a computer and two monitors and a pair of medical display screens, each with a bank of green led lights glowing along the bottom. They moved in different directions. Nel photographed the wired mannequin, and held up for the others to see a TV remote with duct tape across the beam. At the same time Fred was moving everywhere, feeling along walls, sniffing the carpet, picking up a phone and pressing "redial" and writing down a number, dashing to the computer and magically opening Tyne's email and photographing the screen, then clicking on the recycle bin, stuffing the contents of a real trash can into a small plastic bag, popping open drawers and closets. Molly instinctively moved to the artwork with her camera clicking at strange, almost medieval looking paintings, the familiar Masonic drawings, the eyeball over the pyramid and other iconic images she'd half expected; alabaster heads of unfamiliar people of various ethnicities; and over the stairs apparently leading to the first floor, a white canvas flag bearing the red Knights Templar cross, practically a cliché in the witch hunt for New World Order imagery. Centered on the cross was an odd overlapping icon, maybe a tool of some sort, a horseshoe-shaped thing with a bar through the ends of the horseshoe, centered on the flag to give it obvious significance. She stuffed her pocket flashlight in her mouth, clicked a photo, and moved on.

Suddenly she saw Fred waving and dashing across the room toward a window facing the road. As he moved, surprisingly agile for a heavy sixty-five-year-old man, both she and Nel heard it – a switch clicking in the garage. All the lights went off.

"This way," Fred whispered. By now they could hear the sound of the electronic gate opening no more than twenty-five yards away at the road. "Oh, shit," a female voice moaned, and somebody banged into something loudly. *"Don't move!"* Fred whisper-shouted. "He'll have to come through here!"

Half tanked, as he often was in the evening, Dr. Hunter Tyne watched his $14,000 gate close in the mirror of his snow-smeared red '56 Corvette. At the edge of his slightly blurred vision, as the second of the motion-detector spots came on, was a fresh path in the snow alongside his driveway, but it did not register just now. He pushed the other button on the remote and the garage door slid up quietly. As he pulled in he was enjoying the feel of Carolina Delight's warm hand between his legs. She tugged at him and giggled something in a foreign language, and he nearly smashed into the row of garbage cans. The garage door came down as he climbed out of the car, wobbled to the wall – a trim man of medium height – and when he turned to wink at Carolina she winced at the pencil thin black mustache the media loved to mimic. Pressing an intercom button, he called out in high-pitched voice, "Friedmann? Bring a bottle of cognac up, will you?"

"Chocolate!" Carolina said from the other side of the car.

"And see if you can find some chocolate."

A toilet flushed upstairs. Footsteps creaked. Huddled together in the dark, Molly and Nel glanced terrified at each other.

"Come on, sugar pussy," said the Secretary of Communications. Pushing off the Corvette, Carolina did not notice the punched-in window in the door behind her. She hobbled to the steel entry door, then cursed and removed her black heels and pushed it open, reaching easily to her right to switch on the lights. Tyne slipped in behind her, wrapped both arms around her and grabbed her breasts, moaning, never for an instant looking through the room, and followed her up the carpeted stairs and into the house.

Sixteen feet away, crouched behind the computer desk, Fred Geschwantner blinked against the light, but did not move yet. Molly and Nel were actually embracing, immobile as the rifle rack behind them, standing beside a floor lamp in full view of anybody who cared to look.

The light was still on. Friedmann evidently would be coming downstairs. He'd been up there the entire time, and the image pierced into Nel's thundering heart, the houseman bursting in, calling the police, disgrace, horrors, Tyne roaring toward her, ripping a gun off the wall, blowing her legs off, smashing Molly in the face with a rifle butt, it was all too horrific to breathe, and she had to press down into her body with all her strength to stop this madness and collect herself. Feeling the strange tightness beside her, practically within her, she opened her eyes to realize she was gripping Molly like a child with a doll. Immediately she relaxed her grip, and she heard a voice whisper, "It's okay. Let's get out of here." Rising from his desk, Fred pointed two fingers toward the garage door, and they moved quickly but silently into the garage, Fred with a plastic bag stuffed with stolen property hanging out of his heavy coat, and they slithered behind the warm Corvette to the side door they had broken into, when Molly slipped on the fresh snow from the car tracks. She let out an involuntary wail, crashing on her back and head with a soundless thump, but it didn't matter now, instantly a voice called out from upstairs, *"Willa? You back already?"* and they all saw it was life or death. Fred whipped around, his face contorted and wild, and grabbed Molly's upheld arms and yanked her up, looked for a full half-second into her face for signs of trauma, then turned and ripped the door open and ran. The women were right behind him. In fact Nel quickly passed him in the crunching, slippery gravel driveway, Molly right with her, lights suddenly blazing like a prison camp in the freezing night, Molly wailing *"Oh God! Oh God!"* plunging into the path to skirt around the gate, angry voices shattering the night behind them, Friedmann roaring out with a weapon of some kind, screaming into the darkness, and they charged full tilt up the hill to the car and leapt in just as the night lit up with a horrific blast from a shotgun. Molly screamed and plunged into the back on top of Nel as the rear window exploded on their heads. The car jumped to life. Tires spinning, Fred gasping, Friedman coming around the gate aiming the shotgun at the car, and the tires finally grabbed gravel and the car roared off, spinning and shooting snow and gravel as the shotgun fired again, a blinding white light, and they were at the highway and speeding back down the canyon.

Their breath kept fogging the windshield. Wiping with his gloved hand, Fred shuddered with frantic pleasure, yanking the booty in the plastic bag out of his jacket, then stuffing it back in, snickering, looking in the mirror at the women sitting with half traumatized, half ecstatic terror on their faces.

Eventually, sanity returned. At Fred's presentable rambler below the foothills near the University, he slipped the camera chips into his computer and let Molly work out the copying of the illegal photos while he set to making a meal, now wearing the retired man's extra large plaid wool shirt and blue jeans and slippers. Over hot chili and cornbread, they actually had a laugh about the insane escapade, particularly the part about how they could all go to prison if Tyne's perimeter defenses included hidden cameras. Fred wiped his mouth with the linen napkin tucked into his shirt, and noted that all the rich people had fancy devices these days.

After dinner Nel lined up the readable photos and the stolen trash, and sat back trying to grasp what it all meant. Fred scanned the contraband, fiddling with his mustache.

"My general sense, said the great detective, is that we just flew over what the department calls a 'cuckoo's nest.' That is to say, Dr. Tyne is not only a politician, no offense Ms. Sligo, but he's a nut job of the first order. We'll never know what half of this stuff means, and if we ever do find out it'll be from studies at the state loony institution. I will say we made a heck of a haul, but the truth is," in that slow-motion drawl that he had dropped into granny low here in his home, "there's everything here but evidence."

"But we nearly died getting it," Nel protested. "What do you mean, no evidence?"

"I mean admissible in a court of law, ma'am. For one thing, it's all stolen property. For another, we're interested in motive, means and opportunity relating to an incident the FBI has deemed an accident, and none of this points that way. And thirdly, we have nothing here linking Dr. Tyne to anything resembling a matter of interest, past or present, to the state of Utah or to the United States government." He fell back, out of breath.

Molly interjected her thinking from left field. She was profoundly exhausted from the long day, the intensity, the horrific flight from a shotgun-wielding Friedman. All she could think to say was, "Isn't it weird none of us had laid eyes on each other before today! And here we are, thick as thieves, going after one of the most nefarious bad guys in the country! As my mother would say, good gravy Marie!"

"Yes," Nel said, "and right smack in the thick of a government cover-up of Viola's murder! And the cover-up of whatever it was she was investigating!"

Beside her Molly sipped tea and added warily, "And it would appear to involve a member of Cabinet as well as the most powerful conglomerate on Earth."

The big man fumbled through photos and pressed down crumpled pieces of paper and shuffled the numbers he had written on his notepad. He said, "Your man in Chicago. He has a deposition implicating our friend here, essentially hearsay, non-evidentiary but not exculpatory either, and it has to do with Dugway. Let's not forget that. In addition –" He pulled at his lower lip. "That red cross wall hanging, it means something or it wouldn't be hanging there. Maybe a family coat of arms. The crazy science exhibit, anybody can have one of those. I've been in barber shops that look like that. These email addresses and phone numbers will have to wait until morning, but they could easily be nothing, and a man as intelligent as Dr. Tyne wants us to think he is would leave nothing around the house the likes of retired cops and syndicated columnists and Congressional wives would bother with. True?"

Molly shot a look at the retired cop. "Tyne was supposed to be out! What was that, Fred? Geez!"

"I, uh, well, the woman was told... He came home early."

"You're forgiven."

"I'm going to call that phone number you found," Nel announced. She had to do something. She had to get home. She needed a bath, and had no place to sleep, and had to call Courtman, and her husband was missing and a camera may have recorded her breaking into Hunter Tyne's residence. She was picking at her cashmere sweater, and she was having a hot flash. She was coming apart.

Still embarrassed, Fred hedged. "Well... there were two numbers. This almost illegible one was in the trash, and that other one the last call made from that phone." Nel snatched the twelve-digit number Fred had copied, studied it for a while, and found her phone and vigorously punched in the numbers, and waited, then pressed the speaker phone and they all listened to a recording in what they presumed to be Arabic. Nel said a very foul thing.

"I have a couple of spare rooms," Fred said gently, now mixing in the grandfatherly inflection with the country boy drawl. "Plenty of fresh bedding, pillows, everything you need. You ladies need some rest. I am such a lousy host since Shirley died. Well, that's a petty excuse." He grinned sadly. "It's been four years. Just the grandkids come."

Calls were made to airlines, to Molly's neighbor on Nel's safe phone to see to her dog, to Courtman to have him arrange transportation for Nel from SeaTac and to find BJ and get the staff to her home tomorrow evening, to the forensics lab to check on progress, to the local police in Sandy at the mouth of Little Cottonwood Canyon to confirm Fred's suspicion that nobody had reported a break-in, to a trusted colleague of Fred's at the FBI – over Nel's vehement protest – to check on the status of Congressman Sligo's disappearance. Finally Molly insisted on calling a local rock station to learn what the news guy knew about this DB Cooper business that was all over Fred's car radio. A man who called himself "The Marshal" explained that DB Cooper had been spotted in seventeen locations around the country this afternoon, he was running for President, and he was being sought for shoplifting and fleeing the scene at a Kwalmart in Beckley, West Virginia.

Part Two – The Evidence

50

It was after midnight when they peeled off I-5 in Mount Vernon, Washington. Wired to the stop sign at the end of the off-ramp was a poster. Before the Subaru had stopped, Victor recognized himself. They only looked for a moment. "Abducted Jan 15th," the poster blared in squat black letters. "$1,000,000 reward. Please call the FBI immediately." They didn't bother to listen to the voice-print disk below the poster. No doubt it would be Edwin's voice, the frantic recording with Toon on the Cessna radio.

Following a winding drive up Highway 9, Edwin stopped in the middle of a tight, pitch black S-turn in the two-lane road. Railroad tracks crossed just in front of them. Edwin sat for a full minute, still as a corpse.

"Flatcars," he whispered.

They pushed on, and shortly turned onto a narrow country lane. Only the road itself was visible in the mist and darkness, although Edwin had to brake for a beaver struggling to cross the road with an unwieldy branch. "River's over there," Edwin noted sleepily. Down a gravel driveway, and finally they stopped. Instantly a huge brown dog emerged, clamoring for attention, trying to jump in the car.

"This way," was all he said. He dug out his backpack and started into the darkness behind the dog. Victor walked tentatively along after. It was so dark he could scarcely imagine there was any life anywhere. Then came footsteps on wooden stairs, a door opened, a light flicked on. They were on the front porch of an old log house.

"Welcome to the stump ranch," Edwin Foulks said.

The Congressman entered through homemade Dutch doors

with ornamental black barn hinges, into a country kitchen. Another light came on.

"I have to sleep," Edwin said. "We'll get started whenever we wake up. I'll show you your room."

His conversation had changed. He spoke now like a man living alone in the wilderness, short on words, speaking in simple gestures, although Victor had a thousand questions, primary among which was, where the hell are we?

Up a split log stairway, Edwin said, "Only the one bathroom," pointing to a door. "Or the outhouse." He directed Victor into a small wood-floored room that contained a double bed, a worn dresser, and big windows with no curtains. He clicked on a lamp.

There was a momentary embarrassment. Edwin ran a hand through his hair, looked around. "All right," he said. And turned and shut the door.

Seconds after Victor hit the pillow it was morning. He got up and limped to the bank of windows. His legs had stiffened up over the long flight yesterday. He needed some exercise. Light drifted through a curtain of mist across a forested valley. In the middle distance a mountain loomed much higher than he might have imagined on the night ride, the entire ridge silvered by a smear of January sunlight behind it. Brown rectangles along the shoulders of the mountain told of loggers at work. With some effort he opened the wood frame window, and immediately heard the rush of the nearby river. Cold air flushed into his lungs, and the lush smell of forest came with it, wet cedar and peat and rotting leaves. Above the flow of the river, silence shimmered down the forest.

My God, he thought. I've died and gone to Van Zandt.

He smelled coffee. Something sizzled in a frying pan. Shortly he got himself downstairs, through a rectangular log cabin living room complete with a large home-built wood stove already fired up, many books both shelved and scattered, and hand-fashioned furniture. Humming atonally, Edwin was working on potatoes and eggs and toast in the kitchen.

"Sorry, no bacon," he greeted the Congressman. "Found half a cantaloupe though, and a mess of mushrooms and stuff for the eggs. Hungry?"

"Man, I'm famished. And I really need a shower."

Edwin threw a towel at him and pointed upstairs. "Get any sleep?"

"Oh, yeah. Slept like a Newfie – no dreams! But I need clothes." Wincing down at the red coveralls.

"Check that closet just in the main room. My cousin's stuff's in there. He's in Colorado."

He found checked flannel work shirts and folded, faded blue jeans. He showered and returned to the kitchen looking like he'd lived there all his life.

"Better," Edwin said. Once again they were dressed alike. Over breakfast Edwin told the history of the homestead. His great-grandparents had migrated from Oregon into virgin forest when a company was hiring workers for a logging railroad that followed along the river. It was after the First World War. Edwin's grandfather and then his father stayed on the land. His father married a British Columbia woman, Edwin's mother. They had five children. Edwin was the oldest.

He stopped speaking abruptly and tended the stove.

Victor was distracted by a rooster urgently crowing. He saw a vegetable garden settled in for winter, a full woodshed and what looked like a shop building, also made of logs and shake roof.

Beneath the placid exterior, both men were aware of a mildly feverish undercurrent – they were fugitives. The country was in an uproar because of the havoc they'd created. There was a pressing need to act. But in this place there was no sign of political oppression. CBC radio, the only station Edwin could receive here between mountain ranges, noted that the United States electorate had once again hit the nail with its head, preparing for the second Inauguration of Burligame and Hellman by creating a cacophony of Biblical proportions in the streets, compliments of a single disgruntled pilot dressed in frontier clothing, snatching up a US Congressman as if collecting bodies to reinvent civilization on a deserted island, the *Lord of the Flies* returned to haunt the millions who didn't bother to vote. Today in Parliament, discussion continued on whether to close the borders, on speculation that the fear and loathing spreading through the United States might spill into Canada.

51

Shortly they toured the homestead. Both wore knee-high rubber boots and mismatching rain gear. Everything they touched was wet or rotting. Winter finches flitted about, indignant over the invasion of their feeding routes. The eagle migration had started late. When Edwin was a kid, he said, it got colder in Alaska earlier, and the bald eagles were fishing here on the Seyes River before Thanksgiving. Once his sister had counted eleven eagles in a single alder hanging over the river. He spoke with old familiarity about specific trees, deadfalls eight feet through, blackberry patches twice Victor's height and dense as wool, and a patchwork of ferns, shrubs, lichens, ground covers and mosses that completely obscured the forest floor. He talked about early winter floods and summer births and wells running dry every September, and spring so beautiful it made a grown man weep.

Wandering beside him, Victor's mind was on treason, the gas chamber, the thousand ways they could be traced to this spot. He'd have to get to Courtman immediately to get him out of this mudhole. Meanwhile Mgaba'd have to circle the wagons, devise a scenario that put Victor in the rescuer's role with the crackpot pilot of the Cessna, and he'd have to get Lichtenstein back to D.C. as his mouthpiece with Riske in case this popgun rebellion by Edwin Foulks turned into anything. But Nel would have thought of all this. She was his anchor to windward.

They struggled through elderberry and vine maple toward an enormous standing Douglas fir half a mile off the road while Edwin narrated the local history.

"Most of this undergrowth wasn't here two hundred years ago. Mostly the local tribes didn't care to fall the big timber, or couldn't, but when the whites came around 1830 or '40, their eyes must have bulged seeing the dollars standing on these mountains. By 1940 most of the accessible old growth was already harvested. Even before then a new species had arrived, the *state forester.* Their mandate was to protect Washington's economy. They managed to figure out how to get the rest of the old growth timber to market, thereby destroying the ecological balance, eroding drainages and devastating the entire northwest ecosystem. All of a sudden the sun hit the earth. The sun had probably not touched the ground in thousands of years in some places. So all these new species came along. What's down there now, right under our feet, might be a million varieties of insects and herbs and worms and God knows what. We could be walking on the cure for every known disease!"

Congressman Sligo was in fact feeling diminished by the sheer numbing beauty of the quasi-rainforest. But he had heard all this back in the state legislature, and his thoughts were elsewhere.

"Foulks?"

Edwin stopped and studied the great fir, immense and stirring, occupying half the sky.

"What are we doing here?"

"I'll show you."

It rained off and on, mist, then drizzle, then a sort of indecisive moisture-laden heaviness that pushed the body down. At the base of the big tree, that looked to measure twelve feet in diameter, a shaft of sunlight stabbed unexpectedly through the canopy of branches. "All five of us kids plus our parents could stand around the tree touching fingertips and just make it around. When they logged this area there was no wagon big enough to haul this tree away. So they left it standing. Now it's ninety years older!"

The rough outer bark layer wove ten inches into the trunk. Two hundred fifty feet up it branched out, branches the size of ordinary trees, and just above there it ended. Struck by lightning.

Victor was breathing in the forest.

"Look what you started," Victor said suddenly. "A frigging one-man revolution!" He was half-delirious, trying to be angry at Foulks and overcome with the thousand odors and sounds of the forest, and reduced to a mere human before this tree. He studied the gnarled immensity of the trunk. The scent penetrated clear to his core, and he felt nauseated and ecstatic at once. "There's a lot of angry people out there." He couldn't stop his mind from sputtering. He barely knew this man. He didn't know where he was, he was pissed off, and he hadn't felt so good in years.

52

He leaned back to gaze high into the forest, feeling like an ape being filmed for *Animal Planet*. This enormous genetic freak of a tree was doing it. The tree controlled everything. What was happening to the country did not interest the tree. The tree was here when the Vikings discovered Newfoundland. It would be here after fifty governments had collapsed under their own egotistical wallowing. He felt the forest sizzling in his blood. He could not stop inhaling, leaning back, filling his lungs till he nearly passed out.

"My wife should be home by now," he heard a voice say.

"Yeah, hope so," Edwin said.

A spit of drizzle began, and they slipped their yellow hoods up. With the back of his rain slicker pressed against the tree, Edwin sank down to the great roots, lumpy and twisting, the size of ordinary tree trunks. Victor slid down beside him. Boys in the woods on a rainy day.

Both their heads lay on the enormous exposed roots of the tree. Victor watched the current from his lungs cut a channel in the air. He could not remember feeling so clear about nothing at all. Maybe it was the hypnotic frolic of the river, bearing a thousand minerals and beaver fever. Or the tree, punching through remote wildness into heaven, making him feel like an ant at a giant's bootheels.

"I want to know something, Foulks. You keep – I don't know – *charming* people. The crowd at Independence Hall. That cop in Pennsylvania. Spangloss. Some trick you do. You break people down. You did it to me on that plane, but I was too numb to pay attention. Now what is that?"

Edwin felt the tree beside him. Electricity surged into him from the pungent bark. Everything was so obvious.

"Feel it." Victor rolled his eyes but indulged him and put a big palm on the tree. Instantly his hand jumped away, as Edwin knew it would. He grabbed Victor's wrist, and forced his hand against the massive trunk.

"Ung!" He bit his tongue, and he felt fire pulsing through his fingers, all the way to his shoulder. It felt like plunging a freezing hand into hot water.

"See, I connect to something in people. Accidentally. Don't

know how it works. That cop? What was his name?"

"Nesbitt." He winced. His eyes watered. "Let go of me, goddammit."

"Yeah, Trooper Nesbitt. Good man. Somehow I tapped into his information about the FBI. I don't know how. I look at the man and feel this, this – something like the energy you're drawing out of this tree. I feel it on my face, and we sort of breath in and out of each other, and the man tells me the truth."

Yanking his hand away, Victor pressed it against the wet earth, but made no attempt to understand. "Up in that plane. I never talk the truth about politics because *stop doing that!*" Edwin smiled, and immediately Victor felt the warmth creep into his face, and it made him angrier. "I knew you were playing some trick on me in that plane. Don't be fooling with my head. You hear me?"

"Hey, your job is to get re-elected. Everybody knows that."

"But nobody ever says it out loud. You hauled it out of me like pulling a sliver out of your finger. Next time you –"

Raindrops came squalling down, and they stood and moved to the north side of the tree.

"Here's what has to happen," Edwin told him.

"Wait a minute. I don't care for the way you –"

"Let me finish." He looked up in Victor's scowling face and smiled. "Here's what I need you to do. Get the President and the Vice President together in the same place. Then fix it so that I can talk to them. And all this has to happen in front of a national TV audience."

Victor laughed, louder than was necessary. "You've been living out in the woods way too long, sonny."

"Congressman, this is what I've been dreaming of for years! I've tested it hundreds of times. If it works, maybe something will change. Or at least maybe we can get to understand what in blazes is going on with those thugs running this country."

"Understand what? You know what they want. They want to control the world. There's no mystery, Foulks! It wouldn't surprise me if they *loved* twelve percent unemployment, poor people everywhere, nobody voting!" Thinking, this flying country boy is trying to get us both killed! "And here you are, an elf in a damn rain forest with that silly slicker on, trying to tell me *you're* going to fix it?" He tore a handful of wet moss from the tree, and heaved it to the ground. "A master of the vanishing art of *raising stumps?*" He was staring down at his hand, watching the blotch of pink spread. That thing was zinging up his forearm, and his hand was burning. He said, "I jeopardized my career for a deluded nincompoop!"

"Wrong! You jeopardized your career to get to the truth! You know what the people are asking! What is wrong with those gutless fools in Congress, letting this go on? How could you not know how these criminals keep getting elected? You're too busy being a politician to notice!"

Through clenched teeth Victor snarled, "I voted, Foulks! That's how the program works! You don't vote, the other guy wins!" He wanted to strangle him. But he was feeling weird and vulnerable. The kid was seriously getting to him.

"My point exactly," Edwin yelled back. "It's the Progressives who aren't voting! Don't you get it? Something is terribly wrong with the system!"

"You really think a sign behind an airplane is going to change anything?"

Edwin's patience was diminishing fast. "We have nothing left to lose."

"You have nothing to lose! You dim-witted country bumpkin! Who cares if they confiscate your outhouse! I've got fourteen years in the House of Representatives! I have fought these people in the alleys and on the beaches! I'm damned if I'm going to turn my life over to some jackass forest shaman trying to take on Billy Hellman with moss and blackberry vines and a fucking Christmas tree on Viagra!"

Edwin jumped to his feet. "Nothing will penetrate your steel self-image, will it? You're caught up in the same lies the government's always spewing! You're too important! You're in lockstep with the rest of them." He stood close, the storm-gray eyes right in Victor's face. "You're just occupying a seat in Congress, pushed around at the whim of the people who actually run the country!"

Victor roared and shoved Edwin hard, swinging his fists with blinding speed into the empty air, missing intentionally to avoid knocking Edwin down, aware even in his boiling anger he could not possibly hurt this man. At the same instant Edwin dodged along the tree, and Victor slipped on a huge slick root and pitched forward, and his head smashed against the enormous trunk. His face

jammed against a profundity of bark, moss and mites. The staggering history of the great tree rushed into his nostrils like a snapped
ammonia capsule. All in a split second he saw Indian burial rites,
salmon drying, Spanish explorers, slaves, bulldozers. He gasped and
collapsed, sucking air through his mouth like a drowning man, his
nostrils on fire, and he felt the fire sear into his chest cavity, and
then he heard Edwin Foulks standing over him chuckling.

"Like sucking a big shot of salt water up your nose, huh?"

For a while he lay holding his face. Fireflies exploded at the
extremes of his vision. Finally he muttered, "Christ! What was
that?"

"A thousand years of human history just went straight into
your brain. Eagles' nests, bear scat, totem poles and Forest Service
Agent Orange mingled with all the misery, the disease, the booze
and the depravity white people brought to these shores. And before
that —"

"I get it, I get it," Victor said, rolling over and collapsing
against the trunk. "Shut up, will you?"

At that moment, in the old log house five hundred yards
away, the mobile Code Thirteen in Victor's wallet began vibrating.

All right, the kid had some kind of bizarre innate ability,
mocking Victor's long apprenticeship in the hard-core tribunals of
political power. But no avenue in Victor Sligo's thinking would take
him where Edwin wanted him to go, and all this had infuriated him.
Now he was on the ground, felled by a fir tree.

Exaggerating each word, Edwin said, "Fix it so I can talk to
them. In public, on television. Both of them. You know we can't
continue like this. Doing nothing. That is unacceptable!"

For a few seconds Victor had to stay down and pull himself
together. Edwin sat beside him. Victor found himself muttering,
"I'll tell you, kid. You're like a biker doing the Tour de France with
only one gear. How the hell are you going to get up the Pyrenees?
You can't! You might have some parlor tricks up your sleeve. You
woke a lot of people up with that airplane ride. But you're taking on
an enemy you can't defeat! Period! Not to mention Burligame and
Hellman are never allowed in public together! And no law enforcement outfit in the country will let you within fifty miles of them!
There's no way, man. Forget it!"

They were silent for a few moments. Victor looked at

Edwin in profile, the soft beard, the mesmerizing silver-gray eyes, the easy smile. Something made him recall his first sight of Nel on their wedding day, so splendid and perfect. Like a terrifying angel, bringing him life and chaining him to it at the same instant.

"These people are all professional liars. You can't run a country by telling the truth! It's probably never been tried!"

"Well, sure, I –"

"You lie, you dither with the facts, you convince people black is white. The better you are at it, the farther up the power ladder you go."

"Scum rising to the top. Like a septic tank."

Looking back up the tree, Victor said, "So you hauled me out here to tell me this? I'm supposed to get Burligame and Hellman together so you can – what? Beat them with poison ivy till they agree to find everybody a job?"

"They're going to reveal their secrets." He took a few steps, and pointed back toward the road. "Just like you did. And Trooper Nesbitt."

"You're talking about a sting operation. You want to sting the President of the United States!"

"The Vice President's the man I want."

"Of course you realize they're never together in public?" Ducking under a curling vine maple.

"Yes, that's a problem. After election night, there's only one event every four years when they're together in public."

"Yeah?"

"Yeah, and it's coming in five days." He turned to face Victor, and flicked his palms out at him. "The Inauguration!"

Victor caught his breath. "Well, it is, but –" He thought a moment. "Even if in my wildest dreams I thought this could happen, what I want to know is, what is the sting about? What are you going to catch them doing?"

Edwin started down the path. "Billy Hellman is looking for me." He stopped. "I believe he's going to catch me, right on the steps of the Capitol."

"Foulks, you're out of your mind," Victor told him.

"So was John the Baptist. Another weirdo with a radical message."

"Yeah, and look what they did to him!"

53

Insanity always greets public figures at airports. It never fails.

As she came exhausted into the SeaTac terminal, Nel looked desperately for Courtman, or somebody, to get her out of here before she was recognized.

Dazed and only half in her body, she tried to steel herself for the well-wishers, the fanatics, and the Angry Mob. Descending an escalator to the baggage pickup, she was suddenly at the center of a storm, people pointing at her and applauding and screaming, and almost immediately a fight taking place right beside her. Somebody was clubbing somebody on the head with a sign reading "God is love!" She moved frantically aside, straight into the arms of Sloan Mgaba.

"Hello," he yelled exuberantly, with his classic dark smile. "Come on! Courtman's got your bag!"

Obviously somebody had arranged a rally for Victor. Signs and balloons came from nowhere, and a young woman holding a microphone began to chant "Sli-go! Crock-ett! Sli-go! Crock-ett!" The enormous baggage area was a swelling bellow of humanity. Security people were yelling into phones, even as the woman with the mike shouted, "Let's bring the Congressman in with a true Seattle welcome, folks!" and suddenly buff-clad Army troops swarmed her, three men clamping her into a luggage cart while a dozen more surrounded them, facing out, arms linked. Mgaba had moved behind Nel, and was yelling words she couldn't hear, trying to direct her to a side door. She found Courtman ahead with her big wheeled suitcase, his face like an angry lion, and she rushed toward him just as he turned away. Why hadn't they prepared for this? A new chant arose from a single sign-bearer. "DB Cooper for President!" Using his great bulk, Mgaba was pushing people aside, at the same moment holding up a phone and yelling numbers into it. The mob had surged toward the soldiers, but a small cadre of police, in full riot gear, shields and helmets and ricin spray, burst forth from nowhere and forced the crowd to retreat. In the ensuing fumble, Nel managed to catch Courtman's intent as he struggled toward an unmarked door. She rushed toward it, even as more security people came storming down the wide concourse and plunged into the crowd.

Mgaba slammed the door behind them. Courtman stood breathing heavily. They were in a short hallway with doors on both sides. "I know this place," Mgaba whispered hoarsely. "Two years in PR down here. I remember everything! This way!" He darted to one of the doors and banged on it, yelled into his cell phone again, and instantly it opened and they rushed through. An airport official, coffee spilled down his white shirt, hurried them through a small office to a stairway, and all four of them raced upstairs, Mgaba now hauling Nel's suitcase down a corridor with huge windows giving out onto the tarmac, and from there to yet another hall, another slammed door, and they stopped.

"Ms. Sligo." The official, breathing hard and buttoning a black suit bearing a nametag in English and Chinese, came to her and offered his hand. "Antonio Perez, ma'am. I'm terribly sorry about this." He was out of breath, devastated by the turn of events. "In your position, I'm sure you will –"

"Get us out of here," Nel fumed.

Perez and Mgaba spoke hastily in Spanish. A detail was available for such a crisis, largely to defuse potential lawsuits rising from the transportation of dignitaries, athletes and movie stars. They were rushed to the "Star Bucket," a golf cart disguised to resemble a mobile coffee bar, and they zoomed through corridors, down a construction elevator, then across the terminal bridge to the big parking garage and Courtman's white Cadillac. Shortly they were speeding north toward the Canadian border. The entire escape had taken less than seven minutes.

54

The moment they pulled up to the curved driveway on the cliff overlooking the Strait of Georgia, Nel ordered Mgaba to check the house and gardens for wire devices. She stormed down the block to threaten the two disguised FBI agents tinkering with a Holotech signal-intercept box, then ripped up half a dozen nasty notes stuck on the door from wealthy neighbors. Inside, she deleted another two dozen messages on Victor's Web site. All three were distressed, confused, and feared for Victor's life, or his career – which meant all of their careers. Nel was approaching a nervous breakdown. She could only listen to Courtman's grumbling for so long, and finally she sent him home, insisting he contact her immediately if there was news. BJ had left a message that he was at home recovering. Mgaba had continued to press her about using the Code Thirteen to contact Victor, but she was tortured by indecision and angrily refused. Maybe the government was about to fall. Who knew? People in the airport and on the streets clearly showed the rebellion was spreading fast, and seemed to think Victor was directing the operation.

But the reality was, she did not know if he was alive, or in prison, or disappeared. She was too traumatized to let herself feel anything. When Merlin returned from his morning B12 injection, she told him to leave her alone.

Anxious and sick, she called her mother, part of her thinking Victor might be in hiding there. Pearl Diamond had been switching between I-Media and public television for forty-eight hours, and had learned nothing. She'd have to go off island to see about her new dentures. They weren't fitting right.

The kids were worried but okay. There was nobody else to call. She fixed a pot of tea and stared out at the chill gray sky, deeply conscious of the terror her husband might be going through. She felt anguished. Uncontrollable fears crackled through her mind, life insurance, the will they'd never bothered to secure, her two boys, Ken a graphic artist and Kit a contractor, piling guilt on her for letting Victor start this in the first place, and her daughters Jess and Shani launching a civil suit against Hellman for attempted murder of an elected official.

Stop it! She tossed the tea in a fern pot.

In the exercise room she slipped into sweats and stepped on her virtual reality martial arts trainer. Terrorists rushed at her with scimitars and laser pistols, but she could not get up the strength to resist. They rushed right through her. Finally, a hot bath. Slowly, fragments of her personal nightmare began to form into a somewhat coherent series of events. She needed the rest of BJ's report from Chicago. She needed Fred Geschwantner's separate findings from Tyne's house. What she did have was a copy of the screen photo Fred had taken of Tyne's email page. Fred had isolated a complex code number for an incoming message. He'd insisted she get it back to his NSA contact, Bert O'Donnell. Intuitively, Nel believed

Hunter Tyne had arranged Viola Ferrari's death and would never pay for it. It had been four months. As Fred had observed more than once, there was no smoking gun. Tyne was too powerful and too smart to leave any loose ends.

She would have to keep going. And she had to find her husband. She had no way of knowing he was forty miles away, trying to communicate with her.

55

Shaking it all off, she got dressed, snatched up the yellow phone Raven Menez had given her, and called her office in Bellingham in case there was news. Then the Rayburn building in D.C. Nothing on her voice mail. It was not hard to conclude her home landline was tapped, probably by the old NSA technique of forcing a micro-receiver electronically through her curbside energy monitor. O'Donnell came to mind. He was in the thick of this. There was a phone card. Something about using a public phone.

The Land Rover would have been tapped with a GPS locator. Without a second thought she grabbed a scarf and her father's prize hand-carved cane, and walked rapidly, feeling intensely self-conscious, to the suburban transit bus stop several blocks from the house. The sound of her heels made her wonder where the blond woman could possibly be now. Maybe in a submarine, slipping down the Potomac to blow up the White House with a bomb planted in an anatomically-correct Billy Hellman doll.

The lady bus driver was Inuit. She grumbled half-heartedly about having to work on her day off, since the regular driver had called in sick. She was dark and heavy and talkative, but Nel, sitting opposite her, could not summon the energy to fake interest in the driver's life struggles at the moment.

Shortly they whooshed into an intensely-lit shopping mall. Nel's hand shook as she entered a Web lounge in the food court, where people milled by the thousands, all of them, it seemed, studying her. She found a free phone, inserted the card, and heard the phone ring twice at the other end. She hung up.

Now what?

Twenty seconds later, the phone rang. "Will you hold a moment please?" a voice said. She waited. There was soft buzzing, a click. A different voice said, "Please call this number." She wrote it down, and pressed in the number.

"Ms. Sligo. Bert O'Donnell." It was unquestionably the NSA man's voice. "Have you got him?"

Her heart collapsed. "No, I – what have you heard?"

"Nothing. I'm sorry." His voice was kind, but failed to hide an undertone of resentment. "We're getting our ass kicked in this office. People bailing left and right, calling in sick, quitting. The damn Federal Employees' Union is planning an illegal strike at the end of the week." He cleared his throat. "There is news, however…" Pause. "Need to know only." Pause. "I must tell you, Ms. Sligo, the Vice President is planning to institute martial law unless Crockett comes forward. Hellman and the National Security Council meet tomorrow to discuss this."

"But what does that –"

"Essentially, it opens the door for active rebellion. A real fear-monger might predict worldwide economic disaster. This is deadly serious, Ms. Sligo. Rebellion paranoia has crippled Washington. So they're going for martial law. Do you understand what I'm telling you? This entire charade by Crockett has *backfired!*" O'Donnell's stern voice had become nearly frantic. "This may be the trigger they've been waiting for."

"I'm listening."

"Ms. Sligo. I have devoted my life to serving my country, and the turn it has taken in recent years has… has… " It was a tortured lament for the America that was, or could have been. "Who would have thought one freak in a coonskin cap would bring it all down?"

Nel's blood rushed, and she slapped the side of the phone. "Mr. O'Donnell. Where is my husband?"

She heard a rattled sigh. "I wish I knew. When you see him," he said miserably, "tell him to get Crockett to come in."

She had to pull herself together. People would recognize her any moment.

"All right. Listen. Two things. A man named Jaap Tenkley got out of prison just before Viola Ferrari was killed. He went to see her in Chicago. Then he disappeared. He left a deposition –" She

was suddenly terrified she was talking to the enemy. A horrible image loomed upon her, Victor gagged, duct-taped to a chair sitting
beside O'Donnell at this moment.

No! she thought. *Too many movies.* But her breath was
locked in her chest. She worked the ring on her finger until her
breathing returned.

"He recorded a deposition about... a member of Cabinet.
Connecting him to mind-control research. I haven't seen it yet, but I
expect to."

A moment passed. "The other thing?"

"Your friend Fred gave me some information for you."

"Are you on a public phone," O'Donnell said immediately.

"Yes." She lowered her voice. "A code number. I have no
idea what it means." She read it off: three numbers, four letters, nine
numbers, the percent sign.

"Where did he get this?"

"Incoming message on that person's private email, that man
Fred is interested in. The same man –"

Nobody spoke for a few seconds.

"Well. That is a coincidence," O'Donnell said. "Nobody
can access the files about all this. But I did run across an attorney at
the Chicago office who was a friend of Ms. Ferrari's. We spoke off
the record. He recalled that some years ago Ms. Ferrari helped
prosecute a case involving the phone company that had to do with
touchscreen monitors. The kind they used to use in the voting
booth."

Nel wrote a note.

"That man ran the research division. And he got his wrist
slapped."

"Okay," she said. "I've got to go." She remembered what
she needed from him. "Have you ever heard of a device called the
Code Thirteen?"

"Code Thirteen. No. What is it?"

"A communications device."

He paused. "I can tell you, any satellite signal has to pass
through the NSA network. We use the same technology urban terrorists use to intercept it, or the Chinese government, or a physics
student with access to high frequency signal capture. All you need is
the right frequency and the right codes."

It sounded like bullshit to Nel. He'd never heard of it.

Closing her eyes, she surprised herself by saying, "I'm trying to trust you, Mr. O'Donnell."

Without hesitating he said, "That man your husband took off with. I know his real name."

Suddenly she felt overcome with exhaustion and fear and not knowing. The not-knowing was the worst of it. Forces in government on high alert to crush any reactionary activity on the street. She was torn between her growing desperation to find her husband, and the horror that federal agents could locate him if she did something stupid. He could wind up charged with treason, be subjected to any kind of horrendous miscarriage of justice, kidnapped, beaten... or the unthinkable. But there was no other way. If he was alive, he would answer.

56

O'Donnell was feeling the vice squeezing.

The entire Executive Branch was roiling in a bloody mess.

The so-called rebellion was already a disaster on multiple fronts. The way O'Donnell saw it was, the odds of success were equal to the likelihood that the Imperial Japanese Navy could cross the Pacific ocean undetected and destroy the American fleet at Pearl Harbor. The odds were formidably against it, but it could happen. And vastly more likely, it could fail.

The fact that Sligo had not communicated with his wife meant one of two things: he was on course to foment a true insurrection against the government, or he was dead. A couple of nights of tearing his hair out had left O'Donnell in pain, torn between hope and fear that it might actually take place. He'd wrestled with the complex code number Nel had given him from what she said was Tyne's private email. He had finally identified the sequence as a cabinet-level classified communications number assigned by the White House Communications Agency. No red flag there. Tyne was a Cabinet member. He would communicate with the President using the coded system.

The clear possibility of failure caused the NSA man to meet

with FBI Deputy Director John Lee Davis in the middle of the night on a D.C. subway. A matter of paying a debt to a friend. In his position as chief electronic snoop, he knew everything everybody else in government said they knew. Especially the FBI.

Fresh graffiti sprawled across the Metro entrance, proclaiming DB Cooper the next President. Local National Guardsmen had been awakened and hauled downtown to patrol the streets in urban battle dress, armed with crowd-control gear, rubber bullets, ricin spray and mind Tasers, randomly stopping people on the street, violating their rights, checking papers and asking rude questions. *West Coast Paper* bundles disappeared within half an hour. Late crowds stood in the doorways of bars and internet lounges, people yelling at one another about Davy Crockett and Hellman and the terrorist-vigilantes on the streets, and the airborne pathogen crisis that still pissed off a lot of people and many found deeply suspicious. Others spouted slogans supporting corporate citizenship. A strong market economy meant a strong America. The happiest sight in industry is a long line of men at the gate.

Both Davis and O'Donnell were dressed in casual clothing and sunglasses when they met on the Metro near midnight, broad-shouldered O'Donnell with a fishing hat over his sandy hair, and six-and-a-half foot Davis with a hood up, the long graying braid tucked into his sweatshirt. They looked like late night bums sitting on the Metro as it squealed under Chinatown. A couple of bored Guardsmen passed in front of them. John Lee Davis peered over his dark glasses past O'Donnell, down the aisle of the subway.

"What have you got?"

"I need you to know, Hunter Tyne is being squeezed. They're circumventing the Bureau," O'Donnell said quietly. "Soon as this present mess is cleaned up, his ass is going to be in a bucket. Stay away from it."

Davis squinted down the aisle, nodding, brain synapses clicking down to the matter. Not moving his lips O'Donnell went on, telling Nel Sligo's news about Jaap Tenkley and his own hasty check into it. "This guy Tenkley went on supervised release, and then got lost by the Probation Service. Went to see some US Attorney in Chicago, the one who sent him up, and then he disappeared. Anybody could read this in the Sentencing Commission Supervised Release log. So the Secretary of Communications probably did." He waited for Davis to get this. "I was told the US Attorney may have taken a deposition from Tenkley implicating Tyne in illegal mind-control games." Again he stopped. "But we can't find the info. The prosecutor's dead, nobody can find her boss, Tenkley flew the coop, and the goddamn files have been sealed by executive order."

"So that's it," Davis said with an exaggerated sigh. "Tyne. It's in the protocol sheet. He sealed the files himself. I got wind of it since they were DoJ files. I've seen nothing on your guy, or this US Attorney. So that's sealed too. And the trial implicating Tyne. Sealed." He added, "It's legal, for a Cabinet member."

The train stopped. Nobody moved on or off the mostly empty car. They glided smoothly back into darkness.

"Okay," Davis said. He shifted in his seat. "This Crockett thing. Homeland Security's really got their tit in the wringer. Needham Strange is going to declare martial law on his own if Burligame doesn't. At that point it's St. John and the Defense Department against Homeland Security. Strange is too stupid to handle it with any kind of class. He's a violent egomaniac. He'll blow up the Pentagon. Either way," he said, "once martial law kicks in, Hellman holds all the cards. Crockett's little rebellion is going to boomerang."

"Yeah. That's too bad," O'Donnell said. "Too many egos here. According to Sukwant, it's gotten real personal. The Secretary of Defense intends to put out a recycle order on Strange. Some kind of public humiliation. In fact I'm told they've set up a private duel. St. John and Strange, *mano a mano!*" He relaxed finally, unburdened, pulled out a small black cigar and put it between his teeth, unlit. "It's all getting too, too –"

"Fucked up?"

"Yeah. And it's about to get worse for you. Personally."

Davis waited.

"Whatever comes down, with respect to national security there's a massive potential for backdraft. I can't be anywhere near it." Looking up, O'Donnell caught the expression of a weary woman across the aisle, heading home from work. "Once the President comes to his senses, Tyne's finished. That's pretty clear. So that's one piece of it. When the smoke clears between Defense and Homeland Security, rebellion or no rebellion Hellman's going to look so bad he's going to have to publicly grind somebody to bits.

And he hates your guts. The Bureau's the only agency with its fist
in all the pies. He's going to go for you, John. He'll charge you with
something, embarrass the hell out of you, and leave you for the
dogs." He adjusted his glasses, and made a noise in his throat.
"We'll need to trust Sligo's people on whatever's coming down
next. I would suggest you be prepared to move swiftly, and have
your bags packed for points unknown by the end of the week."

His eyes hadn't moved from the woman opposite. For several moments Davis also stared ahead of him, his face set, his body
still. When the subway pulled into the U Street stop, he got off.

57

Sleep came like a dragon for Nel. It had been bad for two
nights, and now the violent images drove her to despair. In the
morning she felt violated. She attempted to scrape her skin off in the
shower, not wishing to think, scouring her flesh as if all the insanity
would be washed down the drain and life would return to normal.
Finally after chasing Merlin away she stood at her husband's desk
drumming her fingers on the burnished leather cover of the Code
Thirteen, sinking into despair, not knowing at this moment which
side O'Donnell was on. A career National Security Agency officer.
He'd demonstrated his outrage with the administration, yes. But he
certainly knew enough not to bite the hand that would throw the
switch on the electric chair if he compromised his own government.
There were riots in the streets, protest crowds everywhere. She had
witnessed them. It was impossible to know how the government
would actually respond.

She had watched a lot of news overnight. Government employees were walking out. The NBA and the National Hockey
League had suspended games for fear of violence. The National
Coalition for Peace and Justice had fomented a riot in Chicago by
announcing they were supporting the move to recall President Burligame and Vice President Hellman, declaring the fall election "a
neutral decision," since only 9.27 percent of the registered electorate
had voted for the New Freedom Party ticket. Half a dozen unions
were out. The League of Women Voters had joined them. Someone

had circulated thousands of black armbands with the Statue of Liberty stitched on one side, raising her middle finger in protest. A photo was spread above the fold on Wednesday's *West Coast Paper* – and displayed on Nel's monitor on the early news – depicting an African America child of ten or eleven in a wheelchair being turned away from the Supreme Court building by a shrugging white Federal City guard. The caption read, "Say it ain't so, Mr. President."

On Public Television, grandly composed commentator Julio Reese, grandfather figure to millions of Americans, speculated that Secretary of Defense Graham St. John and Homeland Security Secretary Needham Strange had virtually declared war on each other. In classic media fashion, the camera moved to vivid video clips of the principals while Reese loomed just in view on the side, smoothing his iconic white mustache and trying not to smile.

Gazing steadily at the camera, piggy-eyed Needham Strange sneered with indignation. "No man is above the law! Least of all some scrambled-eggs wearing, six-gun-toting, semi-literate jarhead!" His face split with a huge grin. Looking aside, he said, "Am I on yet?"

From his side angle Julio Reese noted in that aged-honey voice, "Plainly the Secretary of Homeland Security has an ax to grind."

Instant switch to a large man wearing safety goggles and leather gloves, operating a table saw, cutting through a thick board. He stopped the saw and removed his goggles. Serious, steel of jaw, fixed of eye, Secretary of Defense Graham St. John nodded at the camera. His voice had the exact drawl of Gary Cooper. "This is my second hobby. My first one is protecting this country from enemies, foreign and domestic. I apologize to my commander in chief, the President of the United States – but we have a domestic enemy right here in Washington. Mr. Needham Strange. I have exhausted all diplomacy and patience with him. Let the record show: when I find him, I'm going to whip his ass from here to Glocca Morra!"

From his lofty position, Reese could only spread both hands, mouth hanging open in mock shock at the Cabinet officials. The footage shifted to a night protest at the US Capitol building, hundreds of thousands bundled up, holding candles, arms linked, chanting for Victor Sligo and Davy Crockett. Speakers demanded the administration step down or face a recall vote before the Inauguration on Sunday.

"One is tempted to believe the nation is on a collision course with the Burligame administration," predicted Julio Reese from the sidelines.

It was all agitated polemics, of course. Everybody knew there was no constitutional ground for the recall of a President. But Progressive organizers made sure a gazillion copies of the Twenty-Fifth Amendment to the Constitution were passed out, highlighting the fourth paragraph, suggesting that under certain circumstances Congress could decide whether the President and/or Vice President are fit to run the country.

State militias had been brought up to Red Alert status.

Further news sent a chill down Nel's tight spine. A panicky Secretary of Health and Human Services threatened to block Medicaid funding to state governments until Davy Crockett surrendered to the authorities. Some advisor to the Secretary had assumed Davy Crockett, a Robin Hood figure as popular as Jesus, was being sheltered by the poor.

The Davy Crockett Society was mad as hell and threatened to sue everybody.

It was 7 a.m. when Nel released the elaborate catch on the Thirteen and touched the speed dial tab. If she was wrong it could mean the end of everything she cherished. And if she was right, if in fact she could safely talk to Victor, it might mean the end of life as she knew it. It might already be too late. She sensed it coming, the horrid vision, his body in a ditch with a government-issue nine millimeter bullet in the back of his head. Closing her eyes she released the tab, and prayed to her goddess.

"Make him be there, damn you! Victor, come on, where are you?" She bit her lip, looked out the ten-foot windows at the purple spine of Vancouver Island, her fingers going white against the Code Thirteen. The amber light kept blinking. "I know you're not dead." Her eyes fell on a photo on the desk, Victor and Nel surrounded by all four children. Dropping into his leather chair, she remembered the last dream. She was adrift in the sky under a flimsy parachute, pleading with Victor to call out her name, but he wouldn't, the stubborn fool. It was the clear pathway to rescue. Just call out, and I'll be there. But he would not call. And now he would not answer.

58

Ms. Keena Turple, residing in the elaborate three-story nou-veau Tudor home next door, was ringing Nel's doorbell. Ringing and ringing.

"All right!" Nel snapped, seeing her huge and opinionated neighbor on the front door video. "Don't wear your finger out!"

Warily, she opened the door. Ms. Turple in her double-extra-large rain costume and fashionable red rubber boots, burst into a genuine hissy fit.

"Do you know what your liberal husband has done to this town?" she trumpeted, spit shooting in every direction. "There's no *US Times!* They're on strike! Next thing you know, the tide won't come in till your husband, Mr. Know Everything, pulls a rosary out of his rear end and turns it into a bouquet of daffodils!" She had practiced the speech, and she stood like Moses smashing the Ten Commandments, all 240 pounds of her, steam rising from her head, daring Nel to reply.

"Well, Ms. Turple," Nel said, "You better write somebody a letter." And she slammed the door.

Now she was mad. Taking a full five seconds to refocus, she understood the only way to move was to attack. She grabbed the yellow phone and called Courtman.

"Purvis! Get the staff together at my home in one hour. Yes, I'm tired too and we've all lost half a week of our lives, and I don't give a damn. I'm getting Molly Bee up here if she'll come. And I'm trying to find Iona Webster. She's already in on this, and she knows everybody."

"She was in Philadelphia Tuesday," Courtman said.

"And find Doc Nguyen. He runs VoteAmerica."

"He was there too. Look, Ms. Congressman, you need to get a grip here. Victor will get home, probably today, probably towing that kid along –"

"Knock off the obsequious crap, Purvis! This is me!" Yell-ing into the phone, "Get hold of BJ, and have him bring his notes and that CD from Ms. Ferrari. Get the others here too."

"Yeah. All right, then."

She felt the anger rising, and couldn't shut herself up. "We're doing a surgical investigation of that freak in Washington because he's at the bottom of this, and we can't get any help. It's going to require the most invisible person alive to do it. I want the blond woman to get in there as close as she can. Where is she, Purvis?"

"There's never any knowing where the blond woman is. She moves in for the kill, she eats their young, and she disappears!" He remembered then, and snorted into the phone, "She was going to cozy up to Hunter Tyne, the last I heard."

The blond woman was in fact Courtman's responsibility, his agent in the rancid underworld of Washington politics. Nobody else on the staff knew much about her. As intimidated as she made him feel, he'd have to locate her.

"Purvis, please! Get over here and bring everybody along. And don't let anybody see any of you!"

Courtman broke out his unregistered Liquiphone and a list of numbers: a Silver Spring highrise condo; the *West Coast Paper*'s head office in San Francisco; and the numbers of the throw-away phones his staffers had activated last night under the names of Desmond Tutu, Daniel Ellsberg, Nelson Mandela, and Lenny Bruce. Reluctantly he conceded how gutsy the blond woman was to go after the Secretary of Communications, the madman of the Wasatch.

59

Raven was asleep on Sloan Mgaba's futon when she heard a distant phone ring. Then a hand was on her shoulder.

"We're wanted at the Congressman's house," a deep voice said.

She pulled herself up and wrapped covers around her.

Last night Mgaba had gone for her in a most seductive fashion. He was big and very dark, had told wonderful stories and made a wonderful meal, with African women singing in the background somewhere, and peculiarly-scented candles, and had charmed her with a French-accented bass voice that slid right down to her sexual core.

But she was tired, scared and homesick, and actually did not feel right about it. She was pretty sure he was married, with the dozens of photos of children all over the place. He had in fact tenderly told her he had eleven adopted children, all orphaned Central African refugees. After the second glass of wine she began to wonder what lay ahead for her – she did not have the foggiest notion – and she decided to hold Mgaba off.

In his sleeveless white undershirt and pajama bottoms, Mgaba looked rather different than he had last night. Now he resembled an obese ex-boxer.

"Sleep well?" she said, no intended irony in her voice.

But Mgaba heard it. He offered a fleeting shrug. "Forgive me. A man is a man." Crossing the room, he opened a walk-in closet, pulled down a gray pinstripe suit, and left. She could hear his labored breathing, the romantic sophisticate turned middle-age fighter.

In the bedroom, Mgaba's new pink phone chirped once and stopped. He popped it open to read the message. A six word text from a D.C. area code.

"Get her out of the house!"

It was John Lee Davis. They had spoken briefly last night. In a muffled exchange, Davis had told him the FBI was pursuing warrants on Ms. Sligo and the staff on phony protection orders. Leverage on Crockett and Sligo would vastly improve with his wife in custody.

"Raven!" Mgaba yelled. "Get your things together."

60

In his immaculate Chuckanut Drive condo, Courtman believed he was in charge now, and he felt immobilized. It was clear that Crocket was doomed, the entire caper was a preposterous blip in an enormous ocean, and nothing was going to come of it. They were going to lock up Sligo and his bearded little buddy and throw away the key.

He had to decide, and quickly, whether to support this rebellion or not. Could he decide? Or couldn't he? He pressed his hands against the sides of his head. Was it all a stupid prank? Was it real? People demonstrated against bad weather, for God's sake! Any cause would get loonies out on the street. And they were out there today, sure as hell.

"Gotta go, gotta go," Courtman chanted, not moving from his leather sofa. "The country's in flames and I'm supposed to put out the fire!"

All the madness was reduced to a single question: what was Courtman's best career move with respect to a) a potential Cabinet seat on the one hand, or b) an eight-by-ten housing arrangement at Leavenworth on the other. As chief of staff for an intense, in-your-face politician like Victor Sligo, especially since he was the top Progressive on Ways and Means, a man who collected enemies like a frog collects flies, the question was crucial. The wildest hope was that this half-assed nationwide filibuster might actually neutralize the administration until the Supreme Court could be pressured into allowing a plebiscite to recall Burligame and Hellman. But with the notable exception of Chief Justice Chloe Shapiro-Fujimoto, an old girlfriend of Burligame's who had unexpectedly become a moderate late in life, the high court was stacked with New Freedom Party zombies.

The morning freight train rumbled along Chuckanut Bay. Courtman stood up. "Screw it," he said. "Let's do this."

61

The Code Thirteen had ceased throbbing when Victor and Edwin returned to the log house. Each man grabbed an armload of firewood to haul into the wood crib beside the stove.

"It does bring in spiders," Edwin Foulks admitted. "But the spiders make cool patterns on the ceiling. Besides, I just sweep 'em up a couple of times a year, send 'em back outside."

Victor was still rocked by everything taking place. Something had occupied his brain there at the big tree for two or three minutes. He'd felt invaded somehow. Much like the experience in the Cessna. Now he knew of Foulks' intention to mount a one-man sting operation against the Vice President of the United States. The sheer insanity of it! And the kid didn't even know how to pull it off! Foulks was a passively-deranged, complex figure, a paradox – absolutely fixed on bringing justice to the common man, and at the same time too naïve to realize his life was at risk for just contemplating the damn idea.

But he'd already demonstrated a kind of brilliance. Just as he'd intended, the word about the rebellion had exploded almost instantaneously, and America had shifted in an eyeblink from a herd of disgruntled sheep to malevolent mobs rioting across the land. Angry dissenters on the news and flooding the Internet blogs were so incensed with the national leadership they were even willing to support DB Cooper, a half-forgotten criminal and mythological folk hero.

It was all completely bizarre. A country bumpkin, flushing the scum out of Washington. Really.

It would be as simple as pulling the plug on the ocean, draining it and refilling it. Corruption was so deeply entrenched in government, the man on the street had quit voting to change it.

"We need to get back to D.C. and pull together a coherent group angry enough to take them on," Victor told him. "We have insiders at Justice and Defense and some in Congress. But nobody knows who's listening to who. We've got to organize people who can influence Congress in a serious breakdown. We have to undo that damned election! You know what that was? That was Julio Reese flipping his pencil in the air and saying, 'Don't vote,' and everybody watching stupefied, going, 'uh... okay.' That was not the people speaking! That was the people muzzled!"

"You forget. Julio catches his pencil and says, 'I'm being ironic! Get out there and cast your ballot, folks.' Remember that? 'Democracy only works if you make it work!'"

"No kidding. Julio used your name?"

"All the time."

Victor paced, grinding a fist into his palm, forming a course of action. "We can't do anything here! We need people in every city in America! The military! The guy running the Pentagon was at Independence Hall, that Admiral. He'd better be one tough son of a bitch, for what's about to happen! It's crucial we get to Burligame. That means assassinating Billy Hellman." He was trying to hold himself from going manic now, and counting on long hard fingers. "Somehow we need to be able to communicate with the people, and that means shutting out Communication International! How the hell can a handful of renegades –" Strafing his hair with his hands, looking out at the drizzle. He swiped condensation from the window. "Did that guy say he was going to gas the House of Representatives? What was it? Sodium pentothal? That's what they used to call truth serum, isn't it? Half of the people in Congress will be impervious to it." He was feeling strangely light-headed. His voice was shrill. Spinning around to Edwin, "Congressmen are *supposed* to lie! It's our God-given right! That's why people elect us! That's why they elected Billy Hellman! Hellman hasn't told the truth intentionally since he was five years old!"

Flicking on overhead lights kitchen, Edwin Foulks leaned against the big enamel cook stove. "Congressman?"

Victor shook his head vigorously, slapped both his own cheeks, and blinked at him.

"What?"

"I need your attention, sir."

The younger man held Victor's eyes as he spoke.

"You're right. We will have to get people together. What's going to happen is we are going to create a situation where I speak to the President and the Vice President in public, on I-Media, and ask them a few questions. It's the only possible –"

Victor's head jerked back in astonishment.

"Hold it! I already heard your Pollyanna concept of politics. It ain't gonna happen, Foulks!" Edwin stood before him, waiting for the tantrum to run its course. "All right, I admit –" He felt a bit out of body as he spoke, "– you might have some unearthly ability to, I don't know, create a little sideshow at the Inauguration, embarrass Hellman, make him admit he was conceived in a Petri dish. In front of half a billion people on the Web! Is that what you want?" Part of him feeling Edwin's power, part of him hard-core politician, constantly separating bullshit from reality. "But people don't vote, so why should they watch the Inauguration on TV? What if *American Idol's* on? I know Senators, Supreme Court justices, who'd rather stay home and diddle the upstairs maid than watch Hellman take the frigging oath… Which is just a bunch of hooey anyway – he ain't gonna defend the Constitution, he's going to *dismantle* it! So you thundering in there on your white horse like Don fucking Quixote ain't gonna do shit, Foulks! You're just going to get yourself killed!"

At this moment he heard it, the low humming vibration of the mobile Code Thirteen. He raced upstairs and tore through his paper bag of belongings, grabbed the slim transceiver and pressed a finger to the red key.

"Nel!"

A voice pushed through the micro-speaker. "It's Davis. Can you talk?"

Davis! The FBI! "Yeah, yeah. Go ahead."

"Don't know if they have this thing locked in," Davis said fast. "It's hell or be damned for me anyway."

"Okay."

The Deputy Director barked, "More trouble brewing! People are on the way to your home as we speak. Our satellite tracker shows your wife is there. Get her the hell out of there before they snatch her! I'm calling her right now. They've got a warrant on her on the pretext that she might also be abducted. And they have warrants to detain your whole staff on national security grounds."

"How much time do we –"

"Listen to me. Don't trust anybody about anything any more. Do you understand? Including me. If this thing fails, you are the man facing the firing squad."

The Thirteen stopped blinking.

"Foulks!" He was on full adrenalin. There was no way to call Nel without alarming the countryside. He didn't dare use the Thirteen again. He snapped it closed and felt the last vibrations run through his arm into his heart. Somehow it reactivated the weird sensations from the big tree.

Crashing back downstairs he yelled, "We have to get to my place! They're coming after Nel! We've got to get the staff out fast. This mudhole of yours is probably the safest place in America." Hyperventilating, he glanced out the big window at the garden. White chickens huddled beside a rain-glazed red wheel barrow. So much depended on them!

"Goddamn it, let's go, man!"

Edwin gave him a look, then turned toward the kitchen. He snatched an ancient white push-button phone on the kitchen wall and pressed numbers. The big brown lab was at his side instantly, panting for a ride.

"Hey, Ms. Rush. It's Edwin." He let out a breath and

slowed himself down. Victor stared boggle-eyed at him. "Wanted to thank you for the cookies you sent over. Yes, yes, the bachelor life. Say, I need a favor. Is it possible your truck might be around? I have to pick up some stuff in town. Well, that's so kind of you. Sure. Hey, I can pick up a rebuilt starter at the junk yard. I'll throw her in there for you. Thanks a lot."

Victor was frenzied now. "Yeah. Car's too small. Let's go."

"The truck's coming here. I know it's a national emergency, but we're on Van Zandt time, Congressman. So cool your jets a minute."

It was several minutes, actually, before a horn tooted outside.

A battered four-by-four farm truck rumbled in the driveway. Victor's heart fell at the sight: a kid of about fourteen sat at the wheel revving the old GMC beater to hold its idle. It had a seriously crumpled roof and sideboards constructed from the outside strips of a big cedar log cut by a home sawmill. Bolted to the front was a beat up winch, and a couple of choker cables and chains dangled from the sideboards. A horseshoe-shaped clevis hung from the heavy rear bumper, stout enough to handle a big choker hook. On the door was the faded legend, "Mother Rush's Cookie Line." It was a sight to behold.

"You've got to be kidding! You're going to pick up my staff in that?" Squinting, "What is that?" Hastily Edwin stuffed a backpack, and they raced out and leaped in the passenger door, nearly tearing it off its hinges, leaving the brown lab whining on the porch. The muscular towheaded youngster at the wheel crunched the floor shifter forward and the truck lurched ahead, nearly knocking down the garage. The three of them rumbled out to the road, mashed together in a heap. The truck had no windshield.

Edwin explained. "This is the neighborhood hay wagon, gravel hauler and logging truck. Ms. Rush has a small herd of Guernseys. People around here buck hay for her in the summer. Then in the winter, say you need to move a load of manure or some Congressman's staff, there she is!"

Victor was thinking his teeth were going to rattle out of his head any moment.

"We can't haul humans in this thing!" he said. "This Tobacco Roadmobile wouldn't outrun a one-legged Republican, much less US Marshals in their Crown Vics. That damn crumpled roof! Anybody can identify this rig a mile away. What happened to the roof?" he yelled over the screaming, balking, smoking engine.

The boy yelled, "I was fallin' a big twisty alder and it barber-chaired on me. I forgot about the truck sittin' there. Tree split right where I was makin' the back cut, and the dang thing flew straight up in the air and dropped right on the roof, *bang!* Woulda drilled me into the ground like a fence post! Popped out the windshield clean as a heifer's titty."

They dropped the boy off and followed the river back out to the highway. Edwin laid out a simple plan to smuggle Courtman and the others out – if they could find them – as he crashed through the gears like a demented long-haul trucker. Victor's mind was going two hundred miles an hour. He steadied himself to look at the busted gauges and watch Edwin's grip on the shuddering steering wheel. Wet air blasted through the cab into his face. If the truck didn't break down, they might beat the feds.

"Step on it," he said.

Edwin checked his watch. He squinted ahead, wiping his face for the tenth time. A twitch came to the corner of his mouth. "There's a phone in that gas station up ahead. Give me your friend Davis's phone number. Write down the names of your staff. And their cars. We gotta catch a bus. And hope like hell it's empty!"

They jounced through the foothills, then squealed north toward Sunrise and the Canadian border. As they roar away from the mountains, the air began to thicken. They were fifteen minutes from Victor's house. Edwin's foot was jammed right in the carburetor. The truck sounded like a runaway tank.

62

The Code Thirteen blinked on Victor's desk in Sunrise. Nel grabbed it, frantically hoping it was him. John Lee Davis's face came through clearly on the small display. Her heart fell.

"Nel! Are you okay?"

"Where is he?" she demanded.

"Victor's okay, he's fine. I've just heard from him. Right

now, people from Counterterrorism are on the way. They'll be arriving at your door at 10:45 your time."

"Ten-thirty here," Nel said breathlessly. "Fifteen minutes! We have to get out!"

"There's a bus. I know it sounds nuts, but you're to get on a bus named Sunrise. Get off at the library. I have no idea what this is about but —"

"Yes, yes, I know the place," Nel nearly shouted, not knowing whether to be elated or terrified. "But who —"

"A friend set it up. Get to your people and tell them to listen to the bus driver! She'll be on your street at 10:42!"

"Couldn't you have cut this a little closer?" Already her mind was flying. Credit cards! Kids! Food! Mother!

The Code Thirteen made a lightning sound – *fzzt!* Led lights blinked sharply, and it shut down.

The staff was already on the way. Hands shaking, she found Courtman's new number and told him to make sure Mgaba and BJ were alerted, and for him to ride his scooter to her place and park it in the bushes.

BJ arrived first. He was rounding the bend below the Sligo compound, and had to screech to a stop in front of a full-size city bus blocking the road. Instantly he knew something was off. He'd been told to get to the house fast, and now – what was this? An attack? Like the others, he'd been flipping his own coin, leaning towards submitting his resignation. In fact he and his wife had talked it over, and Leah had agreed there was no predicting the outcome, except guaranteed nightmares, federal prison, loss of everything they owned.

But his country was going to hell. He was torn between plunging into a desperate escapade, and protecting his family and his career. Why hadn't he just become a professional golfer? Life would have been so simple.

A heavy, uniformed Eskimo-looking woman lumbered out of the empty bus carrying a sheet of paper. She looked BJ over as he jumped out of the black Lexus and approached her.

"Mr. Lichtenstein?"

"What is this?"

"I'm Toby. I was asked to stop my bus here and wait for you? And the other guys?" Her voice had that unmistakable native softness. She looked straight at him. Black eyes, large, gentle face, confident and imposing. The gray armband told its tale.

"Who told you to wait for me?"

"Hey, I got a call, okay? You're supposed to be driving up this road right about now in a black Lexus, and you work for them." Thumbing over her shoulder at the sprawling white house in the cul-de-sac. "You have to get rid of your car. Don't ask me what's going on, I'm just the messenger. The cops'll be here in a couple of minutes? You're going to have to trust me." She held his eyes in a way that told him she was for real.

Still, BJ persisted. "How do I know you're not –"

"I was told to say," she flicked a glance at the paper, embarrassment seeping into her big cheeks, "she's going to slap you again if you don't listen to me."

BJ stared. He blinked. "Okay."

"Good," she said. "For a second I thought I was going to have to use force."

He listened. Quickly he spun the car around and turned into the next driveway. The garage door opened. BJ pulled the Lexus into the garage, and the door shut behind him. He saw nobody. As instructed, he found the side door of the garage, raced back to the idling silver and blue city bus, and climbed inside.

Toby was whisper-shouting into a Blue Tooth at the front of the bus.

"Where's the rest of them? I can't wait all day. I can't wait another three minutes!" Squeezing her eyes shut, her face bunched up, thinking about hidden video cameras.

On the other end of the phone, Nel was shouting while she frantically pulled things together. Courtman was late, and might have to be left. She had no idea about Mgaba and Menez.

"Hold on, hold on," she yelled, "they'll be here. If I'm not out there in one minute, just leave! Don't risk any more than you already are!"

Toby was thinking the same thing. Thank God the bus was empty.

At that moment Sloan Mgaba and Raven Menez were flying up I-5 in his four-year-old canary yellow Lamborghini. He'd taken Courtman's urgent call on the road. Sweat was forming on his brow, and he wore a rather creepy look as he flicked glances in his mirror at Raven. Finally she swung a hand up and shoved the mirror away. For her, it had all started out wrong. Already she was crashing full tilt into a crisis beside this man she had steadily refused last night. He was a compassionate man of the world, a good listener with lovely brown eyes and a low growl in the back of his throat when he spoke about his life in Africa – and then like a thunderbolt, it had all gone sour. No, not like a thunderbolt. Like a rotten quart of milk.

The car was going eighty when he reeled off the freeway and down the off ramp, shooting through gears, not bothering with stop signs. Freezing, gripping her seat belt for dear life, Raven just had enough mind left to wonder if this is what politics was like all the time. Then they were flying through a glamorous neighborhood, winding streets, big homes with exotic formal gardens, and he was cursing in three languages, ramming down into second and stomping on the brake at the same time, the superb vehicle not even shuddering as it whined to a halt ten inches behind a big silver and blue city bus.

Sticking his head out the window he bellowed, "Get the hell out of my way!"

BJ Lichtenstein waved frantically from the rear window, but Mgaba failed to notice. Toby, again with the sheet of paper, hurried back to speak to him.

"What do you mean, follow you?" His voice lathered with indignation. "Who are you? I've got an important –"

Toby shot a hand in a swift arc in front of his face. "Shut up, big boy." The hand flew out to the side, toward the cul-de-sac. Nel was racing down the walkway, carrying stuffed pillow cases.

"In the bus!" she shouted at him. "You!" pointing straight at Raven Menez. "Nobody knows you. Take the car." Raven opened her mouth to object. "Just take the car! Meet us at the Sunrise Library in five minutes!"

Raven stammered, "But I don't –"

"Move!" Nel snarled. She turned and ran for the idling bus and plunged up the steps just behind Mgaba, muttering, "We'll have to leave Courtman," then bent to watch Raven through the rear window. Toby saw Raven's plight. She slid her window open and stuck her head out.

"Just follow me, Sweetie," she yelled. Instantly the bus thundered off, causing Mgaba to plunge down the aisle. As the bus passed the house, two black cars pulled up behind the yellow Ferrari, then turned into Nel's long driveway, a state patrol Crown Vic and an unassuming square Chevy American, a big SUV every ninth grader knew was an FBI unit. Toby made an odd squealing sound in her throat and slowed the bus to normal speed. She was fanning her neck with one hand, breathing hard, imagining herself already fired and greeting people at Kwalmart by next week for minimum wage.

They all watched out the back. The four men walked to the Sligos' door. Bald, pudgy Merlin stood before them in his chef's apron, a wooden spoon in his hand, as innocent as a priest. Seconds later the bus rounded the wide turn, and a scooter came flying straight toward them. Toby and Nel gasped, "Whoa!" in unison. It was Courtman, tie flying over his shoulder. With frantic miscalculation, he bounced onto the sidewalk, jarring him clean off the scooter. The bus shuddered to a halt beside him.

The big doors opened. Nel was at the top step waiting for him. Courtman was hysterical. He screamed, "I can't hide this damn thing! It's registered to me! My name's all over it!"

"Dammit!" Nel said. The floor was suddenly moving under her, and she jumped back into the aisle of the bus.

"The lift," Toby yelled. "Get out of the way!" Courtman managed to get the scooter half sideways on the wheelchair ramp and Toby had it up as Nel shoved Courtman down the aisle. The lift slid back in, and she stepped on the gas, throwing everybody back into their seats.

Raven had been watching the feds. As the bus roared away, she carefully nudged the fabulous Lamborghini forward, watching in the mirror as the little bald man artfully gesticulated at the four cops, first pointing in toward the kitchen, then pushing between them, bringing the crowd outside, elaborately aiming his wooden spoon at the chimney. Two of the men were writing in little notepads as Raven rounded the corner.

But they wouldn't stay long. She followed the city bus as it wove through the fancy neighborhood, wound out to a busy street and shortly pulled into an empty parking lot behind the town library. On the bus, Courtman thought he was having a heart attack, and he was reevaluating his career for the hundredth time this week. Mgaba was concerned only with his car. Lying down across the seats at the back, BJ couldn't think at all. His legs hurt. His brain hurt. He'd finally caught up with Leah and now he was being taken prisoner by his own boss. Clutching a silver pole, Nel bent low watching the rear. The black Chevy American was cruising slowly down the street toward the library.

"There he is," Toby announced, pointing a stubby dark finger toward some kind of mid-Twentieth Century farm vehicle idling nearby, putting out a screen of blue smoke and shaking like it was about to explode.

"There who is?"

"That's your ride, ma'am," the driver said. "I have to get back on route. Right now!"

In the driver's seat of the catastrophic truck, Edwin Foulks studied the bus, then gave Toby a hearty wave. He cautioned Victor to stay low in the cab as Toby leaped off the bus, looking over her shoulder at the street behind her, and rushed over to the ancient two-ton haywagon, hidden from the street by the big bus.

"Hey, man!" she greeted him. "Where you been! Sick?"

"Like a fox," he said. "I owe you, honey. You got 'em?"

"There's a little thing," she said. "A scooter."

"A scooter?"

"Yeah, with the guy's ID all over it. Cops are right behind me! I got to drop the lift."

Edwin watched. A shiny yellow sports car turned into the lot and pulled to a far corner, and an attractive young woman ran toward the bus as the wheelchair lift was coming down. Getting the picture, Edwin banged the truck into reverse, and made a wide backwards circle till the back of the truck approached the side of the bus. In the mirror Toby saw the American slowing. Cursing, she eased the lift down onto the rear of the truck. The angle was bad, but it landed. Nel raced back to Courtman, babbling in his seat, and grabbed him by both shoulders. He shook himself all over, blinked at her, and stood up. He backed the scooter onto the lift and dragged it onto the rotting bed of the truck. The others were jumping on the back as Edwin appeared, pulled a battered brown tarp over the side-boards covering the entire crowd, scooter and all, and was tying the tarp down just as the FBI vehicle stopped on the street in front of the bus stop. Immediately Toby moved the bus forward into the street, took an exaggerated look at her watch and tried to look irritated. Both car doors opened. The men, in matching dark suits, came toward her. Edwin coaxed the shuddering clutch out and moved the noisy truck around to face the other direction. At this moment Raven came nervously toward the truck, pretty but grave, uncertain what to do. For the first time Edwin thought the ruse was about to collapse. He took a deep breath and waved her to the back of the truck with a whirling motion of his index finger. Nodding, Raven ran for the truck. He pressed the accelerator, not at all sure where Raven was, but felt weight shifting behind him, and he rolled into the street and lurched away. By now both FBI men were standing in front of the driver's side window, chatting with Toby. She affected her worst Indian accent, and told them her scheduled departure from the library was three minutes ago. She'd just had a visit with her brother in the farm truck.

"The creep owes me fifty bucks," she whined. "He's hauling a load of manure over to my place instead of paying me. Lord, does that ever stink!" Checking her watch again she showed them her serious face. "Got a schedule to keep! You guys need a ride somewheres?"

The taller agent wrote her name down in his notebook, recorded the time, and sent her on her way. Turning then, he watched the ancient manure-hauler rumble down the main drag, bearings squealing, front end askew, the load of manure covered with an ancient tarp. He shook his head. The guy probably never had fifty bucks in his life.

63

Cacophony erupted under the tarp. Raven Menez was squashed against the sideboard in the half-darkness, terrified, trying not to touch the filthy truck bed. In front of her, Nel was desperately clawing through the staff people searching for Victor, calling his name – but Victor would not answer. Courtman and Lichtenstein had wound up in a heap, and were yelling at each other, struggling to separate themselves with extreme embarrassment, while Mgaba was acting as referee trying to help by grabbing all the wrong body parts. He kicked over the scooter and it smashed on its side, pinning Courtman's legs under it. An animal snarl tore from Courtman's lips.

"What is this," Nel yelled over the ghastly exhaust-belching ruckus of the truck. "Where are we going? Who is that guy?"

Raven said, "It's... it's..." But she had no idea, no idea at all, only that her life was in tatters and she was being abducted by a gang of lunatics and it stunk like chicken poop and that smell on her hands! *Arrrgh!* She screamed when she smelled herself.

Agonized Purvis Courtman understood everything. This was the hard nature of rebellion against despotism. They would have to be strong now. He touched Nel's wrist merely to comfort her, a kind gesture, but she yanked her arm away and back-fisted him hard in the face. He spun back and felt blood on his nose. Now both Courtman and Raven were moaning, and BJ, completely out of body, scrambled across Mgaba and the scooter to get to Raven. He kicked Mgaba in the chest.

"What did you do with my car!" Mgaba bellowed, trying to grab for Lichtenstein's foot. BJ wound up in Raven's lap. Her whimpering stopped abruptly.

"It's going to be okay," he started to say. "The worst of it's already over. Just try to relax. Breathe. Okay? You'll be –"

"Get off me, asshole," she shouted, shoving him against the scooter again. Then, "Oh, God , I'm sorry, I'm sorry, I didn't –"

"All right, people!" Nel screamed at the top of her voice. "Get a grip!"

Light suddenly streamed in from the front of the truck. Raven saw BJ plainly shocked at her verbal abuse. Trapped under his scooter, Courtman was holding a bloody nose and sounded like he was drowning. Mgaba was bellowing about his car keys, and Nel was bellowing at everybody. Then a voice said, "Hey."

Nel whipped her eyes toward the front.

Her husband's face was framed in the sliding rear window of the cab. He had wiggled a hand into the back to hold up the ratty tarp. He was gazing at her with a deep, satisfied calm, like a dead man resurrected. She gasped, then clambered over bodies and filth to get to him. "Oh my God," she said over and over, struggling to embrace him through the window, crying and laughing and then suddenly furious, shrieking, "I ought to kill you, you idiot," pressing her cheek against his through the tiny window, trying to get a look at the man driving the truck, the others all stunned and squinting into the light to see Victor Sligo, rescued congressman.

He acknowledged them all one by one, including Raven Menez, then asked Edwin to stop and make room in the front seat for Nel. She climbed up in the cab, almost as disgusting as the bed of the truck, and embraced Victor as he attempted to introduce Edwin. Edwin rammed the truck into second and it banged forward just as the Code Thirteen blinked.

Looking back, both Sligos would remember the next few moments as the most devastating in the saga of the Foulks rebellion.

Hauling the slim device out of his jacket, Victor touched the blinking green light.

A female voice said, "Please hold."

Seconds passed. Then, "Ms. Sligo? Hello. I'm not sure your video is outputting correctly. I'm only getting an audio signal." The voice was familiar but undercut with static and the violence of the truck. Victor handed Nel the mobile Thirteen with an uncertain shrug. Maybe O'Donnell? Hal Riske?

"This is Nel Sligo."

"Ah. This is Billy Hellman speaking. How are you bearing up, Ms. Sligo?" A vile haughtiness punctuated his words.

They stared at each other breathlessly. "No, no," Nel whispered, holding the Thirteen at arm's length like some putrid insect. At the same moment Victor whispered, "Hellman? How in the –" She swung her arm out the window, still holding the mobile unit, and turned back to Victor, her teeth bared.

The green light blinked. Nel pulled the unit back inside and tossed it onto the rotting dash. She flipped her middle finger at it. Then managed to subdue her burst of rage long enough to mutter, "Mr. Vice President," in an icy tone.

"Nel, I wanted to congratulate you on your daring escape from federal agents! You are a woman of your convictions, I will say that." The voice was taunting, like a school principal admonishing a troublemaker. The Vice President said, "Congressman Sligo may be the only man able at this juncture to bring the country back to its senses. I implore you, Nel, before irreconcilable damage is done to his career, persuade him to come in. A chopper will be along in a minute or so for you."

"He's bluffing!" Victor whispered, frantically looking behind the truck and scanning the sky. "They don't know where we are!" Edwin looked over, mildly perturbed, and hit the gas.

The voice crackled, "I imagine they'll have a warrant for documents related to your recent trip to Philadelphia. Not to worry. It's routine, part of the investigation preparing indictments against Mr. Crockett. Please don't embarrass the US government more than we are already embarrassed by this matter."

"Stick it up your ass, you bald little pimp," Victor told the unit under his breath.

"You know, I remember your twin daughters graduating from law school not long ago." Nel slammed herself back against the exposed seat springs, unable to breathe. "They're with, let's see, Jeffrey, Klatt, Bennett and Bruner in Seattle, is that right?" The voice hardened instantly. "Don't be surprised if the firm loses all its government contracts, dear. Oh, that's right. They only handle government contracts, don't they?"

A brief, seething pause. Nel's blood pressure shot through the ceiling. "Didn't Olivia Nevens work there also? An old friend of your husband's?"

"Jesus!" she screamed, hands involuntarily over her face. Olivia was an old girlfriend of Victor's from the distant past. They had fought over her.

"Oh, and Nel? When you see your husband tell him we've broken the code."

Victor looked at her, shaking his head, a question in his eyes. Nel simply looked pained.

"I'm talking about the Code Thirteen, my dear." They heard an ugly snicker. "Now I want you to stay on the line and await further instructions."

When she could speak she whispered through clenched teeth, "That NSA guy. O'Donnell? He told me he'd never heard of the Code Thirteen." She clenched both fists. Poison filling her mouth. She leaned toward the device and said quite clearly, "I'd like to tell you, sir, with all the respect I hold for your office, to go fuck yourself."

Victor's eyes flew from Nel to the blinking green light. His jaws were tight. He grabbed it, and leaned over Nel and slammed it against the door handle again and again, smashing it to pieces. Electronic bits flew everywhere, but he kept smashing it, breathing hard, half insane, finally heaving the jagged plastic out the window.

64

The Vice President was feeling malicious and foul, sitting alone in the throbbing communications center he had constructed on the top floor of the Executive Office Building, across the way from the White House. For a few seconds he stared at the blinking green light below the blank thirteen-centimeter screen the Secret Service had seized, the result of an exhaustive search into private military emails and illegal overseas Intelsat data scans. It was a home-built job, patched together in an Air Force communications warehouse in Thule, Greenland, confiscated and rushed south to Billy Hellman's personal domain, which for the government's purposes was the center of US intelligence gathering. That is, against political enemies.

Tracking down the device was a fortuitous result of the collapse of the Worldwide Web and the national Intelsat system. It was Leora Psybysch, pathologically protecting the Vice-President's actions in the War Room during the attack over the Mall of Brotherly Love, who had noticed a single almost invisible white pinprick on the forty-foot screen during the blackout. It was the only perceptible signal in the known universe for a brief period. Leora had earned herself a major boost in career options by quietly having it investigated and reporting the finding to her boss.

Incredibly, federal agents were told the man responsible for building the secret communications device had just left on a seal-tracking expedition with the Animal Channel, even though daylight would not return to northern Greenland for another five weeks. He hadn't been seen since Christmas.

Following the call to Sligo's wife, a brilliant stroke that would surely end this half-assed rebellion, Billy Hellman ordered "home food," a blood rare steak and potatoes au gratin and greens, a bottle of wine and the nation's last six newspapers. He often ate alone. After many years stirring up the vortex of power, Billy had come to understand he only dined with others when he invited them. Of course there were state dinners, Newfie fundraising feeds, mandatory ass-licking by the smug power brokers of the planet, as well as the beggars, congressional and corporate, seeking to gnaw off a scrap of his vast political empire. And occasionally there was a call from S. demanding an appearance. Otherwise, he dined in silence.

*   *   *

By the time Hellman belched and mounted his neon four-wheeler in the underground tunnel to the White House, and roared down to the emergency meeting of the National Security Council, Edwin Foulks' rustic log home was already becoming a revolutionary command center.

The culture shock went surprisingly well, considering they all felt like fugitives, and all lived comfortably in urban areas far from the rain forest. Edwin Foulks beamed at each of them as they arrived, showing off the old stump ranch, clucking at the Leghorns, tossing a stick into the forest for the dog to fetch, laughing at a single question from BJ: "You mean you live here *all the time?*"

Purvis Courtman located Doc Nguyen soaking in a therapeutic hot tub in Boulder reading *Quirk* magazine. Menez took the assignment of persuading Molly Bee to come north, but Molly, not recovered yet from the wild visit to Utah, felt some fear about the invitation, and in the end told Raven she would bring Iona Webster along as a protection against idiots, foreign and domestic. With fistfuls of reservations, Victor set his staff to the strangest project of his career – finding weapons for Edwin Foulks to fight with should he wind up face to face with Billy Hellman. Obviously the nation was aroused to deep passion. People were suddenly conscious that they had been oppressed too long by forces beyond their control, and now a single man bearing a suggestion of change had awakened them from their stupor.

They grumbled about Edwin's hocus-pocus politics, demanded food and alcohol and sophisticated search equipment, and went to work in the crammed quarters.

Nel finally had her meltdown trying to tell Victor what it felt like being shot at by Tyne's handyman, the terrifying break-in, the wild escape, breaking a dozen laws, then cursing the Vice President and wishing to do unspeakable violence to him after his threat to her children.

"I don't know why I'm identifying with that poor Viola Ferrari," she whispered to him, not quite weeping, sitting at a round table in Edwin's country kitchen. "I am a strong person and I can handle this stuff. I can give the Vice President the most disgusting suggestion –" and she laughed suddenly, wildly, for a full second, then fell grim again. "It's just, she got such a lousy deal. They killed her for –" She couldn't finish.

Watching her and listening as well as a politician can, Victor was torn between trying to focus on his wife's trauma, and realizing his entire staff were making it sound like the administration, or the whole country, was about to fall apart.

"BJ's got her deposition on a CD. Believe it or not, she hid it in plain sight at her mother's nursing home! He called me in Salt Lake and said Hunter Tyne's involved in this. Well, we guessed that." An old pepper grinder was in her hands, and she slammed it down again and again on the worn table, her face twisted and teary, unable to speak further.

After drinking some tea Edwin found, she took both men through every shadow of the night at Tyne's house, and told of the photos now on Fred's laptop, Tyne's hanging artwork and the bizarre mock-up of a plastic man's brain connected to monitors, like some kind of android terminator. She told them about Jerome Tse's suicide. But she needed BJ to give Victor a first hand report on the matter of Jaap Tenkley's deposition and what appeared to be Hunter Tyne's involvement in illegal mind control experiments, or worse.

She needed Iona and Molly present to help her think. And she hadn't heard from Fred. She was beginning to worry about what he might unearth.

65

Mgaba and Edwin sub-divided headquarters in the crowded living area, creating a work center from a pair of sawhorses and a sheet of plywood that was shortly crammed with laptops, phones, notebooks and assorted paraphernalia. Lichtenstein had participated in the Kennedy-Nguyen studies on unexplainable election statistics and had a few contacts. While Nel was having her fit in the kitchen with her husband, BJ was crammed against the plywood with a blooming Christmas cactus in his face, on the phone with the GSA deputy administrator in Cleveland, prying out the names of government contractors who might want to talk about unorthodox election equipment. "Call in all your debts!" Victor had demanded, hitching up the faded blue jeans. "Get to all those patriots at Independence

Hall! Use Doc's VoteAmerica resources. Use everything! Sell your souls for information! We need to drain the cesspool where this damn administration came from."

Scrunched beneath the log staircase, Mgaba left messages for both John Lee Davis and Admiral Sukwant Singh to contact him immediately. Victor had delegated to Mgaba the diplomat's job – liaison with the big boys in Washington. Make sure the information keeps flowing both ways. Dissect every tone of voice, every nuance. Keep your ego tucked in.

The Congressman himself was seeking favors in the D.C. media underground with no success. Already frustrated, he began pacing the long covered front porch in a soft mist, wearing Edwin's yellow slicker and his Disko Troop rain hat, phone clipped to the coat, up against the fragile egos of television news producers. He felt their reluctance. Nobody wished to purchase shares in government malfeasance from a fugitive.

Courtman came outside struggling into his jacket, looking more dark and gloomy than usual. He said, "We have to talk."

"Okay. What's up?"

Hunched against the chill, Courtman gazed out at the mountain across the forested valley, filled his lungs with that excruciating fresh air, enough to kill an ordinary city dweller, and not looking at Victor said slowly, "Do I understand you're planning to overthrow the government of the United States by allowing this man to speak to the Vice President on television?" He paused a beat. "Have I got it approximately correct?" He looked at him, poker-faced, perhaps looking for clues that Victor was losing his mind.

Anger shot into Victor's eyes. As he was about to blurt out a response, Courtman touched his arm gently. "The Buddha says anger will burn up all the good you have done," he said. "Get focused."

Smoldering, Victor took a breath, feeling Courtman's understated wrath, or accusation or whatever it was, rising from the perfectly reasonable view that what was taking place here was an escape from reality which could not possibly end any other way than serious incarceration, or the loony bin.

"Until you can think of something better," he said finally, "that would appear to be the plan. I haven't read the full script yet."

They stood in the moist afternoon. Perhaps each man was

waiting for the other to call him a fool. As one they turned and peered through the big picture window into the living area, where everybody was on phones and writing notes and fiddling with laptops. The energy was conflicting. A healing place, and a fractured nation. A decent and sensitive man holding together this gang of hardened street fighters, all reaching out with clenched fists holding nothing but hope and dreams, doing combat against the inexorable force of the times, the reigning authority holding all the cards, sneering at all the people.

BJ was anxious to show the deposition, his surgically-worked part of the drama, but Nel was holding him off until the women showed up from California.

By a miracle, Nel had resurrected Daniel Cool, a Secret Service agent still bemoaning a personal indiscretion involving Nel herself at an official White House black tie function a dozen years ago. Cool was still working POTUS protection detail.

Needing to plunge into the fray, Raven Menez was back on the phone with Molly, arranging transportation and insisting she and Iona both bring clothes that could take a beating, prepaid phones and two computers, and toilet paper. Armageddon was definitely on the way, she told her mentor, although she probably couldn't afford it once it arrived.

Back inside now, Courtman found himself still stuck in first gear, sipping discreetly from a bottle of Old Hickory from his home stock. He knew the blond woman was up to her neck in this, simply by knowing her favorite hobby – seductively slipping a noose around the neck of a Big Shot, then kicking the chair out from under him. Back in Philadelphia she'd sworn to track Hunter Tyne's every move, and Courtman feared she might be taking the task literally. But he could not reach her from here, in this backwater forest with no Internet service. Doc Nguyen had said on the phone he would bring the equipment. If and when he did, Courtman would return to the old spy game with her, communicating on a long-forgotten blog page buried deep in the Army Corps of Engineers Web site, an abandoned bridge project jointly vacated by the state of Maine and the Engineers, and never taken down. The blond woman was to contact him there. In his heart Courtman no more believed in Edwin Foulks' powers than he did in the Easter bunny. But somehow he had been caught up in this madness and now he was compelled to ride it out. What he had come to understand yet again after twenty-five years in back-room politics, following the treasonous meeting at Independence Hall and frantically dodging the FBI today, was that political chicanery was nothing more than a game. Serious, life-or-death entertainment! People in suits pretending to be grownups, flicking pebbles in the sandbox where real patriots once met to make their decisions.

And now here he was in Never-Never Land, snorting pixie dust from the private supply of Edwin Foulks, aka Davy Crockett.

Nel came in from the kitchen, her eyes swollen, holding up a slim finger.

"Purvis." She sniffled. "Your friend from Independence Hall the other night? Victor mentioned him. Didn't he run the Area 51 Intelsat program? What was his name?"

Courtman squinted at her. He held up a hand timidly for her to high-five. "Yes," he said. "I believe so."

66

President Sol Burligame had been listening to officials since dawn, deliberating with Defense Intelligence, the FBI, NSA, the National Counterintelligence Center, and the National Guard. Both the Secret Service and the White House Inauguration Committee met with him, separately, on Inauguration security matters that covered exactly the same ground. In a spirit of decorum he had suffered through a joint meeting with the House Intelligence Oversight Committee – another crowd brought in during the holiday break – in tandem with the swiftly-formed Senate Ad-Hoc Committee on the Philadelphia Area Security Breach. Nobody who wanted to keep his job was going to call it a rebellion.

Attorney General Jim Turcutt, a hard-core, impeccably dressed bureaucrat and childhood friend of Burligame's back in Minnesota, summed up the frustration of the intelligence community.

"Sir, we have interviewed every D. Crockett in America. The man has simply eluded us. The prints at Ney Field are not in the system. His documents were phony. Olfactory scan took us to Independence Hall – some kind of silly joke, I suppose. There was no rental car, no ticket to Philadelphia, no flight school records, no tracing the *Rebellion.com* banner, no crime scene evidence in the plane itself other than Sligo's hair. The iris scan was a prank! The man who runs that airport has a memory like a shovel. The Van Zandt post office box was a red herring. They haven't had a post office in forty years. Our only lead is a seventy-one-year-old African-American woman! And God help us, Mr. President, now Internet junkies are telling us she's the reincarnation of DB Cooper!"

Distracted, Burligame was tempted to bring in the new House Subcommittee on Voting Irregularities, although their work would not begin till the next session of Congress. He already knew what they would find: criminals hired by his own party to throw the election. It was not an absolute certainty in the President's mind, but in his heart, he knew. This is what motivated Crockett. This is what the street uprising was demanding – the truth. Fewer and fewer voters. Billy Hellman, as popular as malaria, with his iron grip on the Executive Branch. And the New Freedom Party still winning elections! What kind of fool did they take him for?

Sol Burligame was biding his time.

This morning Billy Hellman with his lubricious charm had briefed the President – also nominal head of the National Security Council – in preparation for the emergency meeting.

"These hoodlums want to mess with my government?" Hellman said, his beady eyes flashing everywhere in the Oval Office. "What, investigate some voting problem? Fine. The Independent Voters' Council files a complaint. *Our* FBI reports urgent need to examine all voting contractors and machinery. *Our* GSA checks it out. *Our* National Intelligence Center cleans it up! Congress gets the report. *Our* spokesperson Leoro Psybysch passes it on to I-Media. I-Media informs the people. Right? No need to get your knickers in an uproar! The smart thing is turn this rebellion to our advantage." He snapped his eyes to the President. *"Right?"*

So often Burligame did not comprehend the unraveled inner tapestry of the Vice President's mind. But he listened, with increasing resentment, as his executive officer insisted the government not compromise a millimeter in demanding the surrender of Davy Crockett. If Sligo was harmed – well, greater men had paid the ultimate price for freedom. The minute Crockett was apprehended and the public tantrum settled, entities in the White House would ensure that the President receive the credit for his steady and skillful management of what was really a last gasp on the pathway to absolute New Freedom Party domination.

For Burligame it was a matter of misjudgment. What he had failed to consider was the emergence of Billy Hellman as dictator of government policy, making decisions in disregard of the Constitution and of Sol Burligame's personal constituency – the people.

As always the Vice President was the last person to arrive at the National Security Council meeting, today in a short-sleeve black polo shirt to show off his muscular physique. As always he was in a maliciously foul humor that all present knew could deteriorate in a nanosecond. It was true that this crisis exposed the Vice President's primary character flaw – the ruthless humiliation of his enemies. Several upper-level people had committed the unspeakable error of making it known they hated his guts. He took great pleasure in stomping them into the luxurious carpeting of the Cabinet Room. And he delighted most of all when they got up, bloodied and beaten, and apologized to him publicly for being so foolish as to mistake him for an ordinary mortal.

But Billy had no intention of discussing emergencies at this meeting. The sixteen security agencies were doing their jobs. And really, there was no emergency. This was fun. Especially after he'd blown Nel Sligo clean out of the water with that Code Thirteen shocker. Following a little public seizure, the thing would blow over. Crockett would be arrested, Sligo would invent some bad lie and look like a compromising nitwit, and the party would go about its agenda of expanding the US industrial-technological-financial playground into a gold mine for those Billy Hellman served – the ones who mined the gold.

67

By the time Hellman had snatched the first sweet bite of his almond croissant, the Manhattan Federal Building's downstairs night janitor, Slash Zewinta, in his burrow in Queens, had reconnected with his new friend Dalmatinke. This time he had to lay some Paypal cash on the guy in order to access the top secret log recorded by Homeland Security during the freak show over suburban Philadelphia. The man would get back to him.

An hour later, the very information he'd paid for came over the news stream at the bottom of his TV screen. So much for Slash's last hundred bucks. But sure enough, the *Rebellion.com* drama had involved the FAA, the Pentagon, the Office of Naval Intelligence, Homeland Security, and the FBI, all bashing and spraying at each other for the right to shoot down Davy Crockett. They had treated it like the invasion of the Branch Dividians compound. No wonder the FBI'd scooped up Desdemona Crockett so fast! She was a national embarrassment. Here DB Cooper had gone to great length to change his identity to become Desdemona Crockett, and they had detained her on this bogus kidnapping business. It was just more wasteful government intervention into private lives.

Me and Desdemona. The only two sane people left in America. Hassling the evil empire! Inciting riots! Beating up on federal agents! "Yeah!" belched a hyperconflagrated Slash Zewinta, as he turned up Alice Cooper and boogied to the fridge for a Dr. Pepper. "DB rocks!"

The log Dalmatinke sent him showed that over the time of the *Rebellion.com* riot, everybody involved had gone crazy. They were going to shoot that plane down, Congressman or no Congressman. Everybody knew Victor Sligo was a thorn in the side of the administration. So he was pretty certain whoever "Limburger" was – the man who ultimately gave the command – he obviously wanted Sligo dead along with the pilot.

There was no telling who Limburger was. But Burligame was away farting around somewhere, and only he or the VP could put out a kill command. Man, how he wished he could prove it was Hellman. The guy who greased Hunter Tyne's ride through the Senate hearings to have him appointed Secretary of Communications, so he could deregulate his former company. The dirtiest trick in government since the Iraq War.

Slash knew things about Billy Hellman. More than once he'd seriously decided to stand up and take on the little tyrant, but Billy was too slick to stop, and in reality Slash Gewinta was no good at organized attacks. His strength was in undermining. And also in adoring his heroes from afar – Dwight Gooden and Daryl Strawberry, Michael Bloomberg, Molly Bee and DB Cooper. Billy had been running for Vice President over four years ago when Slash got clear on what a natural-born politician he was. Billy's campaign was caught with a big wad of unreported lobby money from CI. In a deal that the one and only Molly Bee exposed, Hellman, in return for a couple of million dollars in back door cash for his campaign, was supposed to act as a high-profile pitchman for Holotech, the state of the art TV system. Although as Slash himself was to learn, it was a system that tended to blow CI fumes into the house, and it featured microchips and semiconductors that didn't appear on any wiring diagrams.

The expensive new TVs blanketed the country anyway. Now they were everywhere. And Hellman never admitted any wrongdoing.

Slick Hellman and Dr. Hunter Tyne were fungi on the landscape of human decency. So Slash Zewinta, manic cyber-terrorist, was going to sharpen his sheers and do some pruning.

But how?

Clicking the captured log off his screen, Slash balanced the Dr. Pepper bottle on his head and settled in for a good think. His first thought was about this crazy airplane called *Rebellion.com.* Trusting his instinct he typed in the Web site just to check out the *Strategies for Survival in a Corporate World,* and what he saw nearly knocked the bottle off his head. The *Strategies* were actually incredibly simple, common-sense notions of how to run a country. Fair IRS laws devised by genuine tax-savvy citizens. Corporate incentives for provable humanitarian work – a deviously intelligent concept. Decent tax proposals, like a fifty percent surcharge on malpractice suits. For political campaigns, only public funds would be used, and absolutely no corporate money. Six-year term limits in Congress. Connecting the family's role in a child's education to housing and medical and food vouchers. Removing all the non-academic responsibilities from schools. Bringing local corporate funds to the school district to finance programs designed by the same corporations. Somebody had proposed a Department of Strategies for Creating a Transparent Government, staffed by nobody over the age of thirty, with investigative authority throughout the bureaucracy. Man! Big Brother watching himself! Locally elected retirees as ombudsmen in all federal contracts. All lobbying activities would by law appear in local newspapers. A national conversation would commence about handgun sales in urban areas. They were trying to overhaul the whole notion of government as it had been practiced during Slash Zewinta's life. Somebody thought participatory democracy could actually be exercised wherever there was public money.

He wanted to do his part. He dug in, poring through his pile of bootlegged emails, public records, thousands of photographs and his personal collection of sound bites, scratching his grungy stubble with his gnawed-raw fingernails, listening to Gracie Slick belt out *White Rabbit* inside his virtual reality headphones.

Well, there was a hell of a good place to start right on the front page of the *West Coast Paper*, at the moment streaming along the bottom of his monitor. He could find Congressman Victor Sligo, and join the crusade. Sligo represented the opposition to the forces of darkness across the land. And Slash had all kinds of skills Sligo could use.

Finding a fugitive congressman turned out to be as hard as it sounds. He called half a dozen Congressional numbers on his Liquiphone – the latest com device from India, featuring video in and out, Internet, worldwide cell connect, and half a million video games. But he got nowhere. Sligo's own Web site was down. He contacted subversive friends, watchdog Web sites and even the police in Sligo's district. He got lots of advice, but couldn't find the man himself. Touching voices answered at Sligo's offices in D.C. and Everett, Washington, grotesquely sincere youngsters telling him how important his call was.

After a while he lost his focus. The bedlam of his brain just could not keep this thread spinning. This was fortuitous, as it turned out. Slash called in to work for the day's shift changes. The second shift maintenance supervisor, Federica Kos, gave him the bad news. Some woman was being detained in the basement jail they never used, and there was serious security clamping down the building.

Nobody knew what was going on. Make sure he was wearing his ID badge. No visitors, no media, no nothing. Whoa, said Slash Zewinta. Bad girl! What did she do? Federica told him, "The feds are refusing to give her access to her lawyer. They think she's the pilot of that plane down in Philly."

68

President Sol Burligame glanced up and tapped his Rolex as Hellman entered and took the seat to the President's right. The president nodded to the Secret Service agent to close the door on his way out. Sol Burligame's presence, his body language, his demeanor, his eye contact, were absolutely commanding. Each of the twenty or so people in the immaculate National Security Council chamber had known the President for years. He was loved and admired publicly. His policies were seriously considered throughout the corridors of power, and then quietly ignored. Cartoonists struggled to avoid his eyes, badly disfigured by the airborne pathogen pandemic. Thus the big man with the barrel chest and big voice was satirized in the underground press wearing enormous sunglasses, and sometimes a mask, often depicted as a hulking blind man led on a chain by a diminutive Popeye figure, Billy Hellman, armed to the teeth and reeking of nuclear waste. Altogether a pathetic image of the national leadership.

They were all present now. Burligame could almost see what they were thinking. Victoria Cross, his National Security Advisor, would brief everybody with infinite details on what didn't happen since yesterday in the manhunt. Attorney General Jim Turcutt, Burligame's closest friend and tennis partner, would present a cogent case, and grumble privately about his obnoxious colleague, the Secretary of Homeland Security, Needham Strange. For some reason Strange was absent. Also absent was the Director of the FBI, hand-picked by the Vice President. He had been run down by a rampaging oxcart in Kabul, and was on the DL. In his place John Lee Davis had showed up. Davis really got in Hellman's craw, which amused Sol Burligame. He enjoyed watching the VP twitch. Davis's holier than thou demeanor, those wimpy little John Lennon glasses, and that sexually suggestive pony tail! He looked like a bouncer in a London whorehouse.

Uninvited, Secretary of Communications Hunter Tyne was present. Tyne was the dark antagonist, a nervous man compulsively rubbing his thin black mustache, middle-aged with tiny brown eyes darting restlessly about the room, with no apparent irony preferring brown shirts and suits, given to gruff speech if he spoke at all, a solitary man known to everybody in Washington and friends to none. He had risen from the power swamp of Communication International, connecting occasionally with Hellman on CI's dirty business out in the nuclear dump fields of Nevada and Utah, and yet they thoroughly loathed each other. Today Tyne had a female assistant with him. Graham St. John, the Secretary of Defense, was absent, but had sent his immediate inferior, Admiral Sukwant Singh, head of the Joint Chiefs, a respected, old-fashioned American hero from India or someplace. And speaking of India, the President nodded to NSA's director Oliver Red Lightning, a full-blooded Cree, sitting grimly in his muscular, silent demeanor, looking like he'd been poured into his hand-made black silk suit.

Davis unobtrusively studied the attractive woman sitting beside Tyne. He'd never seen her before, and wondered if she were a plant from his own Bureau, or perhaps from CI, the hundred-tentacled monster Tyne used to work for. When the President entered, Tyne had introduced her as his Deputy Assistant for Media Regulation, and he said her name at the exact instant Sukwant Singh chose to sneeze voluminously across the table, scattering papers, driving Ms Cross away gasping and searching for a handkerchief.

Yes, of course, everyone said, nodding politely.

Leora Psybysch, Hellman's universally hated chief of staff, sat rigidly nearby in a form-fitting blue outfit with a plunging neckline, sliding notes to her boss. At the opposite end of the massive oval table sat Burligame's Tweedledee and Tweedledum, press secretary Joel Babylon and the President's pestilential chief of staff, Hussein Al-Jakka.

"Let's get right down to it, shall we?" the President said. He felt over-briefed. Everybody in national intelligence had his ear this morning. There wasn't much he didn't know.

"Damn the torpedoes," said Billy Hellman.

Burligame allowed his pontifical gaze to survey the gather-

ing. "We're here to get a sense of what's taking place in our country
these past few days. We're here to arm-wrestle each other to determine the best way to get our citizens back on track. At the same
time –" His pleasant voice conflicted with the pained look in the
eyes, "– we have a fine opportunity here. The New Freedom Party
has taken mighty severe punishment by the underground media
since the fall election..." Glancing at a scowling Secretary Tyne.
"Not your media, Hunter. Those independent people."

The Secretary of Communications said nothing, but the
steady hatred in his face tore into Burligame's chest. A truly malevolent man.

Several pairs of eyes moved, but nobody spoke.

"Now some guy comes out of left field. He snatches Sligo.
We look like bad guys. We!" Patting his great chest, Sol Burligame
set his firm jaw, eyes bleeding into the heart of each person present.
"Look like bad guys!"

They all felt his anguish.

Then he laughed. Not heartily, not with gusto, but he did
laugh. "Is that ridiculous, or what?"

Other than Tyne, the National Security Council had a good
laugh with him. "The Vice President has suggested we make this
half-baked rebellion work to our advantage. Suggestions?"

"Mr. President." Billy Hellman sat next to Burligame. Immediately his body language suggested he was taking charge. He
did not glance at the President. "I suggest we find Crockett and have
him publicly drawn and quartered. I'm serious. Ripped apart, limb
from limb. And the parts fed to the poor." His hands made a ghastly
ripping motion. "Sends a clear message out there, don't you think?"

Sol Burligame looked directly at him. "We operate under
the assumption of ordinary human decency, sir." And to the entire
council, "That is our policy here."

"But Mr. President, wait," Billy Hellman leaned aside and
whispered with an obsequious smirk. "I don't recall any policy in
this government specifically requiring human decency. You're
swinging out of the strike zone there. Sir."

Burligame cupped a hand over his mouth. He whispered to
Hellman, "Don't you come in here telling me what you don't think!
What you *do* think is so bizarre you easily surpass JK Rowling!"

To the attentive group Burligame said, "All right then. Are

we clear? Put this thing to our advantage. Martial law is not good PR, ladies and gentlemen, but we're going to do it come Monday if this thing isn't over. Understood?" He allowed the message to penetrate. Nobody appeared surprised. "Let's get past this. Bring this Crockett in, get him counsel, and we'll go from there. This nation has always profited from constructive dissent. The Vice President will hear your reports. As Commander-in-Chief I am going to remain neutral until all the information is in. We are not going to hang an innocent man."

69

Doc Nguyen, feeling all of his eighty years, had taken a jouncy company jet to Bellingham and had a colleague race him out to Van Zandt, armed with fifty years of voting analysis, studies of election fraud involving touch-screen and ballot-counting equipment, in addition to three laptops and a Ziplink dish and routers to join Edwin's stump ranch to the Twenty-First Century. So mistrustful was Doc Nguyen of the New Freedom Party political apparatus, it did not occur to him people were failing to vote in such historic numbers as an expression of apathy or discontent. It was simply criminal activity nobody had been able to classify. So far.

At the log house in the woods, the humorous, bent over and bespectacled Vietnamese-American was greeted with half a dozen people speaking earnestly into multicolored drug store phones. The place had the smell of a life-or-death endeavor – and right in the center of it was Congressman Victor Sligo, just freed from perdition or kidnap, or else he'd played a hell of a practical joke on the entire country.

Jabbing a finger to his tracheotomy chip, Doc Nguyen yelled in that sour computer voice, "Yo, big guy!" Victor leaped up and came to embrace the much shorter old man. Immediately they were speaking Vietnamese together. Occasionally Victor pressed a thumb against his own throat and imitated Doc's monotone guttural gratings.

"Where'd you get that shirt?" Doc demanded. "Off a dead lumberjack?"

"Off your mother, actually," the Congressman said without blinking an eye. "For services rendered."

"Ah, me sainted mum," Doc Nguyen said, touching his shiny black hair. "Irish as the day is long. Speaking of which, you look familiar to me. Forty years ago I had sex with a water buffalo. Are you my son?"

"Get that man out of here," Nel Sligo sang out from across the broad living room, "before I call the SPCA!"

He and Nel embraced, people were introduced, and Doc gave gravelly instructions to Mgaba and BJ to set up the Ziplink.

Shortly they got down to graphing the results of the November election, and listening to Edwin's absolutely insane plan to undermine the Inauguration four days away.

70

"Let's have it," Billy Hellman gruffed, clapping his thick hands. "Ms. Cross?" In his head he was phrasing his own report for this august gathering, when they were done: "Who among us has not longed for the triumphant march into the great city on the hill! I will lead you! I! Caliban! This Inauguration signals a new era in America, from despair to empire!"

Victoria Cross, the former CIA agent now advising the White House on national security matters, felt intimidated by only one man on Earth, and she was looking at him. She contemplated what it would feel like to kick him in the balls. In her executive taupe suit and dangling soapstone earrings, Cross not only looked spectacular, she felt herself crucial to the protection of the nation. But this man made her feel conflicted. Female, self-conscious, and murderous.

"We're prepared to respond on *the President's* command, Mr. Vice President. You are aware the country is in a state of near meltdown. We are at the point that when any federal agent presents his or her credentials, the subject immediately wants to know where we are hiding Congressman Sligo! National security has become in less than a week a national farce! People are leaving my office out of sheer –" Her eyes darted to Psybysch for a microsecond. She stopped speaking abruptly, folded her arms across her chest, and stared straight ahead. In an instant she'd gone from animated bureaucrat to silent Quaker.

"Go on," Hellman nudged, sensing she wasn't going anywhere.

She didn't. The Vice President's knuckles drummed on the exquisite table. He frowned at her, waiting like an arrogant school principal.

"We are taking the advantage here, madam," he scolded her. "Before tomorrow's meeting I'd ask you to prepare an eyes-only report..." He pushed his big jowls at her and poked two fingers toward his canine face. "My eyes, Ms. Cross, on your actions toward pressing the advantage on this matter for this Administration. Are we clear?" He looked remarkably like an angry English bulldog.

Cross summoned all her will power. "Mine is not a political office, Mr. Vice President. May I remind you that I serve at the pleasure of the President! The function of the National Security Advisor, as you know perf –"

"Thanks, honey," Hellman cut her off with a chop of his hand. "I'll have your stuff on my desk by ten a.m. or your resignation by noon. Now where the hell is Needham Strange? Isn't he running Homeland Security?" He glared at Admiral Singh. "And where is my Secretary of Defense? St. John. He's supposed to be here." As the National Security Advisor stormed out crimson-faced and seething, Hellman threw an arm up at her and glanced at John Lee Davis, who was staring rigidly at him, hands clasped together on the table, his dark eyes unmoving. Davis was on the brink of expressing a mutinous thought.

Admiral Singh burst in. "Sir, if I may?" Singh clicked a remote and two panels separated to reveal a large screen behind the Vice President. Another click, and a full-size live feed came up. Two men, naked except for Sumo-like diapers, wrestled in a pit of mud in a smoke-filled arena. They were utterly filthy, engaged in a violent, surrealistic struggle. Other men, some in uniform, roared from outside the pit, salivating and cheering and smoking cigars.

Stunned silence clawed through the Cabinet chamber. The Vice President's mouth hung open. Singh let the video roll for another five seconds.

"That is Homeland Security Secretary Needham Strange on

the left, sir. The one just biting the other man's ear. The other man is the Secretary of Defense. Sir."

Billy Hellman stared at the screen, unable to grasp the meaning of it.

"They've been at each other's throats for months," Leora Psybysch announced, in that peculiar splintery voice that sounded like she'd been eating blackberry vines. "It all came to a head over this insurrection."

At last he turned to face the council. His dark face shook. He nodded. And then he dropped a fist quietly on the table. The fist fell again, and again.

"Nice," he said, obviously awed. "Couple of tough guys slugging it out. Settling it the American way. That's what we like to see. Stand up guys in my Cabinet! Commitment! A good old-fashioned ass-kicking! All right. I have some important business to discuss. Let's move on. Who's next?"

71

Upstairs, Nel was having a risky chat with Secret Service Agent Daniel Cool. The agent, embarrassed for life over thirty seconds of lusty malapropisms with Ms Sligo that sultry night by the Rose Garden long ago, found himself agreeing to pass on to Nel logistics for the Inauguration four days hence. She was still waiting for the rest of the picture from Fred Geschwantner down in Salt Lake. He was due to call hours ago. And Molly and Iona still weren't here. Coming down to the crowded main room, she went to the window, fiddling with her wedding ring, and finally started into the kitchen to see what was troubling Raven Menez.

In his old oak rocker by the heater, Edwin watched Nel pass. He was beyond wondering the source of the nightmare he had released on the country. He sat honing his pocket knife, waiting, certain and uncertain, feeling the rain outside the French doors.

At the other end of the big living area, long legs crunched under a kid's desk, Courtman was on the phone with Dr. Kuushmann at Groom Lake, paying no attention to Edwin's big monitor fixed to the Web site where his nameless intelligence asset, the blond woman, was supposed to check in with him twenty-four hours ago. Doc Nguyen was breathing tumultuously through his trach tube and listening to his outlaw researchers in Boulder whining that no man of woman born could break through Communication International's data protection walls. Crammed into his alcove among the spider webs and the Christmas cactus, BJ had narrowed his search on election equipment fraud down to a Truman Butts, a computer programmer who might or might not be able to speak about voting booth machinery in recent elections in Ohio. Behind him, Mgaba was drafting a planned call to his friend Chloe Shapiro-Fujimoto, the Chief Justice of the Supreme Court. Bringing her into this fiasco would either stop it cold, or elevate Mgaba to hero status. He thought he'd make a rather dignified Secretary of State. It was always *women*, he realized for the thousandth time. Women were the key to every pleasure, every victory, every misery, every catastrophe. *Toujours les femmes!*

Victor was getting nowhere. The sting hinged on a hundred points, of which one of the most crucial was the live televising of Edwin's interview with Burligame and Hellman. But no producer would touch it. Everybody in Washington was scared to death. Victor could not understand this. A victor his entire life, he hated failure. All he was trying to accomplish was persuading people he did not know to participate in an act of treason, which would end their careers, attempting to film an imaginary event only a certified lunatic would take seriously.

"I'm getting it now," Iona Webster said to Molly Bee. "A laptop, tough clothes and toilet paper. Look out there! We're gonna meet Paul Bunyan!"

Moments ago they had flown past the ash plume spewing from the Sherman Crater on the flank of Mount Baker, and now they were descending into wall-to-wall forest. Webster's brother was piloting the private seven-passenger airplane toward a podunk airstrip somewhere near Van Zandt, Washington, while they read the news on their separate laptops. Just now, *Truth.com,* an independent news stream, was camped outside the emergency meeting of the National Security Council.

"Not only has the President left the meeting," the commentator was saying. "Now Victoria Cross, his advisor for national security, has also hastily departed the Cabinet Room. Clearly a crisis is unfolding on some front yet to be disclosed! Our alert cameraman took this brief footage before the door closed behind Ms. Cross." Instant segue to the enormous oak door opening and a furious Cross shoving past a Secret Service man. The image froze, then zoomed in to reveal a candid shot of the Vice President, with Tyne and other officials visible nearby. The Vice President's arm was in the air, obviously sending Cross off with a "good riddance."

Molly had been relieved when Iona had told her nothing would stop her from coming up to Washington state. Wearing soft green slacks and sturdy shoes and a black wool sweater, she was feeling more comfortable than she had landing at Salt Lake Airport, in spite of today's rocky ride. Iona had described Edwin Foulks from the meeting at Independence Hall, but both women were surprised at what looked like Ireland or the Mosquito Coast.

Iona's taciturn brother, Dushane Marr, announced, "Wheels down shortly."

Molly whispered, "Where's he staying?"

"He wouldn't say. Some woman. Said where he's going is X-rated."

"Men!" Bee shook her head. "Too dirty to live with, and too stupid to use for guide dogs."

The aircraft dropped into low cloud and a dense mist. A river silvered out of the mountains and curled through foothills.

"The Seyes River," said Marr. "Guy lives down there somewhere."

"Weird place to save the world," Iona said, a nervous air traveler. "Specially from itself. It ain't going to happen in my lifetime. Black people have been screwed since God was a little girl." She laughed aloud. "And I was going to fix it! Course I had to play football first! Then I fixed it, all right. Two decades of sticking my nose in corporate boardrooms. Fifteen years of Freedom of Information demands, embarrassing subcommittees, forming the Black Education Union," rubbing her eyes, feeling all the years burning behind her eyeballs. "Then a black President! I thought I'd died and gone to heaven! Then more recession and more unemployment. So here I am back in South Central, and we're still getting torn apart, the black politicians against the corporate watchdogs, and everybody against the poor folks." She smiled at Molly. "It does get old."

They'd had time to peruse *Government Incendiaries*, a mildly subversive Web site, featuring the unauthorized biography of Dr. Hunter Tyne. The bio quoted radical writings from Tallyrand to Ayn Rand, included one of Tyne's favorites, a classic comment by Karl Marx: "Social progress can be measured exactly by the social position of the fair sex, the ugly ones included."

Molly couldn't wait to get a look at the deposition BJ was supposed to have. Apparently it wasn't Tyne's fingerprints on a smoking gun, but it was close.

More stuff had been added in the past two days by some Web vigilante.

Tyne had studied neurochemistry with a minor in psychology, but had switched in mid-career to mass communications. This was actually only a subtle shift in mindset. The biographer termed Tyne "ruthlessly efficient, a neurochemist with Communication West before it expanded into Communication International, known for its experiments blurring ethical boundaries to achieve universal power." He'd worked on contracts with the US Army as well as Eli Lily and Monsanto – before their merger to become Monsilly – and engaged in classified, multi-agency research on remote mind control. Disgruntled former CI employees claimed Tyne was researching the effects of serotonin reuptake inhibitors as catalysts in the science of Brain-Computer Interface, or BCI, including experiments in which "volunteers" were loaded with a variety of substances, lashed to BCI monitoring devices, and subjected to sex videos. The research followed directly from Army experiments with LSD, brainwashing, and post-hypnotic suggestion at Aberdeen Proving Ground in Maryland.

Over Tyne's signature, a paper had been produced, although rejected by the *Journal of Psychiatry,* on "Digitally-induced hypnosis." He was versed in the works of Jeffrey Dahlmers, Karl Rove and Stalin, as well as *Mein Kampf* and Hitler's war diaries and those of his entourage including Goebbels, Göring and Dr. Mengele. Tyne traveled to the Philippines during the bloody crackdown on dissidents, pushing a research proposal on the government involving television and mass hysteria. Attempts to verify the content of the research were inconclusive.

"And listen to this," Webster said. "At a conference at Davos, Switzerland, Tyne delivered a paper naming the Holocaust a

theoretical model of 'media-induced, hysterical psycho-profiling.'
Apparently he changed his tune after he went skiing and found his
Mercedes accidentally squashed beyond recognition by a passing
bulldozer."

Ten years ago Tyne had moved into CI's Research Division
and through corporate successes in no small part due to earmarks
from a certain Nevada congressman, was relocated to Chicago,
where he took over as Research Director. A footnote to the bio had
been appended, dated two days ago, January 16th. Near the end of
Tyne's tenure running the Research Division, a lab subcontracting
with CI had been shut down for doing unlicensed research on human brain stems and the hypothalamus. They called it "neurochemical programming." US Attorney's Office files show a Grand Jury
indicted a high-level official named REDACTED as project coordina-
tor for CI, but REDACTED was not charged in the matter.

Iona and Molly stared at each other.

The footnote added to the Tyne biography was attributed to
a researcher listing his name only as "Slickwatch."

Molly said, "Sounds scary. Neurochemical programming."
A hundred science-fiction images flew through their minds.

72

The Vice President had an unpublished engagement with a
lady and a gentleman at a certain mansion up the river in Potomac,
and the members were babbling on. He wanted to express his grand
concept of the coming Inauguration, although the principal plans
were laid without the input of anybody but Leora Psybysch. Following the shocking video of the Secretary of Homeland Security in a
naked life-and-death battle with the Secretary of Defense, the other
executives had detected a whiff of the surreal, and a couple of them
had left. It was a difficult scenario to get the mind around: the rabid
Vice President steering the ship of state, intent on shutting down the
nation in response to some unarmed kook with a coonskin cap and a
rented airplane.

Upon witnessing the mudbath brawl, John Lee Davis had
nodded curtly at the Vice President and walked out. His brain was

flying in a tight circle. Enacting martial law, a presidential edict literally in the hands of Billy Hellman, now seemed not only insane but inevitable. And he was powerless to do anything about it. He believed the President was astute enough to realize martial law would have a devastating effect on worldwide financial instruments, possibly tipping the precarious balance of international currencies to favor the People's Republic of China. Whatever shred of confidence the global economic community might be clinging to, would vanish.

At the same time, unrelated to all this, Davis couldn't help feeling terribly vulnerable personally, under the withering glare of the Vice President.

The core of National Security remained at the Council meeting: Burligame's best friend, Attorney General Turcutt – who would never leave a meeting in Hellman's hands; Leora Psybysch, various intelligence agency bosses from NIC and DIA, a Homeland Security deputy assistant, NSA director Oliver Red Lightning, Admiral Singh from the Joint Chiefs, and a Secret Service-CIA-National Intelligence Center liaison person who never spoke, plus Hunter Tyne and his new blond assistant. White House press secretary Joel Babylon sat brooding in the corner like a chained dog.

For a couple of minutes, Babylon whispered into a device that resembled a pickle, and read from a tiny display screen.

Hellman could not have known Joel Babylon was in the final moments of a crushing moral epiphany that had wracked his soul over the past forty-eight hours. The press secretary was preparing to either leap out the window, or stand up and call the Vice President and all his minions a bunch of despicable liars. Finally Babylon crossed the threshold. He was overwhelmed with self-loathing. His alarm at his country's future thundered through his bloodstream.

"Mr. Hellman." For four years Babylon had refused to call him "Mr. Vice President," which always made Hellman want to crush his nuts in a bench vice. "I've just learned of a matter pertinent to this meeting. Both national transit workers unions have voted to walk out! Two hundred fifty thousand transit workers. Every bus, every subway, every public transit vehicle in the country will be at a dead standstill by midnight. The walk-out is in support of a recall vote –"

"I don't care if the Pope walked out of the Vatican, Joel!

We've got business to attend to here! So why don't you button up your lip and pay attention."

"The reality is," Babylon pronounced loudly, "Crockett has a First Amendment right to fly a banner with whatever he wants on it! That's not incitement to treason, that's clever advertising! You can't just stomp on the Constitution at your whim!"

"Don't push me, Babylon!" The veins in Hellman's neck were pumping hard.

Babylon felt his breath constricting, but he loosened his bowtie and pushed on. "And that Web site? It contains the future of the United States of America, when decent men and women rule."

Hellman glared. Fire shot out his eyeballs. But his voice was deadly calm. "You may leave this room, sir!"

"You know what the ugliest part is?" The President's spokesman was addressing the other officials now, realizing his day was over, and he was going to stand up and fight. Everybody in the room knew of the Vice President's open disregard for Babylon's photographic memory of government policy. He spoke the words with dignity. "I love Sol Burligame. He is a civilized, patriotic, actually rather honest man. President Burligame would never allow his country to collapse into anarchy over a measly banner flying over people's heads." Whipping his eyes back to the Vice President, "It's you, Mr. Hellman, that the people are rebelling against. It's you who are causing the country to suffocate under your miserable ego, and your need to carry out the orders of your superiors, whoever they are!"

Hellman stood, way over his threshold, his enormous jowls clamped shut, pointing a rigid finger at Babylon, and swinging the finger toward the door. Without so much as flinching, Babylon said, "You want to do a service for your country? You want to seal your place in history? Resign! Cash in your chips, Mr. Hellman! They will praise your name for years to come!" He spun on his heels and walked out.

A black-suited Secret Service man stood at the door, mouth hanging open, flicking nervous glances at Leora Psybysch.

"Hey, Sean," Babylon greeted him pleasantly as he passed.

Dr. Hunter Tyne watched Babylon leave. A grimace was fixed on the Secretary's iron face. He had to peel back layers of his knife-to-the-throat career to pin down his initial meeting with this

foul little wretch, Billy Hellman. Yes, Carson City. That was it. The
infamous Region 9, the EPA's Office of Solid Waste. A lifetime
moving shit! Region 9 did not include the state of Utah but it did
handle toxic material that Tyne badly needed to get rid of without
public knowledge. Communication West had mountains of re-
stricted chemical toxins and hazardous waste scattered all over the
landscape, material the corporation had no desire to appear on public record. Once Tyne and Hellman teamed up, the thing was ac-
complished so efficiently that both Communication West and Billy
Hellman had gone on to make a bundle of money, causing illegal
waste to disappear from various venues from North Dakota to Los
Angeles.

Long before Communication West had dropped the dirty
business and moved into international media enterprises, Tyne and
Hellman had each recognized an ambitious and dangerous megalo-
maniac in the other. No love was lost between them.

Hunter Tyne was always the last man to have his say. As
Babylon marched out, Tyne allowed the Council members a moment to prepare for a superior being to elucidate the situation. He
had studied a thousand famous speeches, and preferred to speak in
absolute terms. No questions asked.

"Not to worry. This punk rebellion's going to drop on the
dung heap of human folly," he said, carefully modulating his pitch.
"Like all the Progressives' other tantrums." His voice contained no
detectable respect for the Vice President. He knew how much Hellman despised him, and he returned the sentiment gladly.

"Don't try to stop it," he said, for no apparent reason. "The
situation is under control. You'll just make it worse."

Beside and slightly behind Tyne, his new assistant had been
waiting all day, one might say many weeks, for this moment. Slipping a hand casually to her breast, she activated the minicam on the
center button of her red satin jacket. The feed went out instantly
through an Internet connection to the officially defunct blog page of
the Army Engineers Penobscot River bridge project. Ever so calmly,
scarlet fingernails gleaming, she twisted the burnished bronze button, widening the angle of focus, at the same moment aiming herself
toward the two men.

Billy Hellman growled, *"You're* gonna stop Crockett?
What, single-handedly?" He almost grinned, recalling Nel Sligo

cursing him on the Code Thirteen. He knew the damn thing was already over.

Tyne rose as he answered. "DComm's intelligence arm," he said stiffly, moving toward the Director of the National Security Agency, "has already located Crockett. His operation is being monitored as we speak." He stopped behind Oliver Red Lightning, and pressed his knobby fingers into the native American's enormous shoulders. Red Lightning knew Tyne was lying. He leaned forward, but showed no emotion. Tyne massaged harder. The impression was clear: I control this man. "In fact, I don't intend to stop there." He glared at Hellman, daring him to object. "I have had enough of this rampaging Congressman. I'm taking him down." His beady little eyes were on fire.

A hand slapped the table in loud disagreement. All eyes snapped up to see the Attorney General fuming. Heat poured from his nostrils. "What's your intention, Dr. Tyne?" Jim Turcutt growled. "Give him the old Dr. Mengele toothache? You dress the part. May as well *play* the part."

Tyne shot poison through his eyes at Turcutt. "When those gangsters broke into my place the other night, I didn't play around with *intentions,* Mr. Secretary! I put the boots to those little hooligans!" He gave a fair imitation of a karate kick. Involuntarily, he glanced at Leora Psybysch, sucking at that moment on a Stop Smoking Now candy stick the size of a cigar and returning his look unblinking. Hellman waited, boiling with indignation, staring into Tyne's face. This was Hunter Tyne's world, the delirious world of violent men ruling nations. He ignored the Vice President, and told Turcutt in a thick German accent, *"Don't vorry! Ve haff our means of perzuasion."*

Hellman's head jerked back. His eyebrows rose in rage. He was not a man to be tinkered with. He was running this meeting, and now Tyne had taken command after that flaming asshole Babylon had slunk out. Hellman's powerful forearms pressed against the table. The broad face puckered inward. Brusque noises came from his nose. By arm strength alone he pressed up to his full five-foot-four, the biceps quivering, the disproportionately large chest heaving. For perhaps two full seconds he flicked his eyes to the remaining Council members. Then turning to Tyne, he spoke through barely moving lips.

"If you want to play, Mr. Secretary, you will seriously regret it."

Turcutt stood and moved toward them.

Hunter Tyne's eyes narrowed. He wallowed in this, the piss and blood of confrontation. Not moving his eyes from the Vice President, he ripped his hands from Red Lightning's shoulders and came forcefully two feet from Hellman's face. They stood eyeball to eyeball. Turcutt was inches away. Slowly, Tyne removed his watch, eyes never moving from Hellman's iron gaze. The blond woman shifted, holding her breath.

73

Slash Zewinta would have given everything he owned to witness this stunning face-off between the two most menacing figures in a government proud of its menace. Well, maybe he would not part with his favorite bong, carved from the tusk of a narwhale, that he'd picked up in a trade for his 1992 black Jeep Cherokee that hadn't run in four years. But most everything else.

At this moment he was standing on the jammed E train in his fairly clean suede jacket over an I-heart-NY hoodie, rumbling toward The World Trade Center stop. It was hours before his shift started. In a panic after learning Desdemona B. Crockett was being held at his workplace, he'd packed his laptop and a makeshift disguise in a backpack, with the preposterous notion that the sitting judge would release Desdemona on his recognizance, him, the janitor Slash Zewinta. Well, hell, he'd been there nine years! They all knew him. And she was only being held on assaulting two federal agents, and suspicion of inciting to riot, aircraft theft, falsifying FAA records, fleeing federal authorities and kidnapping a United States Congressman.

Good thing they didn't know who she really was! Or did they?

In dirty jeans and Penn sweatshirt and filthy hair, young Raven Menez, in her first days out of Philadelphia, was collapsing under the stress. She sat listlessly on a homemade stool at the kitchen table. Hanging from heavy beams overhead were dozens of cooking implements. It brought to mind a Kansas farm kitchen, some mid-century painting she'd seen. Tacked to the kitchen door was a World War I poster depicting Uncle Sam at a voting box, pointing accusingly at her, above the caption, "Freedom! Use it or lose it!"

Everybody else was busy. Nel Sligo had asked how she was feeling, but Raven blew her off.

Edwin Foulks had outlined his intentions to her. She tried to listen, she really did, but instead she felt herself drawn into his enormous pewter-colored eyes and pretty face, although she didn't care much for beards really, except Hagrid's in the Harry Potter movies. But she'd reached out – a totally innocent gesture – and swiped a crumb of burrito from his cheek, and was surprised how soft his beard was. He had changed into a faded black chamois shirt over a bright blue turtleneck, rather sexy for a country boy, and he focused steadily on her as he spoke, although not at all intimidating, and certainly not in any lustful way. His ringless hands were expressive too, spreading for joy, fists for anger, clapped together for emphasis, counting with the thumb first, then the fingers, like her Portuguese uncles back in Cheltenham.

Now she was struggling to hold herself together. She was constipated from travel and emotional upheaval, frightened by Mgaba, and confused by the others. She missed her mother. She was so stressed it was all she could do to keep from screaming. She hadn't eaten it seemed for days. Everybody else was approaching meltdown. They spoke to one another in a code she was not permitted to follow.

Pushing away from the table, she stood up and tried to stretch but banged her hand against an iron pot overhead. She muffled a cry of pain, then, holding her wrist, she crossed the kitchen and noticed a small mirror. In the mirror she saw a frightened little girl far from home. Her shoulder-length black hair looked like a crow's nest. She felt skinny and unfeminine. Nothing was right. In this jungle her hands and feet had begun to swell up. There was no sunlight anywhere. Just trees and moss and drizzle and those damn chickens. That horrible buff-colored rooster scared her to death.

She staggered into the living room, feeling lost and useless. The others were all jabbering about an eyelash and a murder. This

was no place for her. She looked out the big French doors leading to
the back deck, and decided since she was freezing anyway, she
might as well go out and really be miserable.

"Are there any bears around here?" she said aloud, and
opened the door and slipped outside.

The air was heavy with moisture, but it was not raining. A
gray smear that might have been the sun was balanced on the low
mountain looming above the forest. Everything smelled alive, pri-
mal, and she realized her whole body was on high alert, like a
frightened woman in a dark alley. But no. It wasn't fear. A new sensation nudged against her misery. Cedar and wet wool and the smell
of forest and her own dank self mingling with it, is what it was, and
she almost felt relieved. Although it was still morning, she felt worn
out and exhilarated at once. She breathed deeply, just as that vicious
rooster came strutting around the corner of the house.

She turned automatically, wet and freezing, to go back inside. Then her heart froze. Through the glass door, on the big monitor was a clear image of the Vice President of the United States and
the Secretary of Communications, Hunter Tyne, glaring at one another like wild animals, chests heaving, in poor light from a shaking
camera somewhere. Immediately she recognized it as some kind of
candid video of the two men. Courtman stood talking with Victor,
actually looking out the window at Raven as he spoke, unaware of
what was on the screen. All her devastating feelings crushed down
upon her in an instant. She burst into the house gripped with terror,
grabbing for the remote and turning up the sound, screaming, *"Look
at them! Look at them!"* and everybody in the room turned just as
Hunter Tyne slashed a knife-thin hand through the air an inch from
Hellman's face.

They all focused on the screen in stunned silence. The two
most powerful men in Washington were about to draw blood, standing right there in the White House Cabinet Room, obviously unaware they were live on the Web. The Vice President's face was
turning to pure rage. He roared, "Don't play your candy-ass games
with me!" And Hunter Tyne bellowed back, "I think I'm going to
remind you why you're here!"

"Holy shit," Victor Sligo finally said. "What is this?"

Courtman burst out, "It's her! She's in there! In Cabinet!
No, it's –"

And Mgaba couldn't help hooting, "It's a Washington soap opera!"

"Security!" Hellman yelled. "Get the Secret Service before I break this creep in half!"

Tyne didn't move. "You know why you're here, Billy? You don't seriously think people would vote for you!" He laughed caustically, an enraged playground bully. They heard the sound of doors banging open and people moving, struggling to come between them. "Nobody votes any more!" Tyne shrieked. "You know why? *Me!* I'm your savior, you mindless buffoon!" Slapping his own thin chest. "A herd of drunken monkeys would vote you out of office, if they could vote!"

Hellman pointed a thick arm and yelled, "You! Albright! Arrest that man!" The husky Secret Service agent rushed back in and stood beside the Vice President, eyes jerking from one man to the other.

"Hold it everybody!" Victor recognized the powerful voice of the Attorney General, but he was not visible on the screen. "Dr. Tyne!" Jim Turcutt's voice boomed. *"Sit down!* Mr. Vice President! We don't need these histrionics at this dangerous moment." Turcutt came into sight, moving toward Tyne. Then Admiral Singh joined the fray, shoving between the two men, eyeball to eyeball with Billy Hellman. Courtman said, "Come on, Admiral. Pull out a gun. Shoot the little bastard."

They separated. Admiral Singh had not flinched standing before Hellman. He watched warily. The Vice President glared back at him, and the camera shuddered and moved in close. Hellman's furious, deeply lined face filled the screen, choking with violence and frustration. The lips compressed to a tight circle, a million cracks of smoldering flesh. Turcutt's voice said, more calmly, "All right."

Hellman's next words came with raw hatred.

"This little revolt is working perfectly. Don't let it give you an ulcer, Tyne." He sucked in a ragged breath. "Monday I am going to suspend the First Amendment. The President will agree to it. We're going to rewrite that piece of liberal trash anyway. As for you, you fucking genius –"

Again the Attorney General's voice roared in. "The people of this country have a right to –" But Hellman cut him off. His fist slammed into the huge table.

"I don't give a fiddler's piss what the people have a right to! The people elected me! They'll do what I dictate!" He thumped his own chest viciously. "I!" His eyeballs were smoking. "Caliban!"

Bent into a pretzel beside the screen, BJ wrote furiously.

"That remains to be seen!" Tyne screamed. The screen image jerked violently. Suddenly Hellman grabbed Tyne with two thick hands. He ripped Tyne's neck sideways, at the same time tearing his collar back. Behind Tyne's ear was a small mark – but Tyne moved before anybody could get a look at it. He heaved Hellman away from him.

"Look at you," the Vice President hissed through gleaming teeth. "The dripping sputum at the end of a line of great men!"

There came an astonished cry, and the screen flicked white. A moment later they were looking at the Penobscot Bridge construction project.

Nobody spoke. You could hear a log truck whining a mile away on the mountainside.

"That was the craziest thing," Raven Menez finally broke the silence in a breathless monotone, "I have ever witnessed in my life." She was holding her forehead, leaning forward, half delirious. She knew she should breathe. It would help this weird dimming and blazing of the lights, but she was freezing and had to get herself over to the warm stove but Edwin was sitting there gaping at her as if she were an escaped mental patient but really more than that she had to eat something, she was starving, and she yelled at him, "Can't a person get a decent bowl of oatmeal around here?" She took one step toward the stove, and fainted.

BJ was first to get to her. In another instant Edwin was there, and he nudged BJ aside and knelt beside her just as Mgaba leaned down over her. From the stairs Nel came into the crowd, shoving Mgaba into Edwin. Then Victor burst in, trying to take charge, and they were all yelling conflicting instructions about water and air and checking her pulse and Courtman was trying with shaky fingers to dial 911, a confused scrum swirling over the moaning body, when suddenly the dog was yowling and somebody was knocking at the door.

Everybody froze.

74

Edwin released Raven's wrist and pulled himself up. Exchanging a look with Victor, he moved to a window where he could peer out at the front porch. Off to the side was the old flatbed hay truck.

"I have some blankets in that closet," he whispered, pointing, and started to the front door.

Courtman, shaken to the core, said, "Do you want us to –" and then went to the closet.

Edwin looked back through the archway at the group standing helplessly over Raven. His heart hammered through his shirt.

"It can't be the feds." He turned to the door and opened it.

"Hello!" Iona Webster said, sweet as plum pudding. "It must be Mr. Crockett." She offered her hand.

"Uh well, actually –" Instinctively Edwin pulled back, struck by a moral dilemma he could barely comprehend. Two bundled-up women standing there carrying overnight bags. One looked familiar. A strange car parked by the garage. Could they be police? He could hardly tell them he was Davy Crockett, and he certainly couldn't tell them he wasn't.

"I'm Iona Webster," the woman said, removing her floppy hat. "We met the other day at Independence Hall. And this lady is Miss Molly Bee."

"Of course!" he blurted, smiling guiltily. Then instantly remembered everything taking place inside. He brought them into the kitchen, profusely apologizing for no reason, babbling, telling them nobody ever came to the door of this house except Jehovah's Witnesses, and even they didn't like it here much. Iona Webster and Molly Bee! And the Vice President about to throttle the Secretary of Communications right on the Web! And Raven passed out on the floor! Geez!

Nel had brought water for Raven, who was now sitting in the overstuffed armchair, wrapped in an Army blanket quite still and pale, studying the brass firewood rack beside the stove. Kneeling beside her, Nel held her arm and touched her forehead with a damp cloth. The others stood nervously by, one eye on the monitor, the other on Raven. Courtman was still holding his phone, unsure what to do. Looking up at the women with obvious shock, he said, "I'll get back to you," and he closed the phone and approached.

"Molly Bee! The monarch of *Trying Times*," he said with vast relief. "We are honored, madam."

Molly blushed politely.

Webster greeted Courtman with the reminder that they had also met in Philadelphia early in the week, and observing his ubiquitous poly gloves she gave him a powerful two-handed handshake. In the big chair, Raven was making feeble sounds. "Is this Raven?" Bee gushed. "What happened?" Nobody knew exactly. Victor had turned to look back at the monitor, his mouth still hanging open. He told Molly that Raven was in the process of losing her political virginity before their very eyes and certainly could use a familiar face if not a morning-after pill.

"We've never met in person," Molly Bee said. "But I almost feel like she's my daughter!" She went directly to Raven and, in spite of the young woman's collapsed condition, embraced her in the chair. Molly Bee was at least as tall as Nel, though more filled out, her short flaxen hair beaten flat by the trip, her steel-frame glasses hopelessly out of fashion. She had a serious demeanor about her that BJ immediately liked and Courtman had expected, reading her column over the past dozen years. In some ways, Iona Webster was just the opposite. Webster was a light-hearted woman who took herself and her serious work rather casually. She was capable of disarming tension with her self-imitative female NFL place-kicker jokes, and had spent years editing the *Strategies for Survival,* including her own horror-laced history of the successes and failures of racial integration. Ten years out of the NFL, she had not lost the tight figure, the square, trim shoulders and sinewy arms. Her hair was a Brillo pad, thick and black and perfectly shaped. She dropped her wet leather coat and hat on a chair and shook hands with Mgaba. By old habit, Sloan searched her face and hands for the words to describe her skin color, and settled on cinnamon toast ladled with honey. A fine color. Her eyes were a rich red mahogany.

Webster admitted they'd rented the only car at what passed for an airstrip in the name of Rosa Parks, and announced to the gathering that she wanted her freedom now, and not when Billy Hellman said it was okay.

Victor pointed to the screen and prodded them all back to reality. "Doc! We need to get that video! Can you do it?" Doc made

a guttural sound without pressing his throat chip that sounded like
"asking the impossible."

They caught the women up on events of the last five minutes while Nel attended to Raven. Fiddling with his laptop, Doc re-
set the video and let it role. Even Iona was aghast at the violence in
the Cabinet Room. They experienced again the spinal chills and the
fear and loathing. Courtman could not help observing, "It is clear
who runs the country, I will say that."

Watching BJ scribble through a cramped page, Victor called
out, "Hey, Foulks."

He was back in his rocker by the heater. He looked up.

"Can you get this guy a big notebook?" Edwin disappeared
upstairs. Most of them were writing notes, trying to make sense of
the shocking words as Hellman violently exposed the mark on
Tyne's neck. Paused, close up, the object was a blurry dark mass,
vaguely horseshoe-shaped.

"It's familiar somehow," Molly Bee said from the squeaky
couch she had a feeling she would be sleeping on. "But I can't put
my finger on it."

Shortly Edwin came to the top of the log staircase and asked
for help. He and Mgaba hauled down a four-by-six-foot whiteboard,
and leaned it against the sawhorses. At that moment, a phone jangled. Everybody checked. It was Nel's. She was moving toward the
stairs when she said, "Fred? Is that you?"

75

All the waiting was worth it. He had a video to show them.
Hastily he gave her a YouTube address, and he hung up. The staff
gathered. In his customary place in the rocking chair where he could
watch, Edwin Foulks worked his knife blade against the stone,
brooding.

On the screen, still wearing the retired cop's green and
black checked Pendleton shirt and blue jeans, the walrus mustache
drooping sufficiently, Fred told them all about his new friend
Purger.

Forensic Services scored the first hit with the DNA test on

the nearly-invisible black hair found in Viola Ferrari's rental car. It belonged to a felon. Not only are felons easier to locate than the general population, but this one, a man called Paavo Jones, was actually in Witness Protection in Santa Fe. It was as if he had asked the cops to come and find him.

Paavo Jones, aka "Purger," was an alleged exterminator for hire. He had spent half his adult life behind bars, and had wound up a guest of the state of New Mexico on a plea bargain in the execution of a Most-Wanted individual in Miami, part of a "family" drug operation. Fred made some calls, but also wished to be in on the capture, considering the possible implications of the Skull Valley matter. He was put on temporary consultant status by the New Mexico Criminal Investigations Section. A group of officers, including the required US Marshal, descended on Purger's trailer near Santa Fe within an hour of Fred's arrival.

Nobody was home. The information CIS had from Witness Protection was that Purger – Caucasian, 46, five feet nine, 185, black/blue, multiple scars and tattoos, slightly resembling the actor Tom Cruise – had recently purchased a new BMW for which he paid cash. Usually unknown to a protected witness, when he purchases a vehicle it is discreetly equipped with a GPS locator. The police quickly found the Beamer in Chihuahua, Mexico. Bilingual phone calls were exchanged. The car was surrounded and two people hauled out, slammed to the street and cuffed. They turned out to be a pair of teenagers who'd stumbled on the BMW at the border up in Juarez – and took it for a ride and had it painted. That was right after Christmas.

An exhaustive search of Purger's trailer ensued. This was Fred's kind of work. What they found was quite interesting, almost unprofessional for a career guy like Purger. So it could be a red herring. Stuffed down behind the bathroom cabinet mirror were a phone number and four photographs. The number was hard to trace, since the phone was a prepaid cheapie – the kind Nel herself had used down there in Utah – but he hoped to have results shortly.

"The state's sitting on all this for now," Fred said. "Although they're contacting the Greek authorities." His voice dropped lower. "I can hear your surprise. But this part is... Well, let me just tell you. Understand, an international manhunt is out for Purger. Apparently he had a lot of dough. The charade with the car suggests that he left the country some time ago under another name and won't be returning. The four photographs were squashed up, some almost unrecognizable. Viola Ferrari's AUSA photo was there with a black X drawn through it with a marking pen. The second is the President of Greece. The other two pictures I couldn't identify, but I'm sending them all on to your phone in a bundle. Okay? I'm holding on to the other photos we took for now. Nothing evidentiary. Now I'm deleting this video."

The YouTube screen went dark.

In thirty seconds Nel's phone beeped. In fact, five photos came through together. Handing the phone to Mgaba, she told him to download them onto the laptop since the phone screen was so small.

First came the banner hanging in the basement at Tyne's house. The square-ended Knights Templar cross, and in the middle of it the black horseshoe-shaped thing they had just seen on Hunter Tyne's neck. But the video was too blurry. Tyne had been moving too fast. Nobody noticed the similarity.

Then came Viola Ferrari. They all took a lingering look at the official portrait of a serious, perhaps thirty-five-year-old Viola, glowing wavy black hair, a touch of dark lipstick, high Mediterranean cheekbones and wonderful intelligent eyes, and a crude X slashed through her face. The next was a much older man with an enormous chest wearing a classic silver gray suit and vest, according to Fred the President of Greece. At the third photo BJ stirred immediately. "Oh, my God!" he whisper-shouted. "It's Jerome Tse! He killed himself when I was walking up to his door!" They all looked from BJ back to the photo. The Van Dyke beard, the sad smile.

"Viola's boss at the US Attorney's Office?" Nel said.

"Yeah, yeah, that's him. Was him," BJ said. He scribbled more notes and looked up. "Purger never got to him."

In the last picture, Fred had unfolded an aging newspaper photo of some kind of political rally. A young woman with short light hair and a green blazer was standing on the platform among several other people. Her face in the faded photo was circled with the same marker that crossed Viola Ferrari's face.

Iona gasped loudly. Her hand was at her mouth, her eyes were bulging and she was staring at Molly Bee. Molly wore a grim smile, but couldn't take her eyes off the screen.

"It's okay," she told Iona quietly. "Every ten years or so that picture turns up. It's the only one out there. That guy's probably in Argentina by now."

Quickly Nel was by Molly's side, a long reedy arm encircling her waist. She'd already been feeling they had been in combat together and had a lifetime bond.

"Damn right," was all she could think to say. Iona was stricken by the photo. Molly held a hand out for her, and Iona took it and came close. The three women stood in a tight circle. The others held back, watching.

76

Edwin Foulks went out on a major food expedition. The four women had set up operations in the small bedrooms, leaving the downstairs for the men. Doc Nguyen had already claimed his own private space in the living area to avoid climbing the stairs. The big main room resembled a makeshift triage center, with clotheslines, plywood desks, travel bags, several laptops, the big monitor, the rooster outside shrieking and the dog constantly underfoot. Everybody was stressed.

At last BJ was able to show his hard-earned copy of Jaap Tenkley's deposition.

Buttoning up his cardigan, BJ slipped the disk into the laptop connected to the big monitor. In a moment, there she was in life, painfully beautiful, in a black finely-tailored suit, understated gold earrings, the movie star tan, the strong cheek bones, the serious demeanor.

"Assistant US Attorney Viola Ferrari, in the matter of Jaap Tenkley." She was obviously accustomed to video reporting, and possessed a confident alto voice. A middle-aged man sat at a table beside her, and Viola moved the camera herself to depose him. He was small and stiff, with paper-white skin and short hair and cheap suit. Most noticeable about him though, was the leer. This man was absolutely delighted to be squealing.

Viola's voice said, "This is a voluntary deposition, sworn

by oath, from Mr. Jaap Tenkley. Go ahead, Mr. Tenkley."

"I know this won't stand up in court," Tenkley began, his voice soft behind the rabid facial expression. "I ran Prospectus Medical Technologies lab out in Cicero. We contracted with the state and a couple of universities on accidents, birth anomalies, brain research too exhaustive and too boring for the fat cats to do. There's money out there for this if you have the equipment and the mice. But we started moving into neuro-robotics and neuroscience because of the people I had working for me. So I get a personal email from somebody who wishes to discuss a very large project. He'd already checked me out, found out I had a certain understanding with the Illinois Medical Board that enabled me to be... more creative than other bio research outfits. Maybe they even sent him to me. I never found out. So long story short, we deal strictly on the phone. He wants quiet but extremely costly research into neuro-chemical programming, where I would be supplied all the permits and all the funding, and I report directly to his people in Utah. We don't discuss the fact that there are no such permits. Mind-control research is flat-out illegal. That's what this was. Mind-control research."

He spread his small white hands. "I tell him maybe this stuff is immoral and maybe not, but I can't work if I don't know who I'm working for. He says CI. I say Communication International? What do they want with brain research? And why not go to the Riken Institute in Tokyo – what do they call it, yes, Neural Circuit Theory and Behavioral Physiology! Or the one in Manesar, in India, where the molecular neuroscience and brain imaging research takes place. He says, 'Ask them.'" Tenkley grins. "We took it. It was about five years ago. This guy keeps bugging me on the phone for more results, more results, but won't identify himself. Meanwhile we created a chip that will send out an electro-stimulus to generate a ..." He paused a beat and glanced towards Viola. They could all see he was bursting to talk about it but was conflicted. "...where it will be incredibly effective. Look, it's almost impossible to describe highly technical matters on a video like this. Anyway, it surpasses existing BCI processes, Brain-Computer Interface, by direct electro-infusion into the hypothalamus..." He ran a hand through his prison-cut brown hair. "Maybe I shouldn't be doing this." A long pause. "I wanted to know where it was going, you know, since I'm an egotistical sort myself, and finally I just called the CI office in Utah and asked to talk to the research director. They say his name's Dr. Hunter Tyne, but he'll have to return my call. I said I was his mother's physician and there is a problem that will not wait. About thirty seconds later I hear his voice. He goes, 'Who the hell is this?' Real mad. But that was the voice. Absolutely no question about it." He grinned again, that leering smirk. "I finally went back to see who signed the contract. Sure enough. Dr. Hunter Tyne. Now in the Cabinet. Secretary of Communications."

He waited. "Go on, please," Viola Ferrari said.

"Short version, somebody blew the whistle. Maybe one of my lab guys feeling guilty. I never found out. Feds come busting in, I'm locked up. No permits. Dr. Tyne, now, he's questioned because somebody at the US Attorney's recognized the pattern here, the research for CI. They found the contract. Grand Jury nailed my ass, and they returned instructions to question Dr. Tyne, but he essentially got erased from the case by unseen forces. I imagine the FBI, the Justice Department, somebody connected to the US Attorney." Jaap Tenkley stared at the camera. His face went dark. Speaking slowly he said, "I did three years and eight months in Greenville Federal Correctional Institute. You son of a bitch, I will hound you for the rest of your life until you are dead and maggots are chewing on your brain." He did not grin this time. The screen went black.

77

In his corner, Doc Nguyen was so pleased he congratulated Victor on pulling off what he termed "the clown act of the century, where federal guys on stilts walk on clowns like you." Then he laughed and told Victor he was kidding and said, "Don't go getting sensitive on me, tough guy."

"She figured it out," he said, aiming his chin at Nel.

"The country owes you, Ms. Sligo," Doc told her. Nel only nodded, and winked at BJ.

"All right," Victor announced. "Let's get to work. What do we know? That's the question of the moment. What do we know? Let's wear out that whiteboard."

The uneasy group referred to notes and text messages and photographs and laptops. Nel stood up.

"I think," she said, "Viola Ferrari saw something much larger than we're seeing. But I don't know what. I think she looked at all this, and at the voting history over the past three elections or so, and at Billy Hellman and Communication International and their worldwide influences, and I think she was connecting all this to whatever it is that has caused people to stop voting." She paused. "And I think that's what got her killed."

"She'd prosecuted CI before," Iona said from where she sat on the floor by the wood stove. "You told me yourself. Hunter Tyne got his wrist slapped."

BJ got busy writing notes, at the same moment that Raven seemed to find her place in the structure. She carried a stool to the whiteboard, picked out a blue marker, and wrote Hunter Tyne's name in the upper left area. Looking embarrassed and pale, she sat.

Sloan Mgaba was quick to get in this drama. He walked to the center, looming just below the log ceiling beam. "May I remind you all," he said with massive dignity, his dark face shining, "we have started a rebellion, and we have a great deal of work to do in another direction entirely!" He walked back to his seat, the strutting emperor, and took his throne.

Molly Bee had gone to the kitchen for water, and she returned sipping from a mug and said, "Right, then. We have these photographs from Fred Geschwantner. Thank you Raven. You stay right there and organize this mess, will you?" At the top center Raven had written the word "Rebellion". Twisting over his shoulder to see this, Victor snapped his fingers and said, "Yeah, good point, Sloan," and snapping and pointing at the board in a single gesture said to Raven, "Write, 'Billy Hellman.' Over there. Go ahead."

She did. The big board was now balanced. Hunter Tyne's name on one side, and the Vice President's on the other.

Ideas shot toward the whiteboard. Raven recorded with a swift, slightly shaky hand. Most recent, of course, was Tenkley's accusation of Hunter Tyne. Viola had humiliated Tyne in a previous prosecution, and he was a violent egotist who would destroy anyone who got in his path. The photo of Jerome Tse at Purger's trailer, and Tse's connection to Viola came up. Nel again noted the discoveries at Tyne's house, the weird display of the mannequin and the computers, the Knights Templar banner, the three other photographs on Purger's hit list. Somebody had sealed all those files claiming executive privilege.

"Neurological programming," Mgaba said to Raven.

"No, neuro*chemical* programming," BJ said. Maybe a bit smugly.

"Fine," came Mgaba's French accent. "It was Tyne. Mr. Tenkley just told us." Raven scribbled.

"But no actual smoking gun," the realist Victor Sligo said.

"And this Slickwatch character," Iona called out. "Whoever he is and wherever he got his data, it completely corroborated Tenkley's story. That lab was shut down and CI was contracting to do brainwashing research and some unnamed CI exec walked on the deal!"

Doc Nguyen pressed his throat and said, "We need Slickwatch here." Raven wrote it down.

"Yeah," Victor said. "Good. Can you find him?" The old man made an ugly face at the Congressman.

78

For a third time they ran through the blond woman's video. At his station, Edwin checked his watch. Time was flying by.

This time Molly Bee spoke for everybody: "Imagine Hellman and Tyne killing each other! How Shakespearean!"

"Remember that news clip of Dick Cheney telling that Senator from Vermont to go fuck himself?" Iona said. "Course that was just a little squirt of Dick compared to these two."

Raven recorded cryptic phrases as people repeated them. The Vice President, possibly hysterical, had called himself "Caliban." It was Nel who recalled the deformed slave from *The Tempest,* and said an old boyfriend had an ugly Jeep by that name. She went on to note other obvious state secrets – Tyne claiming nobody voted because of him. Hellman intending to rewrite the First Amendment. That whole thing with Tyne's tattoo and – what did he say? "Sputum at the end of a line of great men!"

BJ said, "No great men in history lead anywhere near these

two guys."

Victor walked to the whiteboard and took the marker from Raven. "I can't resist this," he said. And he wrote in the Hellman column, "Mindless buffoon."

"All right then." He let a loud breath explode from his lungs, easing the tension all around. "What the hell are these two people talking about?"

"What they're saying," Mgaba said, "is that this rebellion is going to be crushed like a bowl of eggs."

Nel said, "They were born to dismember the Constitution. Both of them. Those..."

"Pigs," Raven Menez said.

Molly asked, "Wasn't it George Orwell who said, 'This is a government of pigs, not of men?'" Calmly, she took the marker from Victor. In an arc under both columns she printed the words, "People are not voting."

BJ smirked. "It's Tyne. Tyne's preventing people from voting. He just said so. What's he doing? And it's about time we asked, what in blazes is neurochemical programming, and what's it have to do with all this? How are they getting in my head?"

Opinions crisscrossed, and the frustration mounted. The ceaseless babble of talk shows on the Internet reported that insurrection was rolling in state legislatures and in the streets.

Congressman Sligo went back to logistical problems.

"Okay. Hold all this. We have a few good people in Washington working on this crazy man's intentions," holding an open palm toward Edwin, "but I can't find a camera crew in D.C. who'll take a risk and stand up with us. So I'm the one holding this thing up at the moment. We're going to have to change the fundamental concept here if –"

With obvious surprise, Ms. Bee said, "No! No, we do. We have a camera crew. I can fix that. Just give me the when and the where and the how soon do we need what."

"Three days and eighteen hours from now," Victor said, eyebrows raised in anticipation. "You have production people in Washington?"

"Well, sure!" She brushed back her light hair, smiling. "Is that the problem? Let me get my phone. What time is it in D.C.? Eight? Okay. You don't mind subculture people? Producers in leathers and bone necklaces? The guy's name is Bliss, the producer. Can you work with a guy named Bliss?"

Victor shot a look at his beaming wife, then looked back at Molly. "Bless you, madam," he said. "You are a godsend. I'll dance at your wedding."

Courtman stood. "Come with me, young lady." And Molly Bee, a sophisticated woman of the world, followed Courtman to the command center sprawled on a sheet of plywood over two sawhorses. He outlined what was already planned at the Groom Lake center for military snoopery and Intelsat maneuvering. Dr. Sage Kuushmann was intending to sabotage the entire US communications network for two minutes during the Inauguration.

"This is Area 51?" Molly whispered, a bit agog. "For real?"

"No," Courtman whispered back. "There is no Area 51."

79

A couple of hours earlier and three time zones to the east, Slash Zewinta had dashed out of the subway, taking the steps two at a time up onto Church Street in chill January sunset, wearing a suede jacket and a tattered backpack. He felt like Spiderman soaring into Gotham to make a daring rescue. Walking full speed, he banged into a woman amidst a group of protesters. She carried a sign reading, "Christians for Crockett."

He had to force himself to rein in the mad instincts of the manic depressive overloaded with chocolate. Rushing in to work, wondering if it was safe to wear the old suede jacket that could tell so many stories if anybody bothered to listen. But this was New York! Who would be listening?

The Federal Building squatted among giant neighbors. He ran through the various scenarios, either to get her out, or to join her, or to just keep walking. In reality, Desdemona had pulled off the crime of the century back in Washington state forty-some years ago. She would be the one to know all about escaping from the feds. But still. What if she was on some kind of undercover assignment for the FBI, investigating – what? – if the janitors were terrorists? Could the feds have turned her? What if she were spying on *him?*

He shook it off. He wasn't that nuts. He focused on the front doors as a couple of armored personnel carriers loaded with troops rumbled past, broadcasting reminders of the nine p.m. curfew. A high school kid shook a poster at the trucks: "War is insane!"

Feeding his ID chip at the entryway, he passed over the sub-floor HDD – the Harmful Devices Detector – snapped on orange poly gloves from the dispenser at the door, and crossed the elaborate marble foyer, nodding as he passed the bored security guy fussing with the airborne pathogen sensor at the heating vent. Down two flights of stairs to the basement, passing armed troops scurrying in both directions, and new heaps of paraphernalia along hallways, making up his mind. His job was a piece of cake. The money was good. He couldn't screw this up. But these were in fact the times that tried men's souls, Slash told himself. No sunshine patriot he. A terrible miscarriage of justice was about to take place, and he understood the feds and their fetid judicial system intimately. They would lock her up and throw away the key and proclaim the rebellion ended. Shortly after, the real Davy Crockett would announce the rebellion was still on, and wake up the people with some new mind-blowing demonstration of civil disobedience. The FBI would go apeshit... but Desdemona B. Crockett was already locked up. The key thrown away. They would have her in Riker's Island for *years* before the truth ever came out. Because they knew damn well she was DB Cooper and had made fools out of them! And they weren't about to let her do it again.

"Yo, Joey," he greeted the enormous guard at the bottom of the stairwell. "Whazzup?"

"You early, Slapdash," Joey said, reaching to touch his screen with his orange gloves.

"Wait, wait," Slash insisted. "Don't sign me in. I'm just stopping by for a minute." He swiped the ID chip through the slot, and Joey buzzed him through the heavy door into his domain, the bottom floor of the grand old building.

High ceilings, bright lights, a large central room stacked with new crates of military stuff, enough to stop a Martian invasion. He walked straight across the room and found another guard leaning back in a wooden chair reading in front of the wide open Detainment Center electronic gate.

"Wallaby," he greeted the man. "What's this?"

"G'day, son," said the New Zealand Maori. "I don't know nothing, mate. They think the big riot's coming. Moved Detainment to the sixteenth floor. Mass arrests, something."

"Whoa!" Sudden change of plans. Slash was warming up now, smelling high intrigue, maybe deep do-do, maybe looking at the world from the other side of the bars.

"What sixteenth floor? There's no sixteenth floor in this building."

"Now there is," Wallaby told him.

"Man! This government! Who's up there?"

"Just them two Micronesian cabbies. And some sheila punched up a couple a coppers."

"I need a trick," he said. This was a code employees used to visit a friend who might wind up here. Wallaby stood, lay his ring of color-coded swipe-cards on the table, and drifted to one of the ten-foot-high stacks of new Army cots and began counting them. Slash pushed keys on the computer, found the forms and printed out a visitor's permit, scribbled the Captain's name at the bottom, and walked quickly to the freight elevator. His brain was flying. As his finger reached for the elevator button, he spun around and returned to the desk, grabbed the ring and opened a small office near the back. Inside he rummaged through a steel file cabinet, found another form, and hastily printed out an order and signed the name of the Magistrate of Lower Manhattan, Judge Douglas Salkeld.

The bad news was, he knew nobody on the fifteenth, or now the sixteenth floor. But the good news was, nobody knew him. In the elevator he removed his badge, took off the backpack and tucked the forms in it, straightened his shock of white hair the best he could, and at the top floor he walked directly to the two ancient Hispanic guards posted at the electronic gate.

"Crockett," he said firmly.

"Sorry, sir," the shorter guard began. "You must have a –" Slash made a spectacle of withdrawing the official signed document from his backpack.

"Duane Weber? You're her attorney?"

"I am." He touched the lapel of his suede jacket.

"You must have photo ID, Mr. Weber." He produced a driver's license and a New York State Bar card. The guard made copies of all three documents.

"Okay." A laser beam deactivated the alarm, and the gate slid open. A minute later, he was clicking along the thermal-sensor floor toward Desdemona's cell. There she was. The right height, obviously not a Micronesian cabbie. Light-skinned black woman, ultra short gray hair, distinguished, but angry, wearing an oversized orange prison jumpsuit. He started right in.

"Hey! You're a detainee! They can't take your clothes away!"

She tightened up, bleary-eyed, and glared at him. "Who the hell are you?"

He slipped a fist through the bars, knuckles forward. "Jaroslav Zewinta, at your service."

80

When the dust had cleared and the blood wiped up, Billy Hellman took the opportunity to reveal his intentions for the most remarkable Inauguration the world had ever seen. He stood proudly to speak. Across the silent room, Leora Psybysch smiled at her boss. After all, most of it was her idea, and she had managed to leak the spectacle to select individuals. The Burligame-Hellman Second Inauguration was going to set the standard for national celebrations for a century to come. "The drama will unfold," the Vice President decreed, "immediately prior to the swearing-in ceremony before the Chief Justice, one thousand dignitaries, and the entire planet watching on I-Media. The National Marching Band will be in full crescendo as the Blue Angels make their traditional flyover. At the same instant the Air Force Thunderbirds will come shrieking in from an opposing direction to create a death-defying exhibition of flying skill with the mightiest aircraft in the skies." Billy paused for effect. "At the moment of apparent collision of the eight fighter planes, two hundred paratroopers will descend from a perfectly-timed release a thousand yards above the fighter planes. The entire experience will be so breathtaking, people on the ground will believe they are watching a war." Crossing his arms on his chest, he took a moment to compose himself.

Psybysch could barely contain her delight. The Vice President took a breath, and held up a single finger, allowing his eyes to caress her magnificent figure.

"There's more," he said. "The 101st Airborne will carry billowing red, white and blue flares. At the fabulous climax, the band will be pumping out the final coda of the *William Tell Overture.*" As he spoke, Hellman began flailing his muscular bare arms, conducting the coda. He yelled exuberantly, "On the far side of the Mall, the Navy band will thunder back the *1812,* complete with precisely-timed sonic booms by the Blue Angels." He was practically tearful with ecstasy. Pointing aside he said, "And certainly there will be clowns for the kids, fat as beavers, dressed like Uncle Sam, flipping out playing cards with my hologram on them. Well, and the President's, of course. During his speech the President will talk about peace and points of light and chickens in every pot and all that crap. The seats under the audience will all go cold. And when I myself engage the people about defending the land, combating evil and spreading American democracy on every front, the seats will get so hot," he virtually gasped in triumph, "the people will jump to their feet with cries of rapture."

Psybysch burst into applause, seeing it all, agog with patriotic fervor. She shouted at him, "I-Media will cover every moment, sir! Every bomb bursting in air, every soldier standing erect!"

"Come Sunday!" the Vice President rasped. "History will never be the same!"

They raced around the big table spontaneously and hurled themselves at one another in a sexual frenzy. Fortunately, none of the other National Security Council members was present to share their ecstasy. Everybody else had gone home.

81

Within minutes of his bony knuckles touching hers through the bars, the two were fast friends. Getting a chair from one of the Hispanic guards, he straddled it cowboy style as they began to sort out the depth of the conspiracy against her. Desperate to know that she was the elusive airline hijacker, Slash had to bite his tongue half a dozen times. He had to wait until their relationship solidified. Or she just came out and said it.

"Look, I just want out of here," was what Desdemona came out and said repeatedly. "See this orange suit?" She glared at him, her jaw chiseled, her nostrils wide.

"Yeah'?"

"It doesn't go well with my eyes."

Slash puffed out his cheeks. His head itched. "Ms. Crockett," he whispered. "I got to ask you a question."

She waited.

Bending forward, he gazed into her strong face and lost his nerve. "Do you want to get out of here *legally?*" he said.

"I'm already locked in here. They confiscated my passport which I never use. Look, I'm seventy-one. Probably I have another twenty-nine years of good health and Social Security before I drop dead. My neighbor promised to feed my cats. What's on your mind?"

Unabashedly, he told her. Tearing into the backpack, he handed her a brown caftan, complete with hood, and a pair of his size thirteen Salvation Army sneakers.

"Sit on these. Be right back."

He returned hastily to the elevator, for a few moments overlapping in his mind his deep obsession with Hunter Tyne and the false incarceration of Desdemona Crockett. Somehow there had to be a connection. He watched the ancient dial tell the floors in the freight elevator, pondering these weighty matters and sweating heavily, fearing he might put her in a worse dilemma if they were caught. Suddenly he felt his brain being pierced with a slow-motion bullet. Directly into the central section of the cerebral cortex. Grabbing his head, he fell against the steel side of the elevator, dropping the backpack, tearing his coat off with one hand, gasping for breath, the pain searing down through his skull like spikes rammed into the wrists and ankles of Jesus, and he collapsed on the floor, drooling white fluid from his mouth, fighting for life, chanting deep inside his consciousness, yeah, it was coming, it will pass, it will... He blacked out. The doors opened in the basement. He lay crumpled on the floor of the elevator, unconscious. A rush of air came to his face and hands, and he felt the air cooling his brain, and heard himself saying, it will pass, it was coming, yeah, I knew it was coming, too much at once here, got nervous upstairs, what if I get her in more trouble, where's the Pepsi machine?

It was Aberdeen Proving Ground back to haunt him. The Army. The gift that keeps on giving.

He pulled himself erect and walked blindly to the bathroom. He threw up, washed his face, and drank half a dozen handfuls of water, washed his face again, and felt better. Then he went back to find his backpack, and then find Wallaby.

A year ago, Wallaby had picked up a bonus when Slash hacked into the IRS at great personal risk and added a zero to Wallaby's tax return, causing the Maori immigrant to receive a ten-thousand-dollar check instead of the thousand he had coming.

He needed the money for his wife's gall bladder surgery.

Eight minutes later, Wallaby emerged from the freight elevator on the sixteenth floor, driving a motorized cart bearing two dozen new army cots.

"Hey!" he yelled down the hall. "You screws!"

Both guards were in their seventies. They moved slowly through the empty cellblock toward him. The Micronesian cabbies, in separate cells, looked bored senseless.

"Work order for new cots," Wallaby yelled at the top of his lungs. This is how he spoke most of the time. The lesser guard, a Jimmy Carter Cuban refugee named Martes Domingo-Viernes, read the work order, cursed, and both men began opening cell doors to add two more cots to each cell. Casually, Duane Weber walked out of the freight elevator pushing the bright red Pepsi machine on a manual dolly. The back of the Pepsi machine was closed, but nothing was inside. The guts were in the basement, scattered in cellblock 002.

"Need to switch out that pop machine, too," Wallaby told the two guards, nodding toward Slash. They all knew the vital nature of Pepsi during the long work nights. And they all understood that the elderly guards were too lazy to do the switch themselves. That damn pop machine was heavy! That was why Wallaby, stationed in the basement, made the big bucks. But he was helping them with the cots, so this lawyer *cabron* with the weird hair was doing the pop machine.

In her orange jumpsuit in 1521, Desdemona Crockett sat still as a jailhouse cockroach. They hauled two metal cots into her cell and folded out the legs, and Wallaby inadvertently left her cell door open a crack.

Slash pushed the dolly to the end of the brightly-lit cell-block. He banged the standing Pepsi machine around, cursed loudly, slammed the machine against the wall, then started back down the corridor between cells with the same empty Pepsi machine on the dolly. When he passed Desdemona's cell, she was ready. She was going to ask why his face was wet, but decided that could wait. He checked the others, then turned and opened the back of the Pepsi machine, grabbed the caftan and sneakers from her and tossed them in. He motioned with his head for her to climb in. Immediately she understood. Glancing down the corridor, she saw the others working at the legs of a stubborn cot. Slash held the red back of the machine open, and he smiled at her with his unusually bright blue eyes.

"One thing." His large head came close to hers. She leaned forward. The carefully-quaffed gray head almost contacted his gangsta white hairdo.

He whispered, "Are you DB Cooper?"

Without a moment's hesitation she said, "Yeah. I'm DB Cooper. Let's go!"

Slash frowned. "Right."

She wriggled into the machine and Slash quietly shut the back and whistled as he closed her cell, tilted back the dolly, and headed for the elevator. The stuck cot legs sprang open and Martes and his associate heaved the cot into the empty cell and walked right past Slash.

Going down, he heard her scraping and clawing out of the jumpsuit, and into the caftan. She must be a contortionist.

One thing left. In his backpack was his laptop, and the last job would need it. Nobody was in the basement now. He hesitated. No. He did not dare risk another second getting Desdemona and himself out of the building. He opened the back of the machine in the basement and she climbed gingerly out, adjusting the brown garment while Slash shoved the dolly to the wall and pushed the Pepsi machine upright. They dashed up two flights of stairs and past the entrance guard, busy now as other office workers were passing in and out. Incredibly, nobody noticed the six-foot-tall woman in an Arab caftan and giant Salvation Army sneakers leaving the building.

Back down to the E train. It was more crowded going up-town, protesters and angry graffiti at every platform, people grumbling about the transit strike due at midnight, and Desdemona, hood up and head down, had to wear Slash's backpack, facing away from him, while he worked on the laptop linked to his home unit, using her back for a desk. He had left the original copy of the order on Wallaby's desk in the basement, and now had to tap into the Federal Prisoner Transfer Authority to officially relocate Desdemona Crockett from the Manhattan Federal Building to the stockade at Fort Dix, New Jersey. Next, he notified the MP detachment at Fort Dix that Ms. Crockett would be held for questioning at the 116th Army Intelligence Headquarters at Union Square, and the transfer to Fort Dix would occur the following Monday at 0800 hours. He sent a similar order to the MPs at Fort Hamilton, down in Brooklyn.

About the time Slash and Desdemona crossed over the East River in the gash of afternoon sun, Martes Domingo-Viernes made a shocking observation at the Federal Building. His prisoner count was down by one-third.

"Hey!" he yelled. "Where's that woman? *Chingado!*" He raced as fast as the old legs would take him to the phone to call down to Wallaby in the basement. No answer. He pounded on the freight elevator until it arrived, wondering how his wife was going to kill him. He got to the basement as Wallaby was returning from the main floor with a newspaper. The old man was gasping and obviously frightened. Frantically he told Wallaby there had been an escape and who the hell knew the procedure now? Slamming the paper down, Wallaby grabbed his radio to notify his superiors in Homeland Security on the third floor, when he noticed the triplicate order the Magistrate's clerk must have left on his desk, authorizing the transfer of D. B. Crockett to Fort Dix about five minutes ago.

"Man, that was fast," Martes said. "I never saw nobody."

82

They still had no place to stay in D.C. safe from the lurking media, but now they had Bee's production crew to broadcast Edwin's sting. They had Secret Service Agent Daniel Cool, and Dr. Kuushmann at Area 51. BJ had finally broken through with the wife of a terminally-ill former Communication International software engineer named Butts. Butts was gravely ill, and his wife was wrestling with whether or not she wanted BJ to speak with him. Iona Webster had located her brother at an unlikely place called Malcolm Island off northern Vancouver Island. She browbeat and big-sistered him into taking five thousand dollars for a flight to the East Coast Saturday, and a return flight Sunday, with or without the same number of passengers.

They had already made it known the aircraft had room for seven people, plus the pilot. Doc feared for his unsteady heart, and would not go. They still had one person too many. It was Victor first who looked mournfully at BJ. Then Nel's eyes moved to the little man's suspicious face. Then all the others.

"Just hold on, boss! Don't think for a minute –"

"I'm afraid so," Victor said. "It's for your country, sir."

"My what? Dammit, every time something interesting happens, my country always needs me somewhere else! Make Mgaba stay! He takes up a lot more room! Hey, Edwin can fly the damn plane! You can fly, Edwin!"

"Oh, geez, I –"

"Somebody has to man the communications front here, BJ," Nel said kindly. "You can see that. Even with a larger airplane, you would logically be the one to stay here."

"Your other job, remember," Victor said, "is to claw into every bit of dirt Billy Hellman ever stepped in. It's your best skill and you know it."

BJ grabbed the railing and started upstairs, muttering, "Oh, piss on you people."

Victor had demanded back-up evidence in case Foulks made a complete ass of himself. They had nothing they could go to court with. Worse, he feared the mad scientist Courtman had been courting might be planning some nightmare that would cripple Washington and bust all the plans to hell.

Dr. Sage Kuushmann ran the non-existent Intelsat Override Center at the Nevada Test Site Range, 700 feet below the deserted wasteland of Groom Lake. Public prying had caused the entire spook operation to appear to migrate to an uninhabitable section of central Utah while the actual facility literally dropped out of sight, channeled into the hard ore terrain below Groom Lake. Kuushmann was an Estonian immigrant, and he would never forget the tales his mother told of the Russian invasion in August, 1940. They had raped her at the age of eleven.

In recent years with the dominance of the New Freedom Party, Kuushmann had begun to sense a sort of disinfected, post-modern crackdown on the citizenry. It came to pass not socially as he had expected, but economically, via wealthy corporations buying up public lands and facilities, the selling off of the government, spawning monster conglomerates whose lies and unconscionable treatment of the Earth brought back the stench of Soviet repression his mother had so violently experienced.

Senator Hal Riske did not have to work hard to persuade Dr. Kuushmann to join him in Philadelphia. And whom should he bump into but his old college chum, Purvis Courtman.

The reunion had been sad and joyous, in a melancholy bar on Chestnut Street, where they exchanged convulsive scenarios on the next step after Independence Hall.

Laying his plans, Kuushmann needed to know the exact instant they would want Intelsat to override I-Media broadcasting. The rebels would have one-hundred-twenty seconds. At the one-hundred-twenty-first second, CI's national emergency broadcast system would override the override. His old friend Purvis and his band of saboteurs had two minutes to take over the government of the United States.

83

The whiteboard was jammed with high crimes and misdemeanors. A pair of kerosene lamps cast shadows down the log walls. The house had electricity, but somehow with the darkness, the lamps had appeared. Foulks was missing.

"The Inauguration's at high noon Sunday," Courtman announced. "We travel Saturday. So we have about thirty-six hours."

BJ, working his phones, said, "We'll be hearing from this man Butts or his wife shortly. Some sort of software engineer connected to voting machinery. He's asleep, and his wife is scared to death to wake him up. And I'm talking to the Nevada Department of

Taxation. I'm assuming Billy Hellman left a few bad feelings behind. I think we can persuade the tax guys to help out. We'll see."

Courtman nodded. "Now as soon as –"

Two phones clicked simultaneously. Half a dozen people reached for them. Nel answered one, charged up and only used this morning.

"Mother?" she shouted. "Is that you? Are you all right?" At the same moment, Mgaba was on another phone, and heard John Lee Davis's voice. He grabbed a jacket and walked out to the back deck.

Pearl Diamond, mother-in-law of Second District Congressman Victor Sligo, sat impishly in her Morris chair, vodka and vermouth with a squeeze of lime in hand, watching a glorious sunset.

"I've just heard from Michaela Velasquez!" sniffed the old lady. "Well, she didn't call me exactly. She called my beautician in Friday Harbor. I have no idea how she got her number."

"Mother, but you might be – are you –"

"Don't worry!" Pearl interrupted. "Since you and I spoke Tuesday, I did buy one of those little hotty phones, or whatever you call them. And an encoder." A mischievous quirk layered below her ancient voice. "Michaela Velasquez wants you to stay at her condo in Foggy Bottom. On Virginia Avenue. The key's under the doormat. That's the message I got. Maybe it was an imposter. A man! Do you think? Some kind of sex pervert preying on an old lady?" She mumbled, "One can only hope."

"No, no," Nel said. Her mind flew in all directions. Were they watching her? Recording somehow? She noticed for the first time a fluffy orange cat curled up beside the wood stove. "That's great, Mother. Everything's okay here. I should be coming home for a visit next month." And then with a wild impulse she whispered, "Victor's in Puerto Rico. Crockett left him there, unharmed. In a nunnery. Los Gatos. Los Gatos, Puerto Rico."

"Puerto Rico!" shrieked the old lady. "Oh my Gawd!"

She told Victor everything he needed to know by putting her hand to her own throat and making the universal gagging motion. Her husband scowled at her. The phone chirped again just as she closed it.

"Hey there, it's Fred Geschwantner," came the old cowboy voice. "How's it going up North?"

"Fred!" Nel rejoiced to hear from him. "Not so good, but we're not locked up. What do you have?"

"Okay, here's the news, good and bad. The FBI will not re-open the case on Viola Ferrari. Even with the Purger evidence. They told me maybe Purger rented the car before she did. Or they knew each other. I just can't understand it. The eyelash they missed? Lodged under the gas pedal. That's how they missed it.

"I called Bert O'Donnell at NSA on that code number you gave him from Tyne's email. Got nothing so far, but he's coming unglued, you can tell, and maybe he hasn't been there yet. Next, I paid a visit to Dugway on an Army murder case I invented. The places they let me see, the primary labs, had no sign of medical re-search anywhere. But they sure watch a lot of television! Holotechs in the labs! And last, listen to this! New Mexico traced that phone number stuffed behind the mirror in Purger's bathroom cabinet. That phone was purchased in Maryland in mid-September, a couple of days before Viola's death. More phone calls, more delays. Turns out it came from a chain drug store in Chevy Chase. Somebody was dumb enough to use a credit card." He stopped, maybe to read from a note. "Alfred B. Sorenson, college student, sometime landscaper for a Sievers Tuey, former chief of staff of the Secretary of Com-munications."

She was flipping her fingers at Raven, telling her to make room on the whiteboard. A moment later she clicked the phone closed, and made the announcement to all present.

BJ leaped up from his corner desk. *"Yes!"* he shouted, fist-pumping. *"Yes!"* Satisfaction swarmed through the room. Nel felt vindicated and angry and wretched all at once. She felt her face twist inward, and a horrid shadow cross her breast as she said, mostly to hear herself say it, "You can't help thinking Hunter Tyne had Viola Ferrari murdered."

84

By an odd coincidence John Lee Davis was also sipping a vodka and vermouth, without lime but with a dash of Tabasco, twenty-eight hundred miles east of San Juan Island at his penthouse condo, the top floor of a Georgia Avenue high rise in Silver Spring, Maryland. Headlights flickered far below, south toward Sixteenth Street and on into the murky District. The drink tasted lousy. Since Tuesday night at Singh's Pentagon office, Davis had been wracked with the anguish of the politically-appointed law enforcement official in a world shared by criminals and politicians. Then O'Donnell had reinforced the feeling on the subway. His career was on the line in this stupid matter of criminals disguised as politicians using him as a pawn in their games. His only recourse was to play out the hand he'd been dealt – pretending to guide the Bureau, at least in the perception of the public – until the last possible moment, and then make his move. His career? Or his country? Which mattered most?

With all the intelligence of the greatest intelligence-gathering octopus on the planet available to him, he could not decide if Davy Crockett had a chance in hell, or if his success was more or less preordained because Billy Hellman was so preposterously unfit to rule the nation.

People had been calling in sick all week. While he'd heard no talk of the Bureau's 19,000 agents joining the national walk-out, he could empathize with anybody who was so sick of the administration's agenda they couldn't work. Transit workers were going out. Newspapers, labor unions, truckers, churches, food suppliers, wholesalers, city employees, entertainers, all were expressing discontent. Crockett Fever, they were calling it. Soon people were going to get nervous. By Monday the financial institutions would take over the crisis. The people who ran this country would not tolerate financial upheaval out of their control, under any circumstances. They would bring in the serious artillery. They would grind Crockett and Sligo to dust in a New York minute.

He'd found the time to meet O'Donnell half way, at a rest area on I-95. He could never be absolutely certain of O'Donnell's allegiance – not to mention his sanity – but the man was the most powerful figure in the intelligence community outside the Cabinet, and Davis had to have his confidence.

He did. O'Donnell climbed out of a new black pickup in a black raincoat in a wild gray-black downpour, although it was one in the afternoon, his big, lithe body gliding toward Davis's Shanghai Urban Survival Vehicle. Without a signal he opened the door, dropped into the passenger seat, and said, "No military coup is possible. It's out. Straight from Admiral Singh." O'Donnell was nervous. Kept running a hand through his sandy hair, never making eye contact, speaking curtly and minimally. His office was being picketed. The National Security Agency was effectively useless, he said, until the troops came in Monday at 6 a.m. Incredibly, he had engaged a core group of people who might concoct a way to protect their careers and still engage in the conspiracy. Sloan Mgaba had given him a full report. Apparently Sligo's group had done their homework and had created an end to the rebellion, a totally whacko event nobody could possibly prepare for. But because economic and social catastrophe loomed, and O'Donnell had lost everything including his wife and house in the recession and was goddammit not going to let the country melt down on his watch, he had to take action. Let the rebellion come.

"You know what I think," Davis said calmly. "It's not rebellion. It's hero-worship." He gazed through the big windshield at the storm. "Desperate people clinging to a desperate hope. That smell in the air is not insurrection. It's paranoia combined with frustration." After too many years of unemployment, excessive favors for the financial industry and general mistrust in government, now people were frustrated with their inability to walk into a voting booth or fill out an absentee ballot to get these bastards out of Washington.

Rain thrummed down on the heavy vehicle. "But the worst of it is, the fate of the United States is in the hands of an unstable bus driver in a coonskin hat," Davis said. "I can't believe I'm saying this! This guy's supposed to have a chat with the President and Vice President, and the administration's just going to quit! Jesus Christ, are we all going off the deep end?"

The two officials had a combined total of sixty-one years in government. What those long years represented – rare but not entirely unheard of in upper levels of the intelligence community – was a commitment to justice, decency, and to identifying bad people and locking them up. The way the present administration did business was an excruciating challenge for law enforcement.

At Davis's end, the plans were almost in place. Now, gazing out at the lights on Georgia Avenue, he put his drink aside and touched in Mgaba's number. He flicked on the speaker phone, and braided his long hair as they spoke. It was their third call today.

"Here is my thinking, Sloan," he said. "You may recall my

daughter."

"Of course," Mgaba lied. He was on the porch cooling off. Edwin's house had gotten warm with the stoked fire and all the tension.

"With the baton?"

He remembered immediately. Davis's daughter was the conductor of the National Marching Band. Her name was Euphonia Lee. How could he forget such a name? "Oh, yes, yes, certainly I see her now. We met at one of those functions during the last session."

"How's your connection?"

"I'm scrambled. It's very tense in this place. After this call this gadget goes in the dustbin."

"If a number of other activities take place and we wind up at the appropriate venue –" In spite of the security, Davis would not utter the word *inauguration*, "– it would be conceivable to bring a couple of people into the principal musical group chosen for this year. It will pass quite close to the center of activity."

Mgaba was struggling with the code. If he was reading Davis right, Burligame, or more likely Leora Psybysch, had decided on the Marching Band – formerly the US Military Band – to lead the hundred or so high school bands freezing down Pennsylvania Avenue to the Capitol. And as bizarre as it seemed, somebody might hide himself in the middle of the band. Then as the band passed the Inauguration site – what?

"Yes?" Mgaba said.

"I will have people close in, several security agencies. I am assured for two minutes the intelligence sector will stand down. We're working on the military." He paused. "Once the parts are in place, you're on your own."

It was becoming more outrageous all the time. Mgaba reluctantly took Davis's intentions to Congressman Sligo.

Victor studied the big man's hard walnut-colored face.

"The Marching Band? You're telling me you agreed to this? You're making decisions for me, Mgaba," he said angrily. "Dammit, these matters need to be discussed, analyzed, approved. You know this. You're overreaching your authority. This is the most crucial –"

Mgaba did not flinch. "Enormous problems lay ahead of

us," he said quietly. "A great deal is at stake here, Victor. For you, everything."

Victor curled his lower lip and frowned. He said, "I am so tired of this. All right. It does make sense. We'll have to trust those people." He turned then and found a spot on the crammed white-board. He had to nudge BJ aside, and he wrote, "Euphonia." It almost made him laugh.

85

Slash Zewinta and Desdemona B. Cooper talked politics for nine hours. The "voter apathy" story was a no-brainer for them. Slash's take on it was this: voter apathy these days with this administration would be like ignoring a snake as it crawled up your leg, onto your chest, looked you in the eye and said, "I'm taking over your body!"

Desdemona was not impressed with Slash Zewinta's digs. In fact as he ushered her in the door and she looked around at what might have been a set from *Tobacco Road Meets Dr. Strangelove*, she felt vindicated in her initial feeling that somewhere people were probably looking for him with nets. The man was estranged from ordinary human behavior. A one-pedal bicycle. Gonzo.

And maybe he was. But she was free for the moment. She had definitely felt the noose tightening. They were going to lock her up for good.

The problem was, she kind of liked him. Well, not *liked* him. A kindred spirit, espousing unpopular notions school librarians were not permitted to discuss, particularly that the people running this country should all be lined up and spanked.

She'd had a long day and needed sleep. But the place was filthy. Makeshift computers, scary posters, and a galactic radiation-collecting device were strewn everywhere. This was not the home of your average janitor. The inside of the refrigerator stank like the Fresh Kills dump used to smell. The sink overflowed with dishes that appeared to be growing a fungus. A sort of toxic fluorescence hung over everything. The whole apartment felt like a high school chemistry experiment. She was suddenly missing her cell down at the Federal Building. A clean, well-lighted place. But at least Slash spoke English. Or some version thereof.

"Whether you show up for work or don't, the feds'll be here pounding on the door in a couple of hours," she said. "What's your plan?"

"My plan for the immediate future," Slash said, rubbing his large belly and moving toward the fridge, "is to drink a soda. Want one?"

"Apple juice," she said.

"No juice."

"A bran muffin then."

"All I got's Wonder bread."

"Terrific."

He popped open a Dr. Pepper and explained there was no way in hell his people in the Federal Building would implicate him. Too many outstanding debts, phony birth certificates, reconstructed DD214s, that sort of thing. This moved him to an effusive explanation of all the high-tech stuff lying around, the dartboard with Hellman's picture on it, the bright yellow bumper sticker across the back of the door that said, "Who killed Viola Ferrari?" Then he noted, innocent as a lamb, that he had to find Congressman Sligo right away. It was crucial to the future of the country.

"Is that a fact?" Desdemona eyed him suspiciously. "Well, I'm not staying here."

It was dark-thirty and Desdemona was utterly exhausted, a bone-weary fugitive, and she understood for the moment she was his prisoner. The man himself, fresh from the daring escape downtown, was at the beginning of a manic episode. He felt like Paul Revere, ready to ride and spread the alarm – but where?

The answer lay in a slumping brownstone across Roosevelt Avenue and two blocks south on 68th Street, practically sitting on the Brooklyn-Queens Expressway. Eddie Rickett owned the building and lived in the basement sometimes, a fellow geek who was in Florida or Cuba for the winter, maybe several winters.

Although it was the middle of the night, they hauled hard drives and unwieldy devices and Slash's cat in a borrowed grocery cart – Ms. Crockett now dressed in Mr. Zewinta's black quilt coverall suit – and Slash taped a note to his paint-peeling slab of door. "Dear FBI: in case you're looking for Desdemona B. Crockett, she's not in the basement of Eddie Rickett's place, so don't look there. Love, Slash."

She read the note and shook her head and put a lighter to it, still hanging on the door.

Slash located a key, and found the lock with his fingers in the wet dark basement entryway. Eddie Rickett's apartment smelled like a laboratory where they grafted dead rabbits onto old ladies' bicycle seats. Desdemona immediately turned up the heat, opened all the windows and doors and filled the sink and bathtub with scalding water and poured in bleach. "Disinfectant," she explained. "No way I'm putting my body parts in there." She demanded that Slash go back to his building and find a vacuum cleaner and scrubbing implements. He returned in half an hour to find her in the coveralls, in a fetal position in the bathtub, dead to the world.

86

Congressman Victor Sligo was asleep on the plank flooring of the old log house, tucked against the back of a sofa on which Sloan Mgaba snored rhythmically. Suddenly he was awake. Forest noises, a whole symphony of critters, filled the night. He had to urinate. Rolling up, he reached for his shoes and an odd spasm of light caught the corner of his eye. Fire? His breathing stopped for two full seconds. No. A reflection. Moonlight. As he slipped his shoes on he realized there was no moon, and in a flash he was at the big window. From the depths of the forest came a dim flickering. *Now what?* The feds creeping up? A SWAT guy's night vision glasses? He crept past Courtman. Courtman's teeth were in a plastic container beside him. His mouth was pursed in an anguished frown.

He grabbed the mackinaw and was moving through the dark house when he heard BJ whispering some kind of romantic babble. Beside the front door hung a big red camp flashlight, and he snatched it off its nail and plunged into the darkness, not entirely without fear but simply beyond reason, his mind drained, a fire out in the forest in the middle of the night.

He'd been creeping along on the rough footpath for a minute before he saw it. Switching the light off, he watched the fire snatch-

ing at the cool moisture of the night air. Above and all around him
was black as pitch, so dark he could not see his hand before his face
unless he turned directly toward the flickering light.

Edwin was facing the low fire, head down, wearing the
coonskin hat, hands in his pockets. An old firepit, a circle of river
rocks, a makeshift log bench. He was so still Victor thought he
might be standing up dead, but as he came in close he saw Edwin
was chewing on a weed. He looked for all the world like Davy
Crockett, about to roast a marshmallow.

"Nice night," Victor said.

Not looking up he said, "Evening, Congressman."

They stood shoulder to shoulder before the fire. Victor said,
"You know, people are waiting for you to walk into Washington
and fix this mess."

Edwin moaned. His voice was tender but miserable. "I seriously don't think –"

"Sorry, pal, you don't get to think. Those days ended at the
Mall of Brotherly Love." He plucked a stalk of what looked like the
same weed, held it out at arm's length and squinted at it, and stuck
the stem in his mouth. For a while they listened to the roaring silence curling around boulders in the riverbed.

"We're leaving the day after tomorrow." Victor bent to read
his watch. "Remember, when a government is threatened, they clean
up shop right now. There will not be another chance for you. Soon
enough they'll find a fingerprint, or a laser image, or they'll break
Alonzo Toon or the old Mennonite lady or our friend Dr. Spangloss.
You'll be in the joint forever, and I will be sorry for you, over in my
mansion in Sunrise having a good life and maybe wishing we'd
never met."

"Yes, but –"

"The problem is, on the street people think their votes don't
mean anything. And they think – and I think – Billy Hellman is behind it. You know all this better than I do. You started the damn rebellion!" Heat rose from the fire. Turning to face him, Victor said
carefully, "You are going to walk in there and confront that guy and
make people vote, and nobody is ever going to give you credit for
it."

For several seconds Edwin stared at him. His face glowed in
the firelight. Finally he said, "What if I fail?"

"Jesus failed. Martin Luther King failed. So did Mother Teresa. So did Bobby Kennedy."

Edwin thought about this.

"But they all knew what they wanted and they moved the agenda forward. Ultimately they all succeeded. You might get locked up or killed, but look out on the street, man! Look at I-Media! You have changed the tide. You, Foulks. You have ripped open the big secret that criminals cannot be allowed to govern. You have scared the hell out of investors, corporations, governments, all around the planet. Wall Street probably has a contract out on you!" He spat the weed into the fire. "I'll probably regret saying this the rest of my life, but if you go down, I'm going down with you."

They stared into the low orange blaze.

Victor said, "So I'll tell you what. Be as miserable and scared as you want. When you're done, come on in and we'll put the rest of it together."

87

Desdemona awoke with a start. She thought she smelled smoke, and shot upright alarmed to realize she had not the vaguest idea where she was. By the dawn's early light she looked at her watch. 7:15. It all flooded back then. The brain-damaged man with some serious sleep apnea in the other room, alternately gasping and dead silent, had yanked her out of the Church Street lockup. She'd beaten up two federal agents, and had been subjected to all manner of humiliation in two separate detention centers – body search, fingerprinting, voiceprint polygraph, repeated grilling by people looking for Davy Crockett and his Congressman.

Now she had to get to work establishing her innocence. There was no sense that she was innocent until proven guilty. Oh, no. The prevailing sense was, you are here until you are told otherwise. No attorney, no bullshit, take these orange clothes and shut up.

Then Slash Zewinta had walked in and hauled her away.

"You up?" The voice like an exhausted castaway heaving up on shore.

"Who wants to know?" She could sound ugly too. The place

stank of disinfectant, mold, and mice eating popcorn and farting.

Utterly charmless Slash Zewinta left and returned with two regular coffees and Cheerios and milk, to find her up to her knees in Eddie Rickett's inadequate cleaning implements, scrubbing the floor.

"If I'm staying one more hour," she told him, "we're having a GI party." She had made her decision. For the moment she had no choice about remaining a fugitive. But she felt obligated to find out whether her new best friend Slash Zewinta could, for real, save the world.

So it was time to get acquainted.

"I'm sure," Desdemona told him from her knees, "your story is much more interesting than mine. So I'm telling mine first." She'd been a school librarian for decades, and had in fact once jumped out of a perfectly good airplane over in Jersey. Barefoot, the leg bottoms and the sleeves of the black coveralls rolled up and the front zipped down a bit, she looked to Slash like Katharine Hepburn in *The African Queen,* except she was a dignified African American with extremely short hair. It was the way she smudged her face with her forearm with her hands full of soap. And that voice. Crisp. Direct. No whining.

Incredibly, she hadn't voted in years. Before he died, her husband had predicted the surging fundamentalists would create their own party, and sure enough the New Freedom Party emerged out of the recession and the present dynasty began.

And then came the catastrophe of what some people called Government-on-eBay, the sale of the country's assets to the highest bidder, culminating in the present administration abandoning any shadow of social consciousness, like an angry old man cutting his grandchildren out of his will.

"Even Public Television," she said, laying into the sink. "Watching Julio Reese flip his pencil and say 'Don't vote, it isn't worth it.' Right? Then he'd say, 'No, don't be crazy, go vote.'" Everybody she knew loved Julio Reese and watched his news show all the time. "Anyway, that year I had to work overtime at the library. I was planning to drop off my absentee ballot. But the polling place had closed! Then during Burligame's first campaign I studied Julio. That was when I bought my Holotech. I mean, I watched him religiously. That Old West sheriff's droopy gray mustache he wears. I watched other commentators too. It almost felt like an out-of-body experience, watching these people, feeling really weird sitting on the couch, my ballot clutched in my hand like a schoolgirl holding her lunchbox. Thinking, I'm voting, and they won't stop me. Because the voting numbers were dropping, right? And I got sick! I didn't cast my ballot! Forgot everything for three days. Man, was I ticked! So last November by God I was going to vote or kill somebody. And my mother passed." She stopped a moment, gazing at the greasy casement window. "I packed my stuff and went to Oregon to her funeral, and that mockery of a human being Billy Hellman was back running the country." She shook her head, part disgust, part mourning. "Then to ease my guilt, guess what? I started going to football games!"

Slash was speechless. He'd read stories like this online. Unexplainable failure to vote, freak coincidences, particularly Progressive-minded people. That thing with Julio Reese and his pencil. It was creepy.

After a decent interval he said, "You spent time in Oregon? Well I'll be hornswoggled! So did DB Cooper."

"Oh, drop it, Slash. Some day you'll figure it out."

This comment surprised and amused him and lifted his spirits. So he told her his story.

He'd been drafted. Well, not drafted exactly. It was either the Army, or spend a couple of years in a little room with no toilet seat for conspiring to steal government property – to wit, he wandered into the CIA's Ultra Top Secret strategy to foment war in Iran. He was whisked away in the dark, severely muzzled, his family threatened, and before he realized what was happening he was in Advanced Infantry Training in Georgia, heading for Baghdad. Frantic and fearing for his life, Private Zewinta located people whom he paid to hack him into the Pentagon's Manpower Relocation Center, where in a blind search he uncovered a shortage request for a body at Aberdeen Proving Ground, and cut himself orders for the slot. The entire hour and a half scared the dung beetles out of him.

"You're making this up," Desdemona said. "You wrote your own orders in the Army?"

"Well, hell, wouldn't you?"

It was a defining moment for Slash Zewinta.

"It turns out the Army experiments on everything. LSD, ecstasy, chemical warfare, psychological torture, cleaning fluid, tanks, squirrel poop, bovine growth hormone, motorcycles, menstrual cycles. They used me as a guinea pig, me and about forty other guys over that two-year stint, to experiment on stimulation of certain parts of the brain by using film footage of Hiroshima, playing Beethoven and Jimi Hendrix, all kinds of *Clockwork Orange* types of stuff. Not to mention the dirty movies! It was real spiritual! I had to sign about a million papers saying I'd never talk about it or they'd turn me into a guy nobody would ever invite home to meet the folks. Well, take a look at me. They did it anyway!"

She had shoved the sparse Goodwill furniture into a corner and was disinfecting the walls. She looked him over. "Tell me about it," she laughed. "No wonder you're such a whack job! Here!" She tossed him some rags. "Clean something."

Slash said, "I used to be a boring computer geek who thought the Emperor of Ice Cream was the Good Humor man. Those days are over. Now I'm your basic paranoid janitor, no friends, no hope and a diminishing supply of mind-altering substances." Flicking a rag back and forth on a drawer handle, he told her about his seizure in the elevator, then bent far forward and asked her to take a look at the scar on his scalp. "I think they stuck a chip in my brain and it went punk on them, but they never took it out! Just got me bonkers one weekend – well, all that booze and those mushrooms helped – and I woke up in sick bay on Monday."

"You could sue them! That's torture! That's cruel and unusual!"

"Very funny. That's what my mother used to call me. Anyway, I learned later what they were after. All the outfits. Aberdeen, Dugway, that Research Triangle Park down in North Carolina, a couple other ones. You know what they were doing? Mind control experiments! Say you're a, I don't know, say you're a pitcher for the Bemidji Blue Bombers –"

"That's Burligame's kid's team!"

"Yeah, and the bad guys want to control your game, so they pass on electronic signals to you by this device that communicates with the chip in your brain. They tell you to throw all curve balls."

She made a phone out of her hand and pretended to call a number. "Yes, we have a Section Eight on the loose," she whispered into her hand. "Send the wagon around right away." She smiled at him. "You were saying?"

"Dammit, this is for real! Besides I just sprung you out of the joint, so be nice! Is there any food in this place? Listen. They were trying to make robots out of ordinary GI's. Remember *The Manchurian Candidate?* There's way better ways to do it than the Chinese water torture." His straight white hair fell every which way, and he shoved it aside. He scratched his thick nose and then his crotch as he rattled on. "The Army wanted to make Frankensteins. And not only the Army. Private companies. Stimulation of the brain by remote devices. This was the start of the BCI. The Brain-Computer Interface? You know what I found out? I was snooping on Hunter Tyne, the dung beetle scumsucker, I mean the Secretary of Communications. See, when I was at Aberdeen, Tyne was out at Dugway, in Utah, running the program! He was up to his neck in bad stuff. I found out there was this outlaw scientist dude running a lab doing mind control research. He was tinkering with electro-stimulus to the hypothalamus, creating higher pressures so that the subject responds to certain, like, tweaking. It's the BCI developed to where the interface is done without the chip implant!" Tearing his hair in a psychotic self-parody. "Neurochemical programming! The stimulus goes straight into the hypothalamus. What it does is, it regulates emotions in your head. I swear that's what they were do-ing to me back in Aberdeen! So the lab got busted. And Tyne was working for CI, and he signed the contract with the mind control re-search guy! And he walked! You could tell Tyne was going to high places in government. Corrupt as a New York City alderman."

"Slow down now. Take a breath. You're telling me all this connects to –"

His arms flew outward. "Smells, sounds, sensations like a pinprick or a specific radio frequency. And you do what they want you to do." He paused. His secret was on the tip of his tongue, but his brain was fragmenting like a shattered Christmas bauble. And then it was there – rising out of his mouth like a breaching whale. "You ain't gonna believe this. But I swear to God I'm not making it up. You know what the chemical was they were isolating? Know what really rings a GI's bell?"

"I can imagine."

"Human breast milk!" He sucked in a deep breath, all his circuits overloaded. He'd never revealed any of this before. At least,

not sober. "That's when I was in there. Never heard any more about it. I think they dried that tit up."

She shook her head. "You are truly unbelievable," she said.

"See what I mean?" He held his arms out, palms up. "They been working on remote mind control, medical technology got the BCI highly developed, and then CI got into it! And all of a sudden after two hundred thirty something years of elections and now we got something like two hundred million voters, CI controls the air waves! Get it? You even figured out Julio Reese flipping that pencil in the air. And people stop voting!" A twisted grin was holding his face together. "See, I think Tyne is the result of a nuclear accident, like a freak mutation downrange at Alamogordo!" He swiped drool from his lips. "He could be the guy behind the chip in my head! I told you all about this! That's why I got to get to Congressman Sligo! They're going to kill him! But I can't find him! Been to every hacker goon, every damn web site." His brain was flying faster than he could speak. "Got to get with Davy Crockett, find out if... There's this Chinese guy. His name's Tao Ting –" He felt it coming. Sometimes he could hold it off. But high excitement brought him to his knees.

"Hey, get me some wa–" and he went down, lips blue, body like a rubber band, curled on the floor in an instant.

88

Desdemona handled it. She elevated his feet, checked his eyeballs, rubbed his chest, kept him warm, monitored his pulse, and didn't call anybody. She could not pull the threads of all this into a coherent tapestry. From somewhere he'd gotten the wild idea that forty-five years ago she'd jumped out of a hijacked airplane in Washington state with twenty bundles of hundred-dollar bills. While Slash lay mumbling on the floor, she went to the grungy bathroom and took a long look at herself in the mirror. Rubbing her finger roughly against her cheek, she held the finger up to the light. No way, she thought. Impossible.

In time he began muttering about Crockett again and sucked in air like a drowning man and sat up. She handed him a glass of water and told him where they were.

When he seemed normal, or not normal but like his former self, she had him wash his face and tell her where he worked and his mother's maiden name. His answer was that they had to find Victor Sligo immediately. It was life or death.

He drank off the water, watched his hands until the shaking settled, then wobbled to the chaotic desk, and slipped his thumb drive into the front of Eddie Rickett's computer.

"Hellman is way too good to leave any openings. But I brought along my sound clips and fifty thousand pictures of Billy and Hunter Tyne."

"Yeah?" said Desdemona, pouring more water. "Are you listening to me? You're not well. You need to –"

"I'll show you something." He rubbed his eyes, slapped his cheeks, and clicked a few keys. They were looking at the news broadcast from a couple of hours ago outside the National Security Council meeting. A photo of the President's National Security Advisor, Victoria Cross.

"Watch this." He opened a photo program and clicked in the picture of Cross, and made a square appear on the screen behind her, inside the open door of the Cabinet Room, pushed more keys, and blew up the dark image, then lightened and contrasted it. There stood Billy Hellman, arms raised in a foul salute. Behind him stood Hunter Tyne and a blurred female figure. Again Slash made a square on the background people. The woman came into focus. An attractive blond in a red satin jacket, glaring at Hellman.

"Who is she?"

"Beats me. But the old Slash fifty-gig memory started rumbling soon as I saw her." He fiddled for a moment, looking through files till he found the one he wanted. Clicking it open, he ran through two or three hundred listings and stopped. The screen now showed a *US Times* file photo of Victor Sligo working a crowd in Seattle six months ago. "Look behind Sligo. There." He formed another box around a woman in the background. In a moment they were looking at the same blond woman, obviously working for the Congressman.

Desdemona gasped. "A spy!"

"You got it," he said. "What I think is, she was sucking information out of Sligo, who was real big in Alex Holiday's run for

President. And she passed it on to Hellman. Now. Sligo disappears with Davy Crockett, and the country's about to explode. I got to tell you, lady. I think Sligo figured all this out – that people are not voting because of some kind of weird mind control trick, because if we could figure it out, Sligo could. And Tyne and Hellman are the exact kind of dung beetles who would perpetrate this deal. I think Tyne and this blond woman know where Sligo is, or was, and they had him killed. Or if they didn't, they're going to."

"Kill him? But why?"

"Because he's about to let the whole country know about the mind control trick! That would be the end for them! They can't have that! That would be *insaaaaaaaayaaaayaaane!"* He pulled the last word right out of *The Rocky Horror Picture Show,* spreading gnarled fingers against his face, grinning fiendishly.

"And if we call the cops, we're toast."

The words had an odd effect on her. She realized she would have to take charge of his thinking if they were to make any headway. She was half again as intelligent as most people, she knew. With her one-and-a-half brains and Slash's remaining half a brain, they had a total of two full brains. That was enough.

"If they don't know where he is, they're sure to find out real soon. You're right. We have to find Crockett and Sligo," she said. "And fast!"

89

Three floors below tourist level at the White House, Vice President Billy Hellman was taking a break from his noon bowling routine. He was standing over his score sheet eating a ham sandwich when Ms. Flotilda Lament passed through the back. Wiping his mouth, he walked straight into her path and waited. Ms. Lament looked up. Immediately she pressed her lips together, tilted her aging head sideways, and stopped. Her eyes showed a sort of childlike fear, surprising in a seventy-seven-year-old cleaning lady.

"Mother Lament," the Vice President chanted. "Working late, are we?"

"Mr. Vice President! I've been so worried!"

With genuine chivalry, he led her to a table and they sat, and he demanded she tell him about it.

She stammered and fiddled with her apron and cleared her throat.

"Mother Lament, this government cannot function without you, and you know it! Now please. What's troubling you?"

She blurted it out then. "What if this Davy Crockett character shows up and ruins your finest day," she moaned. "It could happen! It would be the most horrible thing I could imagine." She nearly reached out to touch his face, but restrained herself and clutched her trembling hands together.

He gave her his warmest smile, then took both her poly-gloved hands in his, and shook his bulldog head. "You are a work of art, Mother Lament. No such thing is going to happen. Bless you! Always looking out for the boy from Carson City! Hey, are you hungry?"

"Oh, heavens, I couldn't eat a thing."

He stood. She stood. "I promise you, you have nothing to fear. It's just politics as usual! I am so grateful for your concern. How could this outfit go on without you?" He took her shoulders. They were about the same height. "You know," he told her, "behind every great man is a Mother Lament! It's the only way we can keep going!" Surprising himself, he moved forward and kissed her leathery cheek, and whispered, "Don't worry."

Half crying, half laughing, Ms. Lament went on her way. Billy's smile faded to a scowl. He tore a small black notebook out of his breast pocket. On a blank page he scribbled, *"Inauguration – Crockett???"*

90

"What did you just say?" Slash stared at Desdemona like she was nuts.

"Go ahead. Call his house."

"You don't just call no Congressman at his house. The feds'll be here in fifteen minutes looking for Crockett!"

"Pay phone." She thumbed over her shoulder. "Half a block

down in the arcade. For a smart guy, you do have your –" She studied his calamitous white hairdo, the black stubble, the sapphire eyes.
"Limitations. Get me a phone book."

Disgusted and pouting, Slash flicked on the Webstream. Sarita Chavez was running a filibuster on Real Radio, interviewing
politicians, teachers and labor activists and random callers, yelling,
babbling, singing and chanting her incandescent wrath, intending to
continue until something took place to stop the madness crippling
the republic. She aggressively applauded Victor Sligo's courage in
the face of government mockery of this "street activity," as the administration was calling it.

He clicked over to the white pages.

"Give me ten dollars for a phone card." Her voice was
commanding. An ass-kicker, Slash thought. He imagined her in a
tight white dress and high boots and a big staple gun, stapling Billy
Hellman to the door of the White House.

"Fine. Tell Sligo to get his butt to my new janitorial service:
Cleanoutthehouse. You got it? I set it up last night under the name
of – ready? – Duane Weber." He watched her. Weber was the FBI's
only real suspect in the DB Cooper case.

Desdemona just rolled her eyes, snatched the ten, and
walked away.

Victor was mumbling to himself as he headed out to find
Foulks. He was forming a rousing speech for the troops. As he
stepped down off the front porch, the twenty-pound buff rooster
shrieked and puffed and clawed the moist earth in his path, staring
him dead in the eye. Victor ran straight at him gabbling and clucking, and the rooster scattered in all directions.

This time Edwin was working in the pumphouse out near
the road, surrounded by vine maples and moss in a gloss of January
mist. Edwin had told Victor his great-grandfather had witched this
well. At that moment, Mgaba roared in from the store in Iona's
rented car bearing groceries and the only two cheap phones for sale
in Van Zandt. Victor told Edwin to come in when he was done here.

Sarita Chavez was advocating a mass public strike on Real
Radio, demanding that citizens picket every city government in the
country, stop buying stocks, stop traveling, plug up the freeways,
call in sick, threaten their representatives, and create chaos until a

recall election was forced on Congress. You could hear Chavez thump her desk. She cried, "Rule by corruption in Washington is about to be overruled."

Papers shuffled through the speakers. "Listen up, folks!" Chavez shouted into Edwin's living room. "An hour ago the state of New York voted to submit a constitutional amendment, the Twenty-Eighth Amendment, which would create an automatic recall vote of the President and the Vice President in the case of proven federal election fraud! Illinois and Indiana are considering the same move! In Texas there's talk of seceding from the Union! Florida, Michigan, Maine – it's moving like lightning, friends! Can you believe it?" She paused a long moment. Nobody in the house moved.

"Hear that sound?" She waited a second longer. "That's the sound of Billy Hellman packing his bags!" The words thundered through the house. "The ugly truth is, we'll never know what happened. No politician is going to tell us what secret conversations are taking place over the gilded urinals of the White House. My God, did I just say that?

"My question now is, where is Congressman Victor Sligo?

"If he is dead, our prayers go out to his family. If he's in a position to direct this rebellion, I say come out, Sligo! Come on out and bring the full weight of your authority to this constitutional crisis. Don't cower behind Davy Crockett's coonskin shadow! It was you who fought like a mad dog against the last three administrations. It was you who ran this flag of rebellion up our national flagpole! Don't desert us now, Congressman. Stand up and fight!"

"*Salut,* Victor" Mgaba called, raising a glass of orange juice.

Victor scowled from the card table. "What's she whining about, stand up and fight? Give her a call, Mgaba. Tell her Sunday we're going to blow her socks off."

The big man shifted in his chair.

"No, don't. She'll find out soon enough."

A phone rang. Half the group jumped up, but Courtman opened his, and moved immediately toward the stairs, away from the radio and the murmuring staff. With one finger in his ear he yelled into the phone, "Merlin? Merlin? You'll have to shout at me! I'm in Timbuktu!" His face scrunched as he struggled to check his scrambler and listen to Victor's houseman. "Yes, I know. The whole country's coming apart!" He lowered his voice as Chavez droned on. Victor stood wiping his mouth with a paper towel.

"Turn down that radio. Purvis, punch that speaker button," Victor said.

Merlin's dignified baritone came through now. "They either want to kill him or elect him Pope," he said. "Tell him all the kids called."

"Is your connection okay?" Courtman said.

"Yes. Yes. All the kids are good and worried and have no idea. Wait." A moment later, he sounded as if he was reading from a list. "That fellow who arranged that football game? Yes? He says everything's going fine. Okay. Let's see. The tux is back from the cleaner's. The Lion's Club called, the Progressive Caucus, the Governor, twice, Terry Gross, twice, somebody who said his name was Babylon – don't ask me – left no message. Ms. S's mother thinks the Vice President is a disgusting prune face who should have been beaten more often as a child. Oh, and this woman keeps calling, a Ms. D. B. Crockett. She's on the other phone now."

Victor smiled, shaking his head. He said, "Yeah, that type. A humorous constituent."

"I'm going to get rude with her, her and her friend Slickwatch. She keeps insisting this Slickwatch needs to get hold of the Cong – the boss."

"Slickwatch?" Victor shrugged. "Whoever he is, just handle it the same way you –"

"Slickwatch!" It was Molly Bee, from the kitchen. "Wait, wait Congressman –" She was coming into the main room, followed closely by the brown lab. She glanced up looking for Victor, and instead found Edwin Foulks sitting by the stove, staring at her in an intimate, astonished way. Bee stopped still and frowned at him.

"What?" she said, her space suddenly crowded.

"Uh, sorry. Nothing." Edwin pulled away, embarrassed. "I, uh – you surprised me."

Webster was there too, excited. "Hey, Slickwatch, that's the name from that Web site. The guy who stuck in the new stuff about Tyne." She turned, looking back toward her personal banana crate beyond the stairs, under the hanging laundry.

"You'd better get over here, Congressman –"

"The name's Victor!" Victor shouted to the whole room.

"Now where's my laptop," Webster growled, standing with her hands on her slim hips. "Damn, this mess is a mess!" In her bright purple slacks and wide-striped blouse and the tightly-wound hair, Iona looked more like a frazzled French model than an L.A. ombudsman.

Already beside Courtman, Bee was peering down into his phone display. Edwin was still watching her.

"Better talk to Mr. Slickwatch, Congressman," Webster said, dropping at her crate and reading her laptop. "Hunter Tyne has a pirated bio on here. Slickwatch posted it yesterday. Listen to this. 'A lab subcontracting with CI was shut down for doing unlicensed research on human brain stems and the hypothalamus. US Attorney's Office files suggest the Grand Jury indicted a high-level official –'" She looked up. "This exact stuff was in Tenkley's deposition. How the hell did this guy know about it?"

Molly pointed at Courtman's phone. "I don't know, but he's on the phone! Right there!"

Victor moved quickly. "Merlin?" Snatching the phone from Courtman. "Where is he?"

91

Racing back to Rickett's in her black coveralls, Desdemona handed Slash a phone number.

"Congressman Sligo can't wait to meet you," she said.

"'Bout time," Slash said nonchalantly. "This the number? Where's that phone booth?"

He fought himself back into his hoodie and sunglasses. "You got any time left on that card?" A minute later he walked into the arcade. Two kids were yelping over a video game, and a woman lay stretched out in a corner. A note pinned to her sweater read in clumsy lettering, "Do not rob I am asleep not dead."

Inserting the card, Slash punched the numbers. A man's voice answered, but no video came to the screen.

"Hey," said Slash.

"Yes?"

"It's Duane Weber, dude! Let me talk to the man!"

"I'm sorry. You must have connected to the wrong –"

He searched frantically around the arcade. Now what? Had that damn woman set him up? And then there she was, walking toward him with such confidence, such class, she nearly stopped his heart.

At the oval opening to the booth she said, "Give me that, Duane." And she reached out like the Queen of Sheba, taking the phone from him with her slender dark hand.

"Merlin? Slickwatch is coming on the line." She handed it back with an impetuous wink. "Mister save-the-world. You're on."

Quickly Slash explained to Merlin what the Congressman had to do.

Forty seconds later Courtman's phone rang again in the Van Zandt forest. Victor answered.

"Sir, you're supposed to meet this person Slickwatch on his Website. It's *cleanoutthehouse.* Do you have it? You'll need a password. The password is, 'Custer died for your sins.'"

Eddie Rickett's Skype was ready. Running a finger-gnawed hand through his hair, Slash looked up and nodded at her. "Thanks, DB."

"Oh, get over it," she said. An instant later his screen showed a tilted view of another computer screen.

"Hey," he said, starting to hyperventilate. "Greetings, Earthling!" Immediately Desdemona stood beside him, touching his shoulder, calming him.

Somebody said, "Mr. Slickwatch?"

"Mr. Congressman Victor Sligo?" The voice came buzzing through Victor's laptop speaker like cracking peanut brittle, a hesitant tenor underpinned with sea foam and old bubblegum wrappers. On the screen was an odd-looking face. It possessed feverish bright blue eyes and a sort of clown wig of long white bristles slashing crazily all over the large square head. The mouth was a ragged bow, chapped lips fixed in a Batman pout. In the center of the square jaw was a ball chin that looked glued on as an afterthought during the chaotic creation process.

"What's up, man?" Slash cried. "That was a hell of a plane ride! Wow! What a rush! Look, we have to get that camera of yours cleaned up. I'm looking at myself sideways. I'm ugly enough straight up. Man, am I ever wired today! So I don't know where you're going, but I need you to know what I got, cause it will help you. But you're gonna have to do your part, too, because –" At this point Desdemona leaned forward and was actually cradling his head against her breast, telling him to slow down, breathe, don't screw this up, big boy. This is your moment. Easy, Slash. Easy.

BJ stood beside Victor. He reached out and re-aimed the laptop camera.

Slash let out a noisy breath. "Yeah. Hey. You look good. You look like Paul Bunyan! Where are you?"

Victor said, "I've just been informed of your knowledge of some matters, Mr. Slickwatch. You are obviously intimate with –"

"Call me Slash," he said. Nel stood beside Victor, staring in disbelief, whispering, "Can you imagine what he smells like?"

"I'm intimate all right," Slash chuckled. "Can we cut right to the chase here? And don't call me mister. I work for a living."

Victor relaxed. "Where you from, Slash?"

"Originally? The Bronx."

"Ah. Rosa Scarpe's district. A fine congresswoman. Even wearing the pink shoes."

"Yeah. Listen. I got something for you. And you can also help me with something also."

Doc Nguyen had materialized, looking wan and ancient in his ratty cardigan and slacks, barefoot, wheezing and horking to the bathroom. Now with a mug of tea in one hand he moved into the group.

Everyone was in it now, gathered curiously around the screen. Courtman's eyeballs were jumping. He said to Doc, "Okay. We have to confirm this ASAP."

Doc found his lavender phone, and pressed the trach chip and quickly was talking to his people. His group had a longtime info-swap with the intellectuals running *Government Incendiaries* back in Hays, Kansas. He waited, spoke again, clacked his phone closed, and interrupted Victor with his guttural whisper without using the throat box.

"Somebody walked right through an impenetrable double asymmetric key encryption system to insert that Tyne material. I designed it myself! The material is unverified, but nobody can do what that fellow did! We need to get him on the payroll!" He shot his eyes at Edwin and thumbed his throat. "Stoke that fire, will you? My bones are freezing!"

Onscreen, Slash appeared to be talking angrily to somebody standing beside him. Flicking on the mike, Victor said, "I appreciate your getting hold of me. How do I know this communication is secure?"

Slash's attention whipped back to the screen. "It's not. But I figure the odds at around four million to one somebody will blunder onto this site. Do you want to risk it?"

Victor's eyes went to the log joists overhead, the intricate notches framing the second floor. "Tell me what you want."

Slash looked up at Desdemona. She shook her head sternly. He ignored her, and took a husky breath. "I want to know why DB Cooper is being detained in Manhattan under the name of Desdemona B. Crockett, without being charged and they won't let her call her lawyer!"

92

Victor dropped his head to the table, his momentary hope collapsed. Another crackpot. This one a dangerous information pirate. He turned to find Nel to say something, but Courtman was standing over him. The chief of staff held both hands up, not unlike the posture Desdemona had used with Slash, signaling patience to the least patient man in national politics. Victor let out a long foul sound, his lips fluttering, tongue stuck out.

"Well. That's interesting," he told Slash. He found a pen and paper and wrote something down, and handed the note to Courtman, pointing at Mgaba. "I'm persona non grata at the moment, but I'll notify Secretary Strange at Homeland Security that this matter needs urgent attention. Fair enough?"

"Wow," Slash gushed. "Needham Strange? The Homeland Security Czar? Can you trust him?"

"No."

"I like you more all the time, Congressman." He lifted his Dr. Pepper in salute. "So there's a woman either works for you or used to work for you. I do not know her name. But if you watch your screen, I'm going to show you her picture." He continued speaking as he worked on his computer. The image switched to an enlarged photo of the blond woman in the background at some event in Washington state. "Here she is. In red there?" Victor's staff people crowded around, murmuring in surprise. Courtman actually growled aloud.

"Yeah, good work," Victor said. "My assistant for entropy and renumeration. So?" Click. The new photo appeared, slightly blurry – the blond woman standing beside Hunter Tyne in the Cabinet Room yesterday.

"Yes?"

"She's a spy, man!" Slash ejaculated. "If she knows where you and Crockett are now, you're history!"

Sure enough, she was with Tyne! Courtman slapped his forehead.

Victor calmly said, "She's on my staff. Evidently it hasn't dawned on you she's spying for me!"

Applause came from somewhere behind Slash. He shook his big head and grinned.

"I knew that."

Mgaba was scratching his cheek with his phone, reading Victor's note: "Call Davis at FBI. Confirm arrest of Desdemona B. Crockett, NYC."

"What else?" Victor's opinion of the man was expanding. "And what the hell is Slickwatch?"

"I really got to know, Congressman. Is Crockett okay? Is he with you? Have the feds got to you yet? Whataya think they'll give you for smearing the Newfies' public image like this? Banishment? Make you read George Bush's private correspondence?"

Victor rolled his eyes.

"Yeah, well, see, I've been stalking Hunter." He paused. Looked at Desdemona, standing close by carefully watching the screen. She glanced at him and shrugged. "My real job is going after Hellman. That's Slick. Slick Hellman." He stared with deadly earnest at the fugitive Congressman. "I couldn't find nothing! The guy's a Tasmanian devil! Does all this violence, and don't leave no trace!" His hands needed attention for a few moments. "Fine, too bad. So I figured I'd go after Tyne!" He made a horrible face, expelling a demon from his brain. "He ain't Hellman, but he's as bad as Sodom and Gomorrah and my mother and all the CEOs of Communication International put together." Eyes bulging, banging a fist against the table, blurting out angrily, "What's wrong with you people, sticking him in there?"

Victor was moved by Slash's tormented and acute view of the administration, and in fact Congress. Maybe he was mentally disturbed, but he definitely saw things the way Victor saw things. Which said something, Victor thought, about himself.

"What do you have in mind?"

Slash held off on his monumental request. He grunted and launched into the inchoate scribblings on papers in front of him. A long time ago, he said, Tyne was CI's boy in remote mind control research out in Salt Lake City. Something like brainwashing. He explained his own Army experience at Aberdeen, and said there was no way Tyne, who ran Communication West's idiot-research lab, was not involved. Communication West had the contract, Tyne ran the lab at Dugway, and Slash heard Tyne's name repeatedly at Aberdeen. Recently he'd learned about this lab around Chicago doing the dirty work for Tyne, and the dude going to the joint, which totally linked Tyne to this brain stem and hypothalamus research, this neurochemical programming. What it was, it was Brain-Computer Interface turned inside out.

"And all this time, man, people don't keep voting more and more!" He held up dirt-creased palms. "See what I'm sayin'?"

With effort, Doc Nguyen actually whistled. Others exchanged glances. Nobody had said the words aloud. But the hard connection wasn't there. The link was too flimsy, and Slash himself was too... unthinkable. In court, Slash had nothing. Mere innuendo. A pissed-off Web pirate floundering to vilify the administration. Simply put, people would not go to the polls for as many reasons as there were ballots. No. Every person in the room wanted it to be true, but that was mere politics.

"What *is* he saying?" BJ asked. "Mass hypnosis? Touch the voting screen and your finger bends toward Burligame? You pop open your absentee ballot and Newfie atoms fly into your head? Where's this guy coming from? Has he been eating those beans?"

A phone snipped in BJ's pocket. He answered and moved away. Doc's ragged throat voice spilled out from his alcove. "We found a brother in Arkansas, guys! Sure enough, Jaap Tenkley served forty-four months in Illinois federal prison, and was never seen again. Contacted his people from Egypt! And he ain't saying nothing to nobody."

Victor checked his watch. Ten-fifteen already. Should he use this freak?

"Stand by a minute." He pressed the mike off and turned around to gather the sense of the group. Standing behind Courtman, Nel was staring bug-eyed at the screen, wagging a finger at Victor. Courtman, on the phone, gave him a thumbs down. Webster and Bee muttered over Bee's laptop. Bee made a pained face, and Webster grinned. BJ and Mgaba were murmuring into phones and sneaking looks at Slash, as if deciding not to buy a used car from him. Raven Menez needed to say something.

"Look at that face, though. That man never told a lie in his life. Probably people never believe anything he says."

Nel said, "Or don't understand anything he says."

Edwin Foulks sat by the heater, watching, unable to respond to Victor's look.

"Okay, Slash, I'll have to get back to you. Can you hang a while?"

Slash said, "Uh, can I uh… What?"

Courtman sighed loudly and flipped his phone closed.

"They're not going to open any doors today. Certainly not about a member of Cabinet."

"Who?"

"Justice. Figured they must have seen the new Tyne bio material on *Government Incendiaries*. They're all spooked or out of town. Apparently D.C.'s a war zone."

Molly Bee checked her watch. "Let me try," she said.

"Be my guest," Courtman smiled obsequiously. Molly did a double take, and felt like slapping him. She hadn't slept at all, and she was feeling like she had burned a bridge behind her.

At that moment Mgaba called out, "Same with the FBI. I'm on the number Davis left us, but some woman said to try him in an hour. And I've been working all morning on getting to O'Donnell. Now his Web site tells me the National Security Agency is shut down!"

Victor felt the pulse changing through the building. People shoved up against each other in a strange environment, pretending they could keep the country from total anarchy. He turned back to the mike and touched the button.

"Okay, Slash. What can you do for me?" A groan came from Courtman. At the same moment Edwin said, "That's the question, isn't it?"

"I'm telling you about brainwashing, man!" Slash was in a frenzy. "Tyne's got his fingerprints all over it! It's got to be hidden in CI archives. Dugway, Aberdeen, all their stinking contracts. That's how they work! All you gotta do's find the right guy to break down their defenses. And I might know just the dude to get you –"

On screen a brown hand touched Slash's shoulder. A woman's voice rose over his. "Slash's experience does suggest some kind of mind control might be past the research phase," she said. "It can't be in the voting machinery because people don't get near the polls. It could be connected to I-Media, since they're CI's resource for mass manipulation. What I myself suggest you do is watch Julio Reese flip his pencil when he tells you not to vote."

Victor shook his head like he was hearing things. "Who was that?"

"Oh," Slash said. "That was DB Cooper."

Victor exhaled noisily. Holy Moses, there are two of them. Wackos howling at a paper moon.

Slash scowled at the person off screen. There was a momentary scuffle. The screen flicked white, then reopened to a different scene. The ragged white-haired Caucasian man sat beside his exact opposite – a beautiful light-skinned black woman maybe not yet sixty, her face perfectly carved, with a finely-shaped head of gray hair cut close to her scalp. But why was she wearing baggy black coveralls?

BJ crossed the room toward Victor. "It's Truman Butts." Pressing the phone against his chest. "He has ALS. He's dying. I've been talking to his wife. He wants to tell us about work he contracted for CI. But he's got serious paranoia also. Thinks they'll come after his family if he talks."

Victor held BJ off with an open palm for the moment, unable to take his eyes from the woman on the screen.

"How do you do, Congressman. My name is Desdemona B. Crockett." Beside her, Slash looked at his hands, wobbling his great head in unspoken misery.

"Yes?" Thinking, they're playing war games. They want to break me down with these actors.

"Since we're already talking, sir, it is obvious that we have mutual interests."

"I see. Pardon me. Ms. Crockett? I was told you were being detained by the authorities. I can't talk to you."

"You're right. I was. Now I'd like to answer your question, if I may? As a fellow outlaw." A generous smile filled her face. Beside her Slash chewed on his last fingernail. Ever so tenderly, Desdemona reached out and removed his hand from his mouth. "Obviously we don't know your plan." Again that disarming smile. Dimples formed in her taut cheeks. "The country is poised for the removal of the Burligame administration by any means." Shuffling papers before her, Desdemona held up this morning's *New York Street Rag.* "Here's the overnight poll." Reading with blazing clarity, one word at a time: "Eighty-three percent favor a constitutional amendment enabling the removal of a sitting President, Vice President and Cabinet if an independent judicial body proves widespread election fraud." She stared into his eyes with immense strength. "To that degree, Congressman, your crusade is already successful."

"That's fine," Victor said.

"Now. This man." She nodded to Slash. "Has demonstrated unique abilities in the field of – oh, what's the word I want?"

"Government clean-up," Slash moaned. "Janitorial specialist."

"We believe," she said, "we can explore CI's closed files." Glancing at Slash, she looked up, and her dark eyes seared into Victor's. She waited another beat. "But you're going to have to help us."

93

Nel and Edwin were behind Victor, and then BJ was there, shaking the lime green phone at him. Doc was leaning forward, hands under his thick black suspenders, gaping at the woman on the screen. Iona Webster looked up and said, "Wow!"

Then Edwin Foulks, in no way experienced with political

intrigue or the handling of state secrets, blundered.

"It's getting late," he said from behind Victor in that tender voice, wishing to calm Slash. "The Inauguration's in forty-eight hours." Victor shot a furious glance at him. Slash started. Desdemona tilted her head aside, eyes squinting. "Oh," she said.

"Yeah, oh," Slash echoed. "The Inauguration's in forty-eight hours. That's right, ain't it? So that's when you move? Blow up the White House? Perfect! Presidential papers everywhere! Hellman's body parts scattered like a catastrophe of flies! Look out!" He ducked an imaginary body part. "There goes an asshole!"

They encircled Victor like a team enclosing the quarterback. Mouths hung open. Bee and Webster slapped a high five. Nel wanted to strangle Edwin.

"Organs draped over crosses at Arlington Cemetery," soared the demented Slash. Desdemona covered his mouth with her hand.

"All right. Yes, we move at the Inauguration." Victor spoke to the screen as well as to his staff. "So everybody knows. Now we've brought in this, this poltergeist from cyberspace."

Iona Webster said, "I like him."

Through Desdemona's long fingers Slash yelled, "Bones floating down the Potomac, the skeleton of a prehistoric lizard." He erupted with laughter, prying her hand away. "Slick Hellman's mother!"

"All right! Hold," Victor said, containing his amusement. He moved a hand to flick off the microphone, but missed, and turned to his staff. "I don't hire mentally challenged adults as part of my insurrection team. Any further thoughts?"

BJ pushed his phone sternly at Victor. "Computer programmer," he said. "Contracted with CI on voting machinery."

Doc Nguyen was the quickest thinker, if the most difficult to understand. Removing the reading glasses, he tapped them on the monitor for attention. In that gritty throat-voice he said, "What we're hearing, friends, is that these people are experimenting with mind control. Do you all understand that?" Pointing his glasses at Slash on the screen, "This man was a victim of it! Look at him! This is the very nightmare we're trying to awaken from! Well, then, let's wake up. The game is over, Congressman! If we don't employ every available weapon, we may as well jump in the river."

Pretending he couldn't hear, Slash slid his middle finger along his cheek.

BJ's eyes were bulging. With excruciating patience, he said into his phone, "Here he is, sir." He thrust the phone at Victor.

"Yes, yes, I'm sorry," Victor said irritated into the phone. His eyes were locked with Doc Nguyen's. The others all watched him.

Silence on the phone. "It's Truman Butts," BJ mouthed.

"Mr. Butts? It's Victor Sligo. Please forgive me for making you wait. As you might imagine we're in a serious crisis. We are anxious to hear –"

A nearly inaudible voice said into Victor's straining ear, "Good." A moment's pause. "Can you guarantee," Butts said in a grotesque whisper, "they won't come after my family?"

Victor thought fast. To Courtman, the nearest body, he said, "Can we get video on this thing?" Doc answered for him. "Sure, sure, if he has it on his end." He carried his laptop across to the saw-horse table. Pointing a gnarled hand, "Plug that jack in here."

"Mr. Butts, we're going to try to get video on this conversation, if that works for you. I think it will help us understand each other. Do you have a video hookup?" A female voice came on the line, morose but anxious. Yes, the voice said, and almost immediately the video feed was patched through. Doc's screen went white, then to a clear image of an emaciated man sitting up in bed. He looked about eighty, obviously in dire physical condition, although he had thick brown hair and wore pajamas and a sweater. His eyes and flesh were drained of life. The bedside table was covered with medications and fluids. Breathing tubes were connected to his nostrils. Everybody closed in to listen to the thin voice. Lichtenstein came beside Victor to take notes.

Again Butts asked how Victor could guarantee nobody would be coming after his family.

"I won't lie to you, sir. Guarantees are tough when you're dealing with CI. In the worst scenario, a witness protection program is in place –"

"Wait. I'm on dangerous... ground here." Everybody in the room could feel his pain.

"We appreciate that, Truman."

There was a long silence. A phone buzzed upstairs, then

stopped. Nobody moved. Another person came into view on the screen. A woman of perhaps forty-five, wearing a light blouse and workout tights, and a bright yellow ribbon in her long flaxen hair. She bent over him, then turned and sat on a chair beside the bed, a solid-looking woman, sure of movement, fading tan skin, her serious face fixed on the screen.

"My wife," Butts said.

"Ms. Butts," Victor said quietly. "May I express my –"

"Please don't," the woman said. And nodding to Butts, "Go ahead."

Butts breathed shallowly, and steadied his gaze on the big monitor. Then turning aside to his wife, he raised his hand slightly, pointing to something, but stopped, and stared at his hand. Carefully Ms. Butts pressed the fingers back down.

"My company subcontracted with CI," he said with great difficulty. "Until two years ago. Software kept changing. All over Southern Ohio. CI or some sub... sidiary... contracted with the state to install new... machines." He blinked at his wife. She reached for a tumbler with a straw, and held it while Butts took a miniscule sip. "At the last minute... there was a glitch in the vote-counter segment in the... program. They sent the patch for us to... download to each machine. That was the legal requirement... Back then you had to do each machine individ...ually. When the polls closed... another group locked up the computers. Recorded the votes. Somebody else deleted the... patch we had added the night before."

"Did you keep any records of –"

"All of a sudden they didn't need us any... more. Overnight. Just a minute." The woman leaned close and they spoke.

"Let me explain. The idea was to bring in as many different... groups as they needed... to... Sorry. My throat's all –"

A minute passed. Another sip. "To make the trail hard to... follow. But we added that patch. Somebody else checked it out. We didn't. Just routine. A third company deleted it. When Kennedy..." He let out an exhausted breath, eyes closed.

Victor said, "Why didn't you report this to –"

"No way!" Butts said emphatically. Then slumped again. "I couldn't afford that. I would have been..." His eyes closed. "We had kids in college." He waited half a minute. "Go ahead, hon," he whispered hoarsely, and lapsed into a half-sleep.

His wife studied him for several seconds. When her voice came it was harsh, a fidgeting monotone. "A few elections back the investigations began, remember? Florida, Ohio, Texas, Michigan, some other states. Utah. Law suits challenging the results. Charges of touchscreen tampering. Kennedy was investigating for the ACLU or somebody. CI never gave us any guidance, never said anything. Then two years ago, all of a sudden, no contract. It was a big source of income for us. Two of the kids were in college at that time. But Truman wasn't sick yet. Then they outlawed the touchscreen things." She stared out from the screen showing no emotion.

"I understand how hard this is for you, Ms. Butts. You have both been courageous coming forward, and your statements will be instrumental in stopping this. With your permission I am going to send an assistant around to your home in the coming weeks to discuss this further. For now let me clarify a few points briefly, and I'll let you go."

Scribbling fast, BJ slid him a note. *"Does he have a few weeks?"*

"Do you have any idea what changed around that election?"

"They'd been talking about it at Truman's office for the previous year or more. He was diagnosed not long after, so time turned into a big jumble for us after that." She reached out and took her husband's hand, and began speaking in rambling, cryptic phrases. "Fewer and fewer people were voting... Hush-hush research had been going on for years into... well, we just heard the rumors. Chemical something. I have no idea what it was about. The only action anybody was taking about election fraud was these ACLU investigations. It felt like maybe the government was going to do something, and then –" She shrugged. "Then last summer that US Attorney Viola Ferrari died in that accident out West somewhere."

Several people in the house gasped at once. Nel had been listening beside her husband. Her cheeks went hot, and her mouth twisted downward. On the other laptop screen, Slash was saying something.

"Some accident," Ms. Butts added bitterly.

Victor felt a strange sensation in his chest. He said, "Can you tell me the names of others involved in your husband's work?"

"No! No, I – No. I can't." And added in a quiet voice, "It

seemed like, I mean the rumors made it feel like they were going for more experimental – like they were going in a different direction and didn't need us."

He glanced at Nel. Her face showed the pain and disgust Ms. Butts must have felt. Again he tried to pull an explanation from her.

"You mean CI. But what different direction? What did you hear about –"

Suddenly she exclaimed, "I want you to succeed with what you're doing, Mr. Sligo."

The screen went white.

Immediately the room erupted with shouting, including Slash babbling from the other laptop. Nel was pounding her fist down on Victor's shoulder. Everybody wanted more information from Truman Butts, corroboration, his lawyer, his doctor, his company. BJ questioned his political motivation, but then demanded Victor get a seat on the new Subcommittee on Voting Irregularities and subpoena CI's records. Courtman remembered touchscreens had been a huge political deal until the last general election four years ago. They had been examined and standardized all across the country by the Jimmy Carter Institute. But suspicions lingered. Some states eliminated them. Spearheading the campaign for change had been a pesky columnist named Molly Bee. Through this cacophony, Victor was ruminating on his hundreds of nights on the Hill and various Washington watering holes, seeking out any means, legal or criminal, to stop CI, to break their death grip on the voting machinery and their unchallenged influence in Congress. But somehow CI had become sacrosanct in Washington, almost imperial, an extension of the administration.

Slash shouted to get Victor's attention on the screen. "It was chemical something, all right. You there, Congressman?"

He could feel Nel breathing hotly beside him. "I'm here."

"Now you really need to help us! I know how to check into neurochemical programming for you. I told you that already." Slash repeated the words slowly. "That's what CI's doing, and the big boys are in on it, you betcha! And don't you tell me you never knew about Viola!"

94

Iona called across the room, "I don't know how that man thinks we can help him! He don't need a revolution. He needs a hairdresser!" But behind the words was the opposite sense – Slash was the exact injection of energy and criminal innocence the group had been lacking.

Victor struggled to stay focused. Stuffing his hands in his pockets, he stood at the big picture window, looking out past the hay truck at the winter-shabby garden, the moss-covered chicken house, and Edwin, coming out of that shop carrying a handful of tools. Always doing something.

It felt like a wrecking ball was careening through his head. Too much to hold on to. He turned back to the whiteboard for no reason but to take a break and stare at it.

There was classic election fraud all over Southern Ohio and other places, and CI's creepy tentacles all over. His new best friend Slash and whatever he wanted and his ability to unearth state se-crets, and his hints of neurochemical programming, which Victor now saw as digital age voodoo altering people's thinking. The lab director Jaap Tenkley and CI paying him to experiment with mind control, and Hunter Tyne sunk in that quagmire. Several suggestions of felonious activity related to voter apathy. Then Slash's girlfriend with her demand that they watch Julio Reese and his pencil. And the video from the Cabinet Room. There was Tyne, yelling at the Vice President that nobody was voting because of Tyne himself. "I'm your savior," he'd told Hellman.

Control the media, and you control the world.

And there was that damned horseshoe. Turned up twice now. Life or death to Hellman and Tyne, meaningless to everybody else. And Purger. Tightening the noose on Hunter Tyne's neck. The same thing he'd done to Viola Ferrari.

And Dugway. A dead end. All Fred Geschwantner could come up with was that they watched too much television!

Only a single word fell under Billy Hellman's column: *Caliban.* What the hell did that mean?

BJ had scribbled the latest note on a piece of paper and taped it to the edge of the crammed whiteboard: 'Slash' thinks he can access CI files!!

Molly was studying the whiteboard just in front of Victor, wearing a big loose hooded sweater and the same green slacks. She was slapping a phone against her hip. She was a fairly tall woman, but her posture told of long hours and frustration. Turning to Victor, her weary hazel-green eyes locked on his. The instant she turned he saw she was upset.

"I just spoke to my source. At Justice. I asked him if there were any outstanding warrants out for Dr. Hunter Tyne. And I told him there should be."

Everybody looked up. Even Edwin Foulks did a doubletake, sitting by the heater leaning over a wooden crate, working on a tiny carburetor. He said, "You did what?"

"Hold that a minute," Victor said with a pained look. "Mgaba," he said, pointing to the board. "What about this woman, Desdemona Crockett?" Bee rolled her eyes and pulled out of the way.

"I finally got through to Davis," he announced. "I think he's cracking up! Gave me a voice ID check! He says Ms. Crockett's a fugitive." The big man was wearing a maroon cashmere pullover, emphasizing both his ostentation and his huge chest. His eyes went back to his screen. "That's all he has."

"Okay. When he calms down, let him know he's going to have to coordinate the actual details of the sting. We're piling a lot on Davis. But we had no choice."

Iona now grabbed Victor's attention. Bee crossed her arms and stared.

"This neurochemical programming," she said, one eye on Molly. "So far, nada. I was just in Maryland with the former head of UCLA med school. He now runs NIMH in Rockville." She leaned back and put a hand over the microphone on her laptop and smiled. "His name's Dr. Sunny DiGiorno! Says to call Tokyo. He has no information for us. They never heard of it." She checked her notes. "He thought I was referring to neuro*linguistic* programming. But that's a kind of psychotherapy. I'm going to Aberdeen Proving Ground now. I doubt if anybody'll talk to me." She looked back to Molly, now deliberately facing away.

Victor nodded, then went back to Molly. Nobody was getting anywhere.

"Yes, ma'am."

She straightened her shoulders and said, "Whoever made this ridiculous plan to attack Hellman at the Inauguration needs some lessons in criminology." Her voice was icy. She crossed her arms and slapped the phone against her arm. "We'll never have enough –"

"Excuse me," Victor said, not unkindly, "but that would appear to be the situation we're in. Conditions here are very difficult, and time is moving. I assure you I appreciate –"

Looking him in the eye she yelled, "Will you not give me that holier-than-thou attitude just now! Look at this!" She bared her teeth as she whipped back to the whiteboard. Her eyes were furious. "Billy Hellman, running my government? How did we allow this to happen?" Whipping an arm out to point at Edwin across the room. "This man's going to march in there and get himself *shot!* And you! You know how fanatical they are in Washington! You're pushing him to do this! You're the damn representative here! *You're* the one who voted Hunter Tyne into office! *You* are calling all the shots! You are making him do this, and you'll get the credit if it works, and nobody will every connect it to you if it doesn't!"

She glared at him, lips pursed, looking oddly satisfied. Then Nel was there, up close, feeling the anguish behind her diatribe. She touched Molly's back.

"Molly, please. Everything's getting so *compressed* in here! Come on and sit down. Do you want some tea?" But Nel's voice was off, and Victor could hear it. The air was tight.

Molly did not respond. Her breath came in short bursts. She knew she was being pissy but couldn't stop herself. Cabin fever. Too many of them crammed together with the answer right in front of them, and this arrogant congressman controlling the whole charade. She ignored Nel and turned back to Victor.

He felt the blows, but held his ground. "Your source at Justice," he said. And made a fist in his pocket to not ask his name. "What did he say?"

She thought she heard sarcasm in the question. She forced her blood pressure down a notch. "A week ago he told me CI was doing illegal mind control experiments with the Army, and Viola Ferrari went to Utah to investigate. CI's been in court before for meddling with voting machinery. You know this. And he gave me

Jaap Tenkley's name." Her voice was just below a shout. "Are you getting this? We're looking at a major political cover-up here! What my source said just now was –" and she tore a note from her sweater pocket, not that she needed it, she knew the words, and she spat them at Victor, *"This crowd isn't going to be stopped any time soon!"* She heaved the note at him, and again pointed a steady finger at Edwin Foulks. "Certainly not by putting *that* tin soldier on the front line!"

"Madam!" Edwin said, standing. "I am no kind of soldier at all! Remember that when you write the book you're planning about this. Now I want to speak with you in private when you're done with him. Please."

Everybody was embarrassed and edgy, knowing Molly had said what they dared not think, and wanting to get the damn thing over with. All present were fugitives or accessories.

Nel had had enough. She grabbed her husband's hand and moved him firmly toward the French doors. The crisis was spilling into her guts, and she could already feel the next one looming.

"Be right back," Victor said.

That band of sunlight sliced through thick clouds just above the mountaintop. It must have been approaching noon. The day was moist and cold. She turned on the deck and faced Victor, shivering. Their breathing came in odd puffs after the warmth of the fire. Searching his eyes for a long second, she came close and placed her forehead against his chin. She was transmitting fear and frustration and deep weariness. For Victor these moments when she brought herself to him, vulnerable and raw, reminded him that he was a decent person, a parent, a husband and lover, and not exclusively a target for needy constituents.

"Lord," she said with great intimacy, and it was as if she were lying in his arms at home. "This is so fucking hard."

He moved slightly to look at her.

"Just say it."

She did not speak for a long time. He held her and waited. The air was filled with moisture under hanging clouds. Everything was heavy. She wanted to be angry with him for being here. But her strength was disappearing.

"All these people," she said finally.

He'd been ignoring it until Molly's outburst made it clear.

Claustrophobia. Hard personalities. Cold nights on the hard floor. He wanted to say, "Imagine the Founding Fathers, all gassing at each other, choked by their own flatulence." But he kept still.

"They're tearing me apart," she said bitterly. Her eyes were damp and her face was blotched, and she was barely holding herself together. "I feel like Clarence Thomas must have felt during his nomination hearings. They hate me. The boss's bitchy wife. God, you could have stayed teaching high school and our lives would have been so much easier."

"The election's over, dear," he said easily. "You're only allowed to say that every other November."

She tried to smile for him. "Have I said that before?"

He breathed along her moist cheek, longing suddenly for another time, a beach on the Oregon coast, the boys maybe four and six and the girls seven, dusk, a fire, an enormous tenderness filling him, this lovely, bickering family he did not deserve.

From the depths of him came words unrehearsed and tender, aware she was the stronger of them. Nel had moments like this. Victor had whole years like this.

"All of my best memories," he whispered to her, "are before politics. My life is other things, family things. The kids. You. Freezing our asses off swimming naked in Birch Bay that Christmas. Remember? This craziness is just –" He pulled back to look into her wet eyes. "Work. That's all." A pair of eagles emerged just then, soaring along the shoulder of the mountain in front of them, motionless, exquisite. "The country will survive," he said. "It always has."

She watched with him, then raised a hand high to acknowledge the silent eagles. They followed the curve of the mountain, one behind the other, and glided toward the river that would spawn their dinner. The cocky rooster cackled out his conquest on the other side of the house. They were surrounded by birds.

She said, "Victor Sligo, you are so full of shit."

"Hm?" And knew he had her with him.

"Molly'll be okay. I saw a little bit of that side of her in Utah. She reminds me of me. She's right, you know. It's bigger than we ever imagined. They're going to destroy everything if we don't stop them. And the only thing left to stop them is you. You and that Pied Piper in there. The tin soldier."

Her husband looked out for the eagles, feeling the responsibility, and at the same moment wishing they could just go home and
be left alone. "We'll see about Edwin. But you know I can't do it
without help. I mean you. I can't blow my nose or make a sandwich
without you. And if you ever tell anybody, I'll deny all knowledge
of your existence."

"You'll starve to death with your nose running."

BJ burst through the doors. Always with the perfect timing.

"Victor, the guy wants you. He's not going to wait." Pointing in towards the screen. "Slash. He says if you won't help him
he'll find somebody who will."

Reluctantly they felt the moment dissipate. "Come on, Congressman," she gave him the old family mantra. "Time to go in and
fix everything."

95

Molly Bee was standing at the laptop screen with a handful
of notes. She was obviously not finished. Her jaws were tight. It was
a bizarre tableau – the San Francisco columnist lost in a rain forest,
talking to an insane man through a little TV screen. He was truly the
strangest looking man she'd ever seen close up. As Victor and Nel
entered through the double doors, a pierce of sunlight slanted
through the south window. The light cast a brilliant outline behind
Molly. With the steel-rimmed glasses and short hair and rigid, intelligent face, she looked like an angry librarian. They stood still,
watching her.

"I want to call a meeting," she said, not looking directly at
either of them. Nodding to Slash, "His problem's going to have to
wait."

Victor laced his hands together at his chest and studied her
for one full second.

"Okay."

Without warning she scattered her notes in the air and
heaved the pen she was clutching at the wall. Her voice came like a
punch to the face. "Congressman! I'm going to be taken seriously or
I'm out of here."

Victor moved back half a pace. "Okay."

He gestured to the available bodies to stop working and approach. They closed in. Raven, working in the kitchen, did not hesitate. She came straight to Molly, gripped her arm for a moment, and sat. Offering Molly a deferential sign, Victor waited.

She flung a hand toward the whiteboard. "They are blocking voting. There is no other way to look at this. You said so yourself, Nel, that Viola Ferrari saw it! We have direct corroboration from Truman Butts of voting machine tampering by CI! There's a strong suggestion that this neurochemical programming started up just when they shut down his operation in Ohio. CI has a virtual rap sheet involving voting matters. They're criminals with serious motives and obvious opportunities."

"Lemme see that thing!" It was Slash, squealing from the screen. Molly yelled over his voice. "You tell me, Congressman. No obfuscations. No hiding behind your office. It won't be worth a pile of dust in the wind anyway if these people take over the country Monday morning. Are they blocking people from voting? Or aren't they? Or do you even know?"

All eyes in the room darted from Victor to the whiteboard and back. People read up and down and squinted and they all knew she was right. Nobody breathed.

"You got it, girl!" Slash sang out. This brought murmuring through the group and a welcome switch of focus. Victor's brain flooded with cross-currents – swept from a sweet moment with Nel to enraged Molly to Slash, to the whiteboard rife with accusations, the staff cracking under pressure, both Nel and Molly Bee badly needing to take a break somewhere out of here. The clock racing. His eyes whipped around. It did not look good at all. At the end of all the paths was Edwin Foulks. Edwin's sting just now felt like fighting the Russian army with a slingshot. He sat down and closed his eyes.

"All right," he said. Then looking up to Molly, "I can't answer your question. But the answer is somewhere." He gave her a half-hearted grin, not wishing to irritate her further. "Slash! You there?" He readjusted the laptop so the screen faced the big room.

"Yeah, yeah, heavy day at the office, Congress dude! Wow! Who is that broad?"

"Slash. I'm ready to deal. You can get into CI files? You

never heard this conversation, of course."

"No, no, yeah, sure, I don't know for absolutely sure, but yeah. Are we dealing?"

Slash now had a view of everybody. "That's Dr. Nguyen from VoteAmerica. I heard you on Real Radio lots of times. How you doin'?"

"Just lovely," Doc snarled.

"First you tell me something, Mr. Sligo."

"What?" Victor's hands were at his cheeks, his eyes closed.

"On that board there. All this Billy Hellman and Hunter Tyne business. I mean, it's none of my business, but now you're makin' it my business. Now who killed who? I can see you ain't real interested in filling me in, but what's going on? Huh?"

"Son, we are negotiating with you in good faith," Victor said. "Let's get on with it."

"Yeah, but, what is all this? You got to help me figure out what I'm looking for."

Nel came forward without speaking and replayed the blond woman's video on Edwin's big monitor where Slash could watch. Violent screaming by Slash's two favorite thugs. Hellman ripping open Tyne's shirt and revealing the horseshoe-shaped tattoo. Beside Slash, Desdemona was writing notes.

BJ, already entranced by the madman and the beautiful black woman, asked Slash if he recognized the tattoo.

"Man!" Slash said. "I love it! Show 'em this at Times Square!" His eyes rolled back. "Yeah, I seen that once, on a farm upstate." His laughter pierced the air. "On a horse."

He was nuts all right. Nel shrugged at Victor – Slash had forgotten his own question. Victor closed down the audio feed to Slash, and took another hasty vote. Molly refused to speak. Iona Webster said he was no more nuts than some of the slave owners who signed the Declaration of Independence. Mgaba wanted no part of him. Courtman threw his hands in the air, and with a savage face grunted, "Fine!" All the others cautiously approved except Edwin. Edwin, wielding a long thin screw driver, said, "I can't say yes or no if the fate of the nation is in the balance." And he bent down to his carburetor.

Back to the audio. Victor told Slash to speak. Slash whispered to Desdemona, and took a jolt of Dr. Pepper.

"Dr. Nguyen? You're gonna have to help these people get the concept I'm on here, because nobody's gonna understand it except you." He ran both palms along the sides of his white hair as though just realizing they were all studying him. Doc said nothing.

"There's this Chinese guy. I believe he's the smartest man on Earth. His name's Tao Ting. You heard of him?"

"No. Is this a joke?"

"Us hacks call him a programmer-savant. He can break into anything, get past all known systems to retrieve stuff. And disappear like the Cheshire cat. Tao Ting. At least I believe he's Chinese. What's going to happen is, he'll go into Communication International data central to locate files that are designed to stay in there. See? Basically you need to have whatever Tao Ting has to access your own company. But it wouldn't be hidden like that if it was regular legal stuff, right? People need access. Tax guys, lawyers, I don't know."

"Why doesn't everybody call him?" Victor said.

"Oh. Well, he costs forty thousand dollars."

"I see. And for that money, you get what exactly?"

"You get one visit. He slips into existing systems and his program learns the new language form for that encryption. That's what they do these days. New programming languages. Zeroes and ones just get you in the door, man. Nobody gets past there. Like that horseshoe tattoo on your board there. See it? No processor ever built interprets data on a numeric system based on a horseshoe. Right? It's binary, or it's tertiary, or it could be a nine-based system. But no tattoos. See? What Tao Ting does is, he incorporates geometry into the algorithm. Not only that. He encodes and decodes music! That Grateful Dead song, "Uncle John's Band", maybe that could be the basis for a mathematical language for, say, a plutonium bomb! Or the diagrams to the vaults at Fort Knox! And he can take a random sound, like a car engine or a drill motor, and break down the sound pattern, assign numeric value to the decibel variance, and create a language that way!" He let out a hard breath, and found himself looking at blank faces. "Well, it's impossible to explain, and I ain't no expert. Mostly we use zeroes and ones where I come from. But I think he does it in two or three-dimensions. Like, you could make a computer language from the predictable points of a sphere, say, or a human genome. It's real gnarly! Artwork. Three Dimensional icons.

I've been told Mr. Tao figured out how to create an algorithm for a three-dimensional system, and then he uses it to beat the defense structure he's hacking into. You with me here? Doc? You getting this?"

Doc and Purvis Courtman, the musician, were whispering the Lord's name. But Doc was smiling.

"What's the catch?" Victor asked him.

"Besides it's illegal, well there is one thing. You only get one thing. If you want the guy the second time, it's fifty grand more."

Everybody spoke at once. Doc had one thumb stuck at his throat, and was studying the floor and sputtering. Mgaba walked outside and expectorated off the porch. Molly was absolutely still, arms across her chest. By the fire, Edwin was fascinated. He pulled all the cash from his pocket. Seven dollars and eighty-one cents.

Doc said to the screen, "From your point of view, what will we get with this?"

Slash stared at him curiously. He appeared to fall asleep with his eyes open. Suddenly he gasped for air, like a drowning man. He took a couple of breaths, and said quietly, "You'll get Billy Hellman."

You could feel every person present going inward. You could feel the fear and the loathing.

Courtman was nodding and shrugging at once. He plugged the mike with his hand and said, "If we go ahead, we've made the decision to launch Edwin Foulks, alone, against the full might of the United States of America." Looking at Victor, his head tilted, then at the others. "Is that what we're doing?"

Doc Nguyen shuffled toward the screen, in his white shirt and suspenders and the Yoda look in his eyes. He was not looking at Slash, but at Sligo.

He said, "I'll put up the money."

"Cool," Slash said. He glanced at Desdemona, his feral eyebrows raised, mouth puckered. Everybody saw the gesture. He did in fact look like a con man who had just scored. Squinting at the screen, Doc pondered.

"What's your take in this? You work for Tao Ting?"

"No way. I'm a sanitation engineer, man! I got a chance here to sanitize Mr. Billy Hellman, I believe. I hope to Jesus.

Maybe. And maybe that other dung beetle. Hunter. The Hunter is about to become the hunted. I believe I can get into the US Attorney's Office, but only Mr. Tao gets into CI."

The old man's wizened body, slumped for a day and a half, was now pulling straight. His chest was enlarging to the size of a teenage boy's. A brown thumb caressed the throat chip as he switched his gaze to Victor, thoroughly wallowing in the moment. He grinned. A gold tooth winked at his old friend. He'd made up his mind.

Victor said, "Keep in mind what we're doing here, Doctor. Don't look so damn smug. We're trying to remove a sitting President and Vice President. It's never happened in history."

Doc's black eyebrows furrowed.

"The day after tomorrow!" Victor snapped.

"I gotta tell you, troops," they heard Slash say, and everybody looked back to the screen. "This Tao Ting, he's careful. You don't just look him up in the Yellow Pages. I heard from my buddy Evileye, getting this guy's as hard as training a camel to piss through the eye of a needle in a haystack. But he's worth it."

96

Things escalated immediately. With a spasm of kiddie obscenities and a search through the thumb drive he'd brought to Eddie Rickett's, Slash found the procedure for contacting Tao Ting. He was gasping and frothing himself into a patriotic delirium when several thoughts hit him in a staggered series of tremors.

Shit! What if Tao Ting's already connected to CI! Why wouldn't he be? Slash stopped dead. But he'd punched the numbers, and he watched his screen flip to a Chinese version of Twitter. He wasn't sure Rickett's Home Translator would protect his privacy, but now he was already talking to somebody. As he typed, the words gyrated into one of those Asian alphabets, and he was already clicking down about a money transfer, and he could not get his breath, and he collapsed against the wall, his mind fluttering at warp speed, floaters before his eyes, and then *yes!* That wonderful feeling that comes without words, the one that comes when you've broken through with a fellow cybersleuth, and you *know* it's gonna be all right. He was reaching for a Dr. Pepper when he spotted his employee ID badge on Eddie's rickety table.

Oh, shit! Work! With all this madness he'd forgotten to go to work! Then he saw it all. The adventure on the sixteenth floor. The phony papers for Desdemona. His brain had been flash frozen. He had given absolutely zero thought to what he was supposed to do when all this came to light. The guards in the upstairs cells, he didn't even know them. But they could pick him out of a crowd the size of Shea Stadium! What he had fixed in his neurotic cranium was this: Get DB out of jail. Find the renegade Congressman. Already half the country is out for Billy Hellman's blood. Sligo and Davy Crockett will organize the other half, and them two and me and DB will lead the most radical movement in history, and we'll get rid of all the vermin in Washington and the world will be cool.

At that instant he felt his cellphone voicemail zinging in his pocket. Mohindar Virpaljeettinder, night manager of the Federal Building, had received word from Frederica Kos, Slash's supervisor. "I'm concerned, Mr. Zewinta," her message said. "I'm so concerned I'm going to fire your sorry ass if you're not here in fifteen minutes or come up with at least two broken legs."

Shit!

Desdemona came out from the back room preparing to go out. Taller than Slash, her face like an African princess. She wore Rickett's winter coat and wool hat pulled down low, and had actually painted on a mustache.

"Going to get supplies," she said. "Don't worry. I've got no place to stay but here."

"Oh, man! What if they catch you!"

"They won't."

Saving his job was now an immediate priority but he had no idea what to do. He had two good legs and liked it that way.

And then, *flash!* He picked up Eddie Rickett's dust-covered landline and called the basement of the Federal Building. He never knew who answered. He took a hard breath and yelled, "It's me, Slash! Don't pay the ransom! I escaped!" And he banged down the receiver.

Next it was back to wherever they were, the Congressman and his ratpack and that fiery blond with the short hair and glasses and, he had to admit he was guessing, Davy Crockett. Nobody was talking about Crockett. And Sligo kept not answering his questions.

Nobody was on the screen to tell he had contacted Tao Ting. He saw only the whiteboard in front of a wall made of stacked logs and a large window. It was just going dusk. Through the window he could make out the back end of a dilapidated farm truck. Hanging from the battered bumper was the u-shaped thing they hang on the backs of tractors to hook stuff to. Everywhere in the distance, mist and trees.

"I'll be damned," Slash said to himself. "They're in Ireland!"

97

About the time he began jabbering the news to Evileye, a squad of Navy Seals was slipping into the dusty village of Los Gatos, Puerto Rico, armed to the teeth, preparing an assault on El Convento de Santa Teresa de Jesús. It was one of many nunneries on the lovely island, none of which sheltered or had ever heard of Congressman Victor Sligo until a couple of days ago on the Internet. About the time Evileye was grumbling that he had better stuff to do than piss off the feds by using Tao Ting as a ram to bust into CI archives, Lieutenant Commander Kevin Hickey was being admonished in sputtering Spanglais by a furious Madre Superiora for presuming to bring weapons into her convent. Hickey was told to get lost or all of his children and those of his *guerreros* would be born left-handed.

In D.C. things were on course for either terrifying success or utter calamity. Choking with the self-inflicted ambition virus, John Lee Davis, now deeply suspect and soaked to the armpits in paranoia, sat in the freezing dark in his Shanghai on a police access road under Memorial Bridge, watching the black Potomac roll past, abstractly pondering suicide. He'd managed to consume two-thirds of a quart of vodka but couldn't get drunk. Tumbling through his proud and disciplined mind was a brutal awakening: the street-tested assumptions he had operated under for fifty years were disintegrating into fantasy.

Mgaba had called half a dozen times. It kept getting uglier.

Thoughts of suicide came as easily to Davis as walking on water. But now events were unfolding so fast he was unable to keep the parts separate. This man who had done unsavory favors for three presidents, who had devised violent stings against organized crime, who had lived as a hypocrite for the past dozen years, despising every action of his own government – for this pony-tailed professional bureaucrat everything now felt unfamiliar, as if he were standing on a cliff's edge and a great animal was eating away the earth beneath him. The thing he knew with absolute certainty was that if the rebellion failed he would be convicted of treason, and probably executed. Sure, this crowd out in Washington state were courageous Americans as far as he could see – although nobody's motives are ever fully revealed. The people Hal Riske had brought in were professionals and patriots. And more were nervously falling in line, all loyal to the Republic, all presumed to be committed to the common good.

But loyalty ceases at the gallows. Everybody knows that.

An armed Navy patrol boat cruised into view, spotlights playing along the foul currents of the Potomac.

This week Davis had consumed half a case of Tums, at least another full bottle of Stolichnaya, and not much else. At his discreet prodding, an agent from the New York office had unfolded the strange tale of the transfer of Desdemona B. Crockett from the temporary federal detention facility on Church Street either to Fort Hamilton or Fort Dix. Three military intelligence commanders had told FBI field investigators a different outfit had her in custody, and they had the documents to prove it. The FBI was overwhelmed with the chaos across the land and had managed to file no charges on Ms. Crockett. It was absurdly clear she was not Davy Crockett, she was certainly not the bearded Caucasian with the phony contact lenses sitting in the cockpit of the Cessna 400, and nobody knew where to begin looking for her.

The FBI's wanted list Web site had now recorded 4,109 sightings of the pilot Davy Crockett, from Zihuatanejo, Mexico to a restroom in the Executive Office Building in Washington, standing in line behind Vice President Hellman making an obscene gesture.

Davis was keeping O'Donnell and Admiral Singh informed,

as well as his daughter. Euphonia was exuberant but suspicious, and told him plainly she was not risking her career under any circumstances over somebody wearing a coonskin hat.

Davis's real question was, why me?

Other men he knew had the ambition, and the administrative bushwhacking skills to get where he was. And they had good haircuts. But he knew nobody else at this level in national intelligence would dare take on Hellman and the goons and sycophants he'd elevated into strategic positions throughout the Executive Branch.

Maybe in the long view of history, the experiment with capitalist democracy had nothing to do with the common good. Maybe the backwash of the sinking economic tide capsized the smaller boats. The nature of capitalism is that it is conducted by people with capital, on a theoretical formulation that contains no variable for human greed. Maybe the common good was all pipe dreams and clowns on stilts, a concept patched together by the needy, written in holy books by the hungry and the servile, enshrined in Western thought by hoodwinked philosophers as they arranged trust funds for their survivors – or prepared to drink their hemlock or climb the hill to Calvary.

It causes great anguish, a decent man in high politics.

Politics had always been the ugliest part of justice. Now there was enormous pressure to carry the Newfie agenda into the courtroom. Reversing decades of hard work by respectful institutions, to favor megacorporations over the rights of the individual. Slippery laws greased through committee during Congressional breaks, clearly intended to undermine social progress. The country was going to hell, and the temporary Director of the FBI was supposed to stand guard at the nation's gates and watch it happen.

But as the poet said, way moved on to way, and all of a sudden he was sitting in the January fog across the river from the Iwo Jima statue, organizing a rebellion. He held up the Stoli and strangled the neck of the bottle. Muffled hammering sounds drifted through the frigid night, the slam-bang construction of the Inaugural grandstands.

How had it come to this?

In the end, Davis was so overcome with self-loathing he had eliminated all but the two unthinkable choices: death by his own hand, or treason against the Constitution he had upheld his entire life.

Presently he had no weapon. No pills, no rope, no ability to walk in front of a speeding truck.

He drank as the fog swirled, and he felt old Abe Lincoln breathing down his neck not far behind him, and he envisioned the Marines at Iwo Jima on the far bank. There was no place to hide in Washington. They were everywhere. The heroes, the extraordinary men, the fallen warriors, the mud-booted grunts and the mounted generals, the cops, the teachers, the letter carriers, the men and women in the street who bore the daily grind of this democracy.

Damn these suicidal cogitations! He started the engine, but sat idling in the night, stretching his long, thick body. At eleven he was supposed to meet Daniel Cool up on Wisconsin Avenue. He was told by Sligo to push Cool to the limit, demanding he create a diversion at a precise instant in the inaugural ritual. Sligo had wisely not elaborated on the reason for the diversion. Just get the job done, was all he asked.

The reality was, Cool was not going to work. Davis would have to go farther up the food chain for a diversion.

He had assumed many more upper-level people would be in this. A coup required everybody, and as far as Davis knew, they had almost nobody.

His friend Sukwant Singh was in the same predicament. A double agent, holding off until the last possible instant, and then either bringing down the administration, or setting himself up for the gallows. In a tense moment in the Pentagon parking lot last night, the Admiral had slipped a printed note to the Deputy Director:

"Code 100 only on my command. Stand fast." It meant there would be no military action or intervention at the Inauguration without specific orders from Singh himself. In his car, Davis had burned the note.

Incredible as it seemed, Mgaba had told him Chief Justice Shapiro-Fujimoto, delivering the oath to Burligame and Hellman, was in the loop. Davis needed face time with her. Blowing out a stream of vodka-laced breath, he remembered the last bit of it: Somebody had found a highly placed techno-spook – not CIA, Davis knew, not with O'Donnell's paranoid geeks at NSA, not military – who was supposed to be in a position to override the entire North American communications network for a couple of minutes.

What would transpire at that point, Davis had only the vaguest notion. The FBI was to steer clear of free-lance video teams.

Sukwant had meticulously briefed him on what he called the underground "spasm of lunacy" at Independence Hall. To the Admiral it had seemed just another clandestine bitch session, vigilantes contemplating legal ways to eliminate three or four hundred high-level bureaucrats, plus most of the US Congress, then hold a verifiable election and see what transpired. But all the ideas presented at Independence Hall were unworkable or idiotic. Crockett had even announced exactly what he intended to do, and not a person in the room so much as blinked an eye. Not even Congressman Sligo. Sligo had just laughed.

And then the Cessna had taken off and history was suddenly ripped off course. A fireball was about to explode over Washington.

Davis was ready. He dropped the big Shanghai into gear, flicked on the blowers to clear the freezing mist, and headed north toward the Cathedral.

98

Jane Doe, now, was a sixty-three-year-old programmer at the National Institute of Justice. She'd spent some years as a mold person, making pre-fab flower pots for Kwalmart, then had gone back to school to better herself, and eventually landed in an obscure subdivision of the Justice Department known as Digital Evidence Findings Control. As it happened her only child was a scofflaw, a grown-up computer geek devoted to saving the world by pranks and treachery against all authority.

Maybe she had influenced his life's vocation by naming him Justice Will Prevail. Justy, for short.

"Evileye" suited him better. Although the funny thing was, he wanted to remain anonymous in his longing to sabotage Slick Hellman's administration. He certainly didn't relish jail time for pickling the electronic data of the stupidest people on Earth.

Slash had laid another heavy number on him. It was about those files closed by executive privilege in the Chicago US Attorney's Office. All government corruption, Slash said, is like a map

that leads back to Billy Hellman's doorstep. Or in this case to the
doorman, Dr. Hunter Tyne. Slash's fugitive friends wanted to know
what caused Jerome Tse, Assistant US Attorney, to send Viola Ferrari out to Utah. Tse had said he'd been forced by some Senate
committee to send a mind-control expert to check out Dugway
Proving Ground. The expert was Viola Ferrari. That order to Tse
must be in his files. Remember that stuff, Slash had said, that we
slipped into Hunter Tyne's bio in *Government Incendiaries*? Part of
it was that trial, a scientist named Jaap Tenkley. Hunter Tyne was
mixed up in it. And Ferrari and Tse were the prosecutors. Tenkley
was working on neurochemical programming. Evileye had already
seen the trial summary, but that was all he could access. The full
transcript also had been locked up by executive privilege. With all
this information locked up, nobody could track anybody's footsteps.

     He was to get everything he could find, and haul it out.
Then they'd go to Tao Ting, and tell him they were ready for his ex-
cursion into CI.

     Evileye by now knew the US Attorney's data secretorium.
He'd even left a few bread crumbs to find his way back in. But it
still required Jane Doe to cough up the user codes for midnight to
one a.m. So he'd gone back to his mom. It was way more serious
now. He was certain they were close to the evidence that Billy
Hellman and his friends tormented little boys and threw cats off the
freeway overpass.

     "Ma!" he'd emailed her after dinner. "Can you show up
with a bucket and shovel tonight? It will be well worth your while.
Oysters and mussels and clams, oh my!" They were old Chesapeake
Bay clam-shuckers, these two. He pinched his trim belly under the
button-down Oxford dress shirt, admired the two 1935 Baltimore
Transit tokens in his penny-loafers, and waited.

     True, Jane Doe was loathe to participate again – break a
dozen federal laws, spend her last years sewing Army socks in a
minimum security lockup. By late Friday, though, Baltimore had
succumbed to a nervous stalemate between the citywide retail strike
and the shutdown of the entire social services network. No welfare
checks were going out, and nobody was buying anything. Nobody
was working, everybody was angry, and all afternoon the streets
filled with bundled up, poster-wielding pedestrians demanding a recall election.

With blotches of patriotic rash, Jane passed on the 2400-to-0100 user code to her charming thirty-four-year-old boy. At 12:03 they were in. At 12:08 they were back in the archives of the US Attorney's Office, District of Northern Illinois. This time Evileye had the passcode to slip around the "executive privilege" barrier.

And there it wasn't. The US Attorney and the 160 people assisting him, as well as the retired, fired or missing, all had files containing thousands of documents with their names on them. All but two: Viola Ferrari, and Jerome Tse. Their files had been mashed down to random binary code, way beyond retrieval, worse than the dreaded thirty-five pass deletion. It took more time, but they searched deep for the name Jaap Tenkley in the Criminal Division records. There was the trial summary Evileye had seen before, but when he opened the file, nothing. There were no locked files. There were no files at all! No wonder they had claimed executive privilege. The trick worked. Nobody bothered to find out if the files were actually there or not. They weren't.

Slash would have to report the bad news to Congressman Sligo. And he'd have to do it without the answer to the obvious question: Who did it?

99

An hour and a half after she left, Desdemona Crockett waltzed back into Eddie Rickett's dismal apartment, exquisitely made up, wearing a fabulous full-length white leather coat, and a dark suit complete with pearls, and three or four fingers ringed with jewels. Half a dozen plain silver bracelets made that unmistakable *ka-ching!* sound from one slim wrist.

"Wow! Look at you!" Slash gushed.

"I know. I clean up good. And we're going down to D.C.," she said. "Crack of dawn Sunday. We don't want to miss this."

"Going to Washington? Whaddaya mean? There ain't no buses running. No trains. And we ain't got no money."

She smiled her fabulous smile. "Oh, yes we do. Enough for the weekend. And, look at this, boy." She arched an eyebrow at him. " I borrowed a car." She dangled a set of keys in his face.

"Huh?"

But she couldn't sustain the highbrow act, certainly not for the freakish man at the computer, and when she saw that Slash was distracted beyond ordinary human contact she said, "Ah, to hell with it," and leaned against the fridge since she didn't dare sit on the Salvation Army-reject couch, to read the last thin paper available in Queens. The *US Times-NY* was sixteen pages, with no advertising. The entire city was in chaos. People mulled about watching reader boards for news of the Inauguration. Wall Street was frozen. Troops prepared to take to the streets Monday morning. Listening to Slash mutter and wheeze, Desdemona wished she'd never heard of any of these strange people. They were up to their tattoos in sleaze. All of them. The good guys were bad guys, and the bad guys were public officials.

100

It was late in Van Zandt. Everybody was exhausted and nerve-rattled and frantic, they still lacked the hard evidence Victor craved, and they were traveling in the morning. For a lost moment Victor had gotten his hopes up with mad Slash in New York. But he hadn't heard anything, and he realized even if they had this Tao guy busting into Communication International, no institution as big as CI would be so stupid they would store evidence of illegal activity. He was picking up Edwin's negative energy. Somebody was tying the noose for all of them.

From the edge, Edwin Foulks watched Molly Bee. That hand at the forehead. Squinting at the screen. He had told her he wanted to speak with her, but she had fallen into herself after her meltdown earlier, and he debated whether it was worth it to reveal what he knew.

Of all things, Edwin trusted his instinct.

As she passed his spot by the heater moving toward the kitchen, he stood and offered her a soft smile

"Intimidating, isn't he." Nodding toward Victor.

"They all are." Her voice strangely remote, as if she'd been sedated. She didn't need any company just now. But she stood before him, with no place to hide.

"I've been hoping to talk to you about something," Edwin said, bringing another chair close to his rocker. "Do you mind?"

She could still feel herself slightly out-of-body. She said, "I already took my beating for today, thank you. Have to get my stuff together for tomorrow. It's scattered all over the place." For some reason she was not hearing herself properly. "We'd better be staying in a five-star hotel. I just feel so –. Well, they'd all be booked for the Inauguration, wouldn't they? Did you get the word from Nel? We're leaving at the crack of dawn."

"Yes." He gestured toward the chairs, and they sat. She felt desperate for privacy. She needed to be in her big leather chair at home with Dolly Mama in her lap and her head empty.

And it felt oddly comforting sitting beside this man by the fire.

"Molly." He held her eyes carefully, brow furrowed, his face full of care. He took a long slow breath and exhaled, tilting his head slightly toward her. Molly felt compelled to remove her glasses, and allow him to appreciate her pretty eyes, at this moment almost green. Turmoil bubbled in her chest, ever so briefly, then subsided. She did not speak.

"This is going to be extremely hard for you. What if the whole thing falls apart, right in front of the entire country?"

"What whole thing?" But she understood instantly. She knew that he knew, and she wanted to be angry, but shook her head, and flicked her eyes back at Sligo and Webster under the stairs bent over her laptop. It was Sligo she was angry with. Not this man. She studied him, not entirely voluntarily. Her breath caught in her throat.

"Your father," Edwin said. His eyes were filled with kindness. Her first instinct was to shove him away, then to deny, then to disappear. For twenty years she had guarded the secret, but she saw that he was not the enemy, not the police or the paparazzi. It was not conceivable that he meant harm to her. But he was showing something else. This entire bizarre plan these people had hatched, it was no charade. He was demonstrating it right now. All the breath had gone out of her when he'd said the words, and now, instantly, she was breathing with him, somehow *breathing him in,* and feeling safe. Tears welled in her eyes, but she shut down the emotion. Not here. Not now.

"So you know."

"Well," Edwin said, "no. Actually, I need you to tell me. I'm afraid you might not be able to bear up. Or even worse. I can't help wondering if you're —"

"Let's go outside." Without waiting for him, she picked up her coat at the door, and walked out into a clear night. Then they were standing beside the silent hen house, their breaths condensing in odd puffs. No sounds came anywhere, only the ruffling churn of the river a few hundred yards off. Molly stood tall in the darkness, a strong woman, her short hair moving as she spoke, hands in her jacket pockets, looking first at the deep sky, then at the substantial old log house. Aromas of night and earth, and woodsmoke on Edwin's wool coat filled her nostrils. She could feel his eyes steadily watching her. When she finally spoke, it was without looking at him, as though connecting her eyes with his would burn.

"I was born Mary Burligame. My brother couldn't say Mary when he was two and I was seven, so I became Molly." A pause. "I was only eight when Dad became mayor of Bemidji, twelve when he was elected to the state legislature. Then US senator. I'm sure you know the whole biography. By the time I was twenty I was a raging liberal eco-warrior. I had to get away." She found his eyes in the darkness, close to hers, and it felt warm but not burning. "Either get away or expose him for a fraud. He was not... In the Senate I watched him go through the motions of leadership, saluting that flag Billy Hellman was holding up for him backstage. How I despise that man! I believe he destroyed Dad's spirit. Dad's a decent man with ambitions way beyond his intellectual level. Beyond his ability to crush, to repress, you understand? To be political. And Mr. Vicious came along and dangled the power cord in front of Sol Burligame and he grabbed it. That's what we called Hellman, way back. Mr. Vicious." She shrugged. "Obviously I had to erase my connection to Dad for my own career. And for his."

Even watching her own breath in the chill, she felt warm. "How did you know?"

Smiling at her, he rubbed his hand across his forehead the way Molly touched hers, an exact imitation of Sol Burligame doing the same thing many times in public. A muscular twitch. He shrugged pleasantly, as if this connection was obvious to anyone. Then added, "There is also your source. He knows too much. And the way you flinch when you see him on the news. The President's best friend, Jim Turcutt. The Attorney General." Edwin did not wish to look at Molly at this moment, but she moved herself intentionally into his vision, her eyes dark, questioning. "Nobody will ever know," he said softly.

She went still. Without asking, Edwin had the answer, but all the same he had to hear her say it. Too much was at stake now in this crazy game he initially had no intention of ever playing out.

"What if they impeach him?"

In an eyeblink the President's daughter said, "He is a dear man and I wish him well. But he made his bed. He'll have to sleep in it."

101

Frustration was on all their faces. Edwin had found a big square wall clock, and hung it over the archway into the living room. Mgaba had lost his superior attitude and his toothbrush, and was muttering something in French on his phone. Courtman was comatose under the stairs, and Doc had stumbled on a globe and was spinning it mindlessly. Everybody was worn down. Raven Menez, the rookie, the youngest, and the person with nothing to lose, had eaten a meal with Iona's encouragement, and she and Iona had taken a walk in the dark out to the road. When they returned she asked BJ to replay Jaap Tenkley's deposition, and pull up the notes he'd transcribed from his conversation with Mr. Tse. Iona looked a bit wary, but let her go.

The two women sat in front of the whiteboard.

"I think," Raven said, looking ragged in her sweats and blue Penn sweatshirt. She grimaced, struggling with the risk of exposing herself in the very den of the rebellion. She sent an unsure glance to Webster, and then she knew she was going to let it loose.

"Come on, girl, out with it," Iona said.

Taking up the marker and eraser, Raven said, "So we could break it up into four areas, maybe." Doing some judicious wiping and moving, she made a space in the corner of the board. Her voice grew confident as she spoke.

"One, Mr. Tse was instructed by the Judiciary Committee to investigate mind-control research at Dugway. They specifically needed a mind-control expert in Utah, from Chicago, not Salt Lake City. So. All kinds of problems have been coming up with voting machinery in Utah. And that's where Tyne lives, and where the Purger person appears to have murdered Viola. And Tenkley was sending his research there. Neurochemical programming. Right? That phrase is all over house, and nobody's ever heard of it. So."

She had Nel's interest. She eased over from the sawhorse table, followed by Doc Nguyen. Victor was listening.

She held up two slender fingers. "Two. It turns out Viola knew about Tyne from Tenkley's deposition. Somebody wanted her specifically sent out there so they could kill her. So. *Then!* Our friend Slash says Tyne was up to his neck in brainwashing research for *years* before all this came up. And of course he worked for CI. Tenkley says Tyne signed his contract in, where was it?"

"Cicero," BJ said, now joining them. "Cicero, Illinois."

She wrote shorthand names in the corner space. "Yes. By then Tyne was about to be nominated by Vice President Hellman to be Secretary of Communications. *Government Incendiaries* says Tyne and Hellman worked together out West. Even if they did hate each other."

"Oh, they did," came Doc's crackly voice, and she pointed at him.

They were all with her now. Raven's voice had risen a bit oddly. Nobody had seen this side of her. She shook a fist at names on the board as she spoke, squeezing her hatred out of the problem in order to articulate it.

"Three." Spinning around with a thumb and two fingers up. "The Cabinet meeting. Tyne and Hellman punching each other. Wow!" Holding both hands up to that section of the board. "See? Icons on his neck. A long line of great men, he says! Nobody votes because of him, he says." Whirling around to the group, their eyes wide, hanging on her words with real anticipation, the pretty young sleuth in charge. "And four!" Almost manic now, shrill, yelling the most obvious thing in the world, *"People are not voting!* CI has a ten-year history of dirty voting machinery, so bad the government had to step in and clean it up. We think CI is invincible! We just work around them, believing there's nothing we can do! So we do nothing! It's the monster in the living room! And now we're getting *this!"* Slamming a hand against the board at the photo of the Knights Templar banner in Tyne's basement.

She was in a state of analytical rage. "If I have ever seen…" She pulled back her blackbird hair, and looked from face to astonished face. "I swear to God!" Her eyes shot sparks, and whipped from the board to the people. "If I have ever seen a display of actual evidence of the Society With No Name at work in this country, this is it!" Right in Molly's face she yelled, "You heard what that guy said, your source in D.C.? *This crowd won't be stopped!* Of course they won't be stopped!" Shooting her long arms over her head in an angst-riddled invocation she cried, "This is their time! They're taking over *now!"*

She stopped, calamitously, sucking air in heaving gasps.

There were nods of comprehension, a groan of endorsement from Doc. She was overcome by her own hysterics, and she was embarrassed then, still looking at Molly as she said the rest with subdued tones. "It's the perfect combination. You told me yourself, years ago. Control the communications industry and you get control of the voting booth! They're stopping people from voting and nobody is doing anything! If you can make people do what you want, you control the world."

Edwin was as stunned as the others. Courtman applauded, and BJ and Molly joined in. Finally Edwin stood and held his arms out, palms up, and said to her, "Why don't we just ask them to tell us about it?"

"Because that's insane!" Raven cried, immediately back in her frenzy. "You think you're going to stop a violent machine like CI all by yourself? You're crazy!" And she collapsed into the big chair, clenching teeth and fists to prevent the tears from flowing.

102

Victor, in a crisp white tee shirt and denim farmer John, moved into the center of the room and took command. Holding an arm out to Raven, he said, "I believe she's right." And extending the other arm out to Edwin. "And we're betting he's right."

"She's right about him!" Mgaba, the dissenter, called out.

"You've just articulated what we have all been feeling." He paused to let her have the moment. "But we do have the burden of proof. We cannot go to Washington tomorrow without unassailable evidence of high crimes and misdemeanors. No court, no Congressional body will hear the kind of ex post facto pathology we have gathered here. We have to have hard facts." He studied the group. "And I'm talking about the Vice President. Not just Tyne."

Courtman had thought this through. Crossing his arms on his chest he said, "Actually the only provable criminal activity so far is yours. Inciting to riot, treason, flight from justice, public nuisance, and now," pointing at Slash, silent on the monitor, "accessory to theft of digital evidence."

Victor opened the heater and tossed in a big maple log. The fact was, Raven Menez had shaken him right to the core. Not only was she right, but he was the only person present in a position to act. And he hadn't.

He'd always imagined he would call the citizens to arms on the floor of the House of Representatives, with the cameras rolling. But the heart of the rebellion was out here in podunk, Washington. And instead of rousing the nation, he was preaching to the choir.

But it was time to give the speech. He brought his big knobby hands together.

"Among the tools we have forged in this nation," he said slowly, "is the obligation to resist oppression." He bowed to Molly Bee, in acknowledgement for her words. "This resistance is deadly serious. Fraught with legal obstacles if we are to succeed, and severe consequences if we fail.

"The party in power," he said, "is acting against the reasonable expectations of the people. And against the principles set down in the Constitution." Holding an open palm out toward Menez. "It's all about controlling people. We're all politicians. We're all subject to appetites of power and money and a lust to control things."

"And still subject to the rule of law," Courtman said. "At least on days that end in y."

To which BJ needed to add his irony: "But the evidence we have is inadmissible. That's Raven's whole point! The cards are stacked against us! Besides which, every court in the land is loaded with New Freedom Party people. So if this rebellion fails –"

Victor said harshly, "We are not preparing for failure. But you're right, Mr. Lichtenstein. We already have failure. That's what nine percent of the people voted for. We could not vote them out. So we are going to have to drive them out!" He checked his watch. "Pretty damn soon, too. Is everybody ready?"

Molly Bee walked across the hemlock floor to Raven. "You were terrific!" she said. Standing shoulder to shoulder with her, she turned to the others. "We cannot do nothing. We have already tried doing nothing! It's a disaster."

Pressing his palms together, Victor waited a moment, and continued. "We have all heard about this sting operation," he said. "We are confronting the most serious constitutional crisis in our history. People have been killed. Others viciously intimidated. A mob rebellion is under way across the country that may or may not last another week. Martial law is probably coming down Monday." He stopped to make room for the words. "You've all heard the speech. We are facing the real possibility of the collapse of the American social fabric. And they are in charge. Do not believe for a moment we have any kind of legal recourse here. BJ said it. That is absolute folly."

Nel was standing by her husband. "Remember Karen Silkwood?" she said, her voice strong. "Dennis Banks, founder of the American Indian Movement? Viola Ferrari? Nelson Mandela? Alexander Solzhenitsyn? Remember Guantánamo? The thousands of political prisoners worldwide! We have become them."

Nodding to her, Victor focused his indigo eyes on each person in the group. "The Constitution provides no immediate suspension of powers. They are in control. Period. Hellman will stop at nothing to keep his iron fists on the reins of power. No military uprising is about to take place. So we are going to have to suspend our disbelief and our innate skepticism. We, in this room, must bring about a change of government. Each of us has to make up his own mind." Extending an open arm toward Edwin. "I am placing my faith in this man." He studied each face carefully. His tiny army of insurrection. Breathing deeply, he located the place where he had stored the words he had been preparing for years, reworking the speech during his four marathons, and after frustrating defeats in the House, alone on mountain walks, when the ruling party cut another piece out of the safety network patched together over a century for the disenfranchised, the desperate, and the sick.

But there was no speech. Everything had been said many times over.

"In a real sense, the ruling party has spoken for us," he said. "They have disenfranchised all of us. The role of financial institutions in creating the recession is still up for debate, but this recession was certainly not caused by the actions of the other ninety-nine and a half percent of us."

"Amen!" Iona Webster sang out.

"You know all this. You know the list of the diseases our government has allowed to spread among our people."

"It is *real* sick," Webster persisted, head bobbing, taking a step toward Victor.

His voice rose, picking up Webster's rhythm. "Because we are still a *powerful* people!"

Raven Menez grimaced. She wanted to speak, but no words came.

"We don't have to let our country be destroyed!" Victor called out.

"They can't destroy our country!" Purvis Courtman almost echoed, moving closer, hearing the wind section somewhere.

"Where's Thomas Jefferson now, I want to know?" Victor cried out. "Where's General Washington? Where's Thomas Paine? Where's John Adams?"

"Where is Dr. Martin Luther King?" It was Mgaba, feeling himself pulled into the stream. "Where is Archbishop Desmond Tutu? Where is Justice Thurgood Marshall?"

Raven was caught now. "Where's Davy Crockett?"

They all looked. Edwin blushed and waved a finger.

"We have an honorable heritage," Victor chanted. "Fighting oppression! That's what we were *born* to do! We're not gonna *allow* this!" He was yelling and swaying, watching Iona for body signals, feeling it, feeling all the anger and all the failure ripping his chest open, catching Raven's eye and feeling what she was feeling.

"No!" cried the others. Even Molly Bee was in it. "It's not their country! This is our country! This is *my* country, dammit!"

"God bless America," said BJ Lichtenstein, and he laughed, but could not stop himself there. "From sea to shining sea!"

Both Webster and Bee looked at him oddly.

A gravelly whisper came from Doc Nguyen, sitting exhausted but amused by the big window. "When the whole culture bows down to the oppressors, the oppressors give them the shaft."

"Give *them* the shaft!" BJ blasted back, and then worried that he'd said something stupid.

"Amen!"

"We're going to give them something," Victor said in a soft, firm tone.

Iona said, "A plague of locusts."

"A plague of locusts," Victor echoed, louder.

"It's ordinary human decency they need to learn," Mgaba said. His voice was deep and contained horrid memories.

"And *we* need to teach it to them!" Courtman rapped.

"Nobody but us can do it," Victor Sligo said.

"Nobody will do it but us!"

"But we have to *stay together!* Stay together *strong!*" Iona clapped out her rhythm.

"Take back the house!" Courtman wanted this so badly his body ached.

Standing by her husband, Nel Sligo was finally caught in the cathartic fervor. "And the Senate!" she shouted, without the slightest notion where it came from. "Let's just go after them!" Bursting within her was a real need to do this, to be here, to take them on. An unrestrained rumble slid from her throat.

"Whoa, Nellie!" Iona could not resist yelling. "Let's get down to D.C. and go after them! *Yes!*"

Victor turned and grabbed his wife by both forearms. *"Yes!"* he burst out. She was nodding with him, ready for battle. Still holding her and facing the others he said, "Tomorrow we'll get the rest of what we need. Don't worry! Come Inauguration Day, we'll –" He stumbled for half a second. "We'll see. We have the courage and the integrity and the will to do this!" Pausing again, looking at the anxious faces. "We are the whole army of rebellion, people! We have not fought two hundred and forty years just to be pushed back into slavery by a bunch of thugs with flags in their lapels! We are going to fight for our way of life. We're going to fight for it, or lose it."

He looked to Nel. His scaffolding. His promise. She had never failed him. All eyes in the room went her to her. The building

seethed with passion. They were resolved. Nel held her fists high
overhead, and in her face was true determination. She yelled to the
mountaintops, "You know what the man said! If not now, when?"
And she banged the air with both fists, and finished, "If not us,
who?"

Part Three – The Sting

103

Davis's Shanghai pulled up soundlessly in front of a street lamp on Wisconsin Avenue. The man standing on the corner got in. Without looking at Davis, he sizzled, "Carnage at 1600! *Kapow!*"

Immediately Davis understood Nel Sligo had turned Secret Agent Daniel Cool. He was with the program. A tight man, blunt-faced, nearly invisible outside before Davis stopped the car. In his hard face, after a lifetime in service to Presidents, was a message: take no prisoners.

Automatically Davis turned the CD player up loud.

"Everything in place?"

"You're gonna nail Hellman's nuts to a tree. That it?" He sounded anything but cool. "Inauguration in Golgotha."

Agent Cool opened a pack of gum, and pulled out a stick.

"Okay. As the Chief Justice rises to walk to the podium, Burligame and Hellman will be standing there waiting for her," Davis said over heavy pounding of the Kodo drummers pulsing from his speakers. "At that moment we will need a diversion. You know all the security scenarios around the Capitol." He handed a slip of paper to Cool with a name and a phone number on it. "I want you to call this man to assist with whatever you need."

It was the private number for Admiral Sukwant Singh.

Cool crumpled up the paper and stuffed it in his pocket. He chewed, gazed out at the night, then turned to Davis with a scowl.

He said, "You want my fucking blood, too?"

Through a series of discreet calls, BJ managed to locate Michaela Velasquez in Hanoi on an art junket. The old lady told him both her banks in Singapore and Hong Kong were forming an emergency consortium, preparing to move in like vultures should the US economy collapsed. She also gave him the unusual security code for her Foggy Bottom condo. If it was not safe, they would have to make other arrangements. To which Raven spoke up. She suggested a friend she thought might be helpful in rural Maryland. She made a call.

Bert O'Donnell, the NSA renegade, had misidentified the interesting seventeen-digit number Nel Sligo had passed on after breaking into Hunter Tyne's winter palace outside Salt Lake City. In fact, this was O'Donnell's second mistake with that communication channel. For a man who had spent his life with codes, information and secrets, it was out of character.

He was in fact coming unglued.

Moments after meeting Iona Webster at Independence Hall and being thoroughly fascinated by her, O'Donnell had experienced a sort of frisky adolescent twitching when she'd gone after Hal Riske with such courage and intelligence. Before this marvelous woman was done at that meeting, particularly the artful way she had exposed the government cover-up of Viola Ferrari's death, Bert O'Donnell was already half in love with her.

Affection at dizzying heights of power is often articulated by demonstrations of power dizziness. NSA's stricken Deputy Administrator dug into last September's classified DoJ communication register to learn what he might about Viola Ferrari, only to make the devastating discovery that it was Senator Hal Riske himself who had set up the US Attorney's Office to send Ferrari off to her death. In his position, O'Donnell was forced to live with this knowledge day and night with no hope of disclosing it, and nothing possible to gain by confronting Riske while the insurrection was bubbling.

Tonight it all went to hell.

Ms. Sligo had delivered the code number of an incoming classified message to Hunter Tyne's personal computer. O'Donnell had dismissed it. It was simply the half-baked sleuthing of the missing congressman's frantic wife, working with O'Donnell's eccentric acquaintance Fred Geschwantner. But suddenly he flashed on the numerical sequence in the code. The full impact of the nightmare taking place in the country hit him like a punch in the face. At that horrible instant he lined up in his mind the code number on Tyne's email with the electronic signature on the order from the Senate to Jerome Tse, the one telling Tse to send a mind control expert out to Utah. Something sank in the pit of O'Donnell's stomach. At one a.m., knowing he'd never sleep, he made the half-hour drive from Cherry Hill back to Arch Street to confirm it.

The numbers matched. The electronic signature was definitely Senator Hal Riske, signing for the Judiciary Committee. But the long routing code O'Donnell had not bothered to check a few days ago came from higher up. Essentially out of his domain.

He was going to have to drive down to see Elvis. Two hours south via I-95, with the kind of driver's license he carried.

Feeling extremely paranoid and heavy in the extremities, he loaded up on coffee and hit the road for Anacostia, across the river from Southeast D.C., to visit the White House Communications Agency for a terrible confirmation he did not want to know about. One of NSA's constant burdens is keeping up with White House coding paradigms, the necessary encryption tools the President and Cabinet and other Executive Branch officials use to talk to each other. The codes change daily. In reality, there was zero possibility of tracing the numbers clear back to September – much less actually reproducing the message. But his mind burned to know who would be sending Tyne cabinet-level messages *at home* with that sequence of numbers, back in early September. It was a million to one shot.

But the government never sleeps, and neither did O'Donnell's ex-brother-in-law, Master Gunnery Sergeant Elvis Murdock, RRAM. Elvis had taken to using the acronym – Ready to Retire Any Moment. He had shipped over for the last time before Burligame and Hellman came in, and now he still loved the Marine Corps but hated every moment of active duty. His occupation was to guard state secrets with his life.

Thankfully, he was on duty, which eliminated telephone problems. O'Donnell getting himself admitted to the Naval base was no problem. Finding Elvis was no problem. But then he had to explain what he needed out in his car in the freezing parking lot with the radio blasting, and the rough old gunny sergeant nearly shit his camo drawers.

"You want me to *what?*" he said.

O'Donnell knew Elvis had been monitoring his government's actions with growing disgust for some years. He handed the

Marine an envelope with a long series of numbers and letters written on the back.

"Find out if anybody used this particular code around the twelfth or thirteenth of September last year. And while you're breaking the law, see if you can retrieve the message."

The powerful middle-aged NCO rubbed the back of his head. "There's hundreds of messages a day! All encrypted! Are you crazy? The government's not going to collapse, pal! It doesn't make any difference who's doing –"

"We'll see. Run a search on that number. Please."

"You know we're talking life in prison? I mean if –"

O'Donnell stared him down. Elvis opened the envelope. It contained fifteen one hundred dollar bills. Elvis left.

In twenty-one minutes he climbed back in O'Donnell's car and woke him up. He spoke without looking at him.

"The Vice President did contact the Secretary of Communications on that code sequence on twelve September, 1042 hours," Elvis Murdock said.

"What did the message say?"

Elvis paused a long moment. Long enough for his breath to settle on the windshield.

"It said, *'Deflect this curiosity immediately.'*" Reaching up, Elvis made a fierce slash mark across the condensation on the glass, opened the door, and disappeared.

He was crossing the Maryland-Delaware line when he knew he would have to wake up Davis. There was no time for politeness. The only way it made sense was if the Vice President somehow learned that Jaap Tenkley was about to blow the whistle on Hunter Tyne and CI's mind control research, and this information spooked Billy Hellman very badly.

At four o'clock that morning, Deputy Director John Lee Davis contacted Greenville Federal Correctional Institute, to learn that an FBI agent named Joe Hadrian had spent ten minutes with Tenkley's former cellmate, Rocky Mohammad, on September twelfth, an hour after Tenkley was released. The best groggy Rocky Mohammad could recall was that the agent wanted to know what Tenkley's plans were. Rocky told him.

A 2.09-second search through the Bureau personnel database told Davis there was no FBI agent named Joe Hadrian.

104

It was two-forty a.m. in the rain forest. Nel was beginning to think she might be going insane. She was unable to stop obsessing on the approaching catastrophe. The staff had worked mostly in isolation till after midnight, studying maps, calling loved ones. Iona had checked with her brother on the pickup in the morning, at the same airstrip near Van Zandt. He was working on the problem of where to drop them in D.C. It was going to be a very long flight.

Nel tiptoed downstairs, threading her way between Mgaba and Courtman, nearly stepping on BJ's outstretched arm. A dim light was blinking somewhere. She checked on her husband snoring beside the French doors. His phone was winking. A text message.

She reached to pick up the phone and realized there was also activity on the monitor they'd used to talk to Slash. Assuming the text was from one of the children — who did not seem to know how to communicate any other way to their parents — she got to the laptop and touched the mouse. On the screen was a note propped up by a loaf of Wonder bread.

"Press replay. We're taking a break. S." The initial was so askew, it almost resembled him.

She clicked on the replay icon and slipped on a headset. Instantly Slash was back, still wearing his tattered suede jacket and black turtleneck with what looked like spaghetti sauce splattered on the chest. His snow white hair resembled a cartoon of a man with his finger in a light socket. Slash's warbly tenor came to her ears like somebody sucking on a helium balloon.

"People, I'm recording this. Now listen. We got hold of Tao Ting, but haven't used him yet. But we will. Like I told you, the only way into CI. Meantime, we got stuck on the Ferrari thing. It turns out somebody played a pretty good trick. The files in the US Attorney's Office were sealed all right. But then they were *deleted!* We looked all over for Ferrari and this Jerome Tse and Tenkley, and then even for Hunter Tyne. But guess what? Nothing keeps coming up! We don't know who done it. You gotta know this is dirty politics. As if there was some other kind. We're gonna get back to you, and, you know, talk about when you want to get serious about CI."

A woman's perfectly-manicured dark hand, bearing silver rings and bracelets, came into view, pulling her chair close beside his. She took over, while Slash rolled his eyes and shut his mouth. Immediately Nel was struck with the change in Desdemona's appearance. The black coveralls were gone. She looked like a wealthy socialite, flawlessly made up, dressed for dinner in an understated navy cashmere suit. She looked absolutely stunning.

"We're going to meet you in Washington," she said, and Nel could hear the weariness behind her perfectly articulated words. "Mr. Evileye is still working on this."

The screen returned to Slash's note and his sloppy S.

The phone was still blinking in her hand. Pressing a button, she saw the message on the tiny screen. She had to squint to read it.

"Billy sent the message to Chicago. Evidence firm."

It did not register immediately. She was so worn down, overloaded, fearful of actually going to prison herself as an accessory. But it spilled across her consciousness in a few moments. The Vice President had ordered Jerome Tse to send Viola to Utah. When she arrived, a professional killer would take her life.

105

She did sleep now. She felt somehow safer. They had the smoking gun. Instinct told her to sleep while she had the chance.

Only a couple of hours later she was up, and awakened Victor quietly among the other comatose bodies sprawled in the living room. She showed him the message from O'Donnell.

Still in the sleeping bag, he rubbed his eyes and shook his head and did not know what to say. It was as if they had known all along but did not dare think it.

It was Saturday morning. The bags were packed.

Victor went to the computer in his white tee shirt and Edwin's long john bottoms, a toothbrush in his mouth, and watched Slash's message about deleted files. Others were dragging themselves upstairs, forming a disgruntled scrum at the bathroom door.

She watched his fists. They closed and opened and closed, and he turned to look out the big window with pure rage in his face, and spoke words that will not be repeated here and his wife knew there was going to be bloodshed. His face went sour, as if he had tasted something putrid. He had to leave the building before he could speaking to her.

The immediate question was whether to notify the FBI. They had to assume that Davis had been informed, and that there were elements in the upper echelon of the Bureau who were so deeply enmeshed with the Vice President they could not be relied on. Likewise most of the national security crowd. Hellman was too careful to overlook anything. At this point they could only hope Slash was on the verge of providing the crucial missing pieces, and that Edwin Foulks had something more than a snowball's chance in hell of getting anything out of anybody at the Inauguration, twenty-eight hours away.

Everybody was grumpy and conflicted, and Courtman had stopped speaking to Mgaba, and in fact nobody wanted to talk to anybody. They sorted out their belongings and flew east once again, a jarring eleven-hour flight including two fuel stops, without Doc Nguyen or BJ Lichtenstein. Doc was already returning to Denver, and BJ had told his wife that he expected to be home Sunday, either with a job or without. Leah had heard Julio Reese saying the White House had announced, as usual, the tightest security in history was in place for the Inauguration. In an interview with I-Media's Brock Yryzari, Homeland Security Secretary Needham Strange, unaccountably wearing a neck brace, warned that if these insurrectionists had any plans for the coming events in Washington, they'd better check with their lawyers and pack a big lunch.

Even before the wheels were up Nel was showing O'Donnell's text message to the others. It had seemed prudent to wait until they were on the airplane, in case somebody panicked. Raven had assigned herself the title of Whiteboard Watch, and transferred all the collected data to a notebook. Nel's latest news was so enormous, Raven felt no need to record it, but she scribbled it across a separate page, and took the time to make a drawing of herself shoving Billy Hellman out of a speeding train.

Courtman spent the entire flight alternately niggling with his friend Sage Kuushmann at Area 51, and nagging Molly Bee in furious whispers about her friend Bliss, the TV producer, when and where exactly, and what if, and have you considered, matters this obviously deluded Kuushmann was concerned about. It made Molly aware nobody in America was in the position Sage Kuushmann was in. Of course he was deluded! Dr. Strangelove reincarnate!

Lacking sleep and berserk with anticipation, Slash brought in Tao Ting. This required some waiting, and loading specific commands and orders onto Mr. Tao's small, neat metadata box. Shortly they were sitting back gawking and applauding as stuff came in on Evileye's monitor. Exuberant Slash, still in Queens with Desdemona, sent a forty-minute CI infomercial to Webster's laptop as the nervous group cruised east. He amused no one, describing CI's inner sanctum, mainly thousands of government contracts, from postwar reconstruction in half a dozen countries to consulting on paper clip design for the Federal Spelunking Administration. One entire CI data "army" was allocated to federal contracts with the EPA, going back to the period of Hunter Tyne's work in Utah with Communication West and Hellman's Nevada beginnings. In Baltimore, Evileye's request for Mr. Tao to search the name "Hellman" came up suspiciously empty. In Queens, Slash was slapping the sides of his monitor as he foamed at the mouth and worked on a migraine after reading the name ComWest. It made the chip in his head pulsate.

Certain active segments in CI's huge media division were blocked. Slash was pissed. An error box kept requesting a three-dimensional passcode. So it was real. The Machiavelli covenant deep in CI's underground. Mr. Tao, universally recommended and very costly, wasn't enough. Evileye was threatening to go into a meditative state to achieve cyber-Nirvana, and blow everything up.

Sitting alone at the rear of the bumpy aircraft, Edwin Foulks felt the doubts breaking down the domino house of his affirmations. All night he had ruminated on the facts, with no sense of conviction from his committee of advisors. He knew he was right. But he would be left holding a nasty bag if the operation collapsed. Hiring a Cessna to spread the message of his private frustration was one thing. But this! Taking responsibility for a rebellion, watching the nation go into a tailspin, this was another thing altogether.

He'd felt it coming. Finally he began seeing the flatcars. Pitch black, a moonless night, flatcars rumbling past at the S-curve in the road, a scream, and he slammed his head against the window, and wept.

106

The aircraft landed at a private field in Northern Virginia late Saturday afternoon. Victor and Nel felt the cloying fear of being recognized. A lifetime in politics teaches a lot about masquerading, deception, and back roads.

Anonymity was now crucial. Molly Bee was easily the least recognizable of the group. Quietly the others disembarked in a freezing gray overcast, and Dushane took off again and delivered Molly to the private transit area at Reagan International, where she rented the last van, under the unusual name of Ogils Rotciv. She paid cash, including the deposit. After years doing digital searches, she was confident the absurd name would remain hidden in plain sight.

Eventually she wove her way out of the enormous lot, and found herself waiting while a sparkling black stretch limo whizzed past security barriers, departing the diplomatic gate. Which of the new slamboozle rock bands was performing in D.C. this weekend, she wondered. Or was it the Globetrotters?

Vice President Billy Hellman flicked a glance at the cream-colored rental van exiting the parking lot, and reflexively touched his emerald-toned silk tee shirt under the exquisite wool suit. He believed his paranoia to be not only healthy but also a reliable danger detector. Some broad sat idling in the van waiting for him to pass. Looked vaguely familiar. Maybe wanting his autograph, if she could see through the tinted glass. Maybe wanting to kill him. The two lists were about equally long these days. Lighting his one-a-day cigarette, Hellman pressed the window button and let smoke stream out into the frigid evening. Tomorrow the Inauguration. Pomp and fucking circumstance. The sprinkling of trinkets into the cupped hands of the huddled masses, then Monday the end of this damn kneejerk rebellion. It was like church. Make the poor dolts believe they're participating in some kind of magic ceremony that will make them feel superior to some other group of poor dolts. As if the articulation of authority, as he loved to call it, had something to do with anything other than the absolute manipulation of the masses, elevating the herd instinct to a national pastime, with its uplifting clichés, its parades, and its cherished old pieces of paper signed by dead men wearing wigs.

The Friday night flight and return today had seriously crammed his schedule, not to mention his bowels, but when dealing with the Group, Hellman never trusted any form of communication, electronic, terrestrial or psychic, other than face time. The East Asians were closing ranks on him and not speaking. The Saudis and the Israelis were worried the Russians and the Venezuelans would be re-igniting the old Inner Circle. The lady from Banco Singapore had actually suggested the November election was too successful. The Newfies were cutting out the opposition too hard, inducing a fatal eruption of public mistrust. Unemployment was rampant. A whole lot of people were lining up to buy nothing. There was some sort of outbreak of – what was the word – patriotism! The Group did not suffer fools gladly. The world powers monitored this uprising with definite suspicion. Certain economic disaster parameters had been eclipsed already. The Group had insisted, on the very eve of the Inauguration, that Caliban stand before them and entertain their concerns. Billy Hellman was furious when he received the coded message. They knew it was all bullshit, a liberal media conspiracy. The Group's Western Alliance was in charge, and that was that. To prove it, the Party demanded the creeps and the Rush Limbaughs and the NRA intensify their counterattacks and flag-waving. The Group had forgotten political turmoil was inevitable once a generation. You killed a President, you forced an intern in a blue dress to confess something ugly, you started a war. There would be a big stink, followed by government scrambling, followed by another big stink, and things would settle. That's the American way! There are *supposed* to be dissenters! What did the Group expect as the clamps tightened on these free-thinking subversives? They'd just go belly up and accept martial law? Hell, look at history! The Revolution! The Mexicans against the Spanish. The European resistance against the Nazis. The British against practically everybody. Blood, sweat and tears and all that crap. The people were going to stand up and resist! These damn cowboy Americans think they're *supposed* to resist authority. Like it's an *obligation!*

But when the serious recession hit, everybody shut up and hunkered down.

On the flight to the citadel at S., Billy instructed Psybysch to create an animated video demonstrating what was going to take place next week. Insurgents arrested. Sligo permanently detained, or else his recent activity so negatively exposed he would no longer be a viable public official. Crockett disenfranchised. A swift and substantial demotivation of public support for this rebellion, caused by a broadly-dispersed fear campaign saturating the Internet – the new opiate of the masses – plus unassailable I-Media newscasts by trusted industry authorities, spooking the public with yet another round of bank foreclosures and unemployment. Added to all this, next week the President would appear to endorse the proposed 28th Amendment to recall a sitting administration in the case of proven election fraud. In the meantime, a modified martial law would take effect Monday. This would create an imaginary bargaining chip for the frantic Progressives still in Congress. The whole goddamn thing would go away by the middle of the week.

Hellman raced back to Washington Saturday. In his private suite on his private airplane, he stood admiring himself, sipping his afternoon scotch, gazing at one of true power figures on Earth. The great teeth, the steady hands, the perfectly shaped bald head, the solid musculature, the dictatorial scowl of his mentor and look-alike, J. Edgar Hoover.

But always responsive to the whim of the Group. They tell him to shit, he asks what color. They tell him to take out a busybody Assistant US Attorney, he arranges it.

He breathed fire then, a raw animal sound, and he heaved the whisky at his image. Truly, Billy Hellman loathed this perverse obeisance, divulging battle plans to the fagotty armchair generals ensconced in their plush thrones in S. But that was the way of it. The moles were on every board, every council, every police force, every caucus. The Group's information network was as inescapable as dirt. The whisky dripped across his large, angry head in the glass, and he grasped it for the hundredth time. They were supreme. Billy Hellman simply carried out the details.

He screamed at Leora Psybysch working outside his door, "Get Davis on the phone."

Within fifteen seconds a chime sounded on his phone.

"Sir, it's Deputy Director Davis."

"Deputy. Director. Davis." He separated the three words with perfect disdain. "Make a note. I will be armed tomorrow. I don't trust these idiots. I'm only forewarning you so your people and the Secret Service will override the weapons detector to pass me into the Reviewing Stand. Are we clear?"

"I understand."

107

As far as John Lee Davis could assess it, the props were in place. The audience was filing in, the music was cued, and all that was needed were the actors. They were coming in tomorrow from both sides of the war-drama, for Davis the play that would end his career, and at this point he almost didn't care who was standing at the final curtain. It had become too surreal for him to learn the lines, much less to actually play both roles he was required to act out.

The Stolichnaya had made him blab too much to Daniel Cool, without a clue to the man's real allegiance.

The bad guys, costumed to resemble the heroes of Western society, would show up with lavish pomp and top hats and pearls, to the strumming of *Hail to the Chief* and the other patriotic psalms of nationhood. Whatever Leora Psybysch thought would massage her boss's brittle ego. More than a dozen federal spook agencies, including Davis's, would scrutinize every angle, every gust of wind, every gnat on every spectator's lapel.

The good guys, costumed to resemble musicians, would slip onto the scene uninvited, intent upon smashing the party for good. If you looked straight at it, the way a career FBI officer looked at things, there was no way in hell they were going to register so much as a blip on the screen of tomorrow's ritual coronation of the already coronated.

John Lee Davis was stuck in the middle. He was the high profile provider of law enforcement for President Sol Burligame, a man he liked and enjoyed during the few times they'd been together away from public scrutiny. He was not the bodyguard. The Secret Service did that function. He was not the protector of the nation's Presidency. Not the watchdog. Homeland Security took care of that. But Davis, with his giant physical stature and inappropriate pony tail, was the FBI, the enforcer of the law of the land, there to protect and serve regardless of the depth and stench of the slime pit this administration had dug for itself.

His other role was a bit more subtle. He was to help bring down the government.

This past couple of days he'd completely drained his family, his favor bank, and himself. The moments he'd spent with Chief Justice Shapiro-Fujimoto alone were enough to make him want to turn in his badge. He and Bert O'Donnell had conferred at a coffee stand for a final time at the rear of Verizon Center during a Capitals game. Nothing was well. Both men were distraught, mistrustful of each other, certain at this point of on one thing only: the election was fixed. Nobody could keep electing these people. O'Donnell had not surprised him by relating the story of Viola Ferrari.

Three phones were on his person. The FBI-issue belt pouch, the Code Red unit connecting him directly to the President in case of national emergency, and the breast pocket untraceable unit he'd been using to talk to Sloan Mgaba and O'Donnell.

Billy Hellman always used the Code Red phone. The Vice President was a constant national emergency, and he insisted on making every communication critical, to reinforce his relentless egotism. Oddly, Davis had assumed the Vice President was armed at all times. Thirty years in the profession, eighteen of them in the field, had taught Davis that small, aggressive men always believed they were targets. The sharp tone behind his words told Davis something had fouled Hellman's usually ugly disposition, and he had grabbed the handiest underling to bark some quirky orders at. *I'm bringing a gun to the war. Don't tell anybody.*

Both the private silver phone and his FBI-issue unit jangled as soon as Hellman clicked off. He flipped open the office phone.

"We're back to mud-wrestling," his National Security Executive, Blaine Washington, burst in with no greeting. "This damned 101st Airborne landing at the Capitol. They want a GPS blinking on each troop before take-off at Andrews! These people won't stop! Whose idea was this?"

"I heard it was the Vice President's brainstorm."

"Why am I not surprised."

"All right. Wake up Robbie Snyder at GSA. Get the stuff. Bill it to the Vice President's Office."

"The CO of the 101st is on my other line. He's having a hissy fit about this. When he hears – maybe you'd better talk to him. One of these chain-of-command guys. I can't –"

"Just do it, Blaine! Tell him it's SOP for Inaugurations. I have to go."

He blew out a breath and snatched up the private phone. "Yeah?"

"Hello, it's Mgaba here. Can you talk?"

"Briefly."

Mgaba, crunched in the back of the rental van rumbling through dark Georgetown side streets towards Foggy Bottom, had been afraid Davis might have abandoned ship. They had asked a great deal of this man, including demands of his own family. Nel Sligo, longtime friend of the FBI Deputy Director, had detected alarming sounds in his voice the past day or two. She feared for his safety. She had the staff all listen to the last exchange between Davis and Mgaba. He'd sounded depressed, overwhelmed and possibly drunk. And who could blame him.

"Somebody will have to get band outfits to us tonight," Mgaba said. "I had forgotten this detail. I'm sorry." He shut up and let Davis respond, rather than blubber about screwing up.

Davis scribbled a note nobody on the planet could decipher. "Got it." He hung up. Immediately the phone rang again. He clicked it on. "And instruments," Mgaba yelled at him. "I'll let you know where."

108

Washington was cold and eerie. The Friday night streets were mostly deserted, although they avoided the entire parade zone where protestors were grouping even now. Troops squashed into hundreds of armored personnel carriers were concentrated along the perimeters of the downtown area. Angry signs appeared in store windows and on streetlight poles, condemning Hellman. Somebody had sent Hunter Tyne a message at a Metro entrance in blazing brown letters: "The end is sure as hell near now, Adolph!"

Turning into Virginia Avenue, Molly, at the wheel of the rental van, eased past the Watergate complex and stopped across the street from Michaela Velasquez's twelve-story condo. Michaela's place was on the top floor, facing the river. In the front passenger seat, Victor leaned forward to study the well-lighted brick exterior. Behind him, Iona Webster, Nel Sligo and Raven waited with weary anticipation for the word to start hauling bags inside. Courtman and Mgaba were in the back crammed between suitcases. Edwin, in the far back, gazed blindly out, his head empty. Nobody spoke.

At ten seconds before nine o'clock D.C. time, Victor read a series of numbers from a pocket notepad Lichtenstein had stuffed in his jacket this morning, and pressed the corresponding numbers on his phone. Nel focused binoculars on the twelfth floor condo. A light popped on, clear as day. Everybody held their breath. Nine seconds later the light disappeared.

"Oh, my God!" It was Menez, worried she was going to have to take charge. "Someone's in there!"

"Yeah," Victor whispered. "Let's beat it." They wheeled around and bounced across to Eye Street and then up Rock Creek Parkway, shouting to each other about a mole in the system somewhere, and it was a damn good thing Ms. Velasquez figured this out for them. That left plan B. Raven's friend, half an hour north of town in a place called Olney, Maryland. Raven had already been in touch.

Nel withdrew her phone and handed it to Menez. "Call her."

It was simple, really, Michaela Velasquez's home security alarm. Among her thousands of contacts with inventors, artists and floundering writers, Ms. Velasquez had offered a small grant to a besotted woodcarver who said his name was Gay Blade, in exchange for his tricking out her condo with a remote device that would simultaneously power up a lamp and a radio set at ear-splitting volume, through a cell phone frequency. Just like a garage door opener. Presumably a burglar inside the condo would panic and switch the radio off to save his hearing, thereby switching off the light. Which is what occurred, although it probably was not a burglar.

As they dashed up the Parkway and out of town, Victor told Mgaba to get hold of John Lee Davis. He needed to know where they were staying. Every detail was crucial from here on.

Eighty-four-year-old Marianne Belonis was the perfect hostess for a political refugee and his support staff. She operated what she still called a "sanitarium," where alcoholics with serious money came to dry out, a halfway house between the straight jacket and a return to the straight life. Bacon Farm was a former plantation on a sixteenth-section of rolling farm land that was mostly grass now, rose gardens, a tree nursery, a ten-acre lake, plenty of space for the innocent to contemplate their sins and the guilty to lie about theirs. Marianne Belonis was one of those rare individuals who knew everything. Like the central concept of her halfway house for alcoholics, her guiding principle was anonymity. Even the fact that she knew everything, she kept to herself.

Fortunately, January was the month of refurbishment and overhaul at Bacon Farm. Raven advised them that only Ms. Belonis and her bare-necessities staff were present – Francis the cook, Tommy the gardener and maintenance person, and an assortment of Airedales, German shepherds and Irish wolfhounds, Persian cats, Himalayan cats and Manx cats, all of questionable pedigree, all hopelessly devoted to Ms. Belonis.

At the end of a long country lane, the van pulled around a circular driveway and stopped before the pristine white mansion. They hauled themselves out, groaning with the stiffness of travel, and were immediately greeted by curious critters lapping at their flesh. The grand front door opened, and Ms. Belonis, in a fabulous floral kimono, ornamental slippers and her enormous coif of steel gray hair in a bun, welcomed them with open arms.

They were never to learn that she had a longtime association with an outlandish person named Dr. Horst Spangloss, one hundred fifty miles north in Central Pennsylvania.

Shortly they got down to business. Edwin took a distant third-floor room where he could fret and sweat and at least attempt to absorb information as Raven brought it up to him. At Ms. B's insistence, the others created a command center in the rose-colored antebellum living room. Molly, worn down to raw emotions, was on her new chartreuse phone on a yet another conference call with her D.C. news producer named Bliss, and Dr. Sage Kuushmann, feeling deeply conflicted, wishing to remain anonymous and witness her father's second Inauguration.

At this point Sloan Mgaba felt pinned to the wheel of fate. The entire crisis was in his hands – and he had to determine whether they had a plan or not. He pressed a thick finger on his redial pad every hour until finally, at four o'clock Sunday morning, he heard

Deputy Director Davis curse as he picked up. Mgaba told him to pass the word to Cool to watch for the red umbrella.

It took no time for Raven Menez, a Philadelphia girl, to cozy up to Ms. Belonis. They were practically neighbors. They sat on the rose print Chesterfield having tea, catching up on East Coast matters. Baseball, Chesapeake Bay oysters, horses, cherry blossoms, Airedales, and what the President's wife was wearing.

"I know you're connected to everybody in Washington," Raven said. "You know what? None of us have invitations to the Inauguration." She twisted her pert little nose. "Do we need them? It's pretty late to be asking."

"I figured as much," Ms. B said. "A few of the girls had extra tickets which I managed to filch just in case. You'll be fine. But not sitting together."

It turned out "a few of the girls" meant the wives of various Progressive Congressmen, who chose to be in Hawaii and be missed, rather than be noticed at the Inauguration and be miserable.

"Aren't state secrets fun," Ms. Belonis said, twinkling all over.

All the parts were in place. They had hard evidence on Hellman as well as Tyne – a paper trail linking one to unlicensed medical research, and both to Viola Ferrari's murder. In spite of this, they knew Hellman's network was formidable, and his rule by intimidation impenetrable. Tyne was just as bad – unpredictable and vicious. But there was another problem. Edwin Foulks, the centerpiece of the entire operation, had completely dissolved. He was sinking into a projected web of embarrassment, arrest, unimaginable horrors. From downstairs the others could hear him pacing and banging on furniture. Finally Victor slipped up to the third floor and knocked on the ancient walnut door.

"Hello?"

He opened the door a crack. "Can I come in for a minute."

"No last minute pep talk, huh?"

Victor had to bend slightly to come through the doorway. He spoke quietly. "How are you feeling?"

"I forgot to tell BJ where the dog food is."

"He'll find it."

"Yeah, but what if –"

"Keep yourself together, Edwin. It's almost over."

Holding a small hand up, Edwin smiled without conviction. "All that stuff we accumulated. You wanted to tell me about how it connects to these two guys and election fraud and people not voting. But you really can't tell me much, can you?" His voice was harsh. Gone was the gentle, self-assured champion of the downtrodden, the last honest man.

Victor shrugged. "There is real evidence. And you're right. If we subpoena anything from any government agency it will be doctored. Or missing. That's the way the government operates."

Edwin just nodded, past argument, ready for the final judgment.

"I'm going to say this for myself, and for a decent woman who died working for justice. Not to make you feel guilty. It's clear now they killed Viola Ferrari. She had to be onto some extremely serious activity Hunter Tyne was engaged in, something about all of them, the whole system they represent, whatever it is. Maybe Slash and his buddy might learn something else tonight. Maybe not. I just wanted you to keep this in mind tomorrow when you're speaking to Burligame and Hellman. If the sting fails – which it won't – and we all go down, we sure as hell will go down fighting."

In the half-light, Victor slightly resembled a clean-shaven Abe Lincoln. Lean and serious and January pale. He could see fear in Edwin's eyes.

"Is that what it comes down to?" Edwin said. "Blood and guts patriotism? Go down with your ship? Is that it?"

Victor understood this man actually did want the pep talk. Without the hindrance of thinking, he allowed pure selfishness to flow from his heart.

"I do not wish my grandchildren to grow up in an oppressed society. I do not wish my family to have to hide from government, to sacrifice everything they own for a few crumbs of independence. You and I stand on the shoulders of fifteen generations of Americans, Edwin. War heroes and housewives and laborers of every sort, and teachers and businessmen and leaders and people with the guts to stand up to tyranny and greed. I do not wish this –"

"Easy, there, Congressman!" Holding up an open hand. "Thank you. I get it."

"I do not wish this legacy to be ground to dust by fools and power mongers," Victor persisted. "I don't want these people to strangle my country. My family will not pay the price for them to continue in power. Not as long as I'm drawing breath."

He left. Suddenly desolated, Edwin surrendered to the memories. The flashbacks had returned during the long flight across the country. Really since speaking with Molly about her father. The nightmare images had come up less frequently in recent years, but were no less horrific as he grew older. He always felt like he was rushing off the edge of a cliff into another world, a world of violence and twisted steel. Which is exactly what it was.

He was seventeen. The whole family had been to Portland for a weekend visit to Grandma's house. His mother's mother. Dad always insisted on making the long return drive after dark, slipping through Seattle after hours. All five kids and the parents crammed into the ancient GMC van, along with the dog, camping gear, the usual battered effluence of travel. Four miles from home was a long S-curve in the two-lane country road. Train tracks passed through the middle of the two halves of the S turn. The railroad crossing was marked, but without a signal or automatic barrier in those days. And when you've lived in a place fifty years as Edwin's father had, and you're road-weary and you've long ago lost the blazing wonderment of youth, not only do you not see the crossing sign, but your brain is not prepared for a train crossing the road on a moonless September night with a fog down and the family sleeping.

They were flatcars. Passing in endless monotony and somehow silently, no more than four feet high in utter blackness, so that when he negotiated the first curve he must have imagined the distant black-on-black of Racehorse Mountain when the van smashed into the moving train. The van split apart instantly with a single scream, and then moans that still froze Edwin's blood twenty-five years later. In seconds they were all dead. What was left of the van was hurled down a creekside, wobbled hideously, and dumped onto its roof in the creek with a savage *whump*. All went silent. The air was filled with piss and gas and a horrid quivering that passed through his ears into his brain and it was four years before he could hear right. Bodies were all over and under him, insulating him from death. They were all dead. His two sisters and two brothers, all younger. His parents were crushed likes pea vines ground into the earth. The dog was never found.

He had spent most of his young life helping raise them, the brothers and sisters. So that was the end of that. His child-rearing days were over, and he was seventeen, and he went to work in the woods after the mass funeral, the miniature coffins for his sisters, full size darker ones for all the others, and he struggled mightily to endure alone this thing no man should endure alone, focusing on the work to still the horrible moaning in his head.

109

Not far from Baltimore Harbor, Evileye was ready to shoot Mr. Tao.

"We got to figure out how to break this icon thing," he told Slash up in Queens. "Whatever's in there is *bad,* man. I mean, with this frozen-ass parade coming up in the morning and all these people and all these secrets nobody can get to, I feel like the Lord is hanging on the cross just waiting for us to get the goods and cut him down. You see what I'm saying? And Mr. Tao, he ain't doin' it."

Slash wasn't paying attention. He was cogitating on the conundrum.

Obviously the objective was to worm into people's brains. That much they had intuited and in fact had long suspected, as had street hackers and prepubescent geek children for a decade. They were so close, but were actually nowhere. During the night Desdemona had located an iconography on line, but neither of them had any idea what to do with it. They'd fiddled through thousands of icons, tried several hundred three-dimensional holograms, even a horseshoe resembling the tattoo on Tyne's neck – and had given up disappointed and could do nothing but wait for Mr. Tao. The hours were taking their toll. Slash was standing at the open the door of the fridge, staring at the bright, empty shelves. Just standing there. At the computer, Desdemona watched him in dazed exhaustion, half wondering if he was praying or starving. She'd returned to that damned tattoo on Tyne's neck again and again. She played over and over the blond woman's tape of Tyne and Hellman going at each other. She passed out for a while, then woke, used the bathroom, and made more coffee. Two-twenty Sunday morning. Slash was asleep standing up before the empty fridge with the door open.

Then he returned out of nowhere, faceless, texting them from wherever he was, "Hey! You people know something about a *Caliban?* Come on. I told you to give me all your information. Been busting butt here. It's *47370811 Caliban*(.* You told me everything you're looking for, and it's in here. But it won't be enough. I can see this already. You'll need the proper icon to go further. Find it, and I'm available for the next $50,000 8 a.m. your time."

Slash awoke with a jerk at the fridge. The screen was going wild, dozens of files, pages and pages of scientific study. The first document contained an abstract. The history of neurological tampering, from ancient Chinese herbal intoxicants through the Inquisition to Korean War POW's to LSD experiments to waterboarding, and finally to neurological interconnectivity through a specialized DSM, a digital signal microprocessor, interacting with a human subject two to five meters from the DSM chip. Slash was breathing hard reading this. It was real, recorded right in the office memos of the world's major communications player. Papers had been scanned in, including extensive works by Dr. Hunter Tyne et al, during his early years with Communication West's research division, experimenting with hallucinogenic drugs, tryptophan and some other essential amino acids, and then the obvious step into serotonin and electro-stimulants. Kicked around hypothetically at the conclusion, Tyne's team had formulated a theoretical marriage between an "externally managed" federal government and the communications industry, a benign Big Brother arrangement that would enable the managing body to help the citizens understand what was best for them.

It wasn't theoretical for long.

The invention of the Brain-Computer Interface opened the possibility of actually manipulating the cerebral cortex through the hypothalamus. Tyne's research path shifted to BCI. Within a year Communication West researchers were implanting chips into the brains of rats, then sheep, and then *volunteer military personnel*, to make the BCI work both ways, computer to human and back, to complete the neuro-circuitry. No mention was made of dead bodies, people having seizures or going crazy, or failed experiments. But Slash knew they were out there. As he wandered through clinical experiments without a word concerning the health of the guinea pigs, he wanted to rip the chip out of his head and shove it down

Hunter Tyne's throat.

There was so much more Slash's mind had to move over to make room for it all. And he was feeling sick. Sick enough to put his fist through his monitor as he read.

This business of non-invasive brain-imaging BCI experiments really tore the roof off. First the poor slobs had to wear chips or buttons, and then somehow specific brainwave imaging, evolving from the electroencephalograph, did the job with no implant in the patient. He was reading slowly now, fighting off knowledge of his own nightmares and seizures. They called it Permanent Transcranial Magnetic Stimulation, blasting certain neurons in the brain without implants, maybe even without the guy knowing he was being experimented on! After this came wave-recognition patterning. CI grabbed everything they could use. It looked like real science. It smelled like real science. But the whole purpose was to get inside your brain using a microprocessor, to make you into a robot. If you were sitting six to sixteen feet from the chip, you were toast. They had you.

"They can really do it," Slash whispered to Evileye, reading with him down in Baltimore. He felt like he'd stepped in a cesspool in Hell. "They can break into your brain and make you do whatever they want! I knew it! My brain was part of the damn study!"

Evileye said, "Now you can sue somebody." It felt like they were peering through a time warp to witness the birth of evil. They had found the monster in CI's closet. Electronic language passing into people's brains. They stared at bio-tech specifics and remote programming formulas, and finally overwhelmed, Evileye's squirrelly voice yelled, "Yo, man! I'm done with this! These people are gonna take over the world! I'm gonna call my mom and forgive her while I still have a chance."

"But you see what's missing, don't you?"

"What's missing?"

"Everything!" Slash grunted. "Who are these people, man? Where are the specifics? How do they do it? See? We don't know nothing yet!"

Already Slash was fingering his speed dial without looking at the clock.

110

Victor answered with a grunt. It was five a.m. Slash was frightened for the first time in years, and he fumbled ahead, explaining his ominous findings. He could not stop himself from telling Victor the bad news, that Mr. Tao could get the icon thing for another fifty thousand dollars. But Slash was going to try first.

Straining for consciousness beside Nel in an old four-poster bed, Victor clicked on a dim lamp and wrote notes on how CI could break into your brain and make you do things.

On the morning of Sol Burligame's second Inauguration, Marianne Belonis shuffled merrily through her halfway house, rousing the guests and chanting patriotic slogans.

"Sweet land of liberty," she sang out in a glass-shattering soprano at Victor and Nel's door, "get ready for a revolution!" She'd been particularly taken with Mgaba last evening, and now she pounded pleasantly on his door. "Ask not what your country can do for you," came her sparkling voice. "Ask what you want for breakfast!"

Victor was pulling on his shirt and moving. "Downstairs, people. Foulks!" he called up the narrow stairway to the third floor. "Out of that fart sack! Senators! Congressmen! Heed you the call!" His mind was bleeding neurochemistry and speeches and band instruments, far too overloaded to feel any fear.

Food smells wafted through the fine old plantation, bacon and mushrooms and strong coffee. Mgaba, conscious overnight of the spirits of people once enslaved here, took time in his room to pray for their souls and to draw their shackled powers into himself. In the corner was the red umbrella he had purchased after the discreet conversation with Chloe Shapiro-Fujimoto. The Chief Justice would have no way of knowing whether all the complex plans were intact, so Mgaba would have to inform her, and at the same time let Agent Cool know. In the white-tiled bathroom, Courtman thought about catching a flight home, and he clutched his small white hands together and clenched his teeth until he nearly passed out. Waiting for him in the hall, Iona Webster went over for the thousandth time what she would say when the FBI arrested her. In the pocket of her bathrobe was her lawyer's card. She'd been holding it overnight, and wondering if she had removed her ex-husband as beneficiary on her life insurance policy. Courtman offered her a fresh pair of poly gloves, but she shook her head.

Molly Bee hadn't slept. Overnight she'd imagined a wild free-for-all at the Capitol, and in irrational non-sleep had begun to worry about feds busting into her apartment and stupidly hurting her dog. She wrote two columns in her head, one celebrating the successful rebellion, the other snuck out of her prison cell celebrating acts of patriotism when the rebellion collapsed. She could feel a tragedy about to unfold. If Edwin's magic worked her father would be fortune's fool. Perhaps the country would heal. Maybe the nation's path would be redirected toward the common good. But she would never forgive herself.

Nel and Victor had not thought about making love. But in the middle of the night Nel whispered that they would take care of that as soon as this was over. Victor told her if for some unthinkable reason nothing happened, if the Inauguration proceeded as intended, she was to go stay with her mother on the island till she heard from him. Her answer was, "Do you think I'm going to stay with my mother if you're in trouble? Do you know me?"

"People, more news." Victor flapped open a linen napkin at the long table smothered with the lavish breakfast. You could feel the restrained tension, the moment before the starting gun. "It's finally happened. The lunatics are running the asylum!" He explained Slash's chilling discovery the best he could – CI was probably tapping into people's brains. "It's illegal, immoral, and monstrous," he growled. "And we got the information illegally. But it's disgusting nonetheless. I have a feeling that wacko Slash will be asking for more dough real soon." He looked around at tired but not surprised faces. He closed his eyes a moment. "Okay. What we're going to do is get hold of earphone devices for myself and Edwin, the kind the Secret Service uses. We should be able to communicate any last minute information anybody comes up with."

"Think of it," Edwin said. "Controlling the world through mass communications! Television! Didn't somebody predict this about 1950? Anybody could have figured this out. Enough monkeys with enough typewriters."

Somehow Edwin's fears had diminished overnight. His

mind was clear. Part of him wished they'd found hard evidence that would put Hellman out. But that was the way of it. The foolish struggles of people to hurt each other, to control, to misunderstand the simple nature of things – it would all go on forever.

At the same time, he was not anxious to go to prison.

111

At the junction of the Potomac and Anacostia Rivers, just within the city limits, was Bolling Air Force Base. This morning an unusual exercise was under way, involving the United States Army.

Apparently a bunch of Airborne paratroopers were going to jump out of perfectly good airplanes and land in downtown D.C. just about the time the Commander-in-Chief was being sworn in. Why anybody would do anything so stupid in the dead of winter with snow predicted was beyond the comprehension of the Air Force people stationed at Bolling. Bigwigs were always demanding weird ceremonies and flashy stuff around Washington. In any case, a military limo bearing the circled stars of the Joint Chiefs of Staff arrived at the crack of dawn. The youthful second lieutenant at the wheel, assistant to the Aide for Admiral Sukwant Singh, bore orders to locate the Airborne troops who had been shipped here overnight in preparation for the jump over the Capitol area. The LZ had been carefully planned for the National Mall, but there were new orders. The officer needed to find Sergeant Major Clark, one of the Airborne NCO's responsible for the jump.

Eventually the lieutenant found Sergeant Major Clark in a freshly painted temporary barracks. The lieutenant approached Clark, carrying a military duffel bag.

"You are ordered to take your drop with a subordinate of your choice and float this banner between you," the lieutenant said. "You have been picked since you have jumped with banners in the past. You understand the aerodynamics and the procedure."

Clark withdrew a pack of cigarettes, lit one, and blew the smoke out the side of his mouth. He had been in the Army twenty-nine years, four months, and eleven days.

"Sir, with all respect, what in the name of Blue Jesus are

you talking about?"

"Your LZ," the lieutenant, who had been in the Army eleven months and one day, said, "is directly before the podium on the Capitol steps, at precisely 1200 hours. Is that clear?" He was uncomfortable making eye contact with this hard enlisted man. So he focused on the olive drab duffel bag and the printed orders. Sergeant Major Clark looked at him with the cigarette hanging from his lips as if he were addressing a visitor from Mars. "Additionally," the lieutenant said, "you are not to read, nor comment on, the words on this banner. These orders come directly from the Pentagon. Are we clear?" he said again.

In a quick moment Clark envisioned what the punk lieutenant was ordering him to do. Had he remembered his Shakespeare, he would have thought it was a tale told by an idiot.

"I'm short, Lieutenant," he said. "Two hundred twenty-eight days and a wake up. Are you sure you got the right Clark?"

The young officer shoved the duffel bag at him, spun on his patent leather shoes, and departed.

112

It was harder doing serious work on the Jersey Turnpike, especially the way Desdemona drove. Slash was getting nowhere. He had to admit his skills were puny compared to the formidable Mr. Tao. He called Congressman Sligo. All humor was gone. He had failed. Twice.

"So let's see," Victor said on his squeaky new white phone. "For another fifty grand you might get what you want?" He already knew the money was in place.

"Yessir," the deeply abashed Slash Zewinta admitted.

"And you might not?"

"Yessir."

"We have the money transfer code here. If you get no further, Slash, I'm sending you a bill. You understand?"

"Yessir."

They were careening madly off the Baltimore-Washington

Parkway when she spotted the Capitol dome just as Mr. Tao's text popped up on the laptop. Stuck in her sun visor were two contraband tickets to the Inauguration, provided by the man mumbling beside her.

"Give me your icon set," Mr. Tao's instructions read. "And the name with each one."

Slash and Desdemona looked at each other mournfully. In unison they said, "Dung beetles!"

Edwin suddenly remembered the uniforms. Racing out to the van, not sure where he was going, he kicked a large carton on the sun porch. No name, no address. Just a big box. He found Ms. Belonis and asked what she knew about it. "Goodness, I don't know," she hedged. "I didn't –"

"Mind if I open it," Edwin said, already with a thumbnail on the blade of his pocket knife.

The box contained two mothball-smelling blue band uniforms in plastic bags, two full-length coats, two purple and yellow military saucer caps, two pairs of boots and spats, and two clarinets broken down in black instrument cases. One uniform was larger than the other. He brought the box to Victor, sipping coffee in the dining room.

Victor held up his uniform, with the US shield across the back, red shoulder braids and insignia on the sleeves. "You scared?" He seemed a bit off kilter himself.

Edwin sat. "Sure I'm scared. It's going to end today, one way or the other. We could wind up in some place where they put bad people! You know what they do. They penetrate your body parts! I'd rather be hanged, frankly."

"No, no, leave that alone," Victor told him. "There will be none of that. I'm too important. They're all scared to death of the Vice President and he doesn't dare to actually lock me up. And brother, my fate is your fate. He might have us assassinated. But what for?" He held up a long hand, elbow on the table. Edwin took it and squeezed, like they were arm wrestling. He looked the Congressman in the eye.

"Do we have a plan? Or don't we?"

Slipping on a pair of black-rimmed shades, Victor Sligo said, "We'll soon find out."

Traffic picked up as Molly steered the rental van toward the district line. It was 10:20 when they reached the Florida Avenue Metro Station and had to walk. Troops were in abundance, wearing berets of various colors and passionately shined boots, some carrying crowd-control Projectile Launchers. A hundred or more school buses lined North Capitol Street and the side streets. High school and college kids in band costumes plugged the boulevard. A Metro cop had been assigned to each bus. Silhouettes of armed men were visible on the roof of every building. Troop carriers were parked on the side streets. It felt like martial law had already been declared.

This was the meeting place.

In full National Marching Band regalia, Victor and Edwin separated from the others without a word, and moved into the throng of chilly musicians.

The atmosphere could not be described as revolutionary. People mingled and wandered in every direction. An inordinate number of very large dogs seemed to have taken to the streets, tethered to an inordinate number of serious-looking men with long coats and bleak faces and black gloves. Smoke drifted from somewhere. Fluttering wind instruments and crashing cymbals occasionally split the air. It was cold and overcast. Not quite miserable, but darkness striated with silver loomed to the west. To the south, a blotch of sunlight. It was twenty-four degrees Fahrenheit. Pretty cheerleaders bearing snappy pompoms walked arm in arm, freezing. More buses arrived, cramming more tympanums and euphoniums and piccolos into the maelstrom of paraders.

On the local Real Radio, Alice Duplantis was broadcasting to the rebels the location and number of military troops, FBI SWAT teams, helicopters and others who might interfere with their interference. In the spirit of the morning, Alice went so far as to name some of the patrol dogs on duty for the Inauguration: King and Duke, Roger, Fang, Trouble and George W.

Uptown about two miles, in his block-long executive mansion on Champlain Street below Columbia Road, the Vice President of the United States tossed back his bald head and gargled. They'd be picking him up shortly for the official start of his next four years. And there would be plenty of years after that. Feeling pretty damn fine today. He studied his impressive tan physique and flexed, glancing at the faded horseshoe-shaped tattoo on the inside of his left forearm. He pulled on the silk long johns, the white silk shirt and black tuxedo trousers. Snapping down the suspenders, he admired himself again. No wonder they'd elected him. What a man! Is this man not deserving of great power! And he clapped his muscular hands together once, as though smashing a bug or declaring the Olympics open. A knock came to the outer door.

"Yeah, okay," he called out, and slipped on the hand-tooled pancake holster.

The United States Capitol Building is a sprawling multi-level architectural masterpiece whose grounds occupy over two hundred acres of the Federal City in downtown Washington. On these grounds, spectators would be crammed in the thousands to witness the swearing-in ceremony. They have done this at the Capitol for two centuries. The swearing-in ceremony always takes place on the steps of the Capitol, witnessed back in the day by up to a quarter of a million onlookers and dignitaries. I-Media reported one hundred million viewers worldwide during the last Inauguration. The Marine Band played on the marble terrace below the actual site of the swearing-in. Afterwards, the whole entourage walked or drove en mass to the Reviewing Stand at the White House, where the rest of the parade passed before the newly inaugurated President and Vice President, the Cabinet, the Joint Chiefs, members of the Supreme Court, and a great variety of toadies and coattail-riders, all more or less in bondage to the new heads of government.

But those days were over.

Now the world was out of control. Urban terrorists and crackpots of all sorts used the Internet to fund, plan and carry out subversive activities, particularly to engage people to blow up Americans. Officials withheld the parade route until the day of the Inauguration. Security was so tight a blind person's companion dog near a Harmful Devices Detector might be shot on sight. Metro Police stopped all traffic going into the area at checkpoints in every direction. Officers did in fact stop the cream-colored van in front of Howard University, along with the stream of vehicles heading into downtown. Molly Bee had simply handed the handsome young city cop her journalist's credentials and driver's license and smiled her sweetest smile at him, and they had proceeded.

This year's substantive change was that the swarms of bands and parade officials, the drill teams and motorcycle groups and mounted police, would parade only to the Capitol building. In fact, there would be no reviewing stand this year. No parade to the White House. Rumors had been floated that the swearing-in would take place at the Washington Monument, the Jefferson Memorial, even on Roosevelt Island. Special Forces, Navy SEALs, and combat infantry were highly visible. Both Marine and Homeland Security helicopters crisscrossed forbidden air space continually. Twenty-seven actors had been hired in look-alike roles, sitting in for the senators and congressmen, two US ambassadors and several deputy assistant directors, who did not wish to risk their lives just to watch the President and Vice President take the oath of office.

By eleven o'clock the official I-Media crews had been in place for an hour and a half and were each shadowed by one of the non-union teams Molly had conscripted through her producer friend Bliss. John Lee Davis had managed to supply Bliss's people – six groups complete with state-of-the-art 3D cameras and broadcast equipment – with credentials granting them access to the Capitol grounds. Some I-Media employees recognized the underground broadcasters and cameramen. A certain amount of nudging and winking took place, some scowling and marking of turf within the Capitol circumference, where only people wearing the large red, white and blue ID badges could enter. Bliss himself, not a broadcaster due to a lifetime hearing impediment, directed the operation from an innocuous hot dog vending truck parked on the south side of the Library of Congress. He wore a spanking new gray armband to honor his working mother. On the windshield of the truck, visible only by infrared scanning device, was Davis's official FBI sticker.

Under the fabled clock at Union Station, Euphonia Lee, conductor of the National Marching Band, watched the time, and spoke in nervous whispers with Congressman Victor Sligo and another clarinetist she had never seen before. With Sligo's week-old speckled gray beard and sunglasses and uniform and saucer hat, she had not recognized him until he introduced himself.

She was built not unlike her father, tall and intense and quite attractive, and just as articulate and tough-minded. She had been directed in person by the Chairman of the Joint Chiefs of Staff, an Admiral named Singh. A harmonious name, she'd thought. Like her own. She would conduct her 120-piece band down Louisiana Avenue and onto First Street. Then instead of continuing around past the Reflecting Pool, she would turn the Marching Band left and come directly toward the Capitol itself, with the tens of thousands of onlookers and police and the entire US intelligence community expecting this to happen, Admiral Singh had said. All the hush-hush plans of the past weeks had changed again. They were to march right up the walkway, through the crowd to the marble terrace and stop, continuing with whatever they were playing – it would be Sousa's *Washington Post* just there – while the two new band members, alone, walked up the steps to join the Inaugural group. For those fifteen seconds or so the world would be holding its breath. It was a daring scheme. The two band members in full uniform would appear to be presenting some gift to the President. It was, after all, his day. No security official or cop would imagine it was not part of the ceremony.

That's what they hoped.

Twenty-six hundred miles away and seven hundred feet underground, Dr. Sage Kuushmann was juicing his morning carrot-prune-grapefruit-raw-egg cocktail and readying himself to sabotage the eastern United States communications grid. His plan would take I-Media down with it. Well, yes, I-Media was purportedly a private enterprise, the media partition of Communication International. But everybody in the country had watched the inbreeding as the Newfies deregulated everything, opened doors for massive trade monopolies, and allowed CI to overwhelm the North American broadcast, news and entertainment industries.

For a man like Kuushmann, this was tantamount to handing the nation over to the criminals. The difference between them and Stalin's Communists in Kuushmann's mind was that the Commies buttoned their wool jackets up to their necks, and the CI boys wore three-piece Armani suits. Both crowds were dedicated to the same premise: take everything, and make the people pay for it.

He was ready. An emergency crew was in place for a bit of Sunday OT. The White House, the military, and NSA had engaged so much satellite energy for the Inauguration, Kuushmann had told his people in Groom Lake, that they had to be prepared to activate the emergency Intelsat override in case of signal failure.

In a little over an hour he would have two minutes to help heal his country. It wasn't much. But it was something.

Mumbling half-consciously to himself, Edwin Foulks wandered among the band members, his face numb from cold, wearing the earpiece and invisible transceiver and microphone, and holding with freezing fingerless gloves the instrument he knew absolutely nothing about. He had memorized a dozen questions to ask the Vice President, but not one came to mind just now.

The feeling in his gut was one of raw terror.

Thirty-five miles northeast, not far from Camden Yards, Evileye was singing an obscene version of *My Country 'Tis of Thee.* On his monitor was the list of icons Slash had compiled related to anything political, chemical, corporate, or technological. From the video he'd seen of Tyne and Hellman thumping on each other in a Cabinet meeting, he'd registered the horseshoe-shaped thing, and when he saw the banner at Tyne's house he knew it meant something. He'd shot the word "horseshoe" to Mr. Tao. In addition, Slash passed on orders he'd gotten from the black lady on Sligo's staff – the one who almost looked like she could have played football once. She told him to get Mr. Tao to program his search engine for inner office memos addressed to only a first name, or "gentlemen" or "Group Consultants," or not addressed to anybody, just instructions. She told him to search for neurochemical programming and BCI and Reese and Ferrari and Tyne. Evileye sent it through to Mr. Tao.

But nothing kept coming back.

113

The stage was set. In her finest winter coat, nearly covering her most revealing black dress, Leora Psybysch knew she had examined every possible contingency. The Inauguration was going to create the standard for all future historic occasions in this grand and ridiculous city. She had spent months in preparation, working with six different police agencies, bending the brain of Needham Strange and his Homeland Security commandoes till the bombs burst in her hair, to make it perfect.

Vice President Hellman deserved nothing less than the grandest coronation ever to be staged on the planet. Yes, and the President too.

She had finagled a seat among the hundreds of rows of Lesser Dignitaries, in the wings perhaps sixty feet from the podium, beside another great American, Philadelphia's Chief of Police, Giuseppe Manicotti. Fat for Psybysch's taste, but well-connected and powerful. She nodded perfunctorily and sat. Everybody was aware that Ms. Sligo had embarrassed Manicotti out at Ney Field a few days ago. Later *Big Shots*, the glamour rag, ran a photo of the police chief drunk in a bar in Manhattan. Their reporter had shoved himself in for an interview. The Chief did not hide his contempt for Congressman Sligo, but made only the cryptic remark that he could have just as much fun shooting at clay pigeons.

Which aroused further lusty speculation from those who speculated lustily on the rich and famous. As it happened, Clay Pigeons was the stage name of a male stripper currently plying his trade over in Jersey.

The big man watched Psybysch sit demurely beside him, took a moment to gawk at her chest, and knew instantly what she was thinking. He growled at her, "If they show up here, I'm gonna get up and piss on both of them."

For the first time in history, a stadium-sized television screen had been mounted over the front entrance of the Capitol, above and behind the Inaugural ceremonies, apparently to provide onlookers with the glaring close-ups the folks at home were even now appreciating. The camera silently swept toward the front, zooming in here and there to catch a basketball player or a retired postal inspector.

The giant screen was no surprise to Leora Psybysch. Her boss had demanded it. After his first inauguration Hellman had to go home to Champlain Street to watch his own coronation – and this time he wanted to be able to see the entire historic event in person. Himself playing himself. Unfortunately he would have to turn around to see the screen high over the main archway of the Capitol. But it was the best Psybysch could do. She glanced up to have a look. The screen now closed in on the fearsome cast of American political authority. Just behind the ebony podium, President Burligame, in white scarf and black full length coat, chatting with his wife and son. As always, the daughter was missing. Beside him sat Vice President Hellman and two shivering Secret Service men. To their left, the entire sixteen-member Cabinet. On the right sat all nine black-robed Justices of the Supreme Court. Behind them, the majority leaders of the Senate and House of Representatives, flanked by their second numbers, the heads of committees, the great and nearly great, the military and civic authorities, and all around them, the wannabe great, the used-to-be great, the probably never would be great. Even Archbishop Goldberg had scored a seat close up with the notables, where he sat nervously scanning the crowd. Overall, Psybysch noted, the most ruthless collection of villains ever to be assembled in one body at one time. She noticed even Tenacia Friggie had a good seat. The irony bit at her. The real perk in Washington, the demonstration of genuine power, was sitting in a heated seat at the Inauguration. Everybody else literally froze their butts off.

Four hundred feet farther back, in frigid folding chairs amongst thousands of others, two renegades sat hunched over a laptop. Dressed for the queen's wedding, in her fabulous white leather coat, Desdemona realized she could be recognized on camera, but she clung to the feeling that something was about to break open. Legs shaking violently beside her, Slash waited for Mr. Tao, still shuffling icons, his microphone open to Sligo's people, completely without a Hostess Twinkie all morning. Desdemona happened to be looking up to the big screen when a strange thing happened. The camera had crunched down to close-ups of Cabinet members, and had passed Attorney General Jim Turcutt and settled on the Secretary of Communications, Hunter Tyne. Obviously unaware of the scrutiny, Tyne, dressed unconventionally in a brown overcoat and white silk scarf and brown leather gloves, was rubbing the back of his neck and talking on a phone, his face distressed as though, well, Desdemona thought, as though the entire process was a pain in the neck.

Slash glanced up. "Man, if we could tap into that big screen! Wow!" He'd forgotten his microphone was open. A few blocks away Bliss heard and was already pulling up a program.

Desdemona's eyes lingered on the screen, which by now had progressed to Dewalt Ryobi, Secretary of Labor. "Hey," she said quietly, keeping her body close over the laptop. "That was our boy Tyne. Who would want to talk to him on the phone? The Hillside Strangler?"

Distracted, Slash misheard, thought she wanted another look at Hellman strangling him. He clicked back to the video on his laptop, but he clicked the wrong sequence with his freezing fingers, and the image popped up of the Congressman's hiding place back in Ireland. The log house, the monitor, the big picture window – it was a cold sunny day there – and the old farm truck parked outside. Nobody was around. Desdemona squinted at the scene.

"Wait, that ain't it," Slash said. He started to click again, but she touched his hand to stop him. They both stared at the image a moment. Sunshine poured through the window of the log house. The old truck. Slash glanced at Desdemona, and then he did click back to the blond woman's video. They saw the Vice President nearly strangling Tyne, tearing his shirt back and revealing the faded red tattoo and yelling something at him. Desdemona said, "Go back." He did. Through the window at Edwin's house, the hay truck stood in the winter sunlight. She bent to the microphone and whispered, "Hey! Anybody there?"

It took a moment. An unshaven BJ Lichtenstein came to the screen in a wife-beater undershirt and dress pants. "Look out the window," Desdemona whispered. "See that truck out there?"

"Is that you, Slash?" BJ said, rubbing his eyes. He was holding a mug of coffee. He glanced at his watch, and began speaking fast. "Listen to this! I just spent two days and two nights on this Holotech deal." He yawned and slapped his face. "Pass this on to Sligo right now. Somebody I know at IRS knows somebody on the Nevada Tax Commission. Turns out Mr. Hellman made substantial investments as Vice President, even though his money was legally unavailable in a blind trust. He made out like a bandit on Holotech Television shares –" He snatched up a notepad, "– just before the Holotech market skyrocketed. Probably at least conflict of interest. Or insider trading. He profited massively. It was about four years ago. Right about the time –"

"Yes, yes," Desdemona said, mortified that somebody might overhear, scrunching down hard to whisper into her laptop. "I

have it. I'll tell him. We need a favor. That thing hanging off the
end of that truck. What is that?" BJ blinked at the screen. Then out
the window. Shrugging, he disappeared. A moment later they could
see him outside, blowing on his fingers, unscrewing something from
the truck bumper. He reappeared, holding it up. It was a horseshoe-
shaped piece of steel with holes drilled through each end. A bolt
screwed into the holes.

"What is that," Desdemona breathed, bending further down,
with Slash close beside her.

"This?" He held it up, slid the bolt through one hole and
screwed it into the opposite hole. "I have no idea. But wait a sec."
He grabbed the other laptop on the plywood desk and in a few moments pulled up the photo of the banner in Hunter Tyne's basement.
The image was there overlapping the red Knights Templar cross. "Is
that it?"

Slash clicked back to the video, and stopped it at Tyne's tattoo. It was a match.

Edwin Foulks was so nervous his stomach was reeling. He
picked miserably at his blue uniform. The band had formed up.
Ahead, the color guard. Immediately behind, the Old Guard, the
Third Army mounted brigade, great black horses snorting and blowing steam in the cold air. At least a hundred groups were lined up
behind them. The roaring and blaring and beating and snorting and
shouting were driving him crazy. He thought he was going to throw
up, standing beside Victor, legs shaking, head flashing from too
much coffee, the Congressman strong as an iron statue studying the
crowd. The thing in his ear had off and on crinkled with activity, but
he felt too wired, and too weird, to pay attention.

Suddenly came a shrill whistle from the front. A baton
lifted. Four sharp blasts on the whistle. The entire band lurched
ahead like a giant centipede, thrumming into *The Stars and Stripes
Forever*. The noise crushed into Edwin's ears, but he held the clarinet up to his lips and pretended to blow, although the woman beside
him was marching vigorously along holding her clarinet in front of
her, not playing. She snuck a suspicious glance at him. Motorcycle
cops and two-man motorcycle-mounted video crews puttered along
with the band. Behind them, frantic citizens waved flags and
shouted at relatives.

"Crockett! Crockett!" a voice hissed in Edwin's earpiece. He was so astonished he tripped, banging his instrument into the man ahead. "What?" he shouted over the blaring of the band.

Slash said, "What's that gizmo BJ's holding up that holds the thing onto the whatzit?"

Breakfast churned in Edwin's belly. He imagined himself heaving into his clarinet.

"Speak English!" he yelled. The woman beside him was getting edgy now, looking at him like he was from some other band.

"It's hanging on the back of the truck behind your house," Slash yelled back.

Edwin squinted. "Hanging on the –? The clevis? Is that what you mean?" The whistle trilled sharply and the band wheeled onto another boulevard. Finally Edwin moved the clarinet away from his mouth just as the woman beside him snapped hers to her lips, glared at him, and began playing madly. Cymbals exploded. Snare drums beat a crashing paradiddle that felt like it rose right in his groin and thundered into his chest. The woman had signaled to the man ahead of her, who now spun around, a big red-faced man holding a piccolo, walking backward, looking like he was about to punch Edwin. Instantly Victor yanked Edwin aside and took his place.

"Who are you people," the guy demanded. "What are you doing in my band?" His face had turned a strenuous reddish-purple. "I'm calling security!"

The brass section blared violently just ahead.

Victor moved in close. "If you speak another word, mister, I'm going to shove that piccolo so far up your ass you're going to see stars and stripes forever. Now turn around!"

The man shouted, "I'm the head of the woodwind section, and I think you people –" Victor tore off his hat and glasses and yelled, "I'm the head of the Progressive Party, and I think you'd better shut up and play!"

The man's jaw dropped. He looked at the woman, equally stunned. Both whipped their eyes back to Congressman Sligo and gasped. Then the woman raised her clarinet over her head.

"Halleluiah!" she shouted. The man blushed and said, "Go get 'em, Victor!" and turned his back.

"All right, all right," Victor said to Edwin, pale-faced and stricken beside him. "Take a breath. Get focused. We'll be there in a few minutes."

The speaker hissed in Edwin's ear. "Mr. Tao? We're going with clevis. Evileye? You're gonna to have to do this. My fingers are froze. Get back to the kid in Ireland and capture the thing he's holding."

114

Evileye, hanging on every syllable, had to come back to Slash to get the spelling of the word "clevis." For the moment Slash and Desdemona hung suspended, watching the big screen and hearing the thundering Marching Band half a mile away. Slash's big Mickey Mouse watch read 11:48. The laptop screen zoomed in on BJ holding the clevis in his hand.

Mr. Tao typed, "Got it."

A full minute passed. The band marched. Slash blew on his fingers. At the podium, Reverend Wildermuth was already shivering through the invocation. On the big screen, the Vice President was cackling with a Cabinet member. Once again Slash's laptop shot to life. But this time it didn't stop.

"Look at this, Mama!" he whisper-shouted at Desdemona.

On the display was the blurry black and white film of the atomic bomb exploding over Hiroshima. This image was replaced by endless columns of four-digit numbers. Pages and pages of files. Evidently the user had to know his way around. Picking a random number, Evileye clicked. A file opened.

As far as he could tell, the language was Korean. It had that look. He picked another number. The file read like a list of CEOs and bank directors and corporate honchos from two dozen different countries. Attendees at some function. A million files to check out. Ten minutes till noon. He clicked furiously, noticing the dates were moving forward in time, searching for anything that made sense. He whipped back up the list, and opened what looked like a parody of the Yalta photo of Churchill, Stalin and Roosevelt, all three of them half-smashed, buxom serving girls leaning over their shoulders. More weird alphabets. A photo of Rosy Greer amongst a frenzied crowd pining down Sirhan Sirhan in the pantry of the Ambassador Hotel. More lists. The WTO, the UN, the White House, a catalog of China's oil interests in Africa, the Tokyo Stock Exchange, Crédit Suisse, Banks in Manila and Beijing and Pyongyang and Medellin, Columbia; para-military organizations, weapons suppliers, and a clipping about somebody's wrecked Mercedes in Switzerland. He flashed past Pope Benedict dining with billionaire socialite Barb Burnett on her private island. Then a blaring headline on the airborne pathogen pandemic. Another weird alphabet. Turkish? No. Hebrew. "Yo, man," Slash whispered. "It's... This must be..."

The band blared down Louisiana Avenue as thousands watched on the enormous screen. Edwin struggled to clear his mind, looking at his shiny black boots and snazzy spats and calling his mother and father in his head, apologizing for whatever agony he was about to inflict upon their memories. The band ripped into *"Semper Fi,"* heavy on the clarinet, but there wasn't much Edwin could do but hold it up to his lips and fiddle with it. A sudden gust of wind whooshed down the column in front of him, and the smell of fresh snow filled his nostrils. He looked up. The front of the band was turning down toward the Capitol. He felt like a fool, a dumb mistake, a logger with a busted chain at the bottom of a ravine. The exile in a strange land. What to demand of the Vice President? His mind was blank. There was nothing of substance. Only the crashing six-eight tempo of the Marine Corps battle cry.

"Now listen," came Desdemona's steady voice into Victor's and Edwin's earbuds. Each man had to press a finger against his ear to hear. "We see you. You still have roughly five minutes. Listen carefully. Hellman profited big time when the Holotech television came out. He had to know something." Victor's brain was on fire. Maybe they did it through the Holotech. Truman Butts flew into his mind. They had shut down his contract with voting machines a couple of years ago. Victor had bought his own Holotech that fall. He felt as if he had always suspected something, but was too hypnotized himself to do anything about it. CI controls your life and tells you when to move and when to stop. Programming your neurochemicals.

Over the past days he had pieced this together, but now it sounded confirmed. He bit the mouthpiece of his clarinet. He had devoted a lifetime of service to a country where people were free to experiment on human brains for fun and profit. To lock up elections for the people funding the experiments. But we'll never prove it, he was thinking. Not in a million years. He shot a glance at Edwin. "Did you get that?"

Chattering with cold and fear, Edwin looked back and shook his head, then nodded, then shrugged. He couldn't focus.

"Stand by for the next bit," Desdemona said. "I don't know what it is, but Slash looks like he's attending his own funeral."

Forgetting to breathe, Evileye scrambled through files, and found a large group in blue numbers. He clicked the first one. Words flew out at his eyes: "Holotech marketing campaign will begin in Indonesia to create the impression..." He clicked blindly. "The HIV epidemic should certainly be advantageous to our..." Now he was getting angry all over again. Another click. "...will continue the disinformation campaign with every member of Congress until they grasp our ..."

Who are these people?

Mr. Tao had another treat for Slash. A formal letter popped onto the screen. The clevis icon was in the corner. It was dated one month ago. He scanned it wild-eyed.

Dear Ms ——:

May we express our deepest sympathy on the passing of your grandfather, Frederick H. ——, II. His contribution to the growth of the Group was immeasurable. Mr. —— suggested this succinct recent history for your perusal.

Mr. Parakrananda, Delhi 4682, will guide you through the final weeks of your indoctrination.

Events in the Middle East from 1956 through 2001 led to amalgamation of entities with the common objective of worldwide economic harmony. The Illuminati, deeply imbedded in the United States and the Moslem territories, joined forces with the European guild known in the West as Bilderbergers. The Group administered political units prior to, and eventually created, the European Union. Since the Group directed economic policy in post-war U.S. and Soviet governments, amalgamation was inevitable. The New Templars, the Zionists and the CFR saw the advantage in membership. This left the Subcontinent, and warring factions spawned from the

"Black Dragon" Yakuso group as well as China's Hung and Ching societies. The Japanese chose to remain independent following the forced devaluation of the yen. Through accord reached in Beijing following the so-called "airborne pathogen pandemic," and several other race-specific bio-terrorist actions, both the Chinese and the Indians were integrated.

His eyes fled through paragraphs like his head was in a noose. His brain screamed, *This is them!* Communication International, huh? Like hell it is!

I-Media was showing a formation of military aircraft heading towards the Capitol from Bolling Air Force Base. In a smaller pane filling a quarter of the screen were the Blue Angels, seven F140's already screaming up from Norfolk, from the carrier *Barach Obama.*

Slash saw it finally: the fate of the free world was in his hands. Nine minutes till noon. For sure a bomb was going to explode any second. Okay. He clicked through to the bottom page, and allowed himself three seconds to scan fragments of messages, all dated in the last twelve months.

"The Eugenics Program poses the danger of unleashing..."

"Mr. Julio Reese, the liberal commentator, will continue..."

"Funds will move through friendly South American entities and be made available to deflect the British government's... "

"...through a slight modification to Article II of the US Constitution, Caliban will maintain the position of Vice President so long as..."

"Crockett!" he shouted into the mike, and had to contain himself when Desdemona slapped a hand across his mouth. "Listen!" He knelt on the frigid grass and held the laptop mike to his face and whispered as loudly as he could. "Clevis is the Society With No Name! They control everything! That's what the tattoo means! Billy Hellman is their main guy! Get out of that parade, man, before they –"

He felt it coming, felt it coming, and banged his head on the chair ahead of him. He could taste blood, but at least it was warm. In intense blackness, he heard himself thinking. Never in his most delusional, drug-induced fantasy had he figured the actual bad guys, the real, no kidding Society With No Name, the guys who ran Wall Street and organized wars and fixed oil prices, were taking over the planet using plain old voters to help their cause.

Warmth beside his face. Blood? No. Desdemona was down with him, blowing carefully on his face, holding his chin up so he wouldn't choke on his own vomit, speaking soothingly, waving off other people beside them.

They were busy faking *Semper Fi*, marching down First Street, listening to every word. Victor checked his watch. Four minutes. They crossed Constitution, the crowd freezing and cheering all around them. A protester boosted up a poster: "Where are you hiding Victor Sligo?" Already the huge screen was visible, hanging on the Capitol, presently focusing on Julio Reese with his magnificent white mustache, along with two I-Media people pontificating somberly from a glass broadcast booth at the east end of the grounds as if nothing were amiss.

Edwin Foulks had never seen the Capitol before. Even with Victor watching him, and Slash's voice woofing in his ears, he raised his eyes in awe at the fabulous structure. Then he located the Inaugural group at the podium, the cutthroats running his beautiful country. God only knew what was true and what wasn't. Regardless of Molly Bee's story about her father, just now looking alone and at peace on the big screen, the violin face, the vivid scars around the eyes. A smaller screen popped up on the big screen beside the President. It was Julio Reese, chatting with the nation. Edwin remembered Desdemona's – and practically everybody's – theory about Julio tossing up his pencil. He was being *ironic*! Didn't anybody realize that?

Sloan Mgaba was also feeling the weight of the entire planet on his broad wool-clad shoulders. The red umbrella lay across his lap. Disconnected as they were, Victor's staff was without information at the moment. All they had was the unfolding of events, mentally keeping an exit strategy handy in case of catastrophe. The band was visible now at the far edge of the grounds. The official program called for the band to stop along the circular drive at the outside fringe of the grounds, and immediately the United States Marine Band would begin to play, on the lower level of the Capitol steps. Nel Sligo had said that if anything went wrong, it would be plainly visible on the big screen. By twelve o'clock the cat would be out of the bag. By twelve ten, she said, the world would be a different place. She'd sounded about as convincing as Santa Claus.

Sitting beside Courtman, mutely bundled against the cold, Mgaba waited for the sign from the Chief Justice. But all he felt was dread. Any moment, he and Courtman would be spotted by one of the five thousand or so Congressional employees he'd come to either admire or despise. The House of Representatives was a fool's paradise and they all knew it. And they were all here, each clutching one rung on the ladder, pulled at from below, spat on from above.

For a full week Mgaba had fought off flashes of the Central African violence. It sputtered in the back of his mind, the torture of the President, the burning of whole villages in the north, and his terrifying escape only days ahead of certain execution by yet another band of rebels. Now he was about to witness the West's version, a bloodless palace coup. Nobody who wanted to continue his career would participate in this madness. In fact, when he checked his office email this morning, he found a note from his NSA connection, Bert O'Donnell, posted from a commercial front in Puerto Vallarta. The note said, "Have a nice day. Regards to Iona."

The Chief Justice was scanning the crowd, searching for him. Mgaba's heart leapt. Were they ready? Was he? Who was Edwin Foulks, really? Was he some kind of post-modern Elmer Gantry, that sweet façade disguising a psychotic butcher? There was supposed to be a major diversion at the start of the ceremony to protect Edwin from the authorities for a couple of minutes. But Davis had not communicated with Mgaba about it. Now on the big screen he saw Shapiro-Fujimoto close up, standing with another vaguely familiar woman, searching the crowd with both hands to her cheeks. This was the sign. He had to return the countersign, that Sligo and Foulks were at hand. Uncertain, his arm numb with fear, he raised the red umbrella and snapped it open, aiming it toward the podium. The eyes of the Chief Justice moved right to left, and suddenly she dropped her hands. She had seen him. Immediately she looked at her watch, spun around, and picked up the Bible from the podium.

Fifty rows closer, Molly Bee, sitting with Nel, Iona Webster and Raven, studied her father. He was about to have the worst day of his life. The final family argument had come back to her during the drive in this morning – that suppressed, suffocating Burligame family version of fighting. It was snowing, as it always did in Central Minnesota when it wasn't hot. She was twenty-one, vigorous

and naïve and desperate for experience, and she had finally gotten
up the courage to announce she could no longer stand any of it, the
whole lot of them hanging on the coattails of her father's career, a
fawning, phony cardboard mock-up of a man in a world of suffering. She'd spat out Progressive phrases – from the books of Hubert
Humphrey and Eugene McCarthy and Walter Mondale – about poverty and injustice, and why in the name of everything sacred did he
have to sabotage the budget for the state mental health facilities in
order to cut taxes for the rich? Why did he cling to those morons
running the state political machine?

Her mother had stood helplessly watching, and her father
simply did not know how to respond.

It was the last time she'd ever seen him face to face. Until
today.

115

11:57. Major Gary Anderson, conductor of the Marine
Band, stood at the ready. One hundred thousand people waited. Ten
million more watched their televisions. Suddenly the cold sky was
filled with billowing red white and blue parachutes. Muted fire-
works exploded around the circumference of the Capitol grounds.
The crowd cheered.

On schedule, Sol Burligame rose, followed by Billy Hellman. They took the four steps to the podium, and stood before the
Chief Justice. The President and Shapiro-Fujimoto were both about
six feet tall, and thoroughly dwarfed Hellman. Attorney General Jim
Turcutt sat immediately to the left, beside the Secretary of Defense,
Graham St. John. Behind Turcutt was John Lee Davis, also in the
required white silk scarf and black coat, profoundly hung over,
squinting at this moment into the sky, for the life of him not able to
recall what the diversion was that was supposed to stop the ceremony till Sligo arrived. He had heard nothing this morning. So apparently Sligo had not been snatched at the Velasquez condo on
Virginia Avenue. Blue Angels soared in from all directions. Out at
the fringe of the crowd he could just see his daughter's band moving
into the circle. They would be turning toward the shivering crowd

any second – yes, they were moving in now. The band blared the *Washington Post* march. It was snowing, but the parachutists were coming straight down. The wind had subsided. Davis was so tense he could barely get his breath. The Chief Justice handed the Bible to a woman he knew he had seen recently, but could not place. The woman wore a red coat and red snood covering her hair, and she accepted the Bible showing no emotion.

Just down from Davis, presidential press secretary Joel Babylon wiped snow from his glasses, wondering what the hell this band leader thought she was doing. Psybysch, he thought. Some new cockamamie plan approved by nobody, just to please her nasty little boss.

Musicians were looking oddly at one another, instruments swaying in the cold, watching Euphonia as she brazenly plunged into the broad aisle of the Inaugural audience, baton prodding the heavens. On the big screen, Julio Reese looked surprised, scanning the official script before him and pointing to the Marching Band. In crisp full-dress uniform, Major Anderson, below the inaugural stand, had his baton already raised. He whipped around with a look of confusion and horror on his face, as Euphonia and her band marched up the aisle toward him. Automatically the outer columns of the band squeezed in behind the central marchers, playing heartily, watching Euphonia. On the long waving blast from her whistle, they stopped, stepping in place, the glorious *Washington Post* march thundering across the Capitol grounds. Immediately Victor grabbed Edwin by one arm and they pushed through to the front of the band, then continued walking past the murmuring crowd toward the marble steps.

A pair of D.C. cops stood between them and the steps, looking bewildered at each other. Tilting his head, Victor said quietly, "Mr. Foulks. I just want to remind you, it would be easier to roll back the stone and bring Jesus out, than to get Hellman to tell the truth." His eyes held steady on the two cops. He flashed a smile.

All morning Edwin had been struggling to locate the core of his being. Something was moving in him finally, here in the center of this historic place. It was always this way, when the pressure was unbearable and everybody else was panicking. He was nervous, still clearing the trash out of his head, this Clevis whatever-it-was forming a tapestry in his brain all by itself. He picked up Victor's cue as they closed in on the cops.

"That farmer," Edwin said in the same low tone. "One of those Mennonites? He couldn't remember to vote." He glanced at Victor. "He watched Julio Reese on Public Television, and he forgot to vote. Isn't that something?" His stomach was churning like a slow blender, but his mind had settled.

"Yeah," Victor said, distracted, eyes glued to the two husky Metro policemen blocking their path. "That's something." Then walking tall and self-assured, Victor called loudly, "Good morning gentlemen!" They marched past, directly up the marble steps toward the podium.

Edwin began pulling in deep, slow breaths.

Leora Psybysch felt an uncomfortable twitch in her body. Obviously there was a problem. These two were not on her agenda. Incensed, she jumped up, unintentionally pushing against Chief Manicotti's massive thigh, and pointed to them. Manicotti growled, "Hey! Sit!" But she didn't sit. She had to alert the Vice President. Already two Secret Service agents were closing in from the front of the crowd. Psybysch quickly pawed through her purse for her phone to notify the Vice President's people something was amiss. Then she froze. Chief Justice Shapiro-Fujimoto nodded openly to the two men in the band uniforms, and turned back to Burligame and Hellman. Shapiro-Fujimoto's creased face occupied the full giant screen, and one hundred thousand people watched her turn her head upward to observe the falling paratroopers. Two of them had maneuvered neatly a hundred yards overhead, and one shot a cord across to the other with some kind of power dart. A silver and blue banner unfolded between them, flapped madly a moment, and settled.

The banner read, *Rebellion.com.*

There was a stunned moment. Then a spontaneous roar erupted from the crowd. Leora Psybysch opened her mouth, but only an anguished gurgle came from her throat. She fell back into her seat like she'd been struck by a bad idea.

The paratroopers landed in tandem in front of the podium. They took a couple of recovery steps, disconnected their chutes and stood at attention before the eyes of the entire United States government. The outrageous silver and blue banner stretched taut between them, the most bizarre scene in political memory.

Within fifteen seconds, twenty million people were glued to

their televisions.

Then everything happened at once. On the great marble platform, a dozen public figures went into action. The two Secret Service men spun instantly and moved toward the paratroopers, jabbering into their head sets. The Vice President shot forward like a torpedo, bellowing, "Just what the hell do you people think you're doing? Mister, get your –" The Chief Justice pushed a white-gloved hand in his face, stopping him cold. Surprise, rage and exhilaration exploded everywhere. Uniformed Homeland Security people were trying to launch themselves through the clamoring mass of humanity, and others in convulsions of anger were preventing them from moving. Below the pandemonium, the Marine Corps band stammered into *"Hail to the Chief,"* which only added to the frenzy. By now Victor and Edwin were standing in front of the banner. The Chief Justice was yelling into the microphone demanding silence, pounding her hand against the podium, and to her obvious surprise, people ceased their roaring to see what would happen next. The band staggered to a stop.

You could feel it in the air. A pendulum was swinging before the eyes of the nation, suspended by the bright banner declaring that the rebellion had arrived at the Capitol, and it was swinging right into the face of the Vice President. Julio Reese lit his pipe on national television for the first time in fifty-two years, and watched. A new group of cameramen squirmed forward with their unwieldy equipment. The huge screen dimmed, then went into a shuddering spasm. The screen went black. In an eyeblink the frenzied scene returned, but with a different coloration, like different televisions in a store window. The screen showed the Inaugural party in shocked confusion at the podium, and the camera moved in closer until the entire nation was watching the two men in band uniforms standing before the President and the Vice President. The two closest Secret Service agents stopped in their tracks, unable to communicate, gaping at each other, pointing at their earbuds and shrugging.

Neither military nor city police nor the sixteen security agencies present could make their phones work. A box in the corner of the big screen appeared as a second camera zoomed in on Archbishop Goldberg, just behind the Supremes. Was he laughing? He was pushing toward the podium, white cassock flying, smacking the air before him with karate blows.

The Archbishop was wondering whether somebody would finally make a Cabinet post for clergy.

All the way down in the enlisted men's day room in Groom Lake, Nevada, they could hear the hysterical laughter of Dr. Sage Kuushmann.

Congressman Victor Sligo again removed his saucer hat and black-rimmed glasses, although it was snowing more heavily now. The other man, whom the entire nation assumed was Davy Crockett, did the same. Just behind the Supreme Court Justices, the Chairman of the Joint Chiefs of Staff, Admiral Sukwant Singh, looked to his right to Graham St. John, who nodded his approval, then to his left to the detachment of Joint Special Ops commandoes at the ready. Singh held a single dark hand high in the air, fingers spread in a commanding gesture. His Naval Academy ring was clearly visible. Unobserved high on the gilded dome of the Capitol, Agent Daniel Cool advised his astonished people this was all part of Psybysch's program.

Nobody moved.

Staring directly at Hellman, Victor said to Edwin, "You have one minute and fifty seconds." He moved a microphone stand in close.

Edwin did not allow himself to think. Smiling with that oddly pained smile, reaching down to the depths of his spirit, his eyes riveted to Hellman, he said, "Mr. Vice President. My name is Edwin Foulks. Will you be good enough to tell me why the secret society known as the Clevis Group, mistakenly called the Society With No Name, has worked so hard to cause people to not vote in the past few elections?"

Viewers across the Capitol grounds, and across the nation, gasped and stopped breathing. Newsrooms everywhere went silent. Bartenders and cabbies turned up the sound. Phones jammed as people called neighbors and relatives. At I-Media headquarters, network technicians desperately shouted orders, fumbled with satellite downlinks, and sensed they would be watching replays of this disaster next week from the unemployment line.

Edwin stood with that intense, beckoning gaze, head tilted slightly, the light beard perfectly trimmed, the deep silver-gray eyes penetrating into the eyes of the Vice President.

In one instant, Billy Hellman felt half a dozen emotions

clamoring in his body. Clevis? Is that what he said? In his lifetime association with the Group no human being had ever said the word aloud. He was on national television about to be re-inaugurated Vice President! I am armed, young man, a distant voice hammered. But no sound came. Time had stopped. He and this, this *musician* were alone in this moment. He was playing some game with his damned eyes. I'm not going to discuss this with you or anybody, the voice in his head sputtered. Not without my lawyer. Where the hell is my lawyer?

"Arrest this man!" he roared, arms whipping outward for his support staff. But to his shock and rage, nobody rushed forward. He felt an odd weight in his hand. In front of him, the Chief Justice of the Supreme Court materialized, glaring at him, smoke coming out of her head, looking for the all the world like his mother, spitting through her teeth, "Put that thing away!" He glanced down. Clutched in his fist was the .38 special. Involuntarily his eyes flicked to the huge screen. There he was, thirty feet tall, pistol in hand, aimed at the heart of the man standing in front of him. He steeled himself. Everybody in America was watching him.

It had to be Crockett! Who else could it be? He must be an escaped lunatic! And now he was repeating the damn question.

"Let me try again," Edwin enunciated slowly, refusing to look at the weapon. "Is it true that your secret society, the Clevis Group, used CI technology and the Brain-Computer Interface chip hardwired into Holotech televisions, to cause people to not vote?" Edwin's eyes burned. But his gaze remained fixed on Hellman. With the charge of adrenalin and fear, his body felt like it was going to explode. Some disjointed part of his brain was certain the Vice President would not shoot him. And the powerful voice of the Chief Justice had made Hellman flinch. If Edwin survived the next few seconds, he could make it the rest of the way.

No other sound came to Hellman's ears. Shapiro-Fujimoto glared at him as if she was going to strike him. The blunt-nosed pistol still pointed at Crockett's chest. With a single gesture, the Chief Justice motioned for the two paratroopers and their banner to move aside.

"A minute and twenty seconds," said Congressman Victor Sligo, his voice surprisingly calm. The woman holding the Bible stood motionless beside him.

Fighting himself out of Edwin's eyes, Hellman screamed, "I'm arresting you for treason, Crockett! By authority of –"

"Mr. President!" bellowed Chief Justice Shapiro-Fujimoto.

Beside Leora Psybysch, Giuseppe Manicotti had risen, eyes bulging. It was as if only last night Nel Sligo had kicked him in the chest, and the humiliation hung on him like tar. In front of the podium was her self-anointed shit king of a husband, obviously about to assassinate the Vice President! On auto pilot, Manicotti searched for the nearest TV camera. Yeah. There it is.

"I'm for that bastard," he snarled at Psybysch, and shoved his way through the mayors and movie stars toward the podium. In seconds a renegade camerawoman recognized him and reported to Bliss in the hot dog truck. Bliss simply let the woman loose, and she zoomed in on the enraged Police Chief. Pushing through the crowd, Manicotti was bent on interfering with the assassination, and installing himself, for the moment, into his rightful position of command. There came a twitch in his ear when he thought somebody might have uttered the sacred word "Clevis." But he was so unaccustomed to the sound, his mind simply dismissed it.

In the enormity of the moment, President Burligame knew what he had to do. He had waited far too long. Outrage and shock poured from the Vice President's eyes. But Sol Burligame was standing tall. And then Chief Justice Shapiro-Fujimoto's voice really got his blood pressure elevated.

The most powerful man on the planet had to take charge.

116

Pressing two fingers to his brow a moment to contain his anxiety, he stepped up to Hellman, and in a voice he had forgotten he roared, "Billy! I want you to answer this man! And put that gun away!"

The Chief Justice and the woman with the Bible moved two steps toward Hellman.

There were seventy-five million viewers by now watching the Vice President's face turn a boiling purple. Synapses concussed through his brain. Somehow this inconsequential maggot Crockett had figured everything out at once. How? A palace coup? No. Burligame was too stupid to be involved in this. Crockett kept staring, as if he expected an answer. The pretend rebel, with his ridiculous outfit and his executioner's eyes. He looked like he was going to burst into *Seventy-Six Trombones!* Couldn't they get a decent class of rebel these days? The whole planet watched. Burligame fumed. Suddenly Hellman was hearing some new commotion. He turned to see that cop, Manicotti, crashing toward him, shoving through the crowd black with rage. But he was shouting *Sligo's* name! Just as Hellman turned to deal with Chief Manicotti, he saw that pestilential jackass Archbishop Goldberg closing in fast from the other side, frothing with righteous overload, eyes fixed on the .38. A conspiracy! Goldberg shoved straight through the immobile Secret Service detail, emitted a scream, and charged Hellman, cassock flapping in his wake. Manicotti, thinking on his feet, saw the action unfolding also – Sligo on one side and the freak Archbishop on the other, and he whipped sideways to cut Goldberg off. Goldberg ducked aside, straight-armed Manicotti, and hurled himself at the Vice President, shrieking, arms and legs and head flailing. Hellman took one step back, pistol in his right hand, and slammed his left fist into the Archbishop's chest, dropping him like a wounded duck. Manicotti, blind with fury and gasping for breath, lunged toward Sligo, his last chance to rescue the President. The woman at the podium pushed Victor aside, both arms up. She whirled in a full circle, and with a roundhouse swing of her leg, kicked Manicotti in the temple. He crumpled to the stage with a resounding thud. Without slowing her momentum, she spun sideways and clobbered Hellman's wrist. The pistol skittered off the terrace, and fell neatly into the bell of a tuba in the band below. At the same moment her red snood went flying, and her blond hair cascaded out like a golden waterfall.

One hundred thousand onlookers gasped in collective horror. They were all going crazy! Philadelphia's Chief of Police was down, the Archbishop was down, and the President was pointing at Congressman Sligo and smiling! Chief Justice Shapiro-Fujimoto and this blond woman were slapping a high five in the air, and now something very strange was going on with Billy Hellman. He pointed his finger as though he still held the pistol. He and Crockett were eyeball to eyeball, straddling the carnage before them. They were so close together Hellman's forefinger was pressed into

Crockett's stomach. The cameras closed in. Over the din somebody shouted, "One minute, Edwin!"

Somewhere in the crowd Desdemona shot both hands in the air, practically knocking Slash out of his seat. She sang out, "Sweet Jesus, sell the farm, honey bunch! We've died and gone to heaven!" Purvis Courtman watched every instant on the big screen. He collapsed into his seat, weeping, shaking a fist at the blond woman and laughing through his tears.

Hellman was breathing hard. As his fist had cracked into the Archbishop's chest, and then that damned woman had smacked the pistol away, his brain had suddenly emptied. The blond woman had saved him from that militant cop Manicotti. But the rest of them were all together. Sol was demanding he answer the question. And this kid Crockett was six inches away, waiting for him. Somewhere cameras were running, and somewhere in his large gray-fringed bald head, Billy Hellman knew history had just gobbled him up. There was no turning back now. Maybe tomorrow he would fire somebody, but today his job was to control the situation. Which meant answering the kid, live on I-Media. He was about to become the hero of Burligame's second Inauguration. Besides, he admitted with a wave of surrender, he kind of liked this Crockett.

Down the first row, directly in front of John Lee Davis, stood Attorney General Jim Turcutt and the excruciatingly nervous Secretary of Communications, Hunter Tyne. Tyne was pressing down his mustache as if it might fly off, struggling to hold himself together but gripped with a mixture of terror and fascination. His mind was tearing through several complex scenarios. Hellman and Crockett were talking about Clevis before the entire nation. It was impossible! Nobody knew! No government could survive without the Group at its core, and these people were about to cause a cataclysmic breakdown of the Clevis program in Washington. It was those damned meddling, homosexual *citizens!* They would undo everything Tyne had worked so long to achieve. The housewives, the schoolteachers, the bus drivers, the egomaniacs running this rebellion, they would destroy everything! Didn't they understand they must sacrifice freedom in order to live in a free country?

Snow was collecting on Tyne's glossy black hair and his signature belted brown coat. He shook with cold. Clearly God had singled him out. It was not snowing anywhere else in Washington.

Just on him! Fine. Let the damned snow fall. Let these people all kill each other. With swift calculation he ran through the succession to the Presidency. Most of the people around him would have to be incapacitated before he could take his rightful, completely inevitable position as Chief Executive Officer of the United States.

Then surprise and revulsion knifed into his chest when he recognized the blond woman. His new assistant! You can never trust anybody in Washington, he thought. Never!

But he needed to remain in character. Certain the cameras were on him, he leaned toward Attorney General Turcutt, and said in a shrill voice, "What's going on here? Isn't that Sligo? The traitor!"

Turcutt had been expecting some kind of charade from Tyne. He turned without expression to assess the tormented madman beside him. What Turcutt thought was, this pig's snout is stuck so deep in the government trough, he doesn't even see the butcher sharpening his knife right in front of him. "We'll soon find out," he growled.

The violence had subsided. Two hundred and seventy-five federal agents waited for instructions, gloved hands close to their weapons, some with orgasmic pleasure watching Billy Hellman about to be demolished. The entire United States military command was glued to the upraised hand of Admiral Sukwant Singh.

Six inches from Crockett, time had stopped for Billy Hellman. He felt heat coming from the kid's face. His finger was still jammed in the kid's belly. No doubt tonight the Group would rake him over the coals. He stared into Crockett's eyes and told himself how simple this was going to be. Might makes right. Everybody knows that. And besides, for the genuine pathological liar – which would include every man and woman on this platform – speaking the truth always sounds like a lie to everybody else.

He shot a last glance at Burligame. The purple eye scars flashed. The President had already decided to give Crockett his moment. A voice behind Crockett called, "Forty-five seconds."

Edwin stood fully conscious, holding the Vice President's eyes. Hellman's index finger burned against his belly, and Edwin breathed through his stomach, causing Hellman to move back a centimeter. Edwin exhaled forcefully, and Hellman sucked in a breath. Spasms of energy flowed between them.

"All right," the Vice President said. "Let's finish it, and we'll get back to what we came here to do." He grinned through quivering lips.

Edwin said calmly, "Tell me about Clevis."

The entire nation was watching.

"Our mission is to unify the labors of all the peoples on Earth," Billy quoted without having to think, his strained tenor sounding like he was speaking through a wad of cotton. "Without regard to ownership. Ownership is the primary obstacle to people and nations who fail to grasp their own potential. The Group will teach them. Break down barriers. Enrich the faithful. Educate the uncommitted. You see? Global economic harmony. One world."

"Yours," Edwin said.

"Yeah. What did you think?" Billy grinned, emboldened, forgetting cameras and Inaugurations, wrapped in Edwin's energy field, confident that he represented the truth. "Did you think taking command of the government was enough? Fomenting little wars, Chechnya, Somalia, Afghanistan? Look!" He counted on stubby fingers. "The system's reliant on three things: the whims of voters, the two-bit corruption in Congress, and these damn trust fund babies running corporations! That's too loose! We can't bank on any of that!"

"Ten seconds, Edwin!" Victor hissed behind him.

"You stopped people from voting," Edwin said. His voice was perfectly level. "You used Communication International to get inside people's brains and hypnotize them! That's illegal, Mr. Vice President! You tarnished the entire foundation of representative democracy. People watched, and didn't vote. That was a terrible thing to do."

"Well, it worked, didn't it?" Billy said. "For the good of ... for the reasonable and prudent objectives of..." He looked into the storm-gray eyes, and he wanted to look away, but couldn't. He wanted to produce the pathetic clichés practiced by Vice Presidents for two centuries. But they were not on his tongue when he opened his mouth. "Clevis." He exhaled, suddenly relieved. "Hey, we learned how to control mass communication six hundred years ago. The Gutenberg Bible! Today it's living better through technology." He laughed, and flicked a glance down to his hand. With obvious embarrassment he tucked his finger into his holster.

There were those who tried to switch channels, thinking they'd blundered onto a soap opera. The impossible was unfolding before their eyes. A man in Sheboygan, Wisconsin, had a myocardial infarction. Billy Hellman was caught being himself. Many who had followed the search for Crockett and Sligo from the beginning, actually wept. They sensed they were witnessing the end of a long and bitter conflict. In prisons and on distant beaches people were saying, I knew it! I always knew it! The bastards!

"Are we done here?" Billy Hellman asked. His steady voice reverberated around the Capitol grounds.

"Just a couple more questions, sir. But first let me clarify: Communication International is directed by Clevis?"

"Sure."

"And CI set up a kind of chemical reaction between the Holotech and the viewer's brain? And the result was that people did not vote? And you did all this knowing your party would win. Is that right?"

"Sure. They watched Julio on Public Television flipping his pencil. And he told people why bother to vote. The program just caused an intense negative neural response right then, while his pencil was in the air. Don't vote. Fairly primitive technology. You know Julio's a hardcore liberal, like the whole damn Public Television crowd. Normal people never watch that stuff. Only liberals! Just in case, we went to the churches and military bases and gun shows and NASCAR races and every Newfie function around the country and told people not to watch Julio because he's insane, because by God we're *voters* and we're not going to listen to anybody tell us why bother to vote!"

"It's over, Foulks," Victor Sligo told him.

But it wasn't over. Freelance cameras were shutting down around the Capitol grounds, at the same time as I-Media video teams and cell phones were coming back on line. Incredibly, I-Media producers had gone through an existential crisis, and allowed the programming to go on. To hell with the consequences. Admiral Singh dropped his arm. US marshals and Secret Service agents moved uncertainly forward. The President's hand shot out when a uniformed Homeland Security agent ventured too close. Up in his glass booth, Julio Reese was having a good laugh with his lawyer and wondering if he could star as himself in a movie he might call

The Foulks Rebellion. Before him, one hundred thousand people stood hushed, trapped in the moment.

"Other than the fact that this whole concept is illegal and immoral, why all the secrecy?" Edwin asked. "Nobody's ever heard of Clevis."

The Vice President scoffed. "Secrecy! It's as American as apple pie and violence! Listen, kid. We're living in the era of forced recession, corruption at every level of government, arbitrary wars, the last desperate scramble before Asian financial institutions take over our economy." He was in his element, pontificating to the masses. He actually turned to face the stunned audience. "Somebody's going to take charge before we all go under. But you can't trust voters. Voters are stupid! Clevis!" he thundered, expanding his chest, searching for a camera to roar into. "Clevis will bring its wisdom to mankind! Clevis will neutralize the nattering nabobs of negativity! And we will thrive, and you will thrive!" He bulldozed down resistance across the land with the sheer invincibility of his logic. "And there will be a turkey in every oven!" He smiled righteously, nodding as if it all made perfect sense.

Edwin let ten seconds pass while the nation absorbed this last profundity. He felt his energy dissipating – the echoes in his head, the burning eyes, the deep hunger for sleep – but knew he had to push through to the end. Across the land citizens were plugging up the Internet searching for information on Clevis, only to arrive at carefully placed disinformation on the Society With No Name.

"Okay. Will you please tell us about the airborne pathogen pandemic."

"Oh, well, that was some years ago," Hellman said calmly. He looked gravely at the President. "Too much industrial pollution in the air. Nothing to do with pandemics or pigeons or anything of the sort. Industrial waste combined with global warming finally overwhelmed the atmosphere. Remember? People were getting real sick. The green crowd got rough. So we had to get rough. We got the CDC to invent the airborne pathogen story, and you were dumb enough to believe it." He chuckled. "What were we supposed to do? Let all those corporations go bankrupt? Impossible! Corporate enterprise," he trumpeted, "is what makes this the greatest nation on Earth!"

Victor Sligo yelled out, "You mindless buffoon! You practically killed your own President! Thousands of people were maimed and disfigured in your phony pandemic!"

The kid hadn't blinked. The uglier the stuff was Hellman told him, the more he liked this Crockett. Was there some kind of *bonding* going on here? The eyes intertwined. Billy felt good. He almost gagged when his brain went mushy and told him, this kid's the son you never had.

Beside them, Sol Burligame's face was agonized. He was feeling the scars. He had already read the million faces across the land without seeing them. He was not a man to fight an unclean fight. The purple scars pulsed, and he placed two fingers to his brow and held them there. Thoughts formed in his mind that startled him.

The camerawoman had moved in tighter also. On the big screen, the Vice President of the United States was saying things no politician is permitted to say. Hellman was eyeball to eyeball with Davy Crockett. Both heads were tilted at the same angle. And they were both smiling.

"Tell me, Mr. Vice President. Who is Caliban?"

"I," said the Vice President proudly, "am Caliban! The Group gave me the name."

Edwin said evenly, "Thank you. Will you please tell me what happened to Viola Ferrari?"

There came the first hesitation. The Vice President pulled back, but Sligo was there at his shoulder blocking him, and holding off the marshals. A struggle came into Hellman's eyes. The face twisted. "For that, sir," he said finally, shoving the words through his teeth, "you'll have to ask Dr. Hunter Tyne." He looked over his shoulder and down the front row, then turned back to Edwin. "I will say," and his face quivered noticeably. He tried to shake his huge head, as if he could hold back an onrushing train. His thick hands went to the sides of his head, and he pressed hard, squeezing his eyes shut, and in a guttural spasm he rasped, "The Group realized... Look, I was powerless to..." And the face twisted into a monstrous silent shriek. Sucking in a horrid breath, he said, "You will have to... ask Dr..."

At that instant the huge screen split in half. On the left was the photo of Assistant US Attorney Viola Ferrari, with the ghastly X slashed across her face. On the right, the most shocking scene in Washington's shocking history: The Vice President standing enraged, glaring at Hunter Tyne, as Tyne screeched hysterically, "Nobody votes any more! You know why? *Me!* I'm your savior, you mindless buffoon!" On the screen Tyne slapped his chest and roared, "A herd of drunken monkeys would vote you out of office, if they could vote!"

It was Raven Menez who read Edwin's mind, and she had held her gaze on Hunter Tyne, waiting. He was already slipping down the aisle of astonished dignitaries with the look of a madman in his eyes when Raven grabbed Molly Bee's arm and pointed.

"There he goes!" Raven yelled, and she plunged through the crowd toward the marble terrace. Molly and Nel both leaped up. Nel charged after Raven. Molly raced to the cameraman standing nearby, spun the camera around at herself, and yelled, "Attorney General Turcutt!" Instantly Molly's face replaced the other images on the big screen. "Jim! Up here!" She gestured wildly. Turcutt spun around. "Stop Tyne! Don't let him out of here!" Turcutt whipped back and saw Tyne crashing through the crowd. Raven was sprinting up the broad steps to the platform, flooded with adrenalin, fixed on the brown overcoat already at the edge of the marble terrace, lunging toward the opposite steps. Nel was three feet behind. Turcutt shouted to Davis, standing close by. Davis was already moving, head throbbing, shoving violently through Cabinet people and their families to cut Tyne off. Two women whipped past him like Olympic hurdlers.

At the podium, Sol Burligame saw. Molly! Right there on the screen, bigger than life. Overcome with conflicting emotions, he roared out, "Hunter Tyne! Stop where you are, sir!" The words echoed like the voice of God. Tyne was plunging down the steps when Raven tackled him from the side, ramming him against the marble wall. They both went down in a scrambling heap. A second later Nel arrived, and as Tyne tried to jump up, she mashed his face into the wall with one foot and pushed down hard. Raven jumped up and stood over him, panting, hands on her hips. At that moment Turcutt arrived. Davis was there a second later. Bending forward with effort, Davis slammed cuffs on Tyne's wrists, and panted his rights at him as though he might bite his face off, and yanked him to his feet. The two men glared violently at each other, then responding to a roar from the crowd both looked up to the giant screen and watched a slow-motion replay of Raven's flying tackle, her head jarring back as she slapped her arms around Tyne, and then Nel grinding his face into the marble wall.

Tyne swung his enraged, bleeding face to Davis, pulling himself erect as he did.

"You're finished, Mister!" he snarled. "You're a dead man!"

"Well, I will be, yes," John Lee Davis told him, breathing hard. "But not today." And he pointed to two of his people to take over.

Raven Menez was not finished. "He killed Viola!" she burst out at Davis and Turcutt. "We have enough evidence to hang him!" She flashed her fiery black eyes at Tyne. "You fucking weasel!" She clawed the air at him as they hauled him off. Then turning to Nel, triumphant, "I told you! The Society With No Name! I knew it!" Nel came to Raven and they embraced. Nel felt shaken but very fine indeed.

Molly Bee, shocked and elated and overcome along with everybody else in Washington, was still standing, unsure what to do next. Her mother and brother were seated close to the President. He had plenty of support. But she had seen the look in his eyes even from a distance as he searched the crowd for her. It was an expression of anxiety and surprise – and love.

Watching Tyne's flight on the big screen was like a door slamming between Edwin Foulks and Billy Hellman. Simultaneously, both understood their brief and fascinating relationship was over. Searching for a chair, Edwin wobbled to it, utterly drained, ribbons of color shooting through his eyeballs. He brushed snow from the seat, and collapsed.

Beside him, Victor Sligo found his wife's eyes in the melee, and he held up a clenched fist and shook it once.

117

At the podium, Chief Justice Shapiro-Fujimoto now stood at the center of a national meltdown. Everybody was either accused of a crime, beat senseless, or furious at everybody else. She felt the sense of standing on the floor of the Roman Coliseum as the throng screamed to feed all the politicians to the lions. Joel Babylon had made his way to the President's side, and they were conferring, Babylon shaking his head vigorously, the President as always calm as Buddha, steady in his instinctive response to trauma. Shapiro-Fujimoto waited, uncertain what her next move was. Others were sucked in by the vacuum around the President. Hal Riske had turned up, along with the Majority Leader of the Senate, Robert Satushek, followed by some of the young Turks, both Progressives and New-fies. Several Justices limped forward. The Chief Justice watched in guarded amusement as police and medical people hauled away Archbishop Goldberg and Giuseppe Manicotti. Arms and voices rose in the circle of public figures surrounding the President. Some-body produced a laptop, and was reading heatedly to Burligame and the others. More than a dozen of them jabbered, all with black coats, silk scarves, and even a dapper top hat or two. Behind them, Victor came and sat with Edwin, vastly relieved, proud, vaguely mistrust-ing what this gaggle of penguins might conjure up to defile yet again the intentions of the Founding Fathers.

Molly had reached the steps, and walked unsteadily toward the podium. Her head reeled with the utter absurdity of the very events she had demanded in print for years. She was standing near the President, invisible in the snowfall. Half a dozen Secret Service people, presuming they would be protecting the Camp David park-ing lot the rest of the winter, moved hastily to intercede, but it was Admiral Singh who appeared from the front row to block them, al-lowing Molly to pass. When the President turned, his daughter stood before him. Neither spoke. In her green stadium coat zipped up against the chill, she looked peacefully at him. Burligame smiled tentatively, then broke into a wide grin and swept her into his big arms. They embraced as the arguing continued in the circle, neither thinking at all, merely being with the moment. Finally Burligame stood back, shaking his head in wonder. Tears were on Molly's cheeks. They still had not spoken when her father gestured toward the family, seated in the second row, and Molly went to her mother and brother.

Somebody had to act immediately, and Chief Justice Shapiro-Fujimoto realized it was she. Confident of nothing except her exalted office, she pushed into the inner sanctum of government, listened a few moments, turned, and perhaps a bit uncertainly took the microphone.

"Ladies and gentlemen," she began, addressing not the hushed crowd but the hundreds of gathered dignitaries still standing in shock and disbelief on the terrace. "There would appear to be no constitutional directive for what has taken place here. We have broad hearsay consensus that wrongs have been committed that may have influenced the vote leading to this Inauguration. In point of fact, there is little we can do at this moment but –"

The President of the United States took the laptop, looked across at his wife and children, then came to the podium and touched the Chief Justice on the arm. A long look passed between them. The Chief Justice moved aside. The President took command.

As he did so, a lumpy-looking man wearing a snow-dusted suede jacket over an I-Heart-NY hoodie, with white hair that looked like he had spent the morning in a cyclotron, appeared out of nowhere and sat down beside Congressman Sligo and Edwin Foulks. Without speaking, he crossed one leg over the other, and waited for the President a few feet away. Victor glanced at him, sniffed once, and pulled back against Edwin's shoulder.

For many moments Sol Burligame did not, or could not, speak. He held out his big square hands as though holding the nation together. Then turning, he nodded to Edwin, his thick lower lip pushed out. Without so much as a glance at the sullen Vice President standing to the side, he took three steps over to Edwin, leaned down and shook his hand. "Thank you, sir," he said quietly. "I did not catch your name."

"It's Edwin Foulks." Edwin tried to stand, but slumped back.

Walking back to the cameras and his nation, the President appeared deeply saddened, but determined. Instinct told him this was to be his finest public moment. And his last. Words came forth from his troubled heart that surprised even him, as he fumbled to find his voice.

"We have recorded the intentions of those we believed to be public servants," he said thickly. "It is my duty therefore to request the resignation of the Vice President and the Secretary of Communications, effective immediately." An undercurrent of approval came from the crowd. He pursed his lips, pondering. "In addition, I will issue before the day is out an executive order that the Justice

Department sue Communication International under Title 15 of the US Code, which prohibits monopolies in restraint of trade. Criminal charges will be filed. Until this action goes forward, Communication International and its affiliates, including Holotech Television, are hereby prohibited from engaging in any lobbying activity, the financing of any political campaign, operating voting machinery, or reporting of political events in any public forum."

People in front of him and on the terrace, began to express louder sounds of support. Still, the cheers caught in their throats. Too much madness today, following years of treachery and lies from the White House. Why should they believe him now?

The President paused to organize his thoughts, fully aware the whole world was watching. "Rest assured," he said grimly, "every division of Communication International will be examined for illegal activity by a disinterested body in the coming days. Now then." He stopped and looked down at the closed laptop. "The Vice President's words have been recorded. One Cabinet member has been implicated, and perhaps there will be others. I take full responsibility –" Sol felt himself slipping. With his thumb and index finger, he squeezed the webbing in his opposite hand. He regained his presence instantly. Snow thickened in the cold air. People pressed together, and Burligame's voice rose. He began to understand what he needed to say.

"I take full responsibility for those serving in my Cabinet. Further, I am aware that the Vice President may have acted in ways injurious to our citizens, for which I am accountable. I fully expect articles of impeachment to be filed against your President with the next session of Congress." Cries of "No!" and "It's your turn, Sol" poured from the chilly crowd pressing in toward the marble terrace. The President popped open the laptop computer. The screen was blank.

"This is terrible weather. Up in Minnesota, we call this a sure sign spring is on the way. But we need to talk." He loosened his scarf as a gesture of pulling up to the fireplace with a hot toddy. "Some of you," and he looked to the camera with profound sincerity in his scarred eyes, "may have read a document called *Strategies for Survival in a Corporate World*." He paused to allow the boos and cheers and raspberries to diminish.

Standing in the crowd, Iona Webster would have fallen to

the ground if she had not been compressed by Raven on one side and Nel Sligo on the other. Molly Bee managed to find Iona from her seat, and shot a thumbs-up. But what could her father possibly say? He was referring to documents the New Freedom Party could no more espouse than fish could read.

Beside Iona, Nel could barely hear anything in the cheering mob. After the abject terror she'd felt as Victor and Edwin had walked up to the podium, and then her own reckless crashing after Tyne, she felt enormously relieved and exhausted and wondered if maybe now, finally, Victor would quit public life. They could slow down, perhaps do some traveling, see the kids more often. Three seconds later she caught herself, and shook her head, and then thought, stranger things have happened. Billy Hellman just told the truth in front of the whole country.

"Let me say," the bold new President said, "this document is both audacious, and American. I did study it," he admitted, "after this man sent his protest into the skies over Philadelphia last week. Academics, economists, social observers of all political persuasions agree that the *Strategies for Survival* has many alternatives worth looking into, particularly –" He pressed his lips together, and swept a hand across his brow, "– as we struggle to pull ourselves out of the worst morass since the First Great Depression. Obviously, what we have been doing is not working." Murmurs of agreement came from all sides. Joel Babylon rushed up to the podium to speak into Burligame's ear. Briskly passing the front row, he sent a warm smile and the victory sign to the journalist Molly Bee.

"Never in my long and interesting life would I have believed it," Burligame said, speaking more confidently. "What we have heard here today..." He shrugged the massive shoulders, squinting through white flurries to find his audience. "This Clevis Group the Vice President and others apparently represent –" He was at a momentary loss. He clasped his hands together, brought them to his lips a moment, and said, "Secret organizations... without regard to nationality, committed to worldwide economic domination... dictate policy to congresses, to parliaments, to governments... and governments simply do what they're told."

No response came. The people were confused. The New Freedom Party faithful waited, as did the Progressives, the underground press, and Julio Reese, captivated and silently cheering.

"There are those who believe it's always been that way." The President's voice softened, and suddenly it felt like a bunch of strangers sitting around a bar chatting. "No wonder nobody in America trusts government any more." He stopped again, nodded to himself, and his voice became richer and he said, "But we're going to fix it. This is not a country of namby-pamby cowards. Our people have always risen in times of war and tyranny. We're in a state of national insecurity, and the government *must* regain the confidence of the people. Because without the consent of the governed, we have despotism and repression, and the exact kind of criminal behavior we are just now exposing, right here on the steps of the Capitol."

The crowd burst spontaneously into cheers. At the same moment, barely visible from the southwest, came a sliver of white light. "*That* kind of activity," the President roared, pointing directly at Billy Hellman, "threatens to undermine our way of life!" He slammed a thick hand on the podium. "They're not going to take over our voting system! They're not going to befoul the process of representative democracy." He was angry, and he sounded angry. "I am not going to put up with anybody making decisions in my government," he boomed to the cameras, "who has not been duly and legally elected by the people!"

They roared across the land, in every home and bar and church basement, every hockey rink and senior center. In Sunrise, BJ Lichtenstein screamed so loud his wife burst into his study, thinking he had won the lottery. As the cheering continued the President shouted, "We can function in this great country without the Clevis Group!"

I am here now, Sol Burligame told himself. This is what I was born to do. I am the President! God help me!

He waited for the crescendo of approval to subside, then spoke over the diminishing storm.

"This historic place is usually reserved for self-congratulation. But I am going to make this clear right now. What this country needs is a restoration of faith in our governing bodies and our financial institutions. Let me ask all Americans to examine two things. First, I want you to examine yourselves, to determine what you stand for, and to deliberate with your families and your businesses and your neighbors about it. And I want to hear from you, this week, how hard you are willing to work for what you say you stand for." Again he slammed a fist on the podium. "Because democracy is not a spectator sport!" the President yelled. "Sitting by watching is what got us into this morass! Including me, myself!" He took a breath and let it out slowly.

"Secondly, I want you to examine your own area of interest in this *Strategies for Survival in a Corporate World*. If you're a professional person, if you're an educator, in the health, technology or science fields, a contractor, a business person, a civic employee at any level, if you're a parent, if you're a laborer, if you're a student or a senior citizen, if you have any interest in this great land of ours, you'll find in these documents insightful proposals created by some of the best minds of our times. At the core of the *Strategies* is the monitoring of every government agency by independent individuals skilled in specific areas and chosen by their peers in fair elections. This is true, verifiable, participatory democracy at every level of human endeavor, from the playground to the White House. It will require you to stand up and be involved. And it still offers corporate America the opportunity to develop our great country."

All of the United States waited one more moment.

Sol Burligame said, "I hereby declare Congress in session effective Tuesday noon. At that time I will deliver this document to a joint session of the Congress, and we will see what they can do with it."

His great country flew into a frenzy of patriotic optimism.

The sliver of light had spread northward into a boomerang-shaped curtain of brightness on the horizon. Umbrellas closed. Even the President pointed toward the suggestion of clearing.

"You may think," he thundered, "what you are hearing is just more rhetoric disguising politics as usual. I am here to tell you, Americans, it is time to change our thinking. It is time to improve what is working for the people, and throw out what is not working for the people."

Again he paused for the crashing of applause across the land.

"I will finish shortly, and get us all out of the storm," he said without irony. He held up the bright red laptop computer. "What I have here on this device is a document that caused the *Strategies for Survival*, and everything else put down in writing on this continent, to come into existence."

Finally came the wintry moaning from hard right-wingers who had spent their lives spewing contempt at suggestions that the corporate posture in America was flawed.

Opening the device, he tapped a finger against the screen, then turned back to his Cabinet with a shrug. Quickly Joel Babylon and Hussein al-Jakka were at his side. They pawed over the instrument, to no avail.

The man with the strange white hair fidgeted, watching snow accumulate on his red sneakers. Congressman Sligo, without looking at him, said, "Go ahead, Slash. Fix the damn thing."

"Yo," Slash said. Carefully, he stood, half expecting a cavity search in this exalted group. Victor signaled to the President, and Slash was permitted to step forward. He examined the computer, popped open the back and adjusted something, and handed it back to the President with a broad, gap-toothed grin.

Wiping his glasses, Burligame studied the screen, then looked up with a half smile. "This is not the first time we have been required to re-examine our strategies for survival," he said. "It is the nature of a democracy. If I may."

He stood tall and read slowly, with an unyielding and eloquent voice, pausing frequently to look at the camera. "'We, the people of the United States... in order to form a more perfect union... establish justice... insure domestic tranquility... provide for the common defense... promote the general welfare... and secure the blessings of liberty to ourselves and our posterity... do ordain and establish this Constitution for the United States of America.'

"*This* is the record of our common strength," Burligame said forcefully. "*This* is our strategy for survival. I am directing that this week every school, every family, every business, organization, and governing body in our nation study this Constitution. People will be made available via the Internet to interpret and to answer questions."

Patches of blue speckled the western sky. The temperature was dropping. Snow continued stubbornly to fall upon the Capitol, but the people looked to the West hopefully.

"My friends, our nation cannot survive on the path we have been traveling. We will be in for more storms, costly court battles, enormous economic challenges. But we are a mature people, and we are fundamentally an honest people. We are going to re-examine our premises, re-evaluate our objectives, and we are going to talk about questioning our blind love affair with television."

A hush came over the exuberant throng. It was twenty degrees in the District of Columbia, and the sky was clearing. A single man rose behind the President and began to clap. It was the stranger with the electric hair-do and the hoodie, eyes closed, clapping firmly to a slow beat only he could hear. Then from the compressed crowd, a tall beautiful woman in a white leather coat joined in. A few others here and there hesitantly applauded.

The President said, "I guess we can still watch baseball."

Unbelievably, the sun appeared at that instant. The people roared mightily. In the Citadel at S., plans were already being reconfigured, funds transferred, hard drives wiped clean. Select officials in major cities around the globe were notified that a long vacation might be beneficial for their health. And strategy for the next worldwide economic disaster was added to the agenda for the spring conference.

In her purse, the blond woman's cell phone vibrated.

Epilog

No journey of this magnitude would be complete without describing the fates of the various figures who made *The Foulks Rebellion* a reality.

BJ Lichtenstein took a variety of paths, from golfing to teaching government to running a fruit stand at the university. He finally found his niche in life spending time with older women in nursing homes. He and Leah stayed together, although the going was tough until he retired at age fifty-seven and took up meditation, whitewater kayaking, and volunteering at the local senior center.

Purvis Courtman created a speaking tour following the presidential bi-election. He retired shortly after, realizing that no vagaries of politics could top the experience of the rebellion he had personally suggested back in November. Polishing up his bassoon, he took lessons from a famous instructor, a distant relative of Dr. Sage Kuushmann, and was invited to join the Flin Flon Symphony Orchestra in far off Manitoba. There he fell in love with a violinist named Pat. They are still together.

Sloan Mgaba never did outgrow his venereal appetite, nor his great affection for the sound of his own voice. He created a UN position in the field of orphan rescue, and over the following years he adopted or placed into foster care thousands of refugee children.

Raven Menez endured a four-year relationship with Edwin Foulks. Over time she came to realize her future was not with goats and blackberries and contra dancing. She had suppressed her love of fast cars, recreational drugs, and journalism, but did enjoy the company of Van Zandt's rumpies – the rural, upwardly-mobile peasants.

Edwin Foulks sent her on her way with his blessings. Edwin struggled with his notoriety for a year or two, debated changing his identity, just as the tabloids had insisted DB Cooper had changed his to an African-American woman living in New Jersey. Eventually things settled down. Edwin is said to be thinking about writing a historical-fictional-pictographic epic of one of the great moral leaders of the Twentieth Century, Mickey Mouse. No publisher will touch the proposal, thus far.

Victor Sligo never ran for President. He served eighteen years in the House of Representatives, and eighteen more in the United States Senate, the last six as Majority Leader. At that point Nel simply told him if he didn't quit she would run against him.

Nel Sligo published a bestseller called *The Love Story of Victor Sligo*. She was instrumental in creating federal funding for Mgaba's refugee adoption program, as well as frequently assisting with the care of BJ Lichtenstein's and her own grandchildren, and fund-raising for Courtman's orchestra. She became a serious bird watcher, and every winter participated in the eagle count along the Seyes River, and stopped in for tea with Edwin Foulks.

The blond woman actually did run for President some years later. She received 973 write-in votes, all by renegade feminists and karate instructors who had witnessed the rebellion on television. One of those voters dictated that she be cremated with the famous *Time* magazine cover photo of the lady in red dropping Police Chief Manicotti in front of the podium at the Inauguration, under the banner heading, *"Who is this woman?"*

Molly Bee kept her secret. She remained with the *West Coast Paper*, and quietly visited her family in central Minnesota, not far from Lake Wobegone, every Christmas.

Iona Webster's extended version of *Strategies for Survival in a Corporate World* became an overnight success. Within two years Iona was elected to the California Assembly, and shortly a committee was testing the waters for her gubernatorial run.

Sol Burligame, Billy Hellman, Leora Psybysch, Giuseppe Manicotti, Slash Zewinta, Evileye, Flotilda Lament, the Zander farmers, the taxi driver L'Ouverture, and the others returned to the waiting rooms of literature, where they are available for future work at your request. Characters Guild fees apply.

9 780615 473086